The Portal to
Halavash

The Token Bearers — Book Six

Books by Derin Attwood

The Token Bearers Series

Book One: The Caves of Kirym

Book Two: The Fortress of Faltryn

Book Three: The Trail to Churnyg

Book Four: The Sands of Valythia

Book Five: The Burl of Meglinor

Book Six: The Portal to Halavash

THE PORTAL TO HALAVASH

DERIN ATTWOOD

The Portal to Halavash

A Wordly Press Publication
Ashhurst, New Zealand
Phone 64 6 326 8066

First published by Wordly Press in 2019

Cover Art Copyright © Llyvonne Barber.

Set in 12/18/24 Adobe Garamond Pro
This text uses English (UK) spelling.

ISBN 978-0-9941478-2-0

A catalogue record for this book is available from
the National Library of New Zealand.

Wordly Press
www.wordlypress.com

Dedication

For my dearest Della,
For John Locke,
And for Ron.

ACKNOWLEDGEMENTS

Being a writer is a solitary occupation. However, there are many friends in the background who ensure my books are written and see the light of day. First and foremost, my husband, Ron. Without him, my writing time would be much diminished, my life, less comfortable, my heart, less complete. He brings me drinks when I need them and ensures I eat. He is patient when on occasion, my whole conversation is to do with the latest plots and problems. Above all, he makes me feel loved, and that means I can write.

My daughter Llyvonne, who is the other part of Wordly Press, creates the wonderful covers, formats my manuscripts and deals with all the technical stuff I can't comprehend. She also understands when I complain about my characters, especially when they refuse to do what I want.

Della Hart and Terresa Herleth, for helping me fine-tune the manuscript from good to Great. For being there for me to talk to when I need to discuss plots and plot-holes.

The members of the Pen-Ultimate writing group. We meet fortnightly, critique each other's work and encourage as necessary. They pick me up when I am down and are brutally honest when something I have written is wrong.

Special friends Norrie Pennel, Christine Campbell, Cliff,

Vanessa, and Quentin Olsen, who all, in their own way, encourage me to get away from my manuscript and see the world from different places. And who drink wine with me.

This series would not have been started or continued without family and friends. I can't name you all, but you are not forgotten. You're in my heart, loved, and appreciated.

And Alistair Morgan. You have a special place in my heart.

Characters on this Adventure

Name   *Relationship*

From the Green Valley

Arbreu   M   Kirym and Teema's token brother-
                    Married to her sister, Mekrar

Ashistar   M   Tree Dwarf. Kirym's weapon holder

Churnyg   M   Tree dwarf, Ashistar's Sire

Danth   M   From the Green Valley family

Dashlan   M   Arbreu's brother

Kirym   F   Loul and Veld's daughter
                    Holder of the weapons

Loul   F   Headwoman, married to Veld,
                    Kirym's mama

Mekrar   F   Kirym's sister. Married to Arbreu

Oak   M   Wind Runner's great grandson
                    From the Fortress of Falrtyn

Rabbit   F   From the Fortress of Faltryn

Rosisha   F   Tree Dwarf, Married to Ashistar
                    Varitza's mama

Sundas   M   From the Green Valley

Teema   M   Kirym and Ashistar's token brother

Trethia   F   Kirym's daughter

Name		Relationship
From the Green Valley		
Varitza	F	Roshisha's daughter
Veld	M	War Lord and Voice of The Green Valley
Teema	M	Aligned to Kirym, Arbreu and Bokum.
Veld	M	Voice and Warlord, Kirym, Mekrar and Mekroe's papa.
Wind Runner	M	Leader from the Fortress of Faltryn Oak's great grandmama
Dragons of Athesha		
Iryndal		
Othyn		
Ubree		
Egrym		
Arymda		
Borasyn		
Faltryn		
Trees from Halavash		
Malsavash	M	Title given to the primary male tree on Halavash. Kirym was met by the current Malsavash
Rolliz		Seed pod given to Kirym

Name		Relationship
Trees from Halavash		
Uguvash	M	One of the first trees Kirym met
Vashetha	F	Leader of the trees of Halavash
Vashmilla	F	A previous leader of the trees of Halavash
Vashmitta	F	Ancient leader of the trees of Halavash
Carers of the Land of Halavash		
Dorchym		Tilysh's family
Lartherin		Tilysh's family
Tilysh		First of those to guide Kirym
Gatekeepers		
Gatekeepers are known by their colours		
Dragons and Changlings		
Bogryn	M	Ubree and Faltryn's father
Faranth	F	Ubree and Faltryn's mother
Ilarth	F	Ubree and Faltryn's older sister
Jomme	M	Fhelian
Kwarfo	M	Dragon
Ling	M	Dragon
Safan	F	Dragon
Sarheet	F	Fhelian
Shalinba	F	Fhelian

Name		Relationship
Dragons and Changlings		
Teonarl	F	Dragon
Thenne	M	Fhelian
Zillib	F	Dragon

1

Arbreu

Arbreu paused as he came around the corner of the dwelling. Mekrar was leaning against the door support, the moonlight and glow from the nearest fire enough to show her extreme fatigue and grief. As he hesitated, she straightened her back and turned to re-enter the dwelling. She smiled when she saw him.

"How's Oak?" he asked.

"He woke again but didn't respond. Wind Runner stayed with him until the guard changed. I'd say I sent her off to rest, except no one sends her anywhere, but she did go when I suggested it."

"You should too. Daylight will be here soon enough. I'll sit with him."

She nodded. "I wish I knew what the problem was. Is he silent because of the poisons, because Kirym and Trethia are dead, or is there another reason?"

"You think Trethia's death had that much effect on him?"

She nodded. "As much as Kirym's, I think."

"It's strange. I'd have thought Teema would have been the one. I mean, he found her. I thought it would bring him and Kirym together again. Do you understand it?"

Mekrar shrugged. "It's Teema doing what he's always done. Got close and then run like crazy. He has such fear of being rejected, he won't even try. Poor Trethia. As soon as she shared one small secret with Kirym, he walked away from her." She paused. "Oh, don't get me angry, I'll never sleep. Call me at dawn."

She saw Arbreu's hesitation.

"Please, Arbreu. Oak will be waking then, and I intend to sort this out before anyone else gets here."

"But the healers—"

"Don't necessarily know what's right. Wind Runner agreed with them, but I think she was as pressured as I was. Anyway, it isn't working. Tiptoeing around never helps. Oak needs to know what has happened. It might just galvanise him out of his misery. At least he'll begin to heal. Wallowing in self-pity helps no one."

"All right, I'll make sure you're awake."

Arbreu watched the clouds move across the moon and wondered if Mekrar was making the right decision.

2

Arbreu

Arbreu held his comments as Mekrar placed a platter of food beside Oak's set.

Oak's eyes were open, but he had neither eaten nor spoken. As good as the food smelled, it hadn't helped at all.

"Oak, if you don't eat, you won't get your strength back. You're no help to anyone like this, and I need your help. Tell me what you remember."

Oak closed his eyes.

"No! You will not do that. I will not allow it." Mekrar grabbed his face and turned it to look at her. "I want Kirym at rest, and it won't happen without your help."

Oak's eyes opened. His first words came out as a whisper. "Why not?" He coughed. "You mean you've not buried—"

Mekrar shook her head.

He struggled to sit up. "Why not?"

"Other things got in the way. What's your last memory?"

He frowned as he thought back. "We came out of the Burl.

I felt strange. The full moon glowed big on the horizon. I remember thinking how much Kirym would love it. It seemed to get bigger and then everything went black. That's all. What happened?"

"You were poisoned."

He looked shocked. "Who'd do that?"

"Kirym!"

"What! No!" He shook his head. "How?"

"One little kiss, Oak."

Mekrar bundled up a rug, placed it behind Oak, and sat beside him.

"I'm sorry, but whatever killed Kirym and Trethia, was so fast moving and strong, when you kissed her hand, it was enough to almost kill you too."

Oak looked stunned. "What else has been happening?"

"Nothing. We concentrated on you. That was more important."

"Kirym and Trethia. Where are their bodies?"

"I meant it. They're still in the Burl. Something closed the entrance, and we don't know what."

"What happened to Gynbere?"

"He's in there too."

Oak's face changed. "What? No! I will *not* allow that murderous monster to lie in the same place. I'll dig through the walls if I have to."

For the first time in days, Arbreu saw emotion, anger mainly. He smiled to himself. Anger would get Oak on his feet. Mekrar certainly knew what she was doing.

Mekrar screwed up her nose. "Neither of us will do anything unless you eat." She handed him a small platter of cooked fruit and took a large piece of meat, enclosed in bread for herself.

Oak tried the fruit. "How long has it been?"

"Five days," Arbreu said.

"Why didn't someone tell me?"

"For the first two days, the healers were really pushed to keep you alive. Then they felt you needed to heal fully." She handed Oak a flask. He swallowed a mouthful and coughed.

"What's in it? Skafarhn?"

"Far too early for that. I added a fair gollop of morlarl juice. It'll give you a bit of energy. Always a bit of a shock if you've not tasted it that strong before."

She turned and saw Arbreu's expression. "Well, he'll need it if he's to attend the meeting today. Getting past Wind Runner and the other healers won't be easy."

"Nor Sundas, I imagine," Oak said.

3

Arbreu

Oak glanced around the dwelling as Arbreu placed some clothes on the set.

"Is this a new dwelling? Why didn't you use one of the wagons?"

"A wagon wouldn't have held Iryndal, Othyn, and ten healers at the same time."

"They all fitted in here?"

Arbreu nodded. "The long walls lift up. It was the only way we could do it." He added a pair of boots to the pile of clothes. "Do you need help?"

"I'll manage. These clothes aren't mine."

"They are now. Mama provided them. Everything you were wearing needed to be destroyed. We didn't know whether they were contaminated. Iryndal made the decision," Mekrar said, as she slipped back into the dwelling and handed Oak a warm robe. "I thought this would be warmer than a cloak. Don't rush, nothing will happen without you."

"That's what worries me. Nothing is happening." He paused. "Mekrar, what did happen in the Burl? I can't make sense of it."

"Iryndal said she'll answer what questions she can when we meet. If Wind Runner agrees, that is."

Wind Runner asked a few questions, expressed annoyance that Oak had dressed without her prior approval, but agreed he should get some fresh air and sit in on the coming meeting.

"But you will rest when I order it. If you don't do as I ask, I will allow Sundas to take over your care. He won't need much encouragement, and he'll be disinclined to allow you to do anything for many seasons. So, heed my words, Oak."

Oak agreed reluctantly.

"Wind Runner never makes a threat she doesn't fully intend to carry out. If I don't do as she says, Sundas will be hovering over me until I'm an old man."

"Sundas wants Kirym out of there too," Arbreu said.

"But if touching her almost killed me," Oak said, "how can we move her?"

Mekrar sighed. "If we can't think of a way, then possibly we need to concentrate on getting Gynbere out and let the Burl be a monument to her, Trethia and Ubree."

4

Oak Speaks

It was nice to be out in the fresh air, but I felt ridiculously weak. Mekrar held my arm, and somehow made it look as if she was leaning on me, and not the other way around.

Iryndal sat near the tree stump and rocks. While the huge dragon appeared to be resting, she opened her eyes as I approached, and I knew she had been aware of everything I had said and done.

"What do you remember? What was strange?" she asked.

"The lamps all went out at the same time. Why?" I sat in front of her.

She nodded. "I can show you what Othyn saw, but her vision was blocked moments before everything went dark."

"Did she see who attacked Kirym and Trethia?"

"No."

"So, there's no telling who Gynbere intended to kill." I frowned. "Or why?"

"That's not an accusation you can make at this stage. Kirym would not allow it. There's no proof Gynbere did this."

I nodded. "I'll still wonder. How are Kirym's family taking it? They've lost so many over the last few seasons. I didn't even think of it when I was talking to Mekrar earlier. And what about Amethyst?"

"They are coping better than I expected. Amethyst has many to love her, and she spends more time with Mekrar, Loul, and Veld now."

"What about you and the other dragons?" I asked.

"Losing Ubree and Kirym has, of course, left a huge hole in us."

"Have you sung to Ubree? Kirym said that was what you normally do when one of you dies."

Iryndal looked unhappy. "We've tried. He doesn't respond. I can't explain it."

"Is there anything else you can't explain?"

She nodded. "I never thought Trethia would be as important to us as Ubree and Kirym. I feel she has always been with me, although I can't remember seeing her before Kirym named her. We miss the large tokens, too. I feel unbalanced with them locked away." She paused. "Let me show you what Othyn saw."

The pictures she showed me were familiar, a view I had seen or been aware of, but from a new angle. Mekrar and Arbreu joined me and I was aware of others sitting nearby and taking an interest in Iryndal's view, although they must all have seen it before.

We came to the point when Kirym picked up a scrap of parchment and read it out. There was a flurry of movement and some cries of protest, but before I could see what caused them, something passed in front of Othyn. Moments later, everything went black.

When light was restored, Kirym, Trethia, and Ubree lay dead together near the shelves. Gynbere was by the northern wall, just as dead.

Iryndal's pictures ended.

"What made you break your connection?" I asked.

Iryndal frowned. "I was distracted when some children screamed. It was so unexpected. When I reconnected with Othyn, all was dark and chaotic."

"Why did the children scream? Were you aware of what went on out here while you were connected to Othyn's view?"

"Subliminally, and I've not really thought about it since then."

She showed me. It was a normal scene, nothing untoward at all. Groups of people sat and watched Othyn's view of the interior of the Burl. A few of them walked around, someone retrieved a wandering toddler, a young woman collected a rug for her baby to lie on, a girl handed a shawl to her mama. A group of girls sat in a circle playing a hand game, and a few boys chased a ball from one place to another. Everything was normal. Then three men began to argue. One pushed another, and he fell backward into the girls. That explained the screams.

Iryndal accepted my request to see both views twice, without commenting or seeming to be annoyed.

"Can you put the two views together?" I asked. "The inside and the outside?"

She raised an eyebrow but nodded. It was strange seeing the view in this way, and again, I needed to see it several times.

I realised there was something wrong. "Who is that?" I exclaimed. I felt stupid when I realised, I was pointing to a spot under Iryndal's chin.

"Explain," she said.

"At the mouth of the Burl. A man appeared only moments before everything happened, the fight, the darkness, everything."

5

Arbreu

Oak found himself unexpectedly surrounded by dragons.

"I never considered him important," Othyn said. She appeared to be looking inward. "Something crossed my vision. The only thing big enough was Ubree. I was trying to figure out why he moved. At almost the same time, the lights went out. The man reached the entrance before then. Someone mentioned that one of the dwarves was feeling a bit overwhelmed by the crowd. Perhaps he went up for some fresh air."

Churnyg frowned. "A Dwarf? Nooooo. We thrive on having our hollow filled with family and friends. The more, the merrier. Nothing finer than a huge crowd o' people, so many, you're squashed in so close you have to breathe in and out in unison. Our hollows are always far more crowded than it was down there. So, either he's disguised as a dwarf, or he was acting. Disguise isn't easy for any of you, our height and width would make it almost impossible. So, I have to ask why he would lie?"

"Are you sure, Churnyg? Look, he does seem to be gasping for air, almost on his knees for a few moments." Veld pointed to the image Iryndal was again showing. "Even when he stands, he's still wobbly. See, he reaches for support."

"Nah!" Churnyg said. "I've never known a reaction like that. Again—why?"

"From there, he would have been seen from inside and out," Oak said. "He'd have a view down to the floor of the Burl and could be seen by anyone looking up. Could he have co-ordinated the whole thing?"

Iryndal again seemed to look inward. "Shortly after he emerged, one man was pushed onto the girls. They screamed taking everyone's attention, and at that moment, he touched the wall."

"If we accept this explanation, who organised the lookout?" Loul asked. "Who told him to be at the entrance, and who needed to see him?"

"There's only one person—"

"I might ha' known you'd work out a way to accuse Gynbere," Vellysh snarled.

Arbreu spun around. Vellysh and Zeffun stood together, watching. Arbreu hadn't seen them arrive and wondered why they were no longer confined to the prison area.

He saw the same shock on Oak's face.

Gynbere and his men should hear what is said in each of our discussions. Then there can be no accusations.

Oak nodded, and Arbreu realised Iryndal's explanation had come to them both.

"No one is accusing anyone of anything," Loul said. "However, the timing of this man's movements at the entrance to the burl is suspect, and we must find out what happened. He could explain himself, of course. Who was it?"

There was no answer, no one stepped forward.

"The answer may be inside the Burl. The problem is, we can't enter," Loul said.

"Perhaps it's not that we can't, but that we don't know how," Oak said. "Kirym used some of the weapons to open the Burl. Can you replace them, Ashistar?"

"They haven't been moved, Oak," Ashistar said. "While we were in the Burl, they were guarded to ensure nothing was touched."

"Something else is stopping us from returning. When did you realise you could no-longer enter the Burl?"

"The following morning. The entrance was guarded overnight. When we tried to enter, it appeared to be open, but no one could step over the threshold," Iryndal said.

"And you can't remember any mention of the Burl from the past?" Arbreu asked.

Iryndal shook her head. "We have spent much of the last few days trying to find something, anything. Even Borasyn has nothing."

"What about Faltryn?" Oak asked.

"That stupid baby makes even less sense than Borasyn does," Egrym said, "and he's sillier than most."

Othyn frowned at him. "It takes time; she is just a baby. However, we can read nothing from her, not even what is usual at her age. We don't understand, and I fear the problem is ours, not hers."

"Well," Oak said, "it wouldn't hurt to ask her. Where is she?"

"Lying on Kirym's set," Morkeen said. "I found her there the morning after I came out of the Burl. She's been there ever since."

"It's not healthy for her to stay there. I'll go get her."

"Don't move, Oak. I'll get her." Sundas almost ran to the wagon.

"That may take Sundas' attention from me," Oak said quietly.

Mekrar shook her head. "I wish I'd known. I didn't think to ask where she was. I do miss Kirym. She would have remembered Faltryn."

"You've had a lot on your mind," Arbreu said. "Too much."

"It's something I'll try not to forget. Part of learning to be headwoman."

Loul leaned forward. "It's a lesson for me too, Mekrar. I didn't think of Faltryn, either. This is how we grow and learn."

6

Oak Speaks

Faltryn looked miserable as she snuggled into my arms.

Her scales were dull, she was listless, and that worried me. She had been so close to Kyrim. I didn't know where to begin, or even if there was a place to start. I had to try though. I felt she was my last resort.

"Do you know where Kirym and Trethia are?"

She nodded.

"I want to bring them out of there. Can we do it?"

Another nod.

"How?"

She clambered off my lap and began to scratch through the grass.

"She wants us to dig through the Burl?" Twig asked. "We've tried. Couldn't even scratch the surface."

"I don't think that's what she means," Wind Runner said.

Faltryn had cleared the grass from a small area and started to scratch in the damp soil. She looked up and searched through the crowd around us. I followed her eyes. From the angle she looked, I knew she wanted one of the other dragons.

"Little one." I got her attention. "Who do you want? Iryndal?"

She shook her head and drew a line through the soil. I almost laughed. It was obvious. "Borasyn?"

She nodded, and the crowd parted to allow the artist dragon through.

"You can't draw unless you have space, child." Borasyn ripped away more of the grass and smoothed the soil. "Now, move back, Oak, and let her begin."

Faltryn dug a tiny claw into the soil and meticulously made a line about the length of Sundas' hand. She left a gap of a few finger-widths and repeated the line. She then used two claws to make lines through the gap. She lifted her claws from the soil, put them back, and followed the marks back through the gap. She looked up at Borasyn, then Mekrar, and then at me.

No one said anything. She sighed and put her head on my lap.

I stared at the lines in the soil, around the area, past the stone figures, over to the stump, and along the top of the Burl. Nothing made sense.

"Oh, of course," Mekrar exclaimed. "The long line. It's the path up the Burl. Is the space in it the door?"

Faltryn nodded.

"That shows us going in and out, but—" she paused.

Faltryn was shaking her head. She rubbed out the picture and redid it.

"It's the same as before. I don't understand," Mekrar said.

Nor did anyone else.

Faltryn again erased what she had done, and now did two short lines with a wide space between them. She looked up at the Burl.

"The entrance?" I asked.

She nodded slowly. Then she reached over and with two claws, one in front of the second, scored two lines, first one way, and then the other.

"Two lines," Mekrar said. "Two directions? We go in. But how?"

Faltryn shook her head. She looked as frustrated as I felt.

"Not in and out," I said. "But what?"

Mekrar frowned. "Through, but not in and out."

"Out and in again."

I looked up at Larqeba. "What?"

"We came out," he said, and Faltryn nodded. "Now we go in again."

"We've tried to do that, laddie," Sundas said. "We can't get in."

"Everyone came out, and then you and Mekrar came out, Oak," Larqeba said.

But Faltryn was shaking her head.

I stared at the picture, trying to work out what the lines meant.

"I came out last. After Mekrar. Do we re-enter in the reverse order?" I asked.

Faltryn looked relieved as she nodded.

Entering the Burl was as simple as that. Mekrar followed me through the door, and once inside, it appeared as black as the first time I had entered. This time we carried an unlit lamp each. I had my knife in my hand, despite assurances from Iryndal that it was safe. I was still unsure, but there was only one way to find out.

I took a deep breath and started down the path.

I took one step, and then another. The light travelled with me, and I remembered Kirym's confident walk down the same path a few days earlier. She does—did have an uncanny instinct, an ability to sense when something was safe.

Except it hadn't been safe at all.

I was pleased to hold a lamp and glad to have Mekrar at my shoulder.

As I reached the end of the path, small lights glowed in the ceiling above. Ubree's body was behind me, and although I wanted to rush over to Kirym and Trethia, Loul had decided we would deal with Gynbere first.

I heard movement above, the others had begun to sort out the order they should enter. Most of them carried lighted lamps.

"I don't understand why lamps are needed for some of us, but not others," I said.

"It may be to do with our affinity with the Burl."

"But I don't have…"

"Your connection with Kirym makes a difference, possibly cos she's dead, it has extended to you."

Loul arrived next, followed by Veld, Findlow, Wind Runner, and Storm. Othyn was the first dragon to enter. Then Arbreu carried Faltryn down, and that opened the door to all who wanted to enter. Iryndal and Borasyn also joined us.

Mekrar glanced around. "There are still a few who won't enter. They're scared the door will close with them inside, I guess."

"Would it?" Arbreu asked.

"I don't think so. If I was worried, I wouldn't be here."

"Interesting point; Gynbere's men are here," I said. "All of them? Why?"

We're watching them, Oak. Iryndal's thought also explained why there were so many dragons inside the Burl this time.

"Teema isn't here," Starshine said quietly. "Should I go get him?"

Mekrar shook her head. "He offered to stay with Sarel and Trayum so Zeprah could join us. He did the same last time."

We waited in the area between Ubree and Gynbere, waiting until everyone who wished to enter, had arrived at the bottom of the path.

Zeffun and Thyshult swaggered towards Veld.

"We demand—" began Zeffun.

"If you want Gynbere's body immediately, take it," Veld said. "Personally, I wouldn't touch it, not with the sword and shield there. Whether they are moved or not is up to Ashistar."

Zeffun held his ground. "We were promised."

"No!" Loul said. "I said we would look at the situation. What happens then depends on what we find. I need to know what happened here, and why. If I am not happy, everything will stay as it is."

"Gynbere has already been accused of killing everyone here, even though he never carried a weapon," Zeffun said.

"There have been, and will be no accusations without proof," Sirasha said. "What happened here cannot be changed. We're here to find out what took place while there was no light. The Beech family will ensure the truth is maintained. If you don't trust them, then you would not trust your own eyes."

"Oh, I'm sure evidence to suit you has already been planted."

Iryndal brought her face close to Zeffun's. "Nothing here has been altered. Do you question *my* honesty?"

Zeffun blanched and backed away.

"Ashistar," Loul said. "You are now the holder of the weapons. Have you chosen a helper?"

He shook his head. "I don't feel I have the right to choose one, Loul. As I understood it, the tie between the holder and helper lasts until the death of one. Kirym held them. I may no longer have the authority to even touch them."

"When Kirym chose you, did your feeling for them change?" Findlow asked. Ashistar nodded. "And have they again changed?"

There was a long silence as Ashistar thought about the question. "I don't think so."

"My thought," Sirasha said, "is that you become the chief holder if you wish, and at some time suitable, you may choose a helper."

"And if you're wrong?"

"Then I suspect Gynbere must remain here. This is definitely not the place for him, so there must be a resolution."

Ashistar closed his eyes briefly. "It doesn't feel wrong for me to continue as a holder. However, I see no one as a helper yet, so perhaps this isn't the time"

"You have as long as you need," Loul said.

The silent wait seemed interminable. Ashistar finally took a deep breath. "If I have it wrong, Loul, I will die. Then no one can touch the weapons or my body. My few possessions will go to my Sire, Churnyg. They're in a basket alongside my set. Amongst them is a journal, he will find it amusing. In it is a note to tell him what to do with one or two special items."

Churnyg pushed through the crowd and grasped Ashistar's arm. "I'm proud you're ma son. I shouldn't have taken your name away."

Ashistar smiled. "And yet I've grown fond of your new choice and I'm happy to be known as Ashistar in the journal of this time."

"If you have doubts, Ashistar," Loul said, "don't touch—" but Ashistar turned and picked up the sword.

There was an audible sigh of relief when nothing happened to him. I think we had all been holding our breath. With the sword firmly in his hand, Ashistar picked up the shield.

"Take extra care," Loul said. "We still don't know what weapon—"

"You said there'd be no accusations without proof," interrupted Zeffun.

"And none has been made," continued Loul. "I was about to say we don't know what weapon was used on any of those dead. Nor do we know where that weapon is now. Assuming Gynbere is innocent, it is possible the weapon, whatever it is, has been placed near him, and I'm sure you, Zeffun, would be as unhappy as I if there was another fatality."

"You agree Gynbere was standing behind Kirym, don't you?" Mekrar said.

Zeffun nodded slowly.

"We need to know what happened next. How did he get from there to here?"

"He had no weapons," snarled Zeffun. "He was searched when he was imprisoned. Everything was taken. I challenge your assumption of poison too. He never used it. Perhaps Slaslow did, but Gynbere was far too noble to do something like that."

"We've seen Gynbere using poison," interrupted Ashistar, "and he obviously felt Kirym was dead enough for him to grab the sword and shield. How noble was that?"

"If you hadn't killed him, you could ask him."

"We have not made accusations against you, do not make them against us," Loul said.

"He's been murdered! You can't deny it."

"Until there is proof, yes we can."

Ashistar stepped away from the body. "Now he may be checked, but take care, we know nothing of what has caused the deaths here."

Zeffun, Thyshult, and Suarsh all moved towards the body.

"Stop!" Veld strode forward. "You will not touch him until he has been searched. I'm sure you will watch most carefully. Would you trust Kwarnar Yew to be one of the searchers?"

"He'll do," called Vellysh. "He may have hated his brother, but he won't see aught wrong done to the family name. Thyshult can help—"

"You don't get to choose who helps," Loul said. "I've chosen Findlow to help."

Findlow pulled on a pair of leather gloves, approached the body and studied it carefully. Then he bent and carefully flicked Gynbere's robe open to expose a wide yellow sash over a red robe. He pulled the sash away, shook it, folded it, and lay it on the floor.

Kwarnar, also wearing leather gloves, carefully lifted one of Gynbere's green boots, removed and inspected it carefully. The second was also examined and both were put to one side.

His men aren't interested in these things, I thought. *It must be something else they want.*

Kwarnar and Findlow worked systematically. Findlow was expert at checking for weapons, and he explained what he intended to do before each movement.

"Gynbere's hair is long enough to hide a weapon, and we'll check it for other substances as well."

Kwarnar pushed the left sleeve of Gynbere's robe up and searched for obvious weapons. Then he inspected his hand and fingers.

"Veld, this is ridiculous," Vellysh called. "It's time you accepted that Gynbere was murdered. Hand his body over and allow us to bury him with the honour he deserves."

"We'll talk about burial when Findlow and Kwarnar are satisfied they've searched him properly," Veld said.

"They have," snapped Vellysh. "Doing it twice won't change things, unless they planted something the first time around."

"Then," Veld continued, "Kwarnar will decide what happens to him."

Findlow now carefully picked up the hem edge of Gynbere's right sleeve. Both sleeves had wide cuffs, but this one had unrolled and covered his hand completely.

"Blade, please," murmured Findlow.

Kwarnar handed him a thin knife. Findlow carefully slit the sleeve to the elbow and dragged the material back.

"Look at this." Findlow extended Gynbere's hand, holding his fingers stiff.

Gynbere's first fingernail was very long and had been filed to a sharp point. The nail was dark yellow, with a thick smear of brown at the tip. Hanging from his cuff was a leather finger-guard.

"That, I suspect, is the weapon," Kwarnar said.

"You can't say that," snapped Zeffun. "There's no proof, and anyway, you said the girl was poisoned. Prove it is poison."

"Oh, we don't need to," Loul said.

Zeffun took an angry breath. "You said no accusations."

"Oh, not an accusation. It's up to you to prove it *isn't* poison," Loul said.

Zeffun went white. He glanced nervously at Vellysh, who pointedly looked away.

"Unless of course you think or know it is, in which case we will accept your word." Loul paused and raised her eyebrow.

"Well, I wouldn't put it to the test, either. Now, for the burial. A box has been made. Gynbere's body will be sealed in it and hopefully, the poison will be contained."

"Wait!" interrupted Suarsh. "That's not how we do it."

"I asked Loul to make those arrangements," Kwarnar said. "I want no more ripples from Gynbere's actions. I've asked Iryndal to take the box to a hidden place. No one will find it again, ever."

"I should make those decisions. I am his closest living friend," snarled Zeffun. "I want a fitting ceremony to salute his greatness."

"He is from the Yew, and I speak for the Yew family. His Maman, wife, and dwarflings don't wish for any ceremony," Kwarnar said. "If you insist, we will allow you to go with Gynbere to look after his resting place. However, if the poisons leach from the box, then you'll get no help from us, and you'll never be allowed to return."

Zeffun, Vellysh, and Suarsh whispered together for a short time.

"When will you tell us where the box has been placed?" Vellysh asked.

"Never," Loul said. "This box will be hidden so well, nothing from it will ever appear again. At no time in the future will anyone be able to claim they have a keepsake from it."

There was a gasp from those around the cave when a long box suddenly appeared in the clear area between Loul and the body.

Vellysh jumped back, visibly shocked.

Very clever, Arymda, I thought. *Invisibility can certainly add to an occasion.*

Kwarnar straightened Gynbere's robe.

"Wait!" Suarsh stepped forward, knelt on the far side of the body, placed Gynbere's arms across his body. He ran his gloved hands across Gynbere's chest, straightening his robe. He bowed his head to the floor in obeisance. His hands disappeared under Gynbere's robe.

"What is he doing?" Mekrar murmured.

Suarsh glanced back to Zeffun and Vallysh who both nodded. Suarsh bowed his head again, brought his cupped hands to his chest, and then stood with his head bowed.

Kwarnar grabbed the shoulders of Gynbere's robe, while Findlow used the hem of it. Together lifted the body off the ground and carried it to the box and lowered him in. They added their gloves and stepped back.

Suarsh bowed his head over the box and stepped away although his hands now hidden in his wide sleeves.

"Large tokens belong to The Green Valley!"

I initially thought Kirym had spoken, she and Mekrar sounded very similar.

Everyone looked mystified. Suarsh froze mid-step and partially turned.

Mekrar walked towards him, her hand outstretched.

"Can I help you, Lady?" Suarsh bowed deeply.

"Taking what was stolen doesn't give you ownership."

"Lady. I have nothing that didn't belong to my family in the past." He spoke quietly; I had to strain to hear him.

"When did your family ever hold a large token?"

He paled slightly. "Large token, Lady? I'm not sure what you mean."

"Tokens are a weighty load at the best of times, but when not authorised to hold them, they grind the holder into nothing. Think carefully. Such a story would have excited a young lad. How old were you when you first heard of such a possession?"

Suarsh's face changed. He frowned and looked down for a long moment. When he again looked at Mekrar, he nodded, reached into his robe, bought out and placed the yellow token in her hand.

"Evidently, Gynbere told Vellysh it belonged to my family," he said quietly.

"And yet when it recently came into Gynbere's possession, he didn't hand it over to you. I imagine Vellysh told the same story to a number of different people." She glanced over to Vellysh and Zeffun Urfit, who were whispering together. "Gynbere never displayed it, and that was most unlike him. You knew there had to be some subterfuge for it to be in his possession. If you truly believed it, why didn't you ask for it, ask us to help you search Gynbere's body?" Mekrar half turned. "Mama, before the men are returned to their enclosure, have it and them searched. Search those who remained outside, also. From now until we decide what to do with them, all of those who venture close to the enclosure must be searched and do the same to everyone who enters and exits."

Loul nodded. "Yes, it's a good idea. Veld, could you organise it please."

All attention was now on Storm and Sundas, who put the lid on the box and hammered fourteen wooden plugs into it.

To another gasp from those around me, the box slowly rose into the air and drifted towards the entrance.

Many of Gynbere's people followed the box out of the Burl although a few stayed to watch the yellow token be placed with the others. Mekrar sat it on the fourth shelf down, and to the right of the red token. They began to sing, very quietly at first, but gradually, the tune strengthened.

"I'm not sure if they're happy or sad," I said to Mekrar.

"Perhaps a bit of both. They're together, and they need to be, but Kirym, Trethia, and Ubree are still dead."

Those who loved Kirym, went to say goodbye before following the crowd up the path and out of the Burl.

Finally, only Kirym's family and a few of her closest friends remained. The tokens' song soared as we approached her.

Arbreu gripped my shoulder as I joined the line of those filing past. "Oak, after we say goodbye, can you bring Mekrar up? I'll help Zelriff."

I nodded. In truth, I was glad to have something to do. I'd felt terribly alone since I'd woken, so it was good to focus on someone else.

With a large crowd around Ubree, Mekrar and I stood back and listened to the tokens. I watched as those who loved Kirym as much as I did, walked from where she lay at Ubree's head, to where his tail thinned, and stepped over it. Then they started the long walk around the wall to the entrance.

Wind Runner was overcome with grief. She looked ancient. I'd never thought about it before, but I realised I may soon lose her too. I didn't know her age but suspected she was much older even than Zelriff and Old Harby, who had each seen more than ninety-five winters.

Sundas nodded an acknowledgement as he walked past us. He glanced up at Wind Runner, sped up slightly until he was beside her. He offered her his arm. She took it and leaned against him; Storm had his hand on her back. At the entrance, he slipped his hand under her elbow.

I hope she gets angry enough to argue with them. That would be the best thing ever. Well, Kirym being alive would be the best thing ever, but next to it, Wind Runner needs to fight against being mollycoddled.

Findlow, Churnyg, Ashistar, and Baketer were together as they walked past me. They all looked terribly sad. They were followed, two by one by three, by all of those I now looked on as family and a few I knew I should get to know better.

I felt for all of them.

For myself, I was empty. I'd had so many dreams and all of

them had Kirym in them. I still hadn't really accepted her death.

Zelriff began her walk up the path, Arbreu on one side, Old Harby on the other. Again, it hit me, Zelriff and Harby, whom I loved dearly, may not be with us much longer. I could see loss upon loss ahead of me. Veld had his arm around Loul, as they walked past, stony-faced and dignified. No longer leaders of the families, but just parents, mourning the loss of a special child and grandchild.

Soon Mekrar and I were the only ones left. I knew this would be the hardest goodbye I'd ever make. We waited until everyone else had said their goodbyes before we stepped over Ubree's tail and walked up the length of his body.

Mekrar knelt as close to Ubree as she could, without touching him.

Something has changed.

It worried me—played on my mind—but I couldn't think what or why. I finally shook it away and concentrated on taking in as much of Kirym, Trethia, and Ubree as I could.

I heard the other dragons singing; their way of saying goodbye. They sounded lost even when the tokens sang with them. More voices joined in; the people outside joined the dragons, their voices echoed through the entrance. I heard Mekroe's pipe, Tarjin's drum, Lantiah and Armos harmonising. It was all beautiful and terribly sad.

Eventually, I knew it was time to leave. I helped Mekrar up and together we walked down Ubree's body towards the path.

As we passed his belly, I stopped. Mekrar took two more steps before she realised, I was no longer with her.

"What's—"

"He's moved."

"What! Who?"

"Ubree. His tail has moved."

7

Oak Speaks

She looked around, obviously not seeing what I had finally grasped.

"When I looked eariler, the end of Ubree's tail was curved this way. Now it's coiled towards the—"

She was no longer there.

I followed her back to Ubree's head.

"What do we do?" I asked.

"You wait here. I'll be back soon."

And she was quick. I thought she would have gone to get someone, Loul perhaps, but she only went to the shelves where the tokens sat and brought the blue and green tokens and the black stone I'd given Kirym.

She lay them in a triangle on the ground between Ubree and Kirym, the black as the apex pointing to where Kirym's hand touched Ubree's nose, the green near Kirym's shoulder, and the blue between Trethia and Ubree.

Iryndal appeared beside me.

"Oh good," Mekrar said. "Iryndal, when more than one dragon dies, how do you call them back?"

"We sing to them as we are doing now; just listen." The dragons were still singing along with everyone else.

Mekrar nodded. "Do you sing to all of the dragons together or one at a time?"

Iryndal looked as mystified as I felt. "To the oldest first. Their voice is needed to waken the younger dragon."

"I thought so. And you've been singing to Ubree."

"Well yes, of course. When only one of us is dead, it's simple. In this case, the poison has—"

"Who can waken dragons from death?"

"Older siblings, but when it's the eldest, all of the younger brothers and sisters are needed."

"And what would happen if you sang to a younger dragon first?"

"They wouldn't understand the call. Mekrar what's—"

Mekrar smiled broadly. "Singing to Ubree hasn't worked, so, sing to Kirym."

"Mekrar," Iryndal said gently, "it only works for dragons. I know you would do anything to bring Kirym..."

"She woke you, Iryndal. All of you. Something happened, and we don't understand, but I wonder if she is now," she shrugged, "oh, I don't know, but she's aligned to you, so perhaps it'll work. Nothing else has, but is it possible she's older than Ubree?"

"Oh!" Iryndal turned and stared at Kirym. "I hadn't thought of that. Anything is possible."

"Try it. Please try it."

The whole tone of the song changed as first Iryndal, and then the rest of the dragons sang to Kirym. The two tokens glowed, and each sent up a ray of warm light. They twined around each other and curved over to touch Kirym's tokens.

Oh please, please make this work, I begged.

I was shocked to see the ray flick to the black stone and feed light into it. After a long moment, it lit up and sent its own beam to Kirym.

However, as much as I wanted it to work, it didn't make sense. This was a stone, the stone I had given to Kirym. I had picked it up off the riverbank just as she disappeared from my sight.

Surely, I couldn't have found a token, and yet here it was doing things the tokens did.

I heard the rustle of movement behind me. Loul, Veld, Wind Runner and Sundas had returned, and the crowd grew as the dragons brought people back into the Burl.

Wind Runner squeezed my arm.

I glanced at Mekrar. She now had Loul, Veld, and Arbreu with her. I put my arm around Wind Runner's shoulder and hugged her. She was trembling, but when I glanced down, she looked as serene as ever.

We waited. The song changed again. Churnyg added his dragon call, quickly joined by Ashistar, Larqeba, and Shormel. Initially, those who were with him when he first used it sang, but soon almost everyone joined in the chorus.

"She moved!" Loul reached back, grabbed my hand and pulled Wind Runner and me forward to stand with her family. "I'm sure she moved."

Kirym's eyes flickered open, closed briefly and then opened again.

Everyone gasped. I felt I was in the midst of a dream, and I was scared I would waken and find it wasn't real.

As if in a trance, Kirym sat up, still cradling Trethia. She glanced up at Iryndal, paused, and nodded in understanding—she knew what had just happened and what she needed to do.

Kirym leaned forward, caressed Ubree's cheek and spoke to him. The cave was filled with a triumphant wolf call, the final note of Churnyg's song, so I couldn't hear what she said, but Ubree's eyes opened.

Cries of wonder, shock, delight, and amazement rang through the cave. People were laughing and crying, Mekrar and Loul appeared to be doing both.

The cut on Kirym's jaw had disappeared, her skin, its usual healthy pink; Ubree was darker than he had been.

The singing stopped.

In the long silence that followed, we were all aware that Trethia's scar remained on her forehead, and she lay as still as ever.

I brushed the tears from my eyes, useless, they continued to run down my cheeks.

Kirym and Ubree bent over Trethia, and for a short time, she was lost to my sight.

An ugly laceration appeared on Ubree's cheek. The dark centre of the cut looked as ghastly on him as it had on Trethia.

Ubree's eyes closed, and in the silence, I could hear Kirym's quiet comments, although I couldn't understand her words.

"Dragonese perhaps," murmured Wind Runner. She had stopped shaking and now looked many seasons younger than she had just a short time before.

Ubree took a deep breath, his forehead healed, his head came up and he slowly got to his feet. He still had the scar on his shoulder, I wondered if it would ever disappear.

I moved close to Kirym and took Trethia off her. Her face no longer had the mark of poison, but her body was quite cold. I hugged her close and remembered Ubree's words to Kirym back at the beginning of winter. 'I can't bring the dead back to life. I can only work on the living.'

I was devastated. Trethia had lived such a horrid life, and now just as it improved, it was stolen from her. *She will be beautiful when we bury her.*

Kirym placed Trethia's hand on Ubree's cheek.

The dragons had begun to sing again, but this was a different song. It gave me the impression of spring, flowers blossoming, butterflies fluttering among them, bees searching busily for pollen, along with animals, lots of hatchlings taking their first steps into the sunshine.

Along with the song, Ubree's breath gusted around us along with that of the other dragons. I was intrigued to realise each breath was different and I recognised each one. Amazingly, Trethia's small body began to warm, her eyes opened, and she smiled sleepily. She snuggled close to me for a few moments and then reached for Kirym.

"Thank you, Ubree, Iryndal," I said. "Thank you, all of you so much." Tears streamed down my face. Kirym was crying too.

I glanced up at Ubree. He looked as distant and as grumpy as ever, but his eyes were soft. I knew he was as fond of Trethia as I was.

I moved aside for Loul and Veld and found myself pushed further away as everyone clamoured to be close to Kirym.

Moments later, Mekrar pushed through the crowd and handed Trethia to me.

"She's still very sleepy and Kirym asked if you'd keep her safe until everyone has calmed down."

I wrapped my cloak around the wee girl, even though she now felt warm.

Mekrar hugged me. "Thank you. I would have walked out of here without ever realising they were actually alive."

I shook my head. "Even knowing it, you were the one to figure out how to get them back. I'd never have made the connection of Kirym as a dragon."

She laughed. "I remembered the huge green splodge in her token, and she called each of the other dragons back after they had died. She has to be aligned to them somehow, although I wouldn't have called her a dragon."

"How did you know to bring those tokens over? Especially the black one, I didn't even know it was a token. It was just a stone I thought Kirym would like."

"I was going to bring them all over, but when I got there, I realised I only wanted those three. Honestly, I didn't think about why the black stone was needed until it glowed. I remembered after the earthquake in the Land Between the Gorges when Teema found the rainbow token. Teema said, 'To me, it was just a stone I happened to grab'. Kirym put it with the other tokens, and she did the same to the black stone, so perhaps she knew."

8

Arbreu

They celebrated long into the night. Teema was there,
although he pointedly avoided Arbreu's attempts to approach.
Instead, he helped Zeprah with Sarel and Trayum.

As the moon passed the meridian, the fires died, and most
people slept.

Dawn saw few awake, but when Arbreu walked out of the
dwelling, Kirym was already in the sunshine with Amethyst,
Trethia, and Faltryn.

Loul called the family leaders together soon after she had
eaten. Kirym too was summoned, and while it wasn't a
formal meeting, few stayed away. Everyone wanted to know
what had happened.

Normally, five or six of the prisoners were released to
listen and take part in the meetings, but in view of what

had happened in the Burl, Veld, as Warlord, decided it was safer to keep them locked up. Instead, the meeting was held near the large cage Churnyg had had built for them.

Veld stood and stated the rules for the meeting before Loul took over.

"Kirym, what memories do you have of your time in the Burl. Do you remember finding a book?" Loul asked.

"Yes. When I handed it to you to read, a piece of parchment fell out of it. I read it out." Kirym frowned as she recalled. "It all happened very fast. Trethia was pushed towards the wall, there was shouting and jostling, and it went dark as I was picking her up. "I remember my face hurt, I saw lots of bright colours and heard the tokens calling. Then Iryndal told me I needed to sing with them for Ubree. I didn't realise Trethia had been hurt until Ubree told me."

"Kirym, do you remember—"

"Don't tell her," Mekrar murmured quietly.

Kirym turned and smiled. "Remember what?"

Arbreu groaned quietly.

"You said the tokens called," Mekrar said, "but weren't they already singing? I was wondering."

"Yes. When the lights went out, their song changed." She frowned. "There was a time their voices were distant, almost as if they were moving away from me, but then they came closer, louder."

Loul nodded. "Ubree. What did you see?"

"People were moving around, more than was usual. It didn't seem right."

"In what way?"

"Gynbere stood behind Kirym, but his men moved away. They were in two loose lines off to the right. They were pushing people aside quite roughly. There were shouts of protest, but before I could do anything, the lamps failed."

"That intrigues me," Wind Runner said. "Why would they

all go out at the same moment?"

"I couldn't say it for all of the lamps," Ubree said, "so much was happening at the same time, but at least three of them had something thrown on the flame a moment before they died."

"Who…"

"All those I saw were Gynbere's men, and before anyone states an objection, I can place faces to those men. At the time, I was concentrating on getting to Kirym and Trethia who were already falling. All I could do was ensure I had contact with Kirym."

"Why Kirym and not Trethia?" Larqeba sounded outraged.

Ubree brought his head down until it was level with Larqeba's. "Kirym holds Trethia's heart. My touching the child was unnecessary. Yet, your loyalty does you proud."

"Why were Gynbere's men pushing people around?" Loul asked.

"It seemed unusual until I realised they had opened a corridor between Gynbere at one end, the weapons at the other." Ubree turned back to Loul. "Even as Kirym fell, Gynbere was running towards the weapons."

"How can you accuse Gynbere of even moving? It was dark. You've admitted it yourself," called Vellysh.

Ubree put his head very close to the bars. "Why were you standing beside the weapons?"

Vellysh shrugged. "Everyone stood somewhere. It's where I ended up. It wasn't so crowded there."

"You stood in a place where it was almost impossible to see what was happening. You were a long way from Gynbere, and yet your usual place is beside or behind him. In fact, none of Gynbere's bodyguards were particularly close to him. A strange way to guard someone, don't you think? Unless, of course, it was part of a bigger plan."

Vellysh went red, but Ubree turned away, as Lantiah stood and was acknowledged.

"I was standing between Kirym and the tokens and was pushed away. I banged into Twig and would have fallen, but for him steadying me. Other people were protesting at the same time. There was a lot of movement around me too."

"Do you know who pushed you?" Veld asked.

"Him." She pointed to Zeffun.

"No-no-no-no-no," protested Zeffun. "I might have stumbled into you. The guard called Blacknight pushed me."

Wind Runner spoke before Blacknight could respond.

"Blacknight was assigned to guard the weapons at the stump," she called. "He never left his post."

"I can guarantee that," Iryndal said.

"Does anyone have anything else to add?" Loul asked.

Sirasha stood. "My Lady Loul. Would it be possible for everyone to come and tell me where they stood when all of this was happening? I will make up a chart, and we can cross-reference everyone's position."

Loul agreed, and the meeting ended.

Arbreu pulled Mekrar aside. "What should I not have asked?"

"Kirym doesn't yet realise she needed to be woken in the same way as the dragons."

"But why shouldn't she know?"

Mekrar shrugged. "I don't really know. She will eventually, but I think she needs to figure it out herself. She holds the tokens. She's coming to terms with the changes in Teema's behaviour, and she has Trethia and Amethyst to care for. Why would she need another burden?"

"All right, I can see the sense in it, but she wouldn't see it as a burden. And what if she asks?"

"Then listen to what she asks and answer only her question."

She laughed at Arbreu's expression. "It's not hard, Arbreu. Most people give all sorts of extra information, just because they don't listen to the question properly. Remember when Parlansho asked where he came from? Peet told him how babies arrived and described his birth in vivid detail. All Parlansho really wanted to know if he was born in The Green Valley or The Land Between the Gorges. Harnita had quite a lot to sort out."

9

Kirym Speaks

Five days had passed between my entering the Burl and leaving it. Some of my questions had been answered during the meeting, but there were still many things I wanted to know.

Before I had a chance to corner someone to ask for further information, Larqeba raced up. "Lady Loul wants you and Mekrar in the new shelter beside the healing area."

The shelter had not been there when I entered the Burl. As we walked towards it, Mekrar told me it had been built for Oak. She didn't quite say why Oak would need it.

Mama and Wind Runner were already inside the dwelling. Storm and three guards were raising the eastern wall and propping it up at the corners with poles.

"A man has been removed from the prisoner's dwelling," Mama said. "He's in a bad way. The other prisoners are refusing to tell us anything other than they have never seen him before. I hoped one of you could confirm his identity."

Gynletha, the healer in charge, stepped aside.

Mekrar gasped. "What happened to him?"

The man's face was a swollen, raw pulp. What I could see of his body was just as bad, if not worse.

"Othyn brought him here," Gynletha said.

"Why didn't you call Ubree?" I asked. "He's a healer and he might be this man's only chance of living."

"He'll be here soon," Mama said. "He's doing something for Iryndal."

Mekrar examined the man's blood-stained jerkin and cloak.

"Do you know him, Mekrar?"

She nodded. "Well, going by these," she held them up, "and assuming he was wearing his own clothes, it's Suarsh, the man who handed me the yellow token when we were in the Burl. Why would he be attacked? I thought he was favoured by Gynbere."

"Gynbere is dead," I said. "Possibly it was a fight for the balance of power. Someone discouraging opposition."

"They don't need a new leader," Gynletha said. "Loul chose Kwarnar to lead us."

"One cannot order people to follow someone they don't want," Mama said. "I wonder at this level of violence though. There must be more to it?"

A noise from the set took my attention. The man pointed to Mekrar and me and beckoned us closer. He tried to speak, but it was indecipherable, the pain and effort were too much. His eyes rolled back.

Mekrar carefully checked the pulse in his neck and shook her head. "He's very weak. He may never tell his story. If he makes it, he must be guarded."

"Ubree is on his way," I said.

Suarsh's body began to jerk.

"This isn't good," Gynletha said.

Ubree and Iryndal arrived at the same time, and suddenly Mekrar and I were outside.

"Well, I guess we'll be called back if we're needed," Mekrar said. "I wonder why they didn't keep you in there though. You're so close to Ubree."

"Dragons do what is best for everyone, keeping in mind their obligation to Mama. They're answerable to her as headwoman. I'm sure we'll hear what we need to know."

Sundas and Oak were caring for Trethia, Amethyst, and Faltryn around a small fire. We joined them, and I pulled Trethia onto my lap. I glanced over at the prisoner's area. Not one of them was outside.

"I've never known them all to be in the dwelling at this time of day. I guess they're having a meeting of some sort. I'd love to hear what they're planning," I said.

In view of what just happened, Othyn is watching and listening. If there's any danger to anyone, we will intervene, came Iryndal's answer.

I turned my attention to the area around me. The statues we had re-erected now looked settled. I knew they all faced different directions, but now I mentally followed each line.

"You know, if you follow the line of each statues eyes," I said, "You often find something important to us."

"What do you mean?" Oak asked.

"Well that one," I pointed to the stone warrior nearest the stump. "He looks in the direction of the stone circles. The woman over there," I indicated a statue near the back, "she looks towards our settlement. The one at the front looks to The Land Between the Gorges."

"I think you're right," Oak said. "So, the known settlements and the circles, but what about the rest of them? Could you use the lines and identify where the ancient settlements were? Could we find Valythia?"

"It's not all settlements. The man holding the boat looks

at the amphitheatre and the girl at the back looks at the Burl," I said. "The older girl in the front looks to the sky."

"Midsummer moon or sun, perhaps? Is this to do with seasons?"

I shook my head. "She's not looking to the horizon. Not quite north, either."

"But you know, don't you," Oak said.

"I think she looks at the Dragon Star, but I wonder why?"

Before he could answer, Arymda appeared. *Kirym, Iryndal wants you*, and before I could ask any questions, I was standing beside Mama, surprised to find Oak and Trethia with me. Old Harby, Mekrar, Enliah, and Sundas were there too, and all the family heads except Bryn.

Garanniis has Amethyst and Faltryn, Othyn told me.

Ubree was still recovering from the healing, but Suarsh was sitting up, wrapped in a sleeping robe and looking much better.

I went first to Ubree. *Are you all right, my friend?*

He nodded. *He was badly damaged, and I'm glad I was here. His story will explain a lot and help you all resolve the issues of what to do with the prisoners.*

We waited in quiet expectation. Suarsh looked uncomfortable with the audience but coughed and cleared his throat. "I'll explain the token first. After Gynbere died, Vellysh Urfit said it was mine, had belonged to my great-great-grandsire. He said it was written in a scroll Gynbere had shown him, and the knowledge of it had been covered up by those in The Green Valley. He said it was mine by right, but I had to have the courage to claim it. If I ever doubted it was mine or handed it to anyone else, I'd die, my family also."

"And yet you gave it to Mekrar when she asked for it," Mama said.

"Lady Mekrar's arguments were compelling. Later, I asked around to confirm her points—indeed, Zeffun and Vellysh had given the same story to most of the men who'd been in Gynbere's protection group. I was the only one with the courage to approach Gynbere's body."

Suarsh bowed in Mama's direction. "I realised, Lady of the Green Valley, that Lady Mekrar was right. Once I began to think clearly, I knew it could never have been held by us. Vellysh said Gynbere had always held it safely for my family, although I'd never heard the story before. Gynbere was never one to hide a special possession, even if someone else had true ownership, so I figured it must belong to you. There were whispers about the tokens inside The Rock. No one spoke openly of them; Gynbere and Slaslow killed people for mentioning them."

"Why were you beaten?" Findlow asked.

"At first the Urfit triplets, well, twins now I guess, since Thipen is dead, I've heard. Well, they thought my discussion with Lady Mekrar was a ploy to hide the token from them. When they understood I really had handed it over, they were furious. I couldn't understand why, until I realised they used me to see if holding it passed on whatever poison killed Gynbere. Gynbere had separately promised both Zeffun and Vellysh the title, Leader of the Combined Tribes of the Trees. They felt the stone, the token, would bolster their claim to the title. Few were happy about it, but no one would say out loud what they muttered behind their hands."

"When did Gynbere begin to talk about the yellow token?" I asked.

Suarsh frowned as he worked it out. "After the battle."

"Are you sure?" Findlow asked.

"Oh yes. That's was when one of his guards told him about the other tokens. Gynbere said they were his by right, and they would give him power over the dragons as well.

Holding them allowed him to hold the weapons as well as other things, evidently. Him telling us these things was unusual, he normally stayed aloof from all except his closest advisors. Slaslow mainly, Zeffun, Vellysh and Thippen as well, although not as often."

"Why did he want the weapons? How did he think he could he hold them?" Mama asked. "There were already two holders."

"He said if Kirym as holder died, so would Ashistar, and with them both dead, he could claim the weapons. He planned to poison the dragons and use the sword on them before Ubree could heal them. He thought if they were all killed by the sword, they couldn't be reborn, and Kirym would be dead so she couldn't help."

"So, after they realised you had handed the token over, what then?" Mekrar asked.

"I knew we had to look to the future. You hadn't punished me for touching the token, you hadn't attacked my family, so I talked to the men about accepting our situation and becoming part of your community. The Urfits heard, and there was an attempt to poison my food."

"They have more poison? How?" Mama asked.

"Many families carry a supply. Although the prisoners were searched when first imprisoned, they haven't been searched since. Visitors are searched, but poisons often look like something else. Seeds are hidden in pieces of jewellery, or sewn on clothes as decorations. There's plenty stored and growing back at the settlement. Some of the red seeds Gynbere uses often were buried in the northern corner of the cage. They've sprouted, so there'll be a good crop by summer."

"I'll have them removed," Mama said. "Anything else?"

"Gynbere believed if he held the weapons, he would become the leader in Kirym's place. The Urfits talked about

46

it when we left the Burl. They decided they could do what he couldn't, but then Kirym came out alive. They plan to try again."

"How?"

"They didn't know yet. She's survived four poison attempts—"

"Four?" Papa looked bewildered. "He tried in the Burl and in the amphitheatre after the battle. When else?" He looked at me. "When?"

I thought back, trying to remember. "Oh, when I was leaving The Rock, someone stabbed my foot," I said. "Churnyg said the poison used was a derivative of the yew tree."

"Only Gynbere used it," Churnyg said. "He must have thought you were a threat if he came after you himself."

Papa cleared his throat. "Well, three. The forth?"

"I don't—"

"Rargo did it," Trethia said.

I wasn't the only one who turned to stare at her.

"Rargo did what?" Mama asked.

"He poisoned Kirym. Gynbere told Rargo to kill her and gave him a special knife. It had a vial of poison in the handle. When Elm turned up, Rargo got kicked out of Gynbere's pavilion for a while, but he kept the knife. Rargo said he would kill Kirym, but he'd kill Elm first and then use the knife on Gynbere. Then he would rule everyone."

"What happened to his knife?" Mama asked.

"I have it." Enliah was pale. "But Rargo was dead when you were cut, Kirym. It means *I* poisoned you. Oh, I am *so* sorry."

"Rargo poisoned me, Enliah, with Gynbere's help. You saved my life. You also had poison in your system, and Rargo had already damaged you badly. The biggest problem with my hand was I didn't allow Ubree to heal it when I should

47

have. Give the knife to Ubree, he'll make it safe for you."

"Oh, I don't want it back." She shuddered. "I've never liked having it. I'll be glad to see it go."

"Bring it to me when it's clean, Ubree. I'll put it in the weapons store," Papa said.

"Ubree, why didn't you tell us both Enliah and Kirym had been poisoned by Rargo?" Mama asked.

"In thinking back, I now recognise the poison in Enliah's system. It was minimal; she had other serious problems, Loul. I had tried to help a lot of people that day and was not fully recovered. Enliah's wounds were very subtle but overwhelmingly emotional, which was understandable. I knew Kirym had cut her hand. Cuts get infected. I didn't know whose knife had been involved. Perhaps if I had…?" He shrugged. "She had been splashed with poison from Sundas also, and I didn't think to look for yet another poison. Poisons do strange things when mixed together. It's no excuse, but I had just dealt with Sundas, and I was still eliminating his venom from my system."

Mama nodded, apologised to Suarsh for the interruption and invited him to continue.

Suarsh inclined his head to her and took a deep breath. "Lady Kirym has a fortunate life, Lady Loul. Every arrow aimed at her seemed to fly away. I talked to the men about it. I felt it was a good basis for becoming part of The Green Valley. To that end, I suggested we accept Lady Loul as our leader. Some agreed. The rest of them were still enamoured with Gynbere's dream of ruling the land. It's why I was beaten up—a lesson to those who agreed with me."

"So, some of those in the cage wish to stay?"

"Yes, Lady, but I doubt they will tell you openly. They fear retribution against themselves or their families."

Mama nodded. "We will not be sending you back there. Tell me your wish for the future. It will be binding, Suarsh.

You no longer support Gynbere, but do you wish to live away from The Green Valley? Perhaps move to live with Raff or Wind Runner's people."

"For my family, I'd like to be a part of this community if you'll accept me. I'll vow to be loyal to you, your family and all following leaders of The Green Valley, Lady Loul. I will sign a covenant saying none of my family will *ever* challenge your office of leadership. I will personally serve your family for the rest of my life."

"It's rather an extensive undertaking, Suarsh, and it's not needed," Veld said.

"Oh, I think it is, Sir. I want to ensure my family is fully aware of what they've been part of. They need to know you hold their lives in your hands. I thank you for allowing me to live. I will do whatever you ask of me, except not fulfil this oath."

"You're suggesting a type of slavery, Suarsh. We don't allow that here," Mama said.

"And yet, Lady Loul, this is something my family and I will do, whether you wish it or not."

"Give him to Kirym."

"What? No!" I stared at Arbreu in horror. "What would give you the impression I'd ever be happy with an idea like that?" I asked.

"He'll protect you. Sooner or later—"

"No! Suarsh, you would be of far more use helping Churnyg with the trees. They need cosseting before they are ready to house your people," I said.

"My life is dedicated to your family, Lady Kirym."

"The Green Valley is better when everyone is housed. If you help Churnyg, it'll happen faster. Then there'll be plenty of work for everyone, growing food, building houses and boats, fishing, and exploring the land. No one will attempt to poison me because those who wish me dead will be gone.

And that, Arbreu, is the end of the discussion."

I turned back to Suarsh. "My name is Kirym. Mama is Lady of The Green Valley and Mekrar deserves the title because she will follow Mama in leadership. They lead the families. I don't!"

Trethia climbed on my lap. "He's a nice man. He always pretended not to see me in The Rock and he wouldn't let his men hit me. He deserves to be happy."

"Suarsh, you may give a long-standing oath for yourself, but not your family. They will first have a choice to decide on their loyalties. If they wish to, they may follow the Urfits," Mama said. "Once the decision is made, I will speak to you and those of your family who stay."

10

Arbreu

Everyone returned to the settlement and the choices were explained to the prisoners. Every family head was questioned privately about their desires for their families' future. Some of Loul's questions were unusual, but the answers were enlightening.

Everyone was spoken to privately and many families were divided.

Most of those who wished to stay offered up the weapons and poisons they had accumulated and hidden. Even so, everyone was searched, even those who had no desire to stay with us. More vials, bags of powder, and weapons, were found. Some of the hiding places were quite ingenious and were found only with help from Ashistar, Borboncha, and Baketer. Those holding them were questioned further.

"This is a lesson to us. We were far too trusting, assuming others would as honest as we are," Loul said.

Gynbere's people were separated according to their

decisions. Many of those who opted to leave were upset when they realised a loved one or the rest of their family would not be joining them. Some parents and older children were separated, which caused massive grief.

When everyone was sorted, Papa stood before the two groups to explain their futuress. "Ubree and Egrym have found an island for you to live on," Veld said. "Initial dwellings will be provided, and you'll be able to make more. With spring and summer ahead, you'll have time to plant crops. We will send enough stores to keep you going until the crops ripen, but you will not return here ever."

"What if something goes wrong?" Vellysh asked.

Gynletha stood. "Then you must cope with it. A number of those going with you are healers and we'll provide a store of remedies to cover your initial needs. The island has the usual medicinal plants growing; you can collect and process your own."

"How long before you return for us?" Zeffun asked.

"We won't," Veld said. "We did explain this to you."

"We assumed you were trying to scare us."

"It was also in the document you were asked to read and sign. We were very particular in what we said, Zeffun. The dragons will take you there this afternoon. You will be safe, but there will be no return. The seas around the island are rough even in summer, and the reef surrounding it is impossible to cross even if you had a boat, which you won't have. You will be able to fish—the area within the reef is rich with sea creatures. You will need to care for your land. There are plenty of animals, but if you over-kill, you will eventually starve. You will need to work the land, but you will have good results for your labours. There are many trees fruit and berry vines there already, you will live well."

"Kirym, when did Ubree and Egrym go search for an island?" Arbreu asked as the meeting finished. "I hadn't noticed them missing."

"They were away when Suarsh was attacked. Ubree already knew the island but was checking to see it was as he remembered. Egrym went to learn."

By morning they were all gone. The dragons, Veld, and the ten men who went with him to see them settled, returned three days later.

The following morning, Loul called a meeting and we all gathered in the open area in front of the porch. Everyone hushed as Loul stood.

"We are now all one family. Even though we will live in different parts of the land, we will get together frequently to celebrate. To that end, everyone will be brought together for early summer and autumn celebrations."

A young man stood and was recognised. "Does it include those who were recently taken to the island?"

"No, Grilif. They've chosen not to be part of our family."

Grilif nodded and sat; he looked quite relieved.

"Iryndal has agreed to keep an eye on the island, just to ensure everyone is safe. She will continue to do so until she is sure they have settled."

11

Kirym Speaks

The celebration was fantastic. It was a long time since we had felt so relaxed.

This festivity was to strengthen our ties, join us as one family and everyone was involved. It had been twenty days since Gynbere's people had been taken away, although the days had gone by quickly as we continued to organise permanent homes for everyone.

There was so much to do, but everyone was pleased to begin preparations for the celebration. We began soon after our morning chores were finished, although the cooks had been working on the food for the last few days.

An area was put aside for those who wished to show off their prowess at sport, running, jumping and wrestling. Those who had items to sell set up tables to show their wares and demonstrate their craft expertise. Normally, there would be a lot of private bartering, but today was different. Guild leaders watched to ensure no one handed over their items for less than their true value; there were many new crafters and the guilds felt there was a need to guide them on how to place value, rules that would continue as time passed.

With so many different groups making up our new enlarged family, they all had an opportunity to show off their talents, even if they had nothing to sell. The weaving guild had suggested the community assist with weaving a wall hanging for the big hall. They had set up a loom nearby, and everyone was expected to add a section. Even quite small children were involved.

Oak's mama, Rainbow, set up a loom to show off her proficiency at weaving and along with other weavers, she taught those who wanted to learn or improve. There were competitions too, for those who wished to participate. We tried things we'd never attempted before.

Targets were set up for us to practice with arrows and spears. Knife and axe throwing were new sports, and many tried their hand at it, to the amusement of the crowd.

The men and women from the trees showed their talent at climbing, branch cutting and debarking. Three teams raced to build a storehouse each. The winning team received the buildings for their community.

A group of boys from Faltryn showed us how to put together a stone dwelling. I was interested in how similar they were to many of the older storehouses we had found in the settlement when we first arrived. I spoke to Mama about finding stonemasons to teach us to restore them for their original use. She agreed to approach Wind Runner after the celebration.

This was Trethia's first Green Valley celebration. She was initially overwhelmed by the crowds, but Shormel and Larqeba took her to be part of their team to challenge the others. She ran, jumped and skipped with the other children, and returned laughing and covered in mud when her team lost at tug of war and ended up all face-down in a large mud puddle created for the challenge. I washed her, changed her clothes, and she raced back to join in again.

"We'll have to make her trousers and a tunic," Oak said, as he hunkered down beside me. "She's having so much fun, but her dress did get in the way when she was part of the team."

I agreed. "It's why the dress she's in now is so much shorter. I should have thought about it sooner. It is time she had something new. All she has are hand-me-downs."

"But all the children do," Starshine said.

"Yes, but they also have something new made especially for them," Oak said. "Mama still has the rug she made me when I was born and my first trousers. I think she plans to give them to my wife when I marry. Um, Kirym. What say I ask Mama for the trousers? They may fit Trethia, and it'd be so sensible for them to be used."

I grabbed his arm as he began to stand. "It's a lovely offer but leave it for now. Trethia is happy as she is, and it'd be unkind to ask Rainbow to leave the fun to search them out. Also, remember, she saved them for a reason and put on the spot, she may feel pressured to say yes when she'd prefer not to. Once the celebration is over, I'll get the material together and I can start sewing."

"She'll never live it down if she relies on your sewing ability," Mekrar said, laughing. "I'll sew, you can make me snacks and read to me while I work."

Oak smiled. "I'll make something too, Mekrar."

"And so will I, and I'm sure Wind Runner will also," Starshine said.

"My goodness, she will soon have more clothes than she'll know what to do with. One or two practical things would be more than adequate, and I'll happily read to you all, and

I'll make snacks."

We watched Trethia as the teams were chosen for the arrow shooting competition. She was the smallest there and the last chosen. I worried she would be upset, but she stood quietly until Mekroe called her name.

A long bag stuffed with hay was laid out. It had two lines drawn along the length of it. Getting an arrow into the space between the lines sent the archer to the next level. If their first arrow missed, they got a second chance.

Trethia's first arrow was just above the bottom line, and despite an objection from one of the other teams, she was sent to stand with the others who had succeeded. From the comments, everyone thought it was a fluke.

The target was then changed for a smaller stuffed bag and everyone tried again.

Trethia steadily shot her arrows into every target, generally only just in, but it was enough to keep her in the team. The targets became smaller and sat further away, until the teams were ready to divide into those who had made a kill while hunting, and those who hadn't.

This was normal. Everyone who hadn't made a kill had one final shot at an extended distance with a much smaller target.

Trethia's arrow hit the centre of the smallest circle. She was the only person in her group to do so.

Again, there were complaints. The prize was prestigious, and many men wanted their sons to win. Papa stepped in as a few of the men got very angry.

"Whether it was a fluke or not, she shot the arrow and it hit the centre of the target. No one else in the group came close. She's the winner."

A few guards stood ready for trouble, but the crowd dispersed, although not without grumbles.

Mekroe carried Trethia over to me, beaming as he deposited

her back in my lap.

"She's a clever little girl," he said. He was as proud as she was.

"Did you know, Kirym?" Arbreu asked.

I shook my head. "Mekroe took her off almost every day. He said it was to teach her about the land."

"We did explore the land," Mekroe said, "but she wanted to learn how to use one of the small bows as well. She's a natural and I thought it was a good time to introduce her talent. I reckon she'll win across the board once she's made her first kill."

This was also Amethyst's first celebration. She was a chatterer, a giggler. She was almost at her birth season, and now she was crawling around when placed on her rug and standing when she got the chance and had something or someone to cling to. Everything went into her mouth.

Through the day, she had spent time with Morkeen, Paluniis, Mekrar, Arbreu, Starshine, and Mekroe. Mama and Papa also took her for a while.

I also took Faltryn with me on occasion. She seemed to be at the same stage as Amethyst, more active, but quick to exhaust herself. Then the two slept on a rug together.

Faltryn was also looked after by one or other of the dragons, generally Iryndal, but Othyn, Arymda, and Borasyn also took turns.

It gave me the opportunity to spend time with Trethia and the dragons, as well as my friends.

As the sun lowered, we all washed and those who needed to, changed into festival clothes.

Mama had spent part of the winter adapting one of Mekrar's festival dresses for me. It had been far too long for me, but the intricate embroidery and beadwork decorating the hem would have been ruined had she just cut it to length, so she laboriously raised it, so it looked right, but could be lengthened later when needed. I had managed to find similar coloured dresses for Trethia and Amethyst. They looked so sweet.

Oak came to meet us as we left the dwelling all dressed in our finest. He handed me a length of fine green wool.

"You can use it to make Trethia something later, and what it's wrapped around could possibly be used now."

He took Amethyst off me to free my hands.

"I thought it was time—" He was interrupted by gasps from those around me. I was speechless.

I held a little cloak and an even smaller robe, both made to match mine, although it was a different black.

"It's fibre from Midnight, isn't it?"

He nodded. "You asked me to trim her. The fibre was longer and thicker than I thought it'd be. Armos made the cloak pin. He refused payment when he realised it was for Trethia. I'd planned to make the cloak for Trethia, but there was enough left over to make the robe for Amethyst. I thought it would be more practical for her."

I hugged him. "They're gorgeous. Thank you so much. I must thank Armos as well." I wrapped Trethia's cloak around her shoulders and showed her how to pin it. Mekrar was trying to put Amethyst into her robe, although she objected loudly.

"Perhaps we can put her in it when she's tired and ready to sleep," I suggested.

12

Kirym Speaks

Mama spoke before we ate. She welcomed everyone to the first of many shared celebrations. We remembered those we had lost in the Battle of the Tor, and others who had succumbed to age and illness. I was pleased she added Salcan's name to the list.

A few people looked surprised, but I knew they would ask questions of Mama and Papa rather than me.

Then Papa gave out the special messages.

"A few babies were born over the summer, autumn, and winter. We'll have a gathering very soon to officially name them. Normally we do this soon after each birth, but the situation over winter and spring has been rather different. With an extended family, we must change some of our customs."

He allowed time for people to comment, before getting their attention again.

"A joining, a marriage is planned. We can congratulate

Enliah and Splinter—" he was drowned out by a lengthy enthusiastic cheer and had to wait until it died before continuing. "It's good news, made better because Morkeen and Paluniis will also join. A joint celebration will allow them a special bond; one they will hold for life. It will also bring their families even closer."

Again, the cheer was long and loud.

Papa waited for relative silence before continuing. "If the canyon is clear of water and mud, the celebrations will be held there, if not, we'll gather here for it."

After the crowds around the two couples lessened, I took Trethia and Amethyst over to congratulate them. All four were glowing with happiness.

Enliah hugged me. "If you can convince Qwinita to wear a dress and stand by me, I'd be eternally grateful. Since Mama allowed her to wear trousers over winter, she won't consider anything else."

During the pause before food was brought from the cooking area, the children entertained us with plays, recitations, singing, and dancing.

Then awards were given out for those who'd won the competitions.

Trethia was called up to accept hers. Many refused to celebrate her win, remaining silent while the rest of us cheered loudly. Trethia ignored them. Mekroe carried back her prize, a chest carved by Findlow.

This prize was one of the few the judges adapted for the winner. Often it was a new bow or knife, but Trethia's bow was relatively new, and the knife would have been more like a sword for her because she was so tiny. The chest was just what she needed to store her growing pile of possessions.

Findlow sat beside me as Mekroe and Sundas helped Trethia carry the chest to our dwelling.

"You're looking happier, Findlow," I said.

"Aye, well Sundas dragged me up to see Maletta in her little cave. A strange experience. Have you been there?"

"Yes, she demanded I attend her at her cave just before she went to the Burl."

"I offered to enlarge it for her." He laughed. "She has a way with words, that one. I came away feeling I expected far too much out of my life. She was happy with that tiny cave once Veld removed one rock."

"Did Tarjin go too?"

He nodded. "Objected at first, but Maletta sorted him out with a simple look. He's been back since, and she's helped him come to terms with many things. He'd asked if he could marry Lyndym, but now they've decided to wait for a season cycle before they consider it. I'm sure it was because of the old lady. Tarjin has gone to one of the new settlements Wind Runner is building. He's learning to work with stone, make new instruments and play them. Lyndym is with Cindra helping at the stone path."

"Are you lonely?"

"Nooooo. I'm content. Sundas shares my dwelling and occasionally brings a guest. Life keeps changing; it's interesting. Maletta said she'd teach me to laugh. Not sure how, but there you have it. I laugh more."

Oak, Trethia, and Sundas returned and brought platters of food with them, and other friends joined us. There was every imaginable combination of foods set out on massive boards. Even when we had eaten all we wanted, many platters were still loaded, and more food continued to stream out of the cooking area for us to snack on.

In the dark time just before the moon rose, the sky lit up with great ribbons of fire. This was the beginning of the dragon's gift to us. Faltryn was too young to be part of it, but she watched with as much enjoyment as we did.

The ribbons slowly faded and Borasyn, Arymda, and Egrym shot fireballs high into the sky. The balls collided and sent out cascades of bright multi-coloured sparks, purple from Borasyn, red from Arymda and bronze from Egrym.

Borasyn and Iryndal created smoke and fire rings to float about as Arymda and Othyn shot fireballs through them. As the rings hovered above the crowd, the dragons sent streams of fire up to weave amongst them. The amazing patterns they created floated above us for the rest of the evening.

Churnyg was beside himself with delight. He danced and yelled with delight as each new display appeared. "M' great-grandsire told me about the fire-dancing. I wish he could have lived to see it. My sire also. I'm glad my son is able to stand by me now, but now it's time he handed me a grandson to share it with."

Arbreu laughed. "He seems to be a bit of a loner, Churnyg. He may take after you."

"Humph, even I gave m' sire a dwarfling, as disappointing as he was."

I laughed and put my arm around Churnyg's shoulder. "Everyone will know sooner or later. Why don't you tell them?" I murmured.

He stared at me. "You know? He said it was a secret; he swore me to silence."

"A secret?" Mekrar gasped. "Oh, you have to tell me."

Churnyg went red. "You did that on purpose, Kirym. Now Ashistar will never tell me anything ever again."

"He asked me to tell you to spread the news," I said.

Churnyg scowled.

"What news?" Mekrar was insistent. "Tell me."

"Ack! He married a lass just after the middle o' winter. Senseless thing t' do. It'll never last. A disaster waiting to happen."

"Whoooo?" Mekrar asked.

"Silly little girl called Rosisha. And he's agreed to take on her child as well. Varitza."

"How wonderful. That makes you a grandsire." Mekrar was ecstatic. "So why are you not sharing the dragon-fire with her? She'd love it. It's obvious she adores you."

Churnyg stopped scowling. "Well, I can insist now, can't I, and Ashistar and Rosisha can't stop me. I'm going to get m' granddaughter." He strode off into the crowds.

I laughed quietly. "He is a darling."

"There are many who'd disagree with you. So, why was the marriage a secret?" Starshine asked. "They should have had a ceremony. We could have helped them celebrate. We'd all have been delighted. Can we organise one now?"

"They specifically didn't want any fuss because so many people died at the tor. They thought it was better that way. But there will be other ways we can celebrate with them. Just respect their desires. And let Churnyg tell everyone."

Starshine nodded. "Look." She turned me around and pointed to Churnyg, Varitza in his arms as he pointed out the wonderful shapes the dragons were now creating in smoke and fire. Butterflies, flowers of every type, dragons, hearts, diamonds, circles, every shape one could dream of.

"They're going to be a very happy family," Mekrar said.

The music, singing, and dancing began, and we celebrated until dawn kissed the horizon.

13

Kirym Speaks

Borasyn flew me to the canyon soon after the celebration. The huge gash at the northern edge of the rim was a little deeper. There were no muddy areas; the grass was thick enough to handle a crowd for a few days. Grass and wildflowers carpeted the canyon floor.

We walked into the cave. It had changed; part of the back wall had been scoured out, but the debris had been swept away by the force of the water.

The tokens began to sing as I laid them on the large flat stone in the centre of the cave, however, the tune changed when I added the black stone. They glowed and lit up the cave, the colours an echo of the fire we had seen in the sky a few days back.

Borasyn and I listened to them until they fell silent. I felt they were settling down to enjoy their space.

Borasyn flew me to the top cave, the cave of dreams, Maletta called it. Water still bubbled out of the wall and ran from the small depression to fill the bowl below it. Now though, the bowl no longer overflowed. Again, I studied the pictures carved into the stone. Starshine and I had first seen them at the beginning of our journey to find Churnyg. At the time, we had no idea of the adventure we had ahead of us.

Borasyn studied everything too but said little. I'd never known him to be so quiet. As I watched him, I realised he'd begun to grow up. He still held more of the dragon history than he should have, even though he was no longer the youngest. However, there was still a lot he didn't remember, but everything new he saw helped him link up to other unclear memories.

A group of workers descended on the canyon two days before the planned meeting. They dug a fire-pit, built a large oven, and erected four large shelters and a dwelling. The dwelling was for the healers; in case someone was hurt or needed some sort of care, even though Ubree took care of healing these days. It would be primarily used to store extra remedies and would be a good space if an expectant mother went into labour.

The shelters shaded us from sun and rain, although we didn't expect rain at this time. Papa had brought walls that could be quickly attached for extra protection if needed.

As we had frequently done since we arrived in The Green Valley, we slept under the stars.

After a busy day and a welcome hot meal, we watched the sun disappear and the sky darken. We deliberately lit no big fires initially. It allowed the children to appreciate the amazing night sky and they learned about the stars we followed.

When the moon rose, the canyon was bathed in light. We then slept, knowing we would be awake before dawn.

Trethia and I shared a large low sett with Morkeen, Enliah, Qwinita, Bildon, and Lyndym, while Faltryn slept at my feet. Amethyst's basket sat beside me. By morning, Trethia and Faltryn were curled around her in the basket.

"She was lonely," Trethia explained before I could say anything.

Before dawn, the canyon was dark. The moon had set, but fires glowed; the cooks had been busy ensuring we would all get a good meal after the first ceremony. We dressed warmly knowing it would be cool in the cave.

The early celebration was for those newly born and nine babies were named. The tokens glowed and sang as each baby had their token pressed into their token holder. Each of these new tokens had a green inclusion in the centre. While many tokens had inclusions, them all getting a similar insertion had never happened before.

Amethyst too was named. Her white token glowed and connected with my white and blue tokens.

Mama came over to talk to me when we came out into the morning sunshine. "What do you think it all means?"

"The inclusion shows they now belong to The Green Valley."

"But Amethyst's token wasn't given the inclusion."

"Perhaps because she wasn't born here. She received her token in her birth land. Today we just confirmed her name."

"And Trethia? Why did you not allow her to take part in the naming ceremony? She belongs here, doesn't she?"

"Of course, she does, but this wasn't the right time, Mama. She's mine, but her roots are unknown. Perhaps I need to know them before she gets a token, and maybe she won't ever get one."

"I don't like her feeling different from the other children."

"She is different, Mama, and I don't think a token would make it any better for her. Many children here have no token. Anyway, none shone for her. Her winning at the celebration did more good than a token would have. She didn't put anyone to shame, and her last shot was perfect. No one could honestly deny her the award."

During the afternoon, we collected flowers and spread them around the cave. Late in the afternoon, we dressed in our festival clothes and again entered the cave, this time to see the two couples join.

Enliah looked lovely dressed in pink. She had her hair loose, instead of the plaits she normally wore. Splinter, obviously mesmerised, couldn't take his eyes off her.

Qwinita wore a green robe as she stood to support her sister. It was plain, with none of the embroidery, lace or beads Enliah wanted to put on it, however, it suited her, and she stood out. Splinter was supported by his brother, Lichen.

Morkeen looked very different. Her most striking asset was her long, thick, straight hair. She wore dark blue. I thought the dress was probably a gift from Wind Runner. Tiannii stood to support her; Storm supported Paluniis.

With different families involved, and the ceremony

being held in the cave, the mixture of rituals was new to everyone.

When both couples had made their promises, they received tokens. The tokens were bronze when they first glowed. Those given to Morkeen and Paluniis turned gold when they first clicked them. The colour reminded me of the sands of the desert they came from. The dark grey tokens Enliah and Splinter now wore were almost the opposite in colour, but again, they were perfect for them. They were a little darker than Enliah's eyes, but I was also reminded of the massive walls of the fortress Splinter had lived in. All four had a small green inclusion.

The evening celebration was wonderful, and we were all delighted to share the sweet loaves each couple cooked.

Soon after dawn, Amethyst woke, and I took her and Trethia away from the rest of those sleeping and into the morning sunshine. Most people would sleep late after the nightlong celebration and I didn't want to disturb anyone.

I was changing Trethia's clothing when Garanniis joined us. He helped me to feed Amethyst and asked if he could take her for the day. I was sure the request came from Paluniis and Morkeen as much as from him and was pleased to hand her over.

Faltryn had spent the night with her siblings, but I wanted Trethia to spend time with her today.

The dragons had claimed an area at the northern end of the canyon just under the great gash in the canyon wall. It was a place they could get away from the sometimes-noisy crowds.

Oak joined us when we were halfway there. He swung Trethia onto his shoulders; she giggled with delight.

"Will the dragons return to Winterisle now we are more or less settled?" he asked.

"I hope not, but it is their choice. We all love having them here. It makes life easier, but they may want some peace and quiet."

"Which we get quite enough of, even back at the settlement," Iryndal said. "This is the best time we've had in many seasons, and I think we are making up for the time when we had no contact with you. We've had enough time being by ourselves."

Faltryn had been running towards us but froze mid-step when she hears Iryndal's comment. She turned and walked away, her head low. I went after her and picked her up. She looked mortified, obviously remembering her actions over hundreds of season cycles.

"You mustn't read into the remark, things that aren't said and aren't meant," I said.

Iryndal settled beside me and touched Faltryn's token spot with her nose. "I wasn't commenting on our history, little one. We all understand what happened. Any of us could have done the same thing. We've all made mistakes in the past. We've corrected as much of it as we could, and no one holds a grudge."

Faltryn relaxed, and after a few moments, I put her down to play with Trethia.

They raced over to climb onto Arymda's back, and from there up her neck to her head. They stepped over to Borasyn's head, worked their way down his back, to his tail and turned to do it in the opposite direction.

Oak shook his head. "Tell me if they annoy either of you."

"Children need the adventure," Arymda said, "It helps them to learn. They won't overly exert themselves or us."

"What will happen today, Kirym?" Othyn asked. "Evidently,

Loul said not everyone will go back to the settlement."

"Some of the builders want to go directly to the stone path to build another storehouse. Others will begin building a small settlement about half-a-day northeast of there. There are some fields of grain in need of attention; three families will settle there for the summer at least. And I gather a few of the hunters have plans on the way back."

"We can help them all to get there," Egrym said, "but Loul just refused." He sounded very disappointed.

I smiled up at him. "We appreciate your desire to help, but everyone needs to learn the paths. The walk will teach the children about distances, where and how to find a safe place to spend the night, how to set up a shelter, and where to find food. Anyway, the younger ones will have fun chasing the ducks at Duck Walk, and the artists will love the evening light and tranquillity at Bildon's Rest. You'll enjoy it too. Sometimes life needs to slow down."

Ubree nodded. "We find there's a special serenity in the canyon here. It's different, something I haven't found anywhere else, except perhaps at Winterisle. But right now, we feel our lives are settled enough for us to look forward to a future with you here in the Green Valley."

"Are you planning to return to Winterisle?" I asked.

"Only if Loul wishes us gone. There is a lot of work we'd like to help with, and while we know you could manage it without us, we enjoy assisting. It allows us to get to know everyone in the family. We're actually hoping for a formal alignment with your family."

I smiled. "You've always been part of us. Even when we didn't know you, we were always searching for something. I know now the something was you."

"Ahh, Kirym, you might have been looking for us," Iryndal said, "but you're special in your family. I became aware of you in the early spring, some season-cycles back. I saw a flash of dark blue, and I knew everything was changing. I think that was the beginning."

I stared at her. "I wonder if the dark blue flash was when my token changed back in Raff's hills. If you can read it, it definitely makes you part of me and my family."

"I thought it was only me," Iryndal said, "but Ubree also felt it. We didn't talk about it until recently. Had we talked earlier; we might have searched for you sooner."

"Faltryn watched over us, and had we needed any of you, I think he would have made it happen," I said.

"It's one of the reasons we wish to stay close to you. Faltryn needs to be with you, I think we all do," Othyn said. "Faltryn has information she should be passing on to us. For some reason, she can't do it. There's a possibility she can somehow tell you. Even though speech at her age is generally minimal, by now we should be able to understand some of her thoughts, and yet we're at a loss."

"When she was first reborn, I asked her questions. I got the impression speech was a long way off. I thought then it might be the way of dragons. Now I'm wondering if speech will ever come to her," I said.

Othyn nodded. "Her progress in that regard is slow, and yet she is very intelligent."

Behind me, there were calls of goodbye. A few people were leaving the canyon's amphitheatre. Many were workmen who had brought their tools with them, and they were eager to get going.

"Iryndal, Teema was part of my token when it changed to dark blue. I seem to have lost him. Do you have the connection?"

She shook her head. "I knew he was there of course, but he has never been as important to us as you. Perhaps he was only there to support you for a short time when you needed it. Then his path went in a different direction."

Oak put his arm around my shoulder. "You miss him. Do you want me to talk to him?"

I shook my head. "It's a nice offer, but Iryndal is right, he has another path to follow. Teema and I will always clash. I can't be what he wants, and he can't cope with what I am. He is much better off with someone who will let him care for them, and think he is part of their decision making."

"You think he and Zeprah—"

"Oh, I didn't say that, but right now he feels needed when he's with her."

"Kirym," interrupted Iryndal, "will you show me the small cave at the top of the cliff?"

"Have you not been up there? I thought—"

"No, no. The land here is yours and we're here by invitation only. We were not invited to see it."

"Oh, I should have thought of it. Let me tell you now, you are to visit and investigate any part of The Green Valley you wish to."

"Some places," Iryndal said, "need to be seen at a special time and with special people. Now, I think is the time, and you and Oak are the people. Faltryn too should see it."

I grinned when I saw Faltryn. He and Trethia were already sitting astride Iryndal's back. Oak and I clambered up behind them. She took off and landed on the small platform beside the pool.

Oh, watch this, came Arymda's thought. We saw our entrance to the cave first as Arymda saw it. It looked as if Iryndal had flown into a solid wall and disappeared. Anyone not knowing about the cave would find it mysterious.

As we walked around the wall to the large flat stone, we could hear the tokens singing.

"I thought they were down in the other cave," Oak said.

"They are." I was as mystified as he was.

We rounded the final corner. The tokens sat on the flat

stone, but these were merely shadows of those in the lower cave. There, I had sat them in a circle with the rainbow and black stones sitting side by side across the centre. Here the two shared the centre, but the rainbow token sat in the centre of the black, looking like its heart.

The song was different here, a sad echo of the happier song we could still hear from the lower cave.

As the two tunes soared, Trethia slipped out of Oak's arms and walked over to the flat stone in the centre of the cave. She looked tiny next to it. She lifted Faltryn up and helped the baby dragon scramble onto the stone.

The music changed slightly as a translucent cylinder rose from the black stone. When it had almost reached the ceiling of the cave it stopped, and the blue shadow-token sent a ray of light upwards which gave the cylinder a swirling blue cap.

The cylinder filled with thick swirling mist, much as we encountered when trying to enter the bay while traveling home from our adventure at the fortress city of Faltryn.

Balls and disks of various colours: pink, blue, cream, yellow, and blinding white appeared on the far side of the cylinder, seen as a reflection approaching and then flashing away and out of sight. One shape looked like three discs intertwined with a tiny ball in the centre.

Faltryn reached up, although I was sure she didn't touch the cylinder, and a dark shape fell through the blue at the top and float steadily downwards. It stopped about two-thirds of the way down, and with a flash of black and red, disappeared.

Slowly the whole scene vanished. But then the shadow-tokens each sent up a ray and a rainbow began to form. As it rose, a thin black column hit it and the other colours entwined around it. They slowly faded, and a white mist filled the cave. When it cleared, the top of the stone was bare. Trethia stood beside it with Faltryn in her arms.

There was a long silence, no one moved.

"Did you see what I saw?" Oak asked.

I nodded.

The tokens song from the cave below again echoed up to us.

Iryndal took a deep breath. "Yes, we did, and I feel I should know what it means."

"Only Kirym needs to know."

I swung around.

Maletta stood in the shadows behind Iryndal.

"But I don't. Do you?" I asked.

"Evil came from Athesha and Halavash requires your help. You have almost everything you need." The old woman spoke in riddles.

"Almost? What else do I need? What is Halavash and where will I find it?"

"The knowledge will soon be handed to you, and then you must make your decisions quickly. You will journey for two reasons; to help strangers and to understand your family."

"Who holds the knowledge I need?" but Maletta had disappeared into the shadows.

I raced after her but returned moments later. "She's gone."

"How did she get up here?" Oak asked.

"I just want to know what she meant. Something is very important, and I have no idea what to do next." I felt totally lost.

"I imagine, as with everything, the meaning will become obvious when the time is right," Iryndal said.

14

Kirym Speaks

Iryndal flew us down to the canyon floor where Sundas waited patiently with the other dragons. The sun was high in the sky, and the canyon was otherwise empty.

"Loul said to catch up with her when you're ready," Sundas said. "I have food; would you like to eat here?"

"Brilliant, Sundas, I'm hungry. I guess we all are."

The basket he opened was a feast.

"Where did you get pamchii nuts from?" I asked, cutting one into pieces for Trethia.

Sundas chuckled. "One of the cooks appreciates my healthy appetite."

His smile faded, and at the same moment, my tokens throbbed. I swung around to see what caused it.

Iryndal, Othyn, and Arymda, lay on the ground, their heads close together. They appeared dead.

I stared; my mouth fell open. "Oh, my stars. This—they—Ubree, what's wrong? It's not how they normally die. Why the change? Did you expect this?"

Ubree shook his head, began to sing, and after a few moments, Egrym and Borasyn joined him.

My tokens trilled and joined in the song. Trethia and I too sang with them. The tokens in the cave also sang, but their song was different, almost a celebration.

The sun moved a hand-span across the sky before the song faded.

"There's no response," Ubree said. "This is not death as we know it. From all I can tell, they're not actually dead, they're just—" He paused, searching for the right word. "Well, they seem content."

I touched Iryndal's token with my three, then went to Othyn and Arymda.

"What do you feel, Kirym?" Ubree asked.

"Serenity," I said. I was mystified.

"How is this not the same as your usual death?" Sundas asked.

"When the dragons die, the youngest goes first, but Faltryn is healthy and very much alive," I said.

"I feel their satisfaction with the situation," Ubree said. "I can't heal them, there seems to be no sickness, no infection."

"So, what do we do?" I asked.

Ubree looked confused. "Why ask—" He paused. "You're right. I'm now the eldest. I just don't feel as if I am." He was silent for a time. Then he leaned down and clicked my token. "Kirym, can we share this? I need your help. What do I do?"

Oak nodded. "Kirym, when you were in the Burl, it was different. The dragons had to sing you awake. They couldn't rouse Ubree until they'd woken you."

"It doesn't make sense."

"Yes, it does," Sundas said. "In the amphitheatre when you

learned Mekrar and Arbreu were promised to each other, something happened to your blue token. When I look into it—well, it's different. There's something else in there. It's shapeless, and I've never been able to figure it out. But I think it changed who you are, or maybe what you are. It altered your relationship with the dragons. Remember, you woke them, but you may be more than a dragon caller."

I closed my eyes and thought over the scene Iryndal had shown me days after Ubree saved my life. Even now, I felt as though it had happened to someone else. My blue token did feel different, but I had always put the change down to Teema withdrawing from me. Now, as I thought about it, I knew my token had changed much earlier. My connection to the dragons had increased from when Ubree kept me alive in the amphitheatre.

"I can find no argument against your conclusion, but what from here. Do we make the decisions together?" I asked.

"We think you should make them, Kirym. I'll help of course," Ubree said. "I assisted Iryndal, and she supported Faltryn when we first came here. Also, it means as dragons, we are still balanced, you, me, Egrym, Borasyn, and Faltryn. Now, as I see it, someone needs to stay here to care for Iryndal, Othyn, and Arymda, and contact the rest of us if there's a problem."

"I'll do it," Borasyn said.

I thought about it and nodded. "What will happen if the river runs while they are here?"

"A protective circle would shield them even under the weight of the water from the waterfall," Borasyn said.

"Would you all prefer to stay here? We could manage without you."

Ubree shook his head. "No, we are still committed to the obligations we made to you, our people. There's work to do. So, we leave Borasyn to his job and carry on. Do you want to collect the large tokens, Kirym, or leave them here?"

"They live with us, and I see no reason to change that."
Ubree, did you three see what Iryndal saw in the cave?" I
asked.

"Yes," Ubree said. "I have no explanation for it. Is it
connected to this?"

I thought about it. "Possibly, but only obliquely. I had the
feeling Iryndal suddenly understood something.

We crossed to the cave. The large tokens still sang softly, but
the song was different now. I felt the tokens were in total
agreement with the circumstances.

"I can't help but wonder what caused this. Why these
three dragons? Why not all of you, or the usual system with
Faltryn first, followed by the each of you by age?"

"But you're not quite right," Ubree said. "Had this been
usual, we would be singing to bring Faltryn back. Then after
some time, death would include her and Borasyn. The third
death would take Arymda, and so on, until we all died,
except Iryndal. When she had called us back, she would die
and be reborn as the youngest. But it takes time. I don't
think Faltryn has been the youngest long enough."

"So why has it changed? Is there nothing you can remember
from your history?"

He shook his head. "All I know is, it'll work out in the
end."

With that, I had to accept the change. I gathered the
tokens together and packed them into my pocket.

Ubree and Egrym flew us to Duck Walk so I could talk to

Mama. The younger members of the families were helping to erect two shelters. There were a few who would use them; most people would sleep under the stars, especially as the weather was mild and the night warm.

Telling Mama about the dragons and our decisions was easier than I thought it'd be.

"Is there anything more you can do for the dragons, Kirym?" she asked.

"No. Borasyn will care for them. What we must do is visit them often."

15

Oak Speaks

Guarding the Green Valley was totally different to guarding Faltryn's tower. In the tower, we had walked the battlements and halls. The most dangerous part of it had been when someone occasionally checked the ridge above the tower or if hunters returned after sundown. Otherwise, everything was walled off and safe.

In the valley, the southern hill couldn't be breached. Even so, men were stationed at the top, above and at both ends of Tarjin's Path. We also watched the perimeter of the settlement, which included the lake. Guards also crisscrossed the grounds, watching the dwellings, and keeping an eye on movement between them.

Over the time we worked our shift, the watch was staggered, with our new partner joining us mid-shift. It meant at least one was aware of what had been happening, and the new companion ensured we stayed awake and alert.

My duty began with Twig when the moon was halfway

between the horizon and the meridian. Bryn took over from him before midnight.

As Bryn was also head of the guards, he occasionally left to check the other guard areas. Normally there would be someone else to partner me, leaving him free to concentrate on the whole unit, but a few of those on shift tonight had been unwell and were given leave to recuperate.

Soon after midnight when Bryn had left to do his third check, I saw a hooded figure carrying a staff, slip into the shadows of a nearby dwelling. The weapon worried me.

I watched carefully, prepared to intercept if whoever it was came into my area, and ready to race to assist if needed. I wished Bryn was back. The two-man system worked better if there were two men at each guard station.

I checked my area, trying to see anything that pointed to a multi-prong attack, but everything else looked and sounded normal.

I signalled another guard, he indicated there was nothing untoward in his area. I warned him to be vigilant and again looked for the figure.

The person slipped from one shadow to another, angling towards Kirym's small dwelling. I wasn't overly worried; I knew she had taken the children up to spend the night with Loul, but I was concerned about an unknown person getting this far into the settlement.

The person was adept at using the shadows and there was a degree of thought in where they walked, not so close to the dwellings as to knock over items left leaning against the walls, and yet still well into the shadows of the buildings so as not to be easily seen.

I was relieved to note one of the other guards, *Walf*, I thought, was moving to intercept the figure as they entered his sector. He manoeuvred himself into the deep shadows around Amos' workshop, to allow the intruder to approach and pass him. As the shadowy figure moved from the darkness around the building, and into the orchard, Walf followed.

I knew Walf's move, I'd seen it many times on the practice field. He would grab his adversary in a bear-hug to pin their arms; lift them off the ground and turn them sideways. With their arms held tight, they were incapable of inflicting any damage.

The wind whispered through the branches of the trees, an added noise Walf would appreciate, but as the intruder stepped over some of winter's fallen branches, I caught a glimpse of a profile and realised Walf was about to get into very serious trouble.

I began to run. I couldn't shout, it would put every guard on alert and create un-needed chaos. It would also waken half the settlement and probably not distract Walf at all. I had to get to him before he made his move.

Although both Walf and his prey were quite visible to me as I raced towards them, the orchard was hidden from every other guard's view. Unless Walf looked in my direction, I would be too late, and Walf would be hard pressed to live down the results down.

Even as I closed in on them, it began. The robed figure flicked the staff around to clip Walf's right hip and spun it around to connect with his left knee. Then in a flawless arc, flicked the staff over and with a double tap, clipped his hand, not hard, but hard enough to make him drop his knife, and then his head. Walf grunted loudly and fell to his knees.

Then Bryn was there, his sword in hand.

I reached Bryn and grabbed his wrist. "Step back, now!" These words meant far more than it would appear to most people.

Veld glanced at me, sheathed his sword, grabbed the figure

by the shoulder and spun them around. The figure looked up, paused, leaned the staff against Walf's shoulder, reached up and turned back their hood.

"Wind Runner! Why are you out this late? Why are you attacking my guards?"

"Are you suggesting, Bryn, I should be locked in my dwelling as soon as the sun sets?"

"No, but—"

"And is it now acceptable for your guards to attack an old lady without cause?"

"No, but—"

"Good! Then you can allow me to continue my walk."

"You did look like an intruder," Bryn said. "The hooded cloak—"

"It's cold."

"You are carrying a weapon."

"The same walking staff I use every single day."

"And you were flitting from shadow to—"

"I do not flit," she said acidly. "I object to your expectation that I should need permission to walk around a settlement I was told to make my own. Anyone would think I was old."

Bryn took a deep breath. "Perhaps Oak can escort you to your destination and back again. He has just finished his guard duty."

"Hmmm! If he must." She turned and walked quickly away.

I raced to catch up. "Can I ask where we're going?"

"Kirym's."

"She's staying with Loul tonight."

"I had forgotten." She changed her direction.

"Grandmama, can I take you home and bring Kirym to you."

"Why? I'm halfway there."

"The hill—"

"Is no steeper at night than it is during the day. I do it often enough to know. If it's too steep for you, you can watch me from the bottom."

"Wind Runner!" I grabbed her arm. "Grandmama. What's wrong?"

She took a deep breath and sighed. "Circumstances are proving me to be a stupid old woman. No, don't look at me like that, Oak. I do know my weaknesses. Come along, you may as well learn what an old fool I've been."

She climbed rapidly to the dwelling, knocked and was through the door before most people could have done more than open their eyes. I was out of breath keeping up with her, but I was only a step behind.

Loul, Mekrar, and Kirym were on their feet. They wore night robes, but I saw the glint of two knives; Kirym and Mekrar may have been asleep, but they were alert and fast.

Loul took Wind Runner's cloak and staff, ushered her to a place in front of the hearth, and added a log to the embers while Mekrar heated water to make drinks for everyone.

"Sometimes I do some fool things, Loul. Kirym, I put it aside, and all I can say is, I forgot. Something so very important and the delay could be devastating." Wind Runner's face was pale, even after the exertion of the climb. She looked genuinely upset and ignored the flask Mekrar placed in front of her.

"After the battle, Kirym, you suggested waiting until I was back here and had the family settled before I read it. Well, they've been settled for two seasons, and I didn't even think about it."

She looked up and realised—none of us knew what she was talking about.

"The scroll, Kirym. Elm's scroll. I knew I should have read it the night you handed it to me, but I was pleased to put it off. Then, well it suited me to forget about it. This evening,

I needed a special thread and when I opened my sewing basket, the scroll was sitting on top. Even then, I almost put it aside again, but fortunately, I read a few lines." She paused, pulled a small scroll from her pocket and handed it to Kirym.

16

Kirym Speaks

"Elm gave Kirym the scroll just before he died," Wind Runner explained for Mama, Mekrar, and Oaks benefit. "Read it out loud, Kirym. Best we all hear now. It'll make the following discussion easier."

I opened the scroll, adjusted the lamp and began.

"He writes. *Wind Runner, I have a confession, and I expect you will hate me for it. I deserve your disgust and contempt. However, I hope I have the courage to face what punishment you have in store for me for allowing the situation to evolve. I know I could have come to you—I should have come to you and possibly you could have stopped them.*"

Wind Runner laughed dryly. "For a man whose ability to cut someone down and shut them up with a few words was legendary, he is waffling on. That in itself told me he had something serious to confess."

I found my place in the scroll and continued reading. "First, I helped Rabbit and Danth escape.

There was a stunned silence as we finally understood why

we had found no trace of Danth and Rabbit when they disappeared from Wind Runner's great fortress of Faltryn.

"Rabbit approached me. Initially, I refused. She made threats. Against Gazania first—but she was dead, and nothing could hurt her. When Rabbit realised I would ignore her threat, she threatened Willow and Starshine. She was a talented liar and her lies always managed to do damage. Had she been threatening her evil on me alone, I'd have done nothing for her. But Willow had done nothing to warrant such an attack and I realised I was fond of Starshine. The girl was always civil to me, brought me a platter of special food during feasts, and gave me a new warm rug each winter. And she supported Willow when people made comments.

"Willow, well I treated her badly, but I couldn't allow Rabbit to do as she threatened. And she would have. Even had I told you then, you could not have stopped her vile fabrications. Some people are ever ready to believe lies, or at least remember the salacious details for many seasons after. The damage done would have been devastating. I remembered others Rabbit attacked—she knew how to ruin lives. So, I agreed to help her."

Wind Runner shook her head. "As soon as he mentioned Rabbit, I knew this was bad."

"Could this Rabbit have been *that* dangerous?" Mama asked.

Wind Runner nodded. "Yes. There had been some suspicious deaths over the seasons. I suspected Rabbit was behind them, but without proof, I could do nothing. She was a master at suggesting things, not accusing outright, but insinuating and inflaming. Ghastly notes and whispers in the dark. She always ensured no one could accuse her of anything."

I sipped my drink and continued reading. *"I hid the two of them. In the boathouse initially, and no, don't hold it against Blacknight. He searched it very well, Wind Runner. I built the place, and there are areas in there no one else knew about, and even you could not have found them unless you had your men take the building apart piece by piece.*

"*So, for four days, they hid. Then one evening I took them south to the southern end of the river flats. We travelled at night, hid the boat and slept on the cliff during the day. Through those days and nights of hiding, they talked, made their plans. They continued to discuss their ideas when they thought I was asleep through the day. But I sleep little. In the boathouse and on the cliff, I heard every vicious word* they said."

"Now you will see how nasty Rabbit is," Wind Runner said.

"*They planned to kill me, of course. I knew their intention before I took them south. I chose my ash-innovation. Yes, Wind Runner, I knew you called my precious boat a vile devil and a nightmare, and you were right. It was a ghastly boat and made for an equally ghastly journey. I'm not a fool and I knew how to use it—to my advantage.*"

Oak began to laugh. "But I bet Rabbit didn't know."

"Know what?" Mama asked.

"The boat Elm used was just ghastly," Oak said. "Elm's first attempt at experimental boat design. Most of the ideas were brilliant, as we later found out. But putting them all together the way he did, made it the worst boat ever. It wallowed, slewed, bounced and jiggered. It was too long, too narrow, and terribly unstable. I went in it once. Drowning seemed a wonderful option before we were a stone's throw from the boathouse. As I remember, I elected to walk home, I was so sick. There was one spot in the boat you could sit, and you'd survive. I bet Elm sat there. It would have been a wretched trip. Rabbit and Danth would have been very happy when they stopped each morning."

Wind Runner was smiling now. "Such sweet revenge. Elm had courage, I'll give him that. Carry on Kirym."

"*It was still dark when we reached the standing stone. I knew what would happen when the boat touched the shore, so I tipped them into the water. Sadly, it was only chest deep, so they weren't in any danger, but I put the width of a deep trench between us very quickly. Danth tried to follow me, he's an idiot, but Rabbit laughed and applauded. Having her*

89

admiration didn't make me feel good, but at least I was alive. It wouldn't have been a quick death at her hands and would have been disturbing for whoever found my body."

"Of course, Rabbit wouldn't have done it herself," Wind Runner said. "She came up with the ideas and took great pleasure in getting someone else to do it, either by threat or because they were very warped. She recognised Danth for what he was."

"Danth was nasty," Mekrar said. "He was happy to mistreat Lyndym, Bokum, and Findlow. I think he would have been eager to do her bidding. What happened next, Kirym."

I made sure I was well north of them when daylight came. Then I hid the boat and slipped back along the cliff to see what they were doing. They were still on the bank, trying to dry out what they had retrieved from the water. They'd lost a lot of their stuff; I was pleased about that. I watched them overnight. They left at about midday next day, going south."

"So Danth intended to return here," Mekrar said.

"No," Wind Runner said. "We could easily have managed if he had returned. Anyway, he would have been here long ago. Read on Kirym."

I found where I had stopped reading. *"Initially I didn't care about Danth's plans. But then Willow died and, well, I was so angry. All I thought about was what I hadn't done and said to her. I was consumed with guilt. When I finally began to think of what I'd done, it was too late. I realised I had made yet another raft of mistakes. I'm hoping this will put some of them right. Danth found something—somewhere. He was going there to raise an army, bring them back here to kill all of those he believed had slighted him, pretty much everyone he'd ever met, by my reckoning. He talked about knowing things even Kirym didn't know. He was quite pleased, said it would give him huge wealth and power. He said he'd rule two worlds or more."*

I studied the paragraph again and re-read it to myself. Then I continued to read Elm's words. *"Initially I disregarded his story. I thought he was talking big to impress Rabbit, but he kept* saying the same thing. Never changed his story. I couldn't understand what he knew. He told her he'd found a door to another world where things were different to anything anyone he had ever dreamed of. He said Kirym showed him the door, but she was too stupid to know what it was, let alone the immense value of it. She'd been so blind; she didn't even realise it was there. Said he'd have been stuck in the new place if it hadn't been for Sundas. So, Wind Runner, for what it's worth, this is what happened. Please forgive me for my part in it. I have many regrets. I'm sure I'll have many more before I die. I seem unable to learn."

17

Kirym Speaks

I slowly re-rolled the scroll while thinking about what I'd read.

"If I'd given it to you immediately, we may have been able to stop him doing whatever he had planned," Wind Runner said.

"Don't say that, Wind Runner," I said, "because it's not true. I held it first and I didn't think to read it. Even if we had the scroll as soon as we arrived back from the tower, we couldn't have done anything. We didn't have enough information. Danth might have just been talking big to impress Rabbit."

"Do you really think so?" Oak asked.

"No, she doesn't," Mekrar said. "But if we don't know what Danth knew, how can we do anything, even now. Did Elm say anything else before he died, Kirym?"

I thought back to Elm's final words. "I thought he wanted me to give the scroll to you, Wind Runner. I got it wrong.

Could I get anything right now, after all this time?"

"Danth knew something," Mekrar said. "You were there or nearby; so was Sundas. Could it have been at the stone circles? What about the path he followed?"

I shook my head. "We didn't follow him. After he hit me, I just sent him away. I didn't see him again until he arrived at Faltryn."

"Tarjin and I followed the path when we got to the stone circles," Wind Runner said. "We found a small shelter about six hundred steps along it. The wind and weather had almost destroyed it by then. There was room in it for one person only, but Tarjin said Danth would have made Jinda sleep outside. The path stopped just beyond the dwelling. There was nothing else there."

"So, whatever Danth found, it had to be somewhere else," Mekrar said.

"Something happened. I was there. Sundas was there." I was perplexed.

"Sleep on it," Mama said. "You'll stay the night, Wind Runner. You too, Oak."

I picked up my cloak and slipped outside. I sat on one of the hammocks Papa had set up on the porch and tried to think. The moon was racing towards the horizon; elsewhere there were masses of stars. I could hear Mama organising everyone inside.

The door opened and closed; Oak slipped onto the hammock beside me. "Any thoughts? Perhaps it was something that happened at the Fortress of Faltryn."

"I can't think of any action that involved the three of us, Danth, Sundas, and me. After Storm put Danth under guard, I had nothing to do with him. I don't think Sundas did either, although I'll ask him in the morning."

"Could he have followed you into Faltryn's cave?"

"No. Wind Runner and Storm guarded the entrance. Anyway, Sundas wasn't with us, he stayed at the fortress. Danth and Rabbit went straight to the boathouse when Danth escaped. They were with Elm until they went south. It had to be before then."

"All right go back to the beginning of the journey to Faltryn. What did you do where Sundas was involved?"

"We went to the canyon. Trayum was named. During the night, the tokens in the cave warned us of danger. Everyone left the canyon and climbed the hill. I thought it would be a simple case of walking around the rim to where everyone else was, and then coming back here. But there was a waterfall at the top of the ridge. We couldn't cross, so we followed the river to its source."

"Both Sundas and Danth were with you throughout?"

I nodded.

"Could he have planned to be there with you?"

"No. I only chose that side of the hill because the water was too deep to get to across the entrance to the other side. Danth disliked me too much to want to be near me. There was an argument about who would lead the group. Papa chose me. Danth objected, but everyone else agreed with Papa. Danth wanted to return to the settlement immediately, but I was leader, and elected to rest at the fountainhead for a few days. Tarjin decided to stay with us, and Danth wouldn't leave without his son—he liked to have a follower. Then we climbed down the hill and started back this way.

"Nothing else?"

"On the way home, there was a bit of trouble with him over guard duty. Danth bullied Tarjin into doing his share. I found out because we had visitors and he wasn't there to challenge them. No real problem, but he was very angry when he realised I knew."

"Visitors?"

"Papa and a group of hunters arrived. In the morning, we talked about the map we had found at the fountainhead. Papa agreed we could follow it—Danth wanted to come with us—but Papa said no. After we left, he followed anyway. Papa sent Bokum to warn us, but we didn't see Danth until we were at the stones."

"You've discounted everything from there, so whatever Danth was talking about must have happened before then. Could it have been when he missed his guard duty?"

I thought about it and finally shook my head. "Sundas was asleep. We arrived too late to see anything much."

"Then you've eliminated everything," Oak said.

"Well obviously not, because there was something. I just can't think what it is."

Oak put his arm around my shoulder and pulled me close to him, so his cloak covered us both. I tucked my feet under me; I was shivering.

"Just relax," Oak said. "It'll come to you."

"And if it doesn't?"

"Then we're no worse off than we are now."

I slept, knowing Oak was probably wrong.

The grey of dawn was just beginning to touch the horizon when I woke. I was still in the hammock. Oak's arm was under my shoulder, during the night, someone had placed a thick rug over us both.

He must have felt me move; he was instantly awake. "Did you sleep well?"

I smiled. "Yes, and I have to speak to Ubree. I should have talked to him last night."

Oak was silent for a few moments. "But you didn't know the dragons when all this happened, did you? Teema said you met Borasyn at The Rock."

"True, but they were active in the land. They may have seen something; know something. If I don't ask, I'll always wonder."

Ubree landed on the grass in front of the porch.

"I love it how you know what I want as soon as I know, Ubree," I said smiling.

He gave me his grumpy look. "We have spent the night thinking about Danth's scroll. None of us were nearby. So, what can you do?"

"Can you take me back to where we found the map? Danth may have seen something when we initially searched the top of the hill, or maybe he read the map differently. If it comes to nothing, I'll have to go to Faltryn to see if it was something there."

"When do you want to leave?" Ubree asked.

"I'll talk to Mama. She may have thought of something. Then I'll find Sundas. He needs to come with us."

Oak left, he'd promised to help Churnyg in the trees today, and I folded the rug and slipped inside. Everyone was asleep, except Trethia, who sat watching the door.

"Can I come too?" she asked. "I've got my robe, cloak, and boots ready. Yours too."

I nodded and quietly woke Mama.

18

Kirym Speaks

Ubree took us first to the canyon to check on the dead-but-not-dead dragons. I still couldn't figure out what was happening to them, and I was worried, although Ubree, Egrym, and Borasyn were relaxed enough about the situation.

"They're not dead, not dying, just not awake," Borasyn said. "They are thinking, but I can make no sense of their thoughts."

"Which may have more to do with Borasyn than the others," Ubree grumbled.

Borasyn cheerfully ignored him, but I was concerned he was spending too much time by himself. For the most social of the dragons, this isolation could not be good.

"Naha!" he said, reminding me a little of the dragon I had originally met. "Egrym can't order me around and Ubree can't grump at me all the time." He paused. "Actually, I do miss people. The children mainly. And talking to Loul, Wind

Runner, and Churnyg. They know sooo many things."

"We'll visit more often, and I'll ensure lots of children come," I promised.

We followed the ridge north, and in the early afternoon, landed beside the bowl that gifted us the bronze token. It was a little over four seasons since I had been there, but so much had happened since then, it seemed longer.

Two broken baskets were snagged in a bush, and the remains of a rudimentary shelter sat nearby.

"This wasn't here when we left," I said, glancing at the shelter, "and no one else has come here. So, it suggests Danth has been here, and this is the right place."

"He may have just stayed here for a while, then left to go elsewhere," Sundas said.

I shook my head. "The shelter is big enough for two people, and Rabbit would only climb the hill if there was a reward of some sort here. I gather she wasn't the type to exert herself."

Before we did anything else, we checked the wooded area Danth had searched when we first found the fountainhead. Nothing could even remotely be described as a door. I again studied the map that had been the beginning of our journey to Faltryn.

"Could Elm have misunderstood Danth?" Sundas asked.

I shook my head. "He said Danth repeated himself again and again. Elm was pedantic. I'd trust his word."

We walked across the meadow to the pool.

I stood and stared at the flat stone where I had placed the large tokens at the beginning of our journey to Faltryn. I now had two more tokens, three if I counted the black, which I did, although it was the only stone I'd ever been mystified by.

Is it because Oak handed it to me, or because I had a preconceived idea what tokens look like? I had five when I left here, and two more arrived not too long after. I accepted the rainbow token without question. "Where do they came from?"

"Where do what came from?" Sundas asked.

"The tokens. They're not a natural phenomenon."

"Didn't Starshine say they were made by the ancient leader of the Green Valley?"

"That was a myth. Remember, it said our Faltryn lived in the cave, has icy dragon breath and stole part of the peace token. We know those things weren't true."

"You've always said the myths hold a whisper of truth. So, Starshine could still be right about the tokens; otherwise, where did they come from?"

"I don't know. They're important, and now I'm wondering if there are more out there somewhere."

Sundas frowned as he stared at me. "How do you figure that out?"

"I haven't, but if the black one is a token, and I'm quite sure it is, then there could be any number of others not yet discovered."

"You found one for each of the families."

"One of the many things we assumed, but I think we got it wrong. They may symbolise all sorts of things. There's so much I don't know about them."

"How can you find out if there are more tokens?"

I shrugged. "If there are more, they'll turn up."

"Or possibly not," he muttered, "and it doesn't tell us why we're here. Nothing happened here, except we figured the water in the canyon came from here." He paused. "Didn't we?"

I nodded and glanced at Trethia, who was sitting beside the bowl, throwing flower petals onto the surface.

"Oh, my goodness, how silly of me. It was right under my nose all the time."

"What?"

"I think I know what Danth discovered. Well, some of it, anyway."

I grabbed his hand, pulled him to his feet, picked up Trethia and ran towards Ubree.

"Come on, we have to talk to Mama."

19

Teema Speaks

I watched, hidden in the shadows as they got ready for the journey. I envied every one of them.

I was angry again.

Almost a full season had passed since I had stopped thinking about Kirym constantly, but now it all came back. I was so deep in my misery I didn't realise someone was behind me until a hand touched my shoulder.

I jumped.

"Oh my, you were lost in thought," Loul said. "Will you share my meal?"

I shook my head. "No. No, I have things to do," I mumbled.

"And what would convince you to stay? An order from your Headwoman, or perhaps a request from your mama."

"That's unfair," I said.

Loul shrugged. "I've tried waiting for you to come to me, but you haven't, and time is running short. So, now we will talk."

She led me over to a seat under a tree and handed me a flask.

"Why are you not going with them?"

I looked over to where preparations were being made for a new adventure. "I can't. I can't go and watch Kirym die. It hurts too much."

Give Loul her due, she didn't ridicule me or tell me I was being stupid. She sat quietly thinking about what I had said. "Why do you think she's in danger?"

"The people she's taking. She has ignored every warning I've given her. It was the same at The Rock, again at the amphitheatre, and before the battle. Then look what happened. She was poisoned. Four times in all. She almost died."

I knew I was raving but I couldn't stop. "Kirym has too much responsibility. She's still a little girl, and she takes care of the dragons, the child and a baby. It's not right. She should be playing, not getting up at night to care for Amethyst. She shouldn't have her own dwelling; she should still live with you and Veld. People go to her when they should come to you. She doesn't have time to play, she just works. She does so much, she has no time for friends her own age."

Loul listened quietly until I had run out of energy.

I thought about what I had said and realised what accusations I had made against Loul. I knew she was furious. "Loul, I didn't mean to imply you've done anything wrong. She ignores what you tell her too."

"I can't think of anything Kirym has ignored me over, but I understand how you feel. What makes you feel you need to protect her?"

"You asked me to when we first found Arbreu, but almost everything she does leads her to danger. She nearly died in the cave at Faltryn. On the way home, she almost drowned. She went to Valythia and faced the fyrsha. It was huge." I shuddered, thinking about the massive cat she had fought. "I was so frightened for her. Ubree was almost dragged into the pack and she was on his back. He managed to escape, but—but it was so close. Had it managed to get its claws into Kirym, she'd have had no chance."

"But she didn't die, and as I heard, she saved a lot of lives. She was the one who saw the fyrsha coming."

"She shouldn't have even been there. None of us should have. Anyway, I can't care for her while she keeps spending time with those men. They'll kill her as soon as your back is turned."

Now Loul looked surprised. "Who would kill her?"

"Ashistar, Baketer, Borboncha, any of a number of others. Even though you've let them stay, I know they're still loyal to Gynbere. I even worry about the dragons' personal intentions towards her. It's not natural for her to spend time with them. But she'll go off anyway, even when she knows I can't go with her because of my other responsibilities."

"Would you go if you didn't have those responsibilities?"

I didn't even need to think. "No, cos Kirym would still ignore everything I told her. As much as you want me to, I can't."

Loul paused before answering. She seemed to be searching for the words.

"This is not about me wanting you to go with her. Right now, it's about what's best for you. To go or stay is your decision. But Teema, my dear, your responsibility is to yourself first, and I suspect you need a lot of healing to even manage that. What responsibilities keep you here and yet make you so unhappy?"

"I'm not unhappy. I made promises to Bokum. I can't walk away from them, and Kirym knows that. It's not fair. She wants me to choose."

Loul took a deep breath. "I don't think Bokum would want you to select one friendship over another, but what promise did you make to him?"

"I have to care for Zeprah and the children. It was his last wish. So, I couldn't go with Kirym, even if I wanted to. Which I don't!"

"I do know what Bokum said to all of you before he died. I didn't realise you had taken it *all* on yourself, but it does explain a lot. It's noble of you to take his request so literally, but the job isn't only yours. We all care for Zeprah, Sarel, and Trayum. Bokum asked you to tell the children about the silly things you both did when you were younger, and to help them do those things also. It's a wonderful gift for you to give them. The things you did when you were boys were fun. You laughed a lot. You had adventures. You climbed trees and fell out of them. You played. You cared, and you shared. They need to do those things too. Sarel is smiling less and less. So now, I'm charging you, to teach them to have fun. Teach them to be happy. Teach them to be children, to play. Do it for Zeprah too and," she paused, "do it for yourself. But spend time with other people as well."

I stared at her in shock. "You think I'm making Sarel and Trayum's loss worse?"

"No! I do not think that, but you could make it better for them. I wish we had talked long before this, and perhaps the fault is mine. I should have approached you sooner. Bokum's request shouldn't come between you and your other friends. You must keep those connections."

I shook my head. "No. Kirym has new friends. There's no room for me."

"Who has she chosen over you? And what about Arbreu? He too is your token brother."

"Arbreu has his family and now he has Mekrar. His days

are full." I felt wretched. As I listened to myself, I knew I had been unfair to Arbreu. It had sounded so much better when I justified it in my head.

Loul pulled me to her, and suddenly, I was crying. For all the things I had lost. No, to be honest, I'd driven them away. I felt so very tired and alone.

"I'm so sorry, Teema. I should have sorted this out a lot sooner. Now we will work at getting things right."

"Kirym will never talk to me again."

She laughed, and I was shocked.

"Kirym has been so worried about you. She'd love the two of you to talk. But it can wait until you're healthy."

"I'm not sick," I whispered.

"You're not well. Now, this is what we will do. You'll move back home. It's not good for you to be living in a wagon by yourself. You'll eat with us. Zeprah is welcome too, whenever she wants, her and the children. In the evening, there'll be someone with her to share the load. I've offered this before, and she has refused. Now I'll insist. We are a family and we will pull together."

I was crying again. Loul pulled me to her and I felt immense relief. Someone else would make the decisions for a while.

"I'm so tired."

"Then let's go home."

20

Teema Speaks

Moving back to Loul's was less difficult than I thought it would be. When I carried my pack up the hill, everyone there seemed pleased to see me, but no one made an embarrassing fuss.

I was home, sleeping on the set I had used when we first built the dwelling. I felt guilty. Someone had been moved out for me, but Loul dismissed my worries.

"No one has used this set over the last season, and it was always yours."

So, I unpacked and stowed my belongings, shaken when I realised how little I now owned.

And then Kirym walked in.

I was so shocked. Somehow, I had thought she would stay away.

She smiled at me as if nothing was wrong, gathered some of her clothes from the chest that sat at the end of her set and began to put them into her travel pack.

"Why do you keep stuff here when you live—" I sounded very critical. My face felt hot; I was sure I was bright red.

"I spend half my time here, so it's sensible to keep things in both places. Papa and Mama love seeing Trethia and Amethyst, and it's good for them to be part of a bigger family." She smiled and sounded quite normal, just as she always had.

"But you're taking them away. You're putting their lives in danger. You shouldn't go. You have responsibilities here." I sounded nasty, but I couldn't stop myself.

"I have to do this journey, Teema. Amethyst is staying here with Mama, Morkeen, and Starshine. Trethia has made her own decision."

"She's *far too* young." I was appalled.

Kirym turned around, her eyes steely. She seemed tall and imposing. I'd seen this before, but it was the first time it was directed at me.

"Trethia has been making her own decisions for more seasons than you have lived. She has been in great danger more often than everyone else alive. I think she has the right to decide."

I couldn't look at her. "If you stayed here, she would too. Let others go."

"Who? Who would you send into the unknown?" She took a deep breath, and her face softened. "Teema, if there was danger, the tokens would tell me."

I was appalled. "Scraps of stone? How on earth can they help? You rely on them too much."

She looked sad; I probably felt worse. I wished I could take back everything I had said. I dropped my head to hide my pain. I knew I'd lost her forever.

A shadow loomed over me. I glanced up, she stood in front of me, and I steeled myself, wondering if she would strike me.

"Do take care of yourself, my dear friend."

I looked into her eyes; she was so close. She clicked her tokens to mine.

I closed my eyes, trying to stem the tears that threatened to fall. I felt so lonely. I wished I'd done things differently. "I'm so sorry," I murmured. I took some deep breaths; wanting to be calm, to start thinking clearly again.

When I opened my eyes, she had gone. I hadn't heard the door open or close, I couldn't believe what she had just done. I had spent so much time rejecting her, taking my token away from hers, and yet she connected with me as if nothing had changed.

My token now felt different, and I didn't know what to think.

21

Kirym Speaks

Everyone came to see us off. I was initially surprised but realised they all wanted to know where the mysterious door was.

I'd explained my belief to Mama and Ubree. Mama was not at all sure I was right, but Ubree agreed it was plausible. Sundas did not want me to tell him what Danth had discovered but had not yet figured it out.

I looked at those who had agreed to join me on this adventure. Oak, Sundas, Mekrar, Arbreu, Ubree, Ashistar, and Trethia. Most were people I had expected to volunteer, but Mekrar's inclusion surprised me. I had thought Mama would counsel her to remain here learning her responsibilities as heir to the land. However, Mama and Papa had encouraged her to join me if she wanted to.

"Her life should not be lived on what may happen in the future," Mama said. "Of course, Arbreu's presence is the bonus you get with her."

I also questioned Ashistar's decision to join us now he had a family.

He overrode my objections. "My promise to you came first. Rosisha married me knowing this and she wouldn't allow me to put it aside. Churnyg will move in and care for her and Varitza. He, of course, can't wait for me to go." He shrugged. "With Churnyg, well no matter what I do, it's not right. Either I abandon my family, or I ignore my obligation to you. Anyway, I know you will get me back as soon as you can, and it could be we're both needed. The weapons are designed to be shared. No one can use a sword and a bow at the same time so, I'm going with you."

It was the longest speech I'd ever heard from him.

Ubree decided he should go with us, Borasyn would remain in the canyon, and Egrym was charged with supporting Mama with the building work and anything else she required.

I returned to the pool that ran off the fountainhead and placed the large tokens on the flat stone beside the water. Now although, I had one for each shadow around the circle, there were two tokens, the rainbow and the black, and only one space left in the centre. When I sat the black token in the remaining space alone, nothing happened. Placing both tokens there, each sitting on half of the shadow, also didn't work. The stones stayed silent.

"Kirym, I wonder if—" Garanniis paused. "Well whether this could help you." He pulled an object from inside his robe and handed it to me.

"This is the stone you found in the desert?"

He nodded. "Valycraag. An acknowledgement to the land we came from. I never told you its name, did I."

"You've carried it all this time?"

"Yes, and if your ancestors helped build Valythia, then it may also have a connection to you. Right now, I feel it belongs with you."

It was the colour of the desert, a deep reddish gold, but as he handled it, it turned black. It was a hand-span high; there was a hole through the centre and one end was smaller than the other. The outer wall was a thumb-width thick.

"It's generous of you to offer it, Garanniis."

He shrugged. "I always felt I was caring for it until it found its real home. Maybe it needs to be with the tokens and this is the right place and time to hand it over."

"And perhaps it proves, as I've always suspected, our families are more connected than we realise," I said.

"If we weren't before, we are now. Your daughter is my granddaughter."

I was deeply moved by his comment.

Valycraag was wonderful to hold and different to any other stone I'd touched. It was smooth, felt thick and creamy and I wanted to hold it close, caress it. I remembered Garanniis talking of a similar feeling when he described finding it.

Initially, I thought it was smooth all over, but then I felt three dimples on the wider end. I looked closely but could see nothing. Garanniis, when I asked him, knew of them, but had no answers for them being there.

I sat Valycraag in the centre of the flat rock. The smaller end fitted where I had previously placed the rainbow token. However, there was still only enough room on the stone to hold one token, and no matter which stone I sat there, it didn't feel right. It just sort-of perched on top. Obviously, there must be a different answer.

I studied the rock, the tokens, and Valycraag. I could hear some people getting restless. I knew there had to be an answer. Then I realised, and it was so obvious, I was inwardly annoyed at myself for not seeing it instantly.

I sat the rainbow token on Valycraag but face down in the hole. Then the black token sat on what I had always considered to be the rainbow token's base. The token and the desert stone appeared as one, much as it had in the cave above the canyon. The two tokens began to hum, but the others didn't join them.

Dashlan peered over my shoulder. "It's missing something, Kirym, and I might just know what it is. Well, it's a thought, and I could be wrong, but it's worth a try. Can Ubree or Egrym help me? It'll only take a moment. Don't do anything until I get back."

"Egrym will, although it'll take longer than a moment," Ubree said. "The rest of you may as well share a meal while waiting."

Dashlan vaulted onto Egrym's back, and they disappeared towards the south. Everyone else moved towards where the cooks were setting out food. I sat and studied the tokens. I was about to turn away when I saw Maletta in the shadow of the trees behind the stone wall. She somehow looked older, more bent over.

"Do I have it right?"

"There's only one way to find out," she said.

"And if I'm wrong?" I asked.

"Then life will carry on, but differently."

"But it won't help Halavash. Will people die?"

"Oh, one can never tell the future. The past now, is quite different. The past can be changed occasionally."

The breeze washed across the water, ruffling the surface, the flowers nodded gently. When I glanced back at Maletta, she had disappeared. It was as if she had never been there. I was more mystified than ever. Were my deductions correct? Was I doing the right thing?

Dashlan returned carrying a large pack. He opened it as he approached the pool and hauled out the head, the top section of the speaking stick his family had held for many generations. I'd last seen it at the Battle of the Tor where it had topped a multi-limbed stick. However, he had left the stick back at the settlement.

"Pa, we can't call this the top of the speaking stick any longer," Dashlan said. "Nor can it just be identified as a head, cos it isn't one," Dashlan said. "I think it needs a special name, something to identify it as the icon it is."

Bryn nodded. "Well I agree with you, Dash, but right now I can't think of anything. Did you have something in mind?"

"Not really, but it needs to acknowledge the dragon it held that help us win the battle," Dashlan said.

"What about Arech?" Qwinita asked. "Remember grandma's story about her great-great-grandpa? The one about him fighting a battle to protect the clan. He was given the title Arech as an acknowledgement of his bravery in facing the unknown. Grandma's story said the speaking stick helped him, but she discounted it because it was just the speaking stick. We all saw how it helped at the tor, so the original story was probably right. Anyway, it's a good name because Kirym is facing the unknown, and Arech may help her."

"And what if it doesn't help her as you think it will?" Arbreu asked.

"We still need to acknowledge the help it gave us at the tor," Qwinita said.

Dashlan picked Valycraag up and rubbed his finger across the top. He paused three times, his smile getting bigger with each hesitation. When he sat Arech on Valycraag, the three prongs seemed to sink into the top of the desert stone.

"Hmmm, better than I thought," he said, and stepped back to stand by me.

With the rainbow token nestled into Valycraag, the black above it, and Arech standing over them all, the stones glowed and vibrated. My tokens joined in. Each of the tokens on the stone, sent a ray of light to twirl around the black and rainbow tokens and into the top of the head, where it was absorbed. After a long pause when nothing happened, we were surrounded by a humming noise. It grew louder and then, light erupted from between Arech's three prongs and seemed to fill the two tokens under it until they were fat and pulsing. The two tokens sent light back and a dark amorphous shape deep inside Arech grew and pulsed.

All around me, there were gasps of wonder.

The tokens began to sing a new song. A deep earthier sound underlined the music. I had the impression it came from deep below me. The water in the pool vibrated, and the stone in the centre of the pool where I had originally found the bronze token, expanded until it covered the pool. It began to spin, getting faster and faster until it was just a blur. When it finally stopped, the stone had split into sixteen wedges, which now splayed out like the petals of a flower, each petal a different colour, the outer half lighter than the inner.

While this happened, the token's song soared, a song of joy, which faded, until with a final sigh, the stone flower settled onto the surface of the water.

"I imagine this confirms your thoughts about the door," Mama said. "What do you want us to do with the tokens while you're away?"

"Kirym is the token bearer," Mekrar said. "They must go with her. She may need them." She moved closer to me. "But tell me, what *does* this confirm?"

I smiled sweetly and turned to Mama. "Yes, the tokens are

our connection to this land. If this is the door Danth spoke of, we may need the tokens to ensure we can return."

"What about Arech and Valycraag?" Papa asked.

"Oh, Kirym must take Valycraag with her," Garanniis said. "I feel it needs to be with the tokens."

Bryn nodded in agreement. "Arech too. They do seem to all go together.

"Are you two sure? These have always been held by one of your family. Although they connect with the tokens, you must think carefully about letting them leave your care."

"We're related through Amethyst, Kirym. We are happy for you to carry it," Garanniis said.

"There's an easy answer for us, Pa," Dashlan said. "I'll go with Kirym."

"No, Dashlan," Bryn said. "You're the one who doesn't roam, remember?"

"Perhaps I never knew of a journey I really wanted to go on," Dashlan said. "Anyway, I need to do this. Arech has always been cared for by one of us."

Bryn frowned. "Arbreu's going, he can—"

"I have no connection to Arech, Pa," interrupted Arbreu. "I only vaguely remember it, but we'll take care of Dash. He'll come back. We all will."

"Pa, I'm old enough to do it without your permission. I have to go."

"And you'll go with our blessing, son." Jeresaya took Bryn's hand. "They all must spread their wings, Bryn. We will watch them go and welcome them back. He will return."

Valycraag was wrapped up and packed in with the tokens.

As I picked Arech up, I caught another glimpse of the dark shape in the centre, but before I identified it, it disappeared.

Mekrar grasped my arm. "That's the shape I saw in your blue

token after Ubree connected to you in the amphitheatre," she murmured.

As she went to collect her pack, the shadow of the black token with the glow of the other colours in its centre appeared on the rock where the tokens had sat.

"Does that mean your assumptions are correct?" Oak asked quietly.

I shrugged and handed Arech to Dashlan, who was to carry it.

"You carry a heavy load, Kirym. Can you manage?" Garanniis asked.

"Of course, I can. No load is heavy if you really want to carry it."

22

Kirym Speaks

Trethia and I were the only travellers not strapped into the harnesses on Ubree's back. Trethia hugged Amethyst goodbye and handed her to me. I kissed and hugged her and passed her to Mama, who with Morkeen and Paluniis, would care for her while I was away.

"Faltryn wants to come with us," Trethia said, as she picked the little dragon up.

"I'll look after her, Trethia," Papa said. "We all will. She'll be safe."

Trethia shook her head. "She needs to be with Kirym."

Mama looked questioningly at me.

I shrugged. "Perhaps she does." I touched the wee dragons' chin. "It's up to you, Faltryn. Will you stay here with Mama and Papa?"

She shook her head.

"Ubree?"

"Well, perhaps she'll learn more about being a dragon

if she comes with us than lying on a rug with Amethyst. She needs to be taught, and that's the responsibility of the oldest."

"It's a responsibility we all share, Ubree," I said. "Now let's go."

Papa handed Trethia up to Oak, and then passed Faltryn to Sundas, who stuffed her into his tunic. He picked me up and hugged me. "You take care, my little one. I'll miss you. Your stories will be welcome in winter, so make sure you're here to tell them."

He lifted me up; I scrambled into my seat and tied the harness straps together.

Try to keep in touch, was Borasyn's last message to me.

I hoped I could.

Ubree took off vertically through the trees. I glanced down at the faces staring up at us.

"Wish I knew where we're going," Oak murmured.

Ubree smiled in response. "It's right under your nose, Oak. You'll see very soon."

When high above everyone, Ubree banked sharply and dived towards the ground.

"Think of Halavash," he said.

Moments before we reached the ground, he folded his wings protectively over us and dove into the pool.

It was strange, not like entering water at all. I could breathe, and in view of the gasps behind me, so could everyone else. Ubree's wings lowered.

I glanced back. Those behind me looked tense. Beyond

Ubree's tail I could see the pool surface; faces peering down at us. Suddenly they shot away, and the pool became a small blue dot in the distance. Mekrar's eyes were open wide.

Fear, I thought.

We were in a long misty-walled tunnel suspended in a vast blackness. Small lights beyond the mist passed us at great speed, or perhaps we passed them, although Ubree did nothing to propel us forward.

I turned to the front in time to see an explosion of brightly coloured lights coming towards us. Then a large streak of light approached from the left. Just as I feared it would crash into us, it twisted around the tunnel and I turned to watch it race into the distance. I was pleased the long tunnel we were in deflected everything.

Huge orbs of various colours—mainly shades of white—but we also saw green, red, gold, and silver, continued to fly towards us all spiralling around the tunnel and speeding away. Some of the spheres had rings or smaller balls circling around or hovering near them. One of the larger orbs was plastered with hundreds of small pink blobs. Another looked as if it was split across the middle; parts of it bubbling out.

I heard occasional comments from behind me, a lot of oohs and aahs, and fragments of conversation from Trethia as she chatted to Oak about what she could see, the colours and the lights.

More spheres flew towards us, a beautiful blue, a small muddy brown. A massive yellow dwarfed the rest of them. They too, twisted around us and along the tunnel before disappearing into the expansive black distance.

Eventually, we slowed and stopped.

We were opposite a dark opening. There had been an ornate double-winged gate barring the way. Now it was broken, one half lay in a mangled mess partly on the tunnels misty surface, the other slumped inwards on its bottom hinge. I was reminded of the door to the cabin on Dragons Quest when we first found her. Beyond the gate was merely darkness

"Is this where we're supposed to be?" Dashlan asked. "Do we enter?"

"It's where we stopped," Ubree said. "We were thinking of Halavash when we entered the pool and that should have guided us." He put one clawed foot inside, paused, took a step, another, and another. Then we were inside, and hopefully on Halavash.

It was not as black as it had appeared from in the tunnel, but it was still dark, grey, and foreboding. As our eyes adjusted, we saw a bleak and featureless landscape. It had an unlived-in feeling that sent shivers down my back. It wasn't cold, but the area felt empty and uncared for.

"It's not as I remember, although my memory is incomplete," Ubree said. "The light is gone, the plants too. Someone, the gatekeeper, should be here to meet us. This must be the right place." He glanced at the dark grey sky. "We need to move away from here, find some shelter before night falls. Until we know what is happening, flying could be dangerous. So, for now, we walk."

We climbed to the ground and each of us took a pack.

"There is one message coming to me. It's most important we do not use fire here. No matter the circumstances, no flame or spark at all. Do you all understand?"

"What about meals?" Dashlan asked.

"It's better to go hungry than die," Ubree said. "This could mean the difference between life and death. Ours and others."

"Travelling food can be eaten uncooked," I said. "You'll survive, Dash. Ubree, does this mean someone knows we are here? The gatekeeper perhaps?"

He shook his head. "The message is in the air. Something

is very wrong."

Ubree took the lead. Oak carried Trethia, Sundas kept Faltryn tucked in his tunic. They would never have kept up.

We followed a narrow path, too unnaturally straight to have been made by animals. It led to a cliff-edge with a wide path angling down into grey clouds.

Instead of following the path, Ubree walked along the cliff. Eventually, the cloud below us thinned and we could see the land. A massive forest stretched to the horizon. The trees were leafless, black or dark grey, the soil beneath them was scorched. A huge fire had recently raced through the forest.

"Oh! This isn't good," Ubree said.

"You said no fire," Oak said. "So how—?"

"We'll talk later. Right now, we need shelter, and I need time to think," Ubree said. *Say nothing of importance out loud. If you think of something, I'll know and pass it on. Accept that everything you meet can hear us.*

A little further on we came across a path that fell steeply into the trees. Although it looked too steep to be usable, Ubree started down. It wasn't the easiest climb, but we all made it past the steepest and narrowest section safely.

We soon reached the treeline. It was a little more reassuring to be hidden, but it wasn't until the trees closed over us that I realised how vulnerable I had felt.

I wondered what had caused such a massive fire. Everything, for as far as my eye could see, looked sad and desolate. There was an air of mourning here.

I reached out and touched the nearest trunk.

It shuddered.

I pulled my hand away, and then tentatively touched it again. This time there was no reaction. Something else happened when I touched the tree, but I couldn't place it. *I'll think about it later.*

Just over three thousand steps into the scarred forest we found a clearing, a very small clearing. Thankfully, the air was warm, we would have a reasonably comfortable night. We settled down, and after a small snack, we chatted briefly about leaving The Green Valley and our families. No one spoke of the journey or our mission; what was said was superficial. *Who do you think can hear us, Ubree?* I asked.

Everything, Kirym, came his answer, leaving me more mystified than ever.

Mekrar and Arbreu took the first watch and woke me when the planet's moon had moved two hand-spans from the horizon. A second moon peaked over the horizon.

"I'll nudge Sundas, he's next for guard duty," Mekrar said.

"Leave him to sleep," I said. "I need a little time to think first." I leaned against a tree and studied the sky.

Halavash, if indeed we were in Halavash, was so different. On the ridge, the sky had been invisible, but down here I could see masses of stars. I didn't recognise any of them, but through the bare branches, one caught my eye. It sat near the horizon and had a distinctive green tinge around it.

The two moons were soon joined by a third, all followed the same path.

I thought over our journey so far and tried to send a message to Borasyn. I got no answer and wondered if he had heard me. It was possible he had and couldn't get his reply to me.

Trethia lay on Oak's cloak; I bent forward to arrange my shawl over her shoulders and then leaned back again. The shock of finding myself flat on the ground took my breath away. I was stunned for a moment.

Rubbing the back of my head, I sat up. "Ubree! The tree! It's gone!" I glanced around. "They've all gone."

"Mmmm. They've probably gone to talk about us."

"What! How? Where? They can't have just vanished into thin air."

"Of course, they haven't. They…"

I leapt to my feet and raced away from the camp.

The trees had surrounded us, so I thought maybe they just put distance between us, in which case, any direction would suffice in the short term. My mind raced at the thought of walking trees.

"Stop! Wait! I need to speak to you."

I wish I had a hooded lamp. Ubree had been adamant we not use them, but I was running blind. The moon was bright, but I couldn't see much at all. I tripped over odd bits of debris on the ground. *Will I be able to find my way back to the clearing? Silly, Ubree won't let me get lost.* Then a thick wall of trees appeared at the far edge of my vision.

I stopped.

"Please," I called. "I need to know what happened here. It's obvious there's been trouble. Perhaps we can help each other."

I waited. Nothing. No movement, no sound. Then I realised what had been bothering me since I had touched the tree trunk when I left the cliff.

"I can't help unless you are honest with me about what's going on."

The biggest tree drifted slowly towards me. Those behind it closed up, leaving no space for it to return.

They're sacrificing it!

A semblance of a face appeared in the bark of the tree in front of me. It was silent for a long moment; I had the impression I was being studied.

"Honest? That's an unusual word to use before we've even spoken."

"Not at all, because so far every message you've given since we arrived has been a lie," I said.

"I've not said a word."

"You pretend! Everything about you is an illusion. A lie."

"What gives you that idea?"

"I touched a burned trunk, but there was no soot on my hand. You appear leafless, but when you move, I hear leaves rustling. A tree of your size must be very old, and your bark would be deeply grooved, and yet you show the smooth trunk of a young tree."

The big tree shivered. Instantly, it was covered in leaves, and the bark appeared as aged as I would have expected for one so ancient.

"I will come back and talk. Then we trees will decide whether you live or not," it said.

The trees behind it shook and shivered. I watched in amazement as the tree sent its roots along the ground to interconnect to those nearest.

When it pulled its roots back, they all moved slowly towards us.

As I turned and began to walk in the direction I had come from, the sky darkened. I could no longer see the stars and moons. However, the big tree caught up with me and guided me. It gave its own light and I could easily see it and the ground around us. It moved easily, despite its massive size and I was intrigued by its movements. The ground under it rippled, the roots obviously moving. The trunk would glide forwards and pause as the roots moved again.

We walked a long way, *much further than I had travelled, even*, I thought, *taking our leisurely speed into account*. I tried not to panic; hoped he was honest in his agreement to speak to us. Through all this time, I heard nothing from Ubree, although I was sure he knew what was going on.

The camp, when I saw it, was different. Reversed. We had travelled in a large circle and we were approaching the back of it. However, everyone there was facing us, Ubree, hunkered down on his belly, looked a lot smaller than usual.

"Hmm," the tree murmured, "not taken in, it seems." A branch snaked around my waist and lifted me off the ground.

Ubree stood, stretched to his full height, his wings outspread. He looked massive.

The tree shuddered.

"I'm fine, Ubree. They're here to talk."

Ubree nodded, closed his wings and settled again on his belly.

"We are no threat, tree," I said.

It relaxed, placed me back on the ground and followed me into the camp.

The stars shone as before, allowing me to see the other trees gathered at the far edge of my vision. I felt that if our conversation wasn't to their liking, they would disappear. The only tree near was the one we spoke to.

"I'm Kirym. We're here because we recently received a request for help. Do you know who sent it?"

"Why should we tell you anything?" the tree asked. "You bring monsters with you, the same monsters who kill our cousins and who threaten us still. Perhaps we should eliminate you before you can join them."

"Would that not make you as bad as those who destroyed your cousins? The message came from Halavash. This is Halavash, isn't it?" I said.

The tree rustled; its twigs and branches reached across the

open area towards the others, but they backed away. With an audible sigh, the tree lifted most of its roots out of the ground, leaned over, whipped some long supple branches around the nearest tree. The captured tree screamed in protest. Other trees reached out to pull it back, but they were all dragged towards us. After a lot of branch rustling, the tree let go and settled its roots back into the ground. The others skittered back to their original positions.

"Is this Halavash?" I repeated.

"Yeeess," came the guarded answer. "We don't want you here. You look like those who have attacked and killed our family. How do we know—?"

"How did they do that?" I interrupted.

"They set fires to destroy those who refused to join their plan to leave here and kill others. Our illusion, our lie to you was so you would think there were no more of us to enslave."

"You know we haven't used fire. You saw us arrive; you've watched us ever since."

Again, the trees rustled, this was how they communicated.

You're right, Kirym, came Ubree's thought. *They're discussing us, trying to decide if they should trust us. Some want to destroy us, but others are arguing against it.*

"Are all of the plants able to communicate as you are doing?" I asked.

The rustling from the surrounding trees increased until it appeared a strong wind was battering them.

I waited quite a while before the tree who spoke turned back to me. "I will trust you, but if I am wrong, they will destroy me as they will destroy you. I'm Malsavash—Patriarch! Yes, we can pass on information in many ways. If need be, all in the land will know of your presence. However, I am restricting the knowledge because some of our people have turned on us; are helping to destroy us. Now you will tell us what we need to know. Did you come down the portal or up?"

"What is a portal?"

"It's what is on the other side of the double-winged gate."

"Oh," I thought about the term, portal. It fitted. "Yes, but as for direction, what is down and what is up in a portal?"

Malsavash nodded. "A good answer. Did the planets come towards you, or did they pass you from behind?"

"Towards us. They were planets?"

"Planets, stars, other worlds. Portals are shortcuts between the worlds. You came down the portal. Why did you bring monsters with you? Were you planning to threaten or scare us?"

"Behaviour makes the monster. Did you know those who came earlier were monsters by looking at them?"

"I take your point."

"We mean you no harm. We want only to help, and then return to our homes and families. What assistance do you need?" I asked.

"The fire-starters need to be destroyed or taken back to where they came from."

I nodded. "Where will we find them?"

"What happened to the gatekeeper?" Ubree asked.

Malsavash looked surprised. "You expected a gatekeeper? Hmmm!" He paused for a while. "Something happened although we didn't see it. We heard a great noise and when we checked, the gatekeeper had disappeared. He hasn't cared for the gate since then. When the monsters arrived, he reappeared and went off with them." The other trees rustled, I had the impression they were arguing. "I've listened to my brothers and to you, and we don't know whether to believe you or not. So, I'm not going to decide. I shall send you elsewhere while I think about it. You will leave at first sun."

I glanced at the sky. The line of three moons was mid-sky, and a fourth smaller moon had appeared. It too was racing across the sky.

"What's the dark thing behind the moon?" Arbreu asked.

Malsavash glanced up. "Oh, my!" His leaves shook for a few moments. The other trees answered and closed in around us.

"We're taking you to shelter. If we don't, you will die," Malsavash said.

I was lifted from the ground; I heard several surprised gasps, and a squeak of shock from Mekrar.

The trees passed me from one to another. It was smoothly done, I felt I was sliding headfirst through a dark tunnel and moving very quickly. I was deposited on the ground in front of a cave. The others had already arrived.

"Go into the cave," Malsavash said. "Quickly! Stand at the back away from the entrance. You'll be able to see what's happening."

"Will you and the trees be safe?" I asked.

"Yes! Go!"

Our packs and everything else we had brought with us were sitting in the cave entrance, we took them with us to the back.

"How did you get here, Ubree?"

"In the same manner as you. They just picked me up and passed me along. Strange feeling. They moved very fast. I'd say we were over a day's walk from where we were."

The trees moved close together in small groups, entwining their branches and flattening out their leaves. In the light of the moons, the land that had been a luscious forest now looked desolate.

As I glanced at the strange humps of trees, something

thudded onto the ground in front of the cave. It was grey, bright, the size of a small bird, and gave me the impression of an autumn leaf. Then there was a cascade of them. After hitting the ground, they fluttered, as if injured. The body of the first I saw fall, slowly rose until it was about two hand-spans above the ground. Its legs looked strange, like thick twigs. Once they were fully extended, thin prongs shot from its body and pierced the ground. After a short time, they pulled up a worm. A long feeler pushed into its body. The worm which began to writhe; its skin melted and within moments, its inner body disintegrated. Soon only a few slimy globules were left pooled on the ground. By then the creature's prongs had gone in search of its next meal—a large insect.

I was stunned and slightly sickened, but I couldn't look away.

The trees fared better than the insects. By rounding their shapes and smoothing their leaves they were almost impenetrable. When the creatures hit them, they slid to the ground. The few that managed to cling on, were shaken off.

Then things became even more strange. The ground began to ripple. Mossy tendrils began to twine around the creature's legs. As it crept higher the moss thickened from the bottom up.

The bird-like creature began to struggle, breaking some of the tendrils, but more of them grabbed hold. As the moss piled onto the creature, they toppled and were overcome. They didn't give up easily, though. The ground heaved and roiled as they fought, but eventually the lumps under the moss became still, and eventually flattened out. Some of the creatures discarded their legs and flew away, thereby evading the moss.

For a short time, the ground in front of the cave boiled

as the creatures fought the moss. Eventually, everything settled. We could see other battles going on further away, and an occasional creature still dropped from the trees, but now when they landed, they were immediately smothered by the moss.

After a short period when no more creatures fell, the trees moved apart, shook and opened their leaves and branches.

We ventured out of the cave to see the first three moons now sat halfway between the meridian and the horizon, while the moon the bugs had followed was close to setting.

"What were those creatures?" I asked.

"Kultria bugs. They're named after the moon that brings them," Malsavash said. "They're born into a huge web in the sky and stay there until maturity. To breed, they need flesh and blood. They land only to eat. If they're successful in finding blood, they fly away. The moss smothers them, but enough survive to continue breeding."

"They attack anything alive," another tree said, "but are mostly attracted to blood. If they manage to get their hooks in to you, they will keep sucking until there is no life left. They also attack my brother trees and steal their sap. They will drain us of life also."

Malsavash suddenly shook his leaves and a single bug slid to a piece of sandy ground. He leaned forward, stabbed it with a sharp twig. He held it pointed towards the rocks, well away from us. The creature was motionless for a moment, and then its prongs shot out. I was shocked at how long they were, how far they went. I understood why we were asked to stand well back from the entrance. The prongs were more than four times longer than their legs had been.

Malsavash carefully snapped the body in two and dropped it on the moss, which immediately smothered it.

"How often do they swarm like this, Malsavash?" Oak asked.

"Kultria crosses the sky every spring. Because of your arrival, we weren't quite as prepared as we should have been. The bugs will impact your journey. You will need solid shelter every time the moon appears."

Another tree reached out and grabbed Malsavash's branches. "If we allow them to go, Malsavash. Not everyone has decided."

"Can you give a good reason for refusing to send them on, Uguvash? More important, will you accept responsibility when others find out? And they will find out, you can be sure of it."

Uguvash reached out to other nearby trees. They stayed connected for a while, and some pulled their twigs and branches away. Soon, only three trees stayed connected.

Eventually, Uguvash spoke. "Your arguments are compelling, Malsavash."

"We will send you on your journey if you can assure us your monsters will not hurt us."

I stared at Malsavash coldly. "Perhaps if you made fewer assumptions on appearances, we would all get on better."

Malsavash paused and then continued. "We can direct you, but you need to go places we can't. You will be met by others who will guide you further. You should see the gatekeeper, but he hasn't been seen in many eons. Not finding him will create problems but others can deal with them."

"We will do what we can to help you rid the land of those who kill your family," I said, "but before we go further, there are a few things we need to know."

"Where can we find the dragons?" Trethia asked.

There was a collective stillness amongst the trees, almost as if they were holding their breaths.

"There are no dragons," Uguvash said. "We've never had dragons here."

"You used to," she said.

"We've never had them," Uguvash reiterated, harshly.

I looked at Malsavash. "Really? And I thought we'd agreed not to lie to each other."

"And why would you accuse us of lying?" Malsavash asked coldly.

"Two reasons. First, had there never been dragons here, you wouldn't have understood Trethia's question. Second, Halavash is the dragon star, so, where else would they be?"

Malsavash's roots crept towards the other trees. After a short time, he turned back to me. "I need to speak with my family. You should take the opportunity to sleep. Use the cave, you will be safe there."

23

Kirym Speaks

The horizon was just beginning to lighten when I woke. I lay still for a moment, thinking about what had happened since we left The Green Valley. It was quiet around me; Ubree had insisted we all sleep.

They've finished discussing Trethia's question, Kirym. What made her ask?

Perhaps it was better coming from her, rather than anyone else, I answered. *We couldn't discuss it; they hear everything we say. It needed to be asked. Is it possible they can hear us now?*

I don't think so. This is one privacy we can rely on.

Malsavash was waiting when I walked out of the cave.

"The simple answer is we don't know what happened to the dragons."

"Why were you so reluctant to tell us?"

"There has been dissension among those who live here," Malsavash said. "When one's life is threatened, one looks at things differently. We haven't been settled in a long time.

Since the gatekeeper went into hiding, anything can enter the land freely and we've felt vulnerable. Those entering the gate tend to come here first, and there is nothing we can do about it."

"That's the simple answer, what's the complicated one?" I asked.

"You must understand, this was not a question we expected, nor wanted to hear because we really don't have the answer. The dragons were here, and then they weren't. There had been disagreement among them. It divided the flight. Some went or were sent to live elsewhere, but even then, the differences continued. The Kultria bugs began to fly at about the same time, and then suddenly the dragons were gone." He paused. "It might have happened the other way, them disappearing before the bugs arrived."

"What was the disagreement?" I asked.

"I was but a seedling when it happened. Seedlings are silly things; they don't really notice what's happening around them. They're too busy—" Malsavash paused, "—well, doing things young trees do. The gatekeeper said—" again he paused. "Well, he said there was nothing he could do for the dragons."

"So, he's hiding," I said. "Why did he not fix the gate?"

"He feared the monster who destroyed the gate would return and kill him if he stayed up on the plateau."

"When was the gate destroyed?"

"Time is different in each world, Kirym. For us, it was almost beyond memory."

"After this monster left," I said, "there was a long time when nothing happened. The gate could have been fixed then. Because the gatekeeper did nothing, the fire-starters, a worse danger, were able to enter."

"Nothing is worse than the Kultria bugs. The fire-starters have a different agenda. They will leave when they are strong enough. Rumour is, they intend to take their army through the portal. Mind you, the Kultria bugs may alter their plan. They're stronger. Well, not stronger, but more numerous. They may overcome us all with their numbers."

"So, we have three quests," I said. "We need to discover what happened to the dragons. The fire-starters and the bugs must both be destroyed or neutralised, and we must find out why the gatekeeper has deserted his position at the gate. I think the questions and answers begin with the gatekeeper. How do we find him and what may we encounter in the journey?" *A fourth quest. We must also retrieve our stolen property and I think so much is wrong here, the theft was almost certainly plotted from here.*

"We have decided to send you to someone who may know where the gatekeeper is. He will make his own decision. It could be he is so fearful because of what is happening here, he will avoid contact with everyone."

"And in doing that, your land is destroyed. I do hope he will talk to us. Together we may have more chance of overcoming the problems because if all here die, other worlds are in danger. So, whether he will speak to me or not, the gate must be fixed."

The trees again carried us to a spot where, in the brightening dawn we saw where our journey would take us. Across a massive desert.

"The place to begin your journey. We cannot accompany you across the sands," Malsavash said, ushering us to the edge of the grey sand.

"Will we reach the other side before Kultria rises?" I asked.

"The journey will take you two days. I believe there is a

stone formation out there for you to rest in overnight. I remember hearing there was a cave there. However, you face another more immediate danger." Malsavash raked his twigs through the sand. "This!"

The animal he showed me was small, grey, as was everything here, about the same length as Sundas' hand and rather cute. Its nose was darker than the rest of it, its back was made of bands of flexible armour interspersed with strips of short stiff hair. Towards the dumpy tail, the hair was lighter and finer. The animal had four feet, little more than rudimentary stumps, each with four curved, blunt claws.

"Don't let it's looks fool you. They have killed everyone who has ventured into their desert. They are attracted to whatever crosses the sand. We have watched our friends die, unable to save them."

I touched the little creature. Its body rippled, *it likes that,* I thought. The claws were quite blunt, it seemed harmless.

"How are these dangerous?" I asked.

"They live below the surface in the sand. Their mass movement alters the viscosity of what is above them. You may manage, you can move faster than we do, but any pause as you walk is life-threatening. You quickly drown in sand."

"How can we avoid them?"

"You can't. No one has ever done it."

"Someone must have."

There was silence. Malsavash wouldn't look at me.

"You know of the cave in the middle of the desert; your people are on the other side, so there must be some way of crossing."

There was an awkward silence.

Malsavash scowled. "Keep moving. There are stone outcrops. If you find them, you can rest. But remember. Kultria doesn't rest!"

"How do we find the stone formation? It doesn't seem to be visible from here."

Malsavash pointed across the sand. "Travel towards the light." It sat on the horizon, more a glimmer than a light.

"Where do we go when we leave the rocks?" I asked.

"Ah, yes." Malsavash paused. "You will need this." His leaves rustled; I would have sworn he was laughing. He stretched four of his branches, two on each side of his trunk, then bent them around, like arms, and pushed the end twigs into a thin vertical crack in his bark. Then he started pulling, stretching the two sides of the crack apart. His trunk groaned and screeched as the crack widened. As he pulled, his twigs pushed in deeper and deeper. The resulting hole would have made a lovely home for a large bird or animal.

He paused, breathing deeply and again flexed his twigs. Then one of his branches whipped around and plunged into the hole. He pushed it in deeper and deeper until I felt the branch end must be quite near his roots. When he stopped, he appeared to be searching for something. Eventually, after a prolonged scrabble around, he pulled his branch out of the hole and triumphantly waved it about.

Had I not known it was there, I could easily have overlooked it as a growth on the end of his branch. It was roundish and as grey as he was, wider than it was high, and a bit furry in parts. The areas that weren't had a beautiful grain, almost like a Burl. Dotted haphazardly around it were lots of oval holes.

"This will help you when you're ready to leave the cave."

"How?" I asked.

"It'll talk."

"Really talk?" Arbreu sounded surprised. "Like we are now?"

Malsavash nodded. "And it'll be a tiring journey for you;

you will need to rest at the rocks tomorrow."

He held the ball up and poked a twig hard into one of the holes.

It snapped shut and there was a crack.

"Ouch!"

The mouth spat the end of the twig out and clamped its mouth firmly shut.

Malsavash held the ball out to the other trees. "One of you want to load it?"

They all backed away fast.

"Oh, no!" Uguvash said. "Not when you've already riled them up. They're vicious and they always get worse. You'll be lucky to come away with any twigs at all once that thing's finished with you."

"Surely there's a gentler way to do this. Isn't it part of you?" Sundas asked.

Malsavash stared down at him and frowned.

Sundas shrugged. "Just asking."

Malsavash tossed the ball up, and as it came down, he thrust a twig in each of the holes. He moved so fast, none of us saw it happening.

The ball made gagging sounds.

I felt sick. "Oh, please don't hurt it."

"It decided to be aggressive. With some things, there is no easy way." He pulled his twigs out, and the ball dropped, to be caught by one of his lowest branches. He juggled it up, from one branch to another, until he could hand it to me.

"How do I retrieve the instructions?"

"When you're ready to leave the stones, shake it. It'll probably ignore you, so you may have to throw it against a rock a few times. That'll encourage it. Then follow the instructions."

"How can I return it to you once I have the instructions?" I asked.

Malsavash flicked his finger-like twigs. "Oh, don't. They're useless. It's best destroyed. Then it'll cause no more trouble, ever. Now you must go, or you will still be travelling when Kultria rises."

As Oak swung Trethia from his hip to his shoulders, the closest trees, gasped and backed away.

Oak glanced around as he flicked his pack over one shoulder.

Everyone else grabbed their packs, leaving mine, the baldric and the weapons. I put the ball in with the tokens, tied on the baldric and shouldered my pack, before turning back to Malsavash.

"What do we do on the other side?"

"You will be met and directed." He was already walking away.

"Thank you for your help," I called.

24

Arbreu

Walking on the sand was not difficult, but it was tedious and tiring. Every time Arbreu took a step, the sand beneath his feet wobbled as if it had become less dense.

Kirym appeared to be more relaxed with it, so Arbreu tried to match her stride; a longer step, with movement from her hips rather than her knees.

"It's easier, but it still feels weird," he muttered. "Makes you want to stop until it stabilises."

"I wouldn't advise it," Sundas said. "It'll stabilise somewhere over your head."

"You believe Malsavash?"

"I've no reason not to."

The sun was well above the horizon before Ubree saw the first stone pad away to their right. They changed direction; it took two or three steps on the solid sand before the creatures caught up.

Reaching the stone was a relief. Everyone dropped their

packs, although Kirym, Arbreu noted, kept the baldric on, and her token pocket remained in its usual place on her hip.

"It's a weird sensation," Mekrar said. "When we first arrived at the amphitheatre and saw Wind Runner's herders making curd from squilute milk, Mekroe asked what it would be like to walk on it. I think this is as near as we'll ever get."

"Do you think we'll make it to the cave thing in a day, Kirym?" Arbreu asked.

"Malsavash said we would. I have no real idea how long a day is here, so we will have to keep walking."

"We'll make it," Ubree said, "as long as we don't stop for long."

Sundas and Ashistar set out a small meal for them all. In the quietness as they ate, Arbreu heard a low drone. He tried to work out where it came from, but it was very indistinct. The sky was clear, even the birds didn't fly here, but he couldn't place the sound. He wondered if it was the desert itself.

Before he could mention it, Kirym opened her token pocket and pulled out the lump Malsavash gave her. Every mouth was grumbling.

Arbreu finally got a close look at it. Grey, round, but flat on the top and base. "Goodness, it's a seed cone, isn't it? Should you talk to it now, Kirym? Malsavash said to ignore it until you needed it. What if it'll only talk once?"

Kirym held the ball at eye level. "I'm Kirym. What's your name?"

Three of the mouths suddenly became eyes. One of them stared distrustfully at Kirym, the others watched everyone else.

The eyes looked strained and sore. Kirym reached for her remedy pack.

"I have a tincture to soothe your eyes." She picked it up,

but the eyes immediately disappeared.

"Kirym puts them in my eyes too. It's nice and soothing," Trethia said. "She won't hurt you."

A single eye appeared and then said dryly, "All right, but if it hurts, I'll bite you. And I'll not tell you the right instructions and I can talk as much as I want too."

Smiling, Kirym brought out a small vial and carefully put a single drop into the eye. It blinked several times, and then the other two eyes appeared, although they appeared in different places to previously. Five more eyes appeared for treatment and after a lot of blinking, they all closed.

"I shall rest now," the seed ball said pompously. "Mind you, there's not much chance of that happening. That nest is so bumpy, I'll be surprised if I'm not broken into bits before the day is finished."

"Perhaps it'll be better if I nestle you in my shawl."

"See, I told you she'd try to smother us," a different voice said.

"Did not!"

"Did so!"

Ashistar rolled his eyes. "Oh. wonderful! Now it's arguing with itself."

One of the eyes moved around the ball until it was looking at him. "Better than arguing with you. Anyway, you're walking. I'm being carried."

"And that's enough from all of you," Kirym said. She held the seed ball at eye level again. "Do you want something to eat?"

It rolled its eyes, in perfect imitation of Ashistar. "I'll tell you when I do. Right now, I need to sleep, although there's not much chance in this company."

As Kirym lined the token pocket with her shawl, a small voice spoke up.

"Our name is Rolliz."

"Why'd'ya tell her that for? Idiot!"

"'Coz she's nice."

"Sucked in again. You're such a pushover. Just wait. It'll start soon. Always does."

"May not."

"Will!"

"Won't!"

"Will!"

"Humph!"

Kirym tucked Rolliz into the shawl in her pocket.

"Won't," a muffled voice said.

Kirym smiled, but then a look of shock crossed her face.

"Look!" She pointed to the edge of the stone. There was a deep whirlpool in the sand.

"My goodness," Arbreu said. "That's where we left the sand. They're searching for us. That'll form under us if we pause as we walk."

Far too soon, Kirym picked up her pack. "Come on, we can rest when we get there."

She set a fast pace, and although it was slower than was usual, the jelly-like feel to the ground drained the power from their legs.

Sundas spied another stone outcrop when the sun was a hand-span past the meridian. They ate quickly before again stepping onto the sand.

In the middle of the afternoon, they were resting briefly on another small rock pad when Oak pointed towards the horizon. The light they were aiming for now sat above a tall rock formation.

"Where did that come from?" he asked. "I'd swear it wasn't there when I sat down. Should we aim for it?"

"Where else would we go?" Mekrar asked.

The last sun that rose had not taken the trajectory they had expected but had crossed just a small section of sky. Now it was setting, and they could no longer see the rock formation. They travelled in deep twilight, with enough light to see where to put their feet, but not much else. The short rests that had sustained them were now out of the question.

"We're not going to make it," Arbreu said quietly to Mekrar. "We shouldn't have stopped at all. I wonder if Malsavash sent us out here to die."

"No, he didn't," Kirym said. "He didn't have to help us at all. Had he said nothing the bugs would have killed us on the night we arrived. We can still see light, so we know we're going in the right direction."

Just before the last light left the land, there was a faint gleam on the horizon.

"This place is so weird," Dashlan said. "It's another sun. Except for the three moons last night, the suns and moons all follow different paths."

Arbreu glanced ahead as the daylight strengthened. Abruptly, the rock formation was much closer than he expected. Taken aback, he paused mid-step. The ground beneath his left foot dissolved. He glanced down. Even in this dim light he could see the sand swirling up over his boot. He stepped forward, but the sand under his right boot wasn't firm enough to give him leverage to pull his left free. As the sand covered his right boot; his left foot sank further; sand covered his calf.

I can't call out. He closed his eyes. *They'll all stop to help me, and they'll get caught too. Mekrar will miss me. I wish I could tell her how much I love—.*

He felt pressure around his chest. Then his legs felt as if

they were being pulled from his hips. He opened his eyes.

Ubree's tail was coiled around his chest. The dragon was trying to haul him out of the sand, which was now swirling towards his thighs.

The pain was excruciating. Arbreu took a breath, his mouth opened.

Don't scream, I can only deal with one of you at a time. Ubree's message came just in time.

Arbreu clamped his mouth shut, biting his lip to distract himself. It worked, but now he had a sore, bleeding lip as well. Then he was dangling above the sand. Ubree moved forward, still holding Arbreu above the sand.

Slowly, the pain in his leg and lip dissipated, and Ubree set him back on his feet.

Keep walking. You can stop when we reach safety.

Ubree kept his tail around Arbreu's chest until he had regained his stride.

Arbreu sent his thanks to the dragon.

Sooner than expected a tall imposing wall; too sheer to climb rose out of the sand and towered over them. Without stopping, Kirym turned left and followed the rock-face. They covered a huge area, but with no hand or footholds in the rock, there was no way of climbing up. They passed an occasional hollow in the wall, but they were all too small for them to use, and the base of them was sand.

They walked around the formation and when the sun was at their backs, they found a tunnel. It was low; it would be a squeeze for Sundas. Ubree would have no choice but fly over the wall.

Kirym, however, continued past it without pausing. Mystified, they all followed her.

"The tunnel is only big enough to allow one person to use it at a time, and I need to check it's safe inside before we all crowd in. Don't stop walking until it's your turn to enter. Don't walk on the spot, you must keep changing your direction," she said. "It would be sad to die when safety is within our grasp."

Arbreu was sure she was looking at him. He was glad the dim light hid his red face.

"Decide in what order you will enter the tunnel so there is no pausing for polite talk. Mekrar, you come with me now." Kirym pulled out her knife, abruptly changed direction, and disappeared into the tunnel.

"Arb, you take Trethia in first," Oak said, walking next to him and handing her over. "Dash, you go second, then Ashistar and Sundas." He readied his bow in case it was needed.

A short time later Mekrar appeared. "You can come in, but one at a time, we want no accidents. The ground in here is mainly rock so we can relax a bit."

"Well, this is not what I expected," Ubree said, when they were all inside.

The space was longer than it was wide, *running east-west*, Arbreu thought, *assuming the first moons rose from the east.* There were two large sand-pools in the centre. The walls had lines engraved on them. *I wonder what Kirym will discover when she studies them,* Arbreu thought. There were a few ledges around the walls, but no growth, not even grass or lichen.

Kirym pointed out the cave in the northern wall. It was big enough for them all, although not as deep as Arbreu would have liked.

"With the reach those bugs have, we'll be in almost as much danger as out in the open," he said.

"I'll put a protective circle over us," Ubree said. "That, I hope, will be enough."

The cave was piled with what looked like short twigs.

"Where do those come from?" Arbreu asked, pointing to a pile of twigs.

"Bug-legs," Trethia said.

Arbreu stared at them. Trethia was right. "There are hundreds of them. How did they get in there? And what do we do with them?"

Trethia opened her little pack; took out her platter and begun to shovel the legs out. "Just move them away, but don't touch them."

Oak watched her for a few moments, then grabbed his platter and went to help her. Moments later, Mekrar and Sundas had joined them.

Kirym dropped her pack, removed the baldric and began to study the walls. It was unlike her not to get everyone settled first, and when she had not moved for a long time, Arbreu went to see what held her attention.

Wide lines in the wall fanned out from a small waist high ledge. Arbreu touched the lines, but although they looked carved, the rock was smooth. Closeup, they looked as if they had grown in the rock.

Kirym opened her token pocket, unwrapped the rainbow token and placed it on the ledge.

For a long moment nothing happened, and then the ground seemed to shift slightly. Not like the shifting sands beyond the walls, nor like an earthquake such as he had felt back in The Land Between the Gorges. To Arbreu, it felt as if the stone beneath them had slid sideward. He put his hands on the rock face in front of him to steady himself.

"It's vibrating," he said quietly.

"Yes." Kirym picked up the token and touched it to her forehead.

"Oh my," she gasped. "Arb, what colour is the rock?"

"Grey," he said. "Just like everything else here."

She nodded. "Just keep quiet, I need to check something." She clicked the token to Arbreu's.

He stared at the stone wall in shock. Most of it was blue. Each of the lines Kirym had been studying was a different colour—they looked like a rainbow. The sand-pools were a lighter blue, and the sky looked like a divine sunset, a mixture of orange, red, and yellow.

Kirym had moved away. Arbreu spun around and saw a look of shock on Mekrar's face as Kirym clicked the rainbow token to hers.

Kirym called everyone to her and asked the same question. "What colour is the rock?"

"Grey," Oak, Ashistar, Sundas, and Dashlan said in unison.

"Blue," Trethia said.

Ubree frowned. "You saw no colour?"

"Until now," Kirym said.

She leaned forward and touched Oak's forehead with the token. Arbreu knew Oak could now see the same colours he could, and by then, she had pressed the token to Dashlan's forehead, followed by Sundas, and Ashistar.

"Something we need to talk about," Kirym said, "but let's wait until we're settled."

25

Kirym Speaks

The last sun had moved across the sky with great speed and was already beginning to set. Mekrar arranged the rugs so we wouldn't have to sit on hard stone. The packs sat where they would be easily accessible.

I untied my pocket and peeked in to see if Rolliz was awake.

Three eyes stared up at me. "It's about time you checked on me. I'm suffocating in here."

He was now a beautiful rich purple.

I lifted him out. "Where would you like to sit?"

The eyes sped around the ball. "Well, I see the best places have been taken." He sighed. "Oh well, I take it the ledge on the wall there is free. It'll be hard and uncomfortable, but at least no one'll sit on me."

I made a nest from my shawl and sat Rolliz in it.

He rolled his eye—the only one I could see. "I knew it. I told you this would happen. Now I can't see a thing. I knew that tincture was simply to blind us thoroughly."

I lifted him out, pressed down one side of the nest and sat him back down. Now he could see everything in the cave, and the open area in front of it.

"Well, I s'pose it'll do," Rolliz grumpy voice said.

"Aww! It's lovely. We can see everything."

"Humph. You mark my words, though. If we don't fall off, we'll be knocked off. Or they'll wait until we're asleep and throw us against a wall."

"Well, she won't throw me."

"Fool. She'll throw me, and you'll come too. She's just lulling you until," he paused, "Nah, she's already got ya. Just wait. She'll turn." He closed two of his eyes and ignored me.

Trethia had cleared the cave of bug legs, even taking those lodged into the corners. Now she was pushing them away from the entrance.

"Trethia, come and have something to eat," Mekrar called.

Trethia continued as if she hadn't heard the call, and because that wasn't like her, I went to talk to her. She carried on pushing the bugs against the walls. Finally, I had a good look at the bugs. A sickly muddy yellow, they were long, about two fingers thick and each had a ridge across the centre. I reached out to pick one up, but Trethia grabbed my hand.

"Don't! Even like that, they can hurt you."

She was now pushing them away from the edge of the sand-pool.

"Why are you moving them?"

"Faltryn asked me to."

I looked at the little dragon. She stared up at me.

"It's so the sand-swimmers can get out to move them," she said.

"How do you know they move them?" I asked.

She shrugged.

"Well now it's time to eat, and for both of you, sleep." With her in my arms, I followed Faltryn back to the cave.

"Ubree, we've not spoken of anything that's happened since we arrived," I said, as I sat. "Can we talk now?"

Ubree nodded. "I don't feel anyone can hear us, although I'm not sure if Rolliz will pass our conversation back to Malsavash."

"No matter what, we have to consider Malsavash a friend of sorts. If he wasn't, I think we'd be dead," I said. "Rolliz, would you pass anything you hear to Malsavash?"

"Might!"

"Won't," another voice said.

"Can't, actually," the little voice said.

"Well, you can't. I might be able to."

"So, would you?" I asked.

"Not if you ask me nicely."

"Kirym, why don't you just wrap him up, so he can't hear us?" Ashistar asked.

"Because one doesn't do that to a friend," I said. "I trust Rolliz. He will care for us as we care for him."

"Until you decide to throw us against a wall," Rolliz grumbled.

"I wouldn't do that. Especially not to someone I like," I said.

"They might when you're not looking," he said, glancing towards the others.

I smiled. "They're nice people. They wouldn't."

"Oh well, I s'pose I'll think about it then."

"So, what do we do, Kirym?" Dashlan asked.

"I trust Rolliz. Now let's move on."

"What's with the colour thing?" he asked. "And how come the token worked for me."

"I have no answers for the tokens, but the more interesting point is the huge anomaly here. Malsavash said the bugs discard their legs after they eat, that they needed blood to breed, and couldn't fly until they had it. So, why are all these legs here?"

"Maybe they kill the—, what did Trethia call them? Sand-swimmers?" Dashlan said.

Sundas shook his head. "The ground here would be littered with swimmer remains, the outer skeletons."

"And if there is nothing for the bugs to eat here, then shouldn't there be lots of bug bodies?" Mekrar asked.

"If Dashlan is right, though, perhaps whatever they do dissolves the shells." Oak shrugged. "Well, that's one explanation, although the bug casing we saw in the forest wasn't affected by whatever dissolved the bodies. Anyway, how would the legs get into the cave? Do you realise we saw no legs in the desert?"

"Well the sand-swimmers would cause them to sink, Kirym, wouldn't they?"

"Trethia knocked one onto the surface of the larger sand-pool. It's still there," I said.

"If the bowl is isolated from the rest of the sand," Mekrar said, "then maybe the sand-swimmers couldn't get to it. Mind you, I wouldn't step on it to check."

"Which brings us back to the question, what do the bugs here feed on to get their blood?"

"And why do they have legs if they don't use them?" Oak asked. "Because none of those we saw took even one step."

We ate in silence for a while.

"The sand-pools are full of swimmers," Ubree said, "Watch over there." He pointed to the nearest bowl. A small dark snout nosed above the surface of the sand and pushed the bug-leg back onto the rock.

"They don't seem to like them, do they?" Dashlan said.

Three sand-swimmers crawled out of the sand—they were all shades of pink—and began to nose through the bug-legs. They selected one, pushed it under a small overhang by the wall and went back for another.

"There are hundreds of legs here, nothing else. What do the sand-swimmers do with them all?" Arbreu asked.

Sand-swimmers were now swarming out of the sand-pools. They snuffled around, making an amazing amount of noise. When one came close to the cave, I leaned forward and picked it up. It snuffled louder but didn't seem to mind being handled. Its body vibrated when I ran my fingers over it.

I turned it over to look at its tummy. It too was covered with shell-like armour, although smaller square plates. The bristly hair was a darker pink than the shell. Its face was little more than a dark pink triangular snout, very hairy, with small dark eyes at the top.

I put it back on the ground and as it snuffled around again, I realised what it was doing. It was blowing all the small insects out of the cracks in the ground and eating them. Its tongue was long and white, the insects stuck to it. But we were no closer to understanding why the sand-swimmers treated the bug-legs as they did.

We sat back and watched the first moon rise over the rocks. Dashlan leaned out of the cave and studied the night sky. "It's brighter than last night. Does it mean anything?"

Faltryn became quite agitated. She put her tiny front feet on Dashlan's leg and pushed aggressively until he moved back into the cave. Then did the same to Ashistar and dragged the rug away from the opening.

"Come on, let's all move back," I said. "She obviously

knows more than she can tell us."

Faltryn arranged Ubree over one side of the cave, with the rest of us squeezed against him. She touched noses with one of the sand-swimmers for a short time, and then they came into the cave together. Faltryn closed her eyes and screwed up her nose. A silver glow appeared around her head but disappeared again almost immediately. She tried again, and as it collapsed, I realised what she wanted us, or rather Ubree, to do.

"She wants you to put a protective circle over us now," I said.

"Why didn't she ask?" Ubree grumbled.

The protection was heavy and made me feel sleepy, but I wanted to be alert. I needed to see what was happening. I carefully measured out a stimulating herb and swallowed it with a mouthful of water. I prepared some for the others if they wanted it, and all of them did except Trethia who didn't seem affected by the dome.

"I didn't know you could cover yourself too, Ubree," I said.

"I've never had to in the past and I'd never thought of it. It feels strange. Interestingly, my circle is thicker than normal. I'm not sure if it's because we're in the cave or on Halavash. Maybe it's because I am now the oldest, except I don't think I am. Then again, it might just be because it's needed."

A small group of sand-swimmers nosed around the edge of the cave, obviously unable to enter because of Ubree's protection.

"Do you think they normally shelter in here?" I asked.

"No," Trethia said. "They're checking to see we're safe. They talk to this one." She held up the swimmer who had come into the cave with Faltryn.

"Can Faltryn talk to them?" I asked.

Trethia shrugged. "They understand each other."

"Can you understand what they're saying?"

"No."

The moons did indeed seem brighter than last night and the sky brightened again when, as the first moon hit the meridian, Kultria rose above the horizon.

"The web is more visible tonight, but I'm sure it's bigger than it was," I said. "If it continues to grow at the speed we've seen, I'd say there's very little time left for anything to be done to save the inhabitants of Halavash."

"Trethia, what do you have against bug-legs? Why did you want them all out of here?" Arbreu asked.

She frowned and glanced down.

"We'd have been most uncomfortable sitting on them," I said, "and Faltryn doesn't seem to like them so that's as good a reason as any."

I glanced down as Trethia slipped her hand into mine. She looked relieved at my answer.

Dashlan laughed. "Those bugs are a bit creepy. Possibly it's as simple as that."

There was a thunk nearby. Moments later, a bug hit the ground in front of the cave, followed by a deluge of them.

The bodies were shiny orange, the undersides brown. I moved closer to the shield to get a better look as the bug began to rise as its legs extended.

"Don't Kirym," Oak said sharply. "We don't know if—"

"If Ubree's protection doesn't work, then we're vulnerable anyway. I need to know about these things, they may have some connection to the dragons."

Here, the legs were not as long, and the bugs did not utilise their prongs as they had in the forest. They stood for a short time and then one by one opened their wings and hovered momentarily, their legs fell to the ground, and they flew away. Many hundreds must have hit the ground in the ground in front of the cave before flying off. With four legs each, I wondered again why there weren't more legs lying about. Eventually, the last bug shed its limbs and flew away.

Ubree's protection remained until the sand-swimmers began to emerge from the sand-pool.

"That was interesting," I said. "Did you notice, none landed on the sand?"

"Lucky for the sand-swimmers, I guess," Sundas said.

"With the numbers that fell here, it's inconceivable they'd all miss," I said. "This means they land where they want."

Ubree shifted so he could look at us all together. "Think about what we saw. They arrived; grew limbs, discarded them, and flew away. What else?"

Oak nodded. "The legs here are shorter and fatter than those in the forest. Why?"

"Perhaps it's environmental. They grow taller in hope they can evade the moss," Mekrar said.

"Here they flew without killing anything," Sundas said. "That means Malsavash could be wrong about their need for blood. Did he think it was true or did he lie? Rolliz, do you know?"

Rolliz stared at us from his perch on the cave wall. "Can't say a thing."

"Is that because you don't want to, or because you don't know?" Ashistar asked.

"It's cos I'm not going to."

"Cos, we don't have to."

"So, because he, they—"

"Rolliz is under no obligation to tell us anything other than where to go when we leave here, Ashistar," I said. "Now, let's get some sleep. We will rest here tomorrow."

We were all awake as the sun rose. The sand-swimmers were already pushing the discarded bug-legs over to the wall.

I watched them for a while. "You know, it's almost as if they're pushing them into the shade. Why? And what happened to the rest of them? I would expect to see thousands more."

"What do you mean?" asked Ashistar.

"How many bugs would you say landed here last night?"

"Near enough to two thousand."

I stared at Dashlan.

"He shrugged. "I took the number that hit the area between the bulge in the rock and the sand and enlarged that to the whole area. It must be at least two thousand. Why?"

"All right, so even at one thousand bugs, that's four thousand legs just last night. So, where are the rest of them? There were only a couple of hundred here when we arrived. That's a lot of legs unaccounted for."

"Perhaps the swimmers use them," Sundas said.

"Why would they move them twice? I need a closer look."

Faltryn rushed over and stood in front of me.

"All right little one, I'll be very careful. Ubree, can you show me a close view of a leg?

It was an interesting sight. The central ridge was rimmed with very fine stiff hairs. It really did look like a strange coloured twig.

"I think they were a lighter colour in the forest."

"They are, Kirym," Rolliz said, "and they're fatter here?"

There was little more I could tell by looking.

I sighed. "I have no idea what it is, and nothing about it makes sense. So, I want to cut one in half."

"To do that, you'll have to touch it," Oak said.

"I'll use the sword to manoeuvre it, that'll keep it as far away as possible."

"Wait, Kirym!" Ubree bent his head down to Faltryn who bunted her token spot to Ubree's nose. Then she again attempted to make a shield, less successfully.

Eventually, Ubree sighed. "It seems—I think, she wants me to create a shield between you and the twig, but not a full shield. What she wants hasn't been done before, but she seems to think I can do it. I'm willing to try, but I don't know how successful it will be. You must cover as much of your skin as possible."

I slipped my robe over my clothes, put on my gloves, and Oak tied the sleeve close around my wrist. I picked up Mekrar's sword. Ubree's shield covered all of me except my sword arm, weird, but manageable, and I pulled the bug leg to a convenient spot with the tip of the sword.

"Oh, my stars! The leg! It's pulsing!" After a few moments of watching, and learning nothing, I cut across the middle of one side of the leg.

I was surprised. The outer casing was thin; the creamy inside was pulsing.

"Eww! It looks like you've cut through a larva," Dashlan said.

I stared at it in shock. "These aren't legs, they're egg-pods."

Both halves of the larva wriggled—oozing creamy goo onto the ground.

"Kirym, all the swimmers are leaving," Mekrar said.

I glanced over at the nearest sand-hole. She was right, they had all dived out of sight. I wielded the sword again, swept another leg-egg-pod closer and carefully sliced through the casing beside the centre ridge. I needed to get a look at the whole larva.

Its face was blunt—well I thought it was the face—the creature looked as if it had walked into a wall. As it oozed out of the pod, I could see how the internal body contractions gave it movement. The larva ended in two small hairy antenna-like growths that waved about independently as it began to crawl in irregular circles. It was the longest, fattest larva I had ever seen.

After a short time, the whole larva found one of the halves. It paused, arched its tail over its head and the two antennae pierced the body.

"Eww!"

"I think we all feel the same, Mekrar," Arbreu said.

We watched the flesh begin to liquefy and dissolve. Most of it was sucked up. When the larva finished, it catapulted over its meal with its tail and continued its wander.

Mekrar looked pale. "Imagine the devastation if they all hatch."

"We can assume a good number will be eaten by their own kind, but it doesn't answer the most important question," I said. "How do we destroy them?"

The larva found an intact egg-pod and again catapulted over its head. Its stinger pierced through the outer casing, and we watched the pod deflate on one side. The larva did a double flip and landed on the second half of the pod. As it deflated, the casing disintegrated, eventually becoming a small pile of dust.

"Well that explains why there's no debris," Oak said. "But why did the swimmers keep some. They're obviously scared of them, and I would be too if I was them."

"Perhaps they're the ones left in the morning," I said. "Look, those in the sun are growing faster than those in the shade. However, we need to decide what to do about them?"

"Why do we have to do anything?" Dashlan asked.

"Because I suspect they will still be hatching when we need to leave tomorrow. Even if they're gone by midmorning, we won't have enough time to cross the remaining desert before

Kultria flies again."

"Oh!" Everyone looked shocked.

"Ubree, could you shoot the larva thing?" I asked.

"Shoot?"

I laughed. "A small ball of fire. Just enough to get it."

"We can't use fire. It's a rule of the land. If we do, we become the enemy."

"How would anyone know? The fire won't spread. I suspect destroying the bugs would be accepted as necessary, if anyone found out."

"She's right," Oak said. "Who would tell?" Oak asked.

"Rolliz," Ashistar said.

I glanced over at our messenger. "Would you?" I asked.

"Ain't gonna say nothin' ta no one."

Ubree still paused, thinking it over.

"Ubree, why would fire-breathing dragons live on a planet where they are not allowed to use fire?" I asked.

"Maybe we were told to leave because our dragon-line was the first to breathe fire," Ubree said.

"Borasyn told me the history of your birth. Nothing was said about fire being unusual. Malsavash said the dragon-flight was divided. Some were sent to live elsewhere. I suspect that was you seven. The rest stayed here, but later vanished. More importantly, there were no bugs when you were here, but there are now and they're a threat to our lives. There's no reason why we shouldn't try to get rid of them."

"Kirym, I've never known you to see someone or something's death, as the only answer," Sundas said. "It goes against everything you believe in."

"I have, actually. I made no attempt to keep Salcan alive, although I had an antidote for the poison he took."

Mekrar's eyes widened. "You never said. Did he know? Why didn't you help him? His leg was mendable."

I thought back to the sad time when I sat beside Salcan

and talked to him through the last evening of his life. "Yes, he did know, and he was grateful I chose not to use the antidote. His mind couldn't be healed. He could never have lived peacefully, and I don't mean with us, but with himself. Loneliness terrified him more than death. All he wanted was someone to sit with him as he died. He knew if he told people his problems, they would always be ready to interpret anything he did or said as a threat, and he was so scared he'd kill someone else."

"Kill? Someone else?"

At Mekrar's tone, I glanced up and nodded. "He killed his mama and brother. There might have been others; I couldn't say for sure, but he knew what he was capable of. He hated what he was, what he had done. He didn't want it to happen again. These creatures are different. They're killing everything. They aren't natural to Halavash, and they've upset the natural balance of the land."

"All right, there's a precedent for killing the bugs here," Oak said. "But will it work?"

"We can only try, but if it doesn't work, I suspect it'll be too late to save the land."

"This is a big step—"

Ubree's sentence was cut short when I grabbed my bow and shot a bolt out of the cave. It hit the far wall. Wings fluttered and sparked in the throes of death. The wings had sprouted very quickly, a shiny iridescent green, it looked rather like a butterfly.

"Your fire may not kill them, but surely it's worth a try," I said. "killing these bugs won't be enough. They'll still reproduce elsewhere."

Ubree grunted, took a breath, and sent a tiny flame towards another larva who had begun to sprout wings. The flame hit it, the wings disappeared in a small puff of smoke, the bug charred, burst into flame, and disappeared.

"Well, it worked," I said. "Now what about a few at a time."

Ubree rolled his eyes. "I feel much better when I heal things."

"Think of it as proactive healing," Dashlan said, "because I suspect if even one of them gets to us, you'll be very busy."

"I hate justifying it," Ubree said, and sent five small fireballs into a pile of larva, whose wings were sprouting. "It'll still take all day, Kirym."

"Not if you target the egg-pods. Try those." I pointed to a small pile of pods sitting in full sunshine.

Again, the fire stream needed was very small, left no residue and gave no smoke. Ubree then targeted a much larger pile of pods. A few more snorts took out the last of those in front of us, and Ubree made short work of those in the other areas of the rocks.

"The sand-swimmers are coming out," Ashistar said, as he returned. "They seem happy with what you've done." He turned to me. "Why did you shoot the first one Kirym?"

"It flew, but it was the way it flew. Didn't you see it?"

He shook his head. "I was looking at Ubree."

"I saw it," Sundas said. "It came prongs first, and straight for us. For me actually, although it may have missed me and hit Ashistar. I wouldn't have been happy with either result. I think you've done the right thing, Ubree. It's a shame it'll be the same tomorrow and every morning after that."

Sundas' words hit me hard. I leaned back against the rock and thought about it as the others set about preparing a meal.

After a while, I walked out to the rock wall where I had first seen the rainbow. It still vibrated. I wondered why.

A shadow loomed up behind me, I turned to see Oak. He handed me a flask of water.

"Interesting isn't it," he said. "Natural phenomenon? It's

almost alive. Does it do that all the time or just because the tokens are here?"

"I wonder if it's because the dragons are here." I suddenly felt better, because I had just had an idea. A brilliant idea, although convincing Ubree might not prove easy.

Ubree looked almost contented as we sat together to eat. "The wee pink creatures seem happy. They're enjoying themselves too. They probably spent most of their time moving those that landed in the shade and hiding from those that hatched late."

"Ubree can you talk to them in some way?" I asked.

"I've tried. There's a lot of chatter among them but I can't decipher it. I get the impression Faltryn understands them. Why?" He paused. "Kirym, what are you thinking now? It worries me when you look like that."

I took a mouthful of food, chewed and swallowed before I answered. "I hoped the trees would know what happened to the dragons. They obviously didn't recognise you as a dragon. While there was fear, it wasn't directed at you specifically. Faltryn stayed out of sight when we were with them. I thought she might be scared, but now I wonder if she was just being circumspect."

"They called Ubree a monster," Ashistar said. "Maybe it's just a name for anything big they don't understand. If they felt threatened, wouldn't they have left us to the bugs?"

"What's it got to do with Faltryn?" Dashlan asked. "I thought she was just a bit tired after the journey."

"She didn't move a muscle while we were with them," Sundas said. "In the desert, she looked out to see what was happening, and when we stopped to eat, she came out and played. And here, she made friends with the wee pink things."

I nodded. "When we asked the trees about dragons, they didn't look at Ubree and say, 'Oh yes, that's what you are,'."

"What's your point?"

"Malsavash must have seen dragons when he was young, so, why didn't he recognise you? Ubree, what did the dragons do when they lived here?"

"Those are memories I don't have, Kirym."

"That's all right." I paused, trying to figure out how to broach my next idea. "I have an idea. Could you fly up and destroy the bugs in their web?"

"We agreed when we arrived that it's not safe for me to fly. I don't want anyone to see me. Especially when the problems here are so unknown."

"And I agreed with you on that. But if you did it at night, then you wouldn't be seen. You'd be able to destroy so many more bugs. Each bug lands and lays eight eggs, and I'd say at least two of them fly away. The problem is exponential, and it's probably at crisis level now."

"You make a good point, Kirym, but while I may reduce their numbers somewhat, it won't be enough in one night to make much difference."

"That's true, but there's the rest of the cycle. If you could do it for the time we are here, you may just get them to a manageable point, or even destroy them completely."

"Fire will be noticed, Kirym. What if someone figures out it's us?"

"I was thinking more a sheet of flame, much as you and Iryndal did at the celebration. I know it would be better with two or more of you, but even by yourself, I think you'd make a huge difference. Once you've done it, Malsavash and his trees will have to accept you did it for good. Why not try tonight. If it doesn't work, then who will know? Of course, you'd have to leave us protected, and protect yourself somehow. It is your choice though. Perhaps it's more than I should ask of one lone dragon."

He snorted, stood and walked out of the cave.

"Oh dear," Mekrar said. "Have you upset him?"

I shook my head. "No, he's trying to figure out how to manage it. He knows it's a good idea, but the reality will be more difficult."

After we had eaten, I took Trethia and Faltryn to wander around the rocks looking in all the nooks and crannies. We were followed by a horde of sand-swimmers.

We returned to eat our midday meal at the entrance of the cave, again surrounded by the pink swarm. As I finished eating, the tokens began humming, so after everything was cleared away, I took them out and sat them in a line in front of the rainbow wall. I studied each of them, thinking of what I knew about them. Finally, I chose the orange. I'd found it sitting on the surface of the portal pool, and the pool led me to Halavash. I knew it was the right token when they all began to sing, and everyone, hearing, joined me to watch and listen.

The scene unfolding on the rock wall in front of us appeared wrong, although I was sure it portrayed this land accurately. The waving grasses pictured here were in shades of pink, the sky showed as orange, the colour it had been since we were first able to see this land in colour.

The leaves on the trees ranged from cream to deep pink; the trunks were a vibrant purple, the same colour as Rolliz. It looked so peaceful.

Animals ranged across the grasslands.

"Dragons," I whispered.

As we watched, the moving painting's darkened skies, a moon settled into orbit. Lightening streaked across the sky, the trees waved violently, the grasses flattened, and the dragons reared up, their faces suffused with terror. It looked as if the land was being wracked by a fierce storm. The storm's violence increased; the lightening was almost constant. Then abruptly, it ended. In the darkness, small creatures fell to the land. Sparks and small balls of fire darted here and there across the land and sky.

"This seems to show the first attack by the bugs," I said. "The dragons did use fire."

We watched as peace came to the land, but only because the dragons continued their attack on the bugs. Then after one night-time attack, the dragon fire disappeared. The wall image showed the bugs begin again to grow in numbers.

"You were right, Kirym," Ubree said, as the picture faded. "What could have happened to the dragons though? Did the bugs manage to overcome them? Will that happen to me?"

I had no answer. "I shouldn't have asked you to do it. Not when I have no idea of the result."

"No, you had every right to expect me to do my best for the land here. I'm a healer. It's what I do and being in a new land shouldn't stop me. I'll make you safe before I go. If I'm not back by morning, talk to Rolliz and get across the desert. If you leave before light, you'll be gone before the bugs hatch, and hopefully, they won't bother you while you're walking. Get to safety. Don't try helping this planet without me. Find a way to get home and warn Iryndal to stay away from here."

Everyone was quiet after that. As much as I wanted to convince Ubree not to go, I knew it would be pointless. I packed the tokens away, ready for the journey in the morning.

We were all tense when the sun settled below the horizon. Ubree saw us into the cave, set our protection and left.

I set two guards and insisted everyone wear their robe. The rest of us slept or tried to. We hadn't talked about watching for Ubree's fire, but we were all awake watching the portion of sky visible, as Kultria rose.

"Do we know what happens to our protection if Ubree dies?" Dashlan asked.

"We talked about it," I said. "The protection will disappear. That's why we're wearing our robes. Come morning, we'll have to manage."

"How though?"

"The same way we would have done it had Ubree not agreed to come with us," I said, sounding far more confident than I felt.

I saw a tiny flicker of light at the edge of my vision. I stared intently, wondering if it was an illusion. It was much higher than I thought it would be.

Then I saw it again, a river of fire was accompanied by what I could only describe as an explosion of sparks. Then there was another and another closer. A few bugs fell, but far fewer than on the previous night.

"He's above us and no sparks have reached the ground," Dashlan said. "It's working."

"Unless the bugs are attacking him as well. What's the point, if he dies?"

I laughed. "You sound like Churnyg at his most foreboding, Ashistar."

Eventually, the fire disappeared from our vision, and everyone settled down to sleep. Sundas joined me on guard. With little else to do, we watched the sky, although there was nothing to see.

Just before dawn paled the sky, the protective circle disappeared with a small crack.

26

Kirym Speaks

The change in pressure woke everyone.

Mekrar sat up with a start and glanced around, her eyes wide in the pale moonlight. "What do we do now, Kirym?"

"Ensure your robes cover you well. If a bug comes for you, let's hope the properties of the robe hold it off. Now, eat and drink, we leave at first light."

"What about Ubree?"

"He'll catch up. He may have already landed."

As the sky lost its inky blackness, I lifted Rolliz off the wall. "What message do you have for us? We're ready to continue our journey."

"You're gonna throw us against the stone when we've told you, so, why should we say a word?"

"I wouldn't dream of hurting you. When you've passed on your message, you'll have a choice. You can stay here on the ledge or come with us."

"Harrumph." His many eyes closed, and three of the

mouths began to speak together. "The dark horizon hides your path." The voice was like an echo from a long way away. "Beware though, fire in the night sky heralds great change. Our enemies may have learned of new ways to destroy us."

"Was anyone hurt by the sky fire?" I asked.

The voice became distorted and I couldn't understand the reply. The eyes opened. "Did'ya mean it about us being allowed to choose?"

"Of course, I did."

"Then I'll come with you."

"What if I don't want to?"

"Then figure out a way of staying, but I was first and anyway, it's my turn to choose."

"Oh, all right, but don't go suffocating us again."

"Would you like me to carry you in the open?'

"Oh! Now she wants to blind us in a sandstorm. Told you she'd hurt us as soon as she had the chance."

"I'll make you a nice cosy nest for you."

I slipped the still complaining Rolliz into my pocket and picked up my pack. "Let's get as far as we can before the sun rises. Don't pause for a moment, even if you see someone beginning to sink. Just make sure it's not you."

We stepped out of the cave. I glanced around it, to ensure we had left nothing behind.

"You lead, Kirym," Oak said. "I'll keep an eye on things from the rear."

"Um, no," Mekrar interrupted. "Sundas, you carry Faltryn, Oak, you have Trethia. Arbreu and I will bring up the rear. It's the most sensible way to do it, we need to share the load."

While they were arguing, I went to the sand hole and placed my palm on the surface. "Goodbye, little ones. I hope you don't follow us too closely."

The walk across the sand was as tedious as it had been two days earlier. I was surprised at how quickly I adjusted my walking again. I thought of the Valythians spending their lives crossing sand dunes. They too had feared for their lives, although from a different source.

The first sun had almost hit the meridian before we saw a rock pad. We stopped, relieved. Dashlan hunkered down beside me as I ate. "The rock formation has disappeared."

I nodded. "Soon after dawn."

"Why didn't you say anything?"

"What could I say? We didn't plan on going back there."

He nodded. "This is a strange land."

"I suspect it will get stranger before we manage to leave," I said.

"Do you think Ubree is dead?"

"No, but then again, I haven't heard from him." I stood. "Let's get going, we have a long way yet."

The dark area we aimed at was small, but it never wavered even when I felt it should be hidden by a sand dune. I wondered if it had anything to do our ability to see the world in colour, but whatever it was, the sight of the dark spot was comforting.

There were fewer places to stop this time. We no longer had Ubree's added height to guide us, and as a result, we were all close to exhaustion.

The last of three suns seemed to take a long time to rise but had dropped onto the horizon with a speed that left me stunned.

It darkened to deep twilight very quickly. The sand beneath me suddenly felt even less substantial. "Keep walking," I called. "Don't stop!"

The ground under me rippled. I struggled to keep my

balance, but as the sand dropped from under me, I fell.

I landed a little awkwardly, but surprisingly, I didn't sink. To my horror, everyone altered their path and came towards me.

"Walk away," I called. "I'm fine."

I tentatively got to my knees, still on the surface, the sand firm under me, I couldn't understand it. Then Oak was beside me, pulling me to my feet.

"Walk!" I snapped. "You carry my daughter."

I pushed him ahead, and quickly followed, not sure what to make of the change in the sand's surface, and not willing to trust it.

The sky darkened further but the dark area we aimed for was still visible, larger now and lighter than the surrounding area, but still a long way off.

A large hill rose out of the sand thirty steps ahead of us. As it grew, the top erupted and rolled down the sides. I altered my direction to walk around. The hill also moved. It seemed determined to block our path. A wave of whatever was erupting from it rolled towards me. I bent, mid-step, and scooped one up.

A sand-swimmer and suddenly, I was knee deep in them. There were thousands. They littered the sand, swimming around my feet, seemingly impervious to being stood on, and I had to stand on them, they were wherever I put my feet, and they still swarmed out of the hill. I changed direction again, and this time, the hill didn't move.

"I found rock," Sundas said. "A big outcrop."

"Walk towards Sundas," I called to everyone. "Don't pause," but even as I spoke, I felt the ground become more unstable; I had already begun to sink.

I fell to my hands and knees, remembering how when I had fallen earlier, I'd not sunk at all. Again, the sand became firm under me, and I was able to scramble up and stumble towards the rock outcrop. The hill of sand-swimmers came closer, I waded through them, occasionally the waves of them rolled to my waist. They thinned as I stepped onto the rock beside Sundas, out of breath and wondering how much my tiredness was affected by fear.

"I know I came for an adventure, but that last bit was a little too exciting," Dashlan said, as the mound of sand-swimmers began to roll onto the rock.

"Get away from the edge," I said, although I stayed where I was, staring into the darkness, trying to see what was causing this change in behaviour.

"Ubree? Is that you?"

His face was in front of mine. And he was smiling. He crawled out of the sand and settled on the stone. We crowded around, with lots of questions, and for a while, it was chaotic, and I couldn't hear anything.

"Quiet!" I snapped. "Ubree, what happened?"

"First, how many bugs fell?" he asked.

"Hardly any at the rock. You made quite a difference."

He nodded. "I hoped so. I followed the moon until almost dawn. I started back but had to go lower and lower as the light strengthened. I made it to the desert. I began to walk, but those sand-swimmers ganged up on me. I just couldn't stay on the surface, but then I found I didn't have to. I copied their movements, realised I could swim through the sand."

"You came a long way?"

He nodded. "And I learned a lot. Under the sand, I can understand them a little easier. They knew I was a dragon. They recognised Faltryn. They think I'm a giant, a freak of nature, but they're happy we're here. They want me to find more dragons and bring them here to help solve the bug problems."

A slight glow on the horizon heralded a fourth sun.

"We must get going, even when we reach the far side, we've some distance to go. Oh, the swimmers aren't trying to kill us, they just want to play. But there are thousands of them. Now, all climb on my back, I can get you some distance before the sun rises."

It was a good idea, we clambered up. Ubree flew, but just above the surface. The ground raced past. From atop him, we could easily see the dark point we were aiming at. Shortly after the sun began to rise, Ubree settled back on the sand, his wings extended.

"Step down onto my wings," he said. "They're stable, and you can continue onto the sand as before."

When the sun was two hand-spans above the horizon, we started seeing clumps of pink at the edge of the sand. I was beside the first clump before I realised it was grass. They quickly got thicker and taller, and then we were on a solid narrow path, and the grasses towered over us. Blue dunes, thicker and taller clumps of pink grass and when the sand was covered with grass, we stopped to rest.

I saw the first tree when the sun reached its zenith. Its leaves were shades of pink, and the trunk was purple, although not as dark as Rolliz. Everything looked as it had on the rainbow wall in front of the cave. Our path took us down a blue sand dune, and when we breasted the next, the tree had disappeared.

We trudged on and finally, the dunes became shrub-covered hills. It was almost evening again when we topped the last hill and faced a solid wall of trees.

A familiar figure stepped out of the ranks.

"Malsavash! How did—"

"I am *not* Malsavash!" Her voice was different, feminine.

"He's an insignificant cousin. I am a child of Vashetha, these," she indicated the trees behind her, "my sisters and our daughters. I will take you to Vashetha."

I felt Rolliz trembling and slipped my hand into my pocket to reassure him.

These trees are female, Ubree told me. *Keep Rolliz hidden, he is terrified.*

A narrow path opened in front of us. The child of Vashetha disappeared into the mass.

The forest was ancient, most of the trees looked as old or older than Malsavash. There were three different shades of purple, aligning with the different sizes, *different ages,* I thought.

The path meandered; I wondered if they intended this to disorient us or if it was the easiest route across this piece of land. It made no difference, we had been lost ever since we arrived.

The path ended in a clearing, and the trees closed in behind us. Ahead was a magnificent tree, her trunk so ancient, parts of her gnarled bark had greyed with age. I couldn't properly tell her size because the other trees were gathered close around her, but the purple of her bark was so dark, it was almost black. Malsavash was a mere child compared to this tree. Her leaves were silver, although when the wind whispered past, I could see the dark pink undersides.

She beckoned us closer, but a web of roots grew out of the ground, halting us.

"Let them come, children." The voice was as aged as the tree. "They mean me no harm."

We halted in front of her, her branches moved around us. I had the distinct impression she was studying us from every angle. Finally, she pulled them back.

"I am Vashetha of Meglinor. I bid you creatures from another place, welcome."

Someone, Arbreu, I thought, poked me in the back.

"Thank you," I said. "I've heard of Meglinor."

She looked surprised. "Oh! How?" She shook her branches. "Oh dear, I am being inhospitable. Please sit and rest. I have many questions, but you must be tired and hungry after your long journey."

Areas of ground around us swelled and became eight grass-covered humps. I removed my pack and cloak, setting them on the ground beside me. Then I helped Trethia as Ubree settled beside us.

"Would your little dragon like to come out?" Vashetha asked.

"Thank you. I'm sure Faltryn would like to stretch her legs."

Sundas lifted her out of his tunic. She looked around at the massive trees and crawled onto his lap.

One of Vashetha's branches reached out, looked at her from all angles, looked at Ubree, and then back at Faltryn. Finally, she settled.

"I know you came from Malsavash." She shook her head. "He never could take responsibility for anything. This time he did the right thing, although probably for the wrong reasons. There is much I need to know. I've heard stories from the sand-swimmers. Generally, they know to avoid me: I cannot abide their mindless chitter-chatter. This time, I persevered and although their story darted around like a wind-blown autumn leaf, I rather suspect they spoke a modicum of sense. Hmm! So, last night there was fire in the sky. Fewer of Kultria's children fell. You are here, and you own dragons."

"Ubree and Faltryn are our friends. We do not own them," I said. "Yes, we too saw the fire in the sky. Did any of it reach the land? Did anything get burned?"

She rustled her leaves and ignored my questions. "I have

to wonder if all these situations are connected."

A movement caught my eye, I glanced away from Vashetha. A hump of ground moved towards us, on the top, a nest filled with strange items and a woven container of something, water, I assumed from its movement.

What will you tell her? Ubree asked.

The truth, I answered.

I turned back to Vashetha. "These things are not a coincidence."

I told our story, the request for help, the horror of the bugs, and Ubree's attempt to destroy them.

Vashetha was quiet and still for a long time. Then she shook her branches. "Eat, drink. It's all wholesome, I have no intention of allowing you to be harmed."

The nest held an assortment of fruit and nuts, the woven container, water.

The little hump scurried from person to person, me, then Sundas, Mekrar, Oak, Arbreu, Ashistar and Dashlan. I shared mine with Trethia, I wondered where they put her in our hierarchy. They obviously knew dragons didn't eat, they offered nothing to either of them.

"Well," Vashetha said. "This aligns with what the sand-swimmers said. As soon as the little one was described, I knew it was a dragon, and therefore, so is the big one. It's good to see they are finally back with their fire. Now they can settle here and build a flight to finally destroy the bugs."

"Ubree and Faltryn live on Ashetha. We all plan to return there; however, we'll do our best to sort out the problems you have before we leave."

She frowned. "Oh! I assumed this was the beginning of them returning. Why do you think we have problems?"

"The bugs are not original to the land, and they're killing everything they find. Something happened to your dragons.

176

We need to find out what, and where they've gone. And why the gatekeeper is not guarding the gate!"

Vashetha made a strange noise. "Gatekeeper! He hasn't seen the gate in remembered time. He refuses to train anyone, or do the job he begged for."

"Then why should we see him?" I asked.

"I don't want to be accused of overriding his authority. Some things must be attempted. Having his cooperation may be helpful in the future."

"What if he refuses to see us?" Mekrar asked.

"If you make the attempt, something will come of it. However, I have heard he's annoyed Malsavash didn't send you back to where you came from. I'm surprised, it's a long time since he cared about those using the gate, and I wonder why he took exception this time. Now, will the dragons fly tonight and continue what they started?"

"I will," Ubree said. "However, I will not fly until after dark. I'm reluctant to have my presence trumpeted throughout the land, until we discover what happened to the dragons."

"And the little dragon?"

"She's too young. She can't yet fly, and her fire-breathing abilities are abysmal."

Vashetha turned back to me. "You said you'd heard of Meglinor. How and where?"

"The Burl of Meglinor was presented to the people of The Green Valley for helping to bring peace. It happened many hundreds of seasons ago."

"You've come here because of a presentation plaque?" She sounded amused.

"I didn't say it was a presentation plaque, but you obviously know about it."

The trees around us rattled their twigs, but Vashetha nodded.

"Yes, I do. I presented it. And I was thankful for the help

given by your people. Why do you not know more?"

"This history was in a journal, written at the time these things happened. It has been stolen."

"Really? How convenient."

"Not at all. The thieves also stole the rest of our history. Can I ask what we did for your land to warrant such a beautiful and generous gift?"

"You averted war, and gave an offer of continued help, should we need it."

I nodded. "When we recently entered the Burl, we found the request for help, and so we came. Did it come from you?"

"No. It didn't come from any of my trees."

"Who could have done it?"

Vashetha looked troubled. "The gate is broken. With no keeper, anyone could enter or leave. However, few know how to enter the Burl."

"Kirym led us into the Burl where she found the message," Oak said. "What help do you need?"

Vashetha was quiet for a long time. We finished eating, night was close. I'll tell you all I can. But the dragon must—"

"There is no must about it," I said. "It's Ubree's decision. Vashetha, we all have names. As you would object if I called you tree or Malsavash, similarly, this is Ubree, his little sister is Faltryn. If you want our help, please acknowledge us properly."

She was silent briefly. "I apologise. I will send you to the gatekeeper at first light. But Ubree, why does Kultria bring the bugs?"

"The bugs aren't attached to Kultria," he said. "They float high in the sky. The wind blows them, so they appear to follow the moon. What happens to them when spring ends?"

"They disappear."

"And Kultria?"

"It too disappears, but that's what it has always done. Why?"

"Because there is no connection between the two of them. Kultria is not new; the bugs are. It's a coincidence that they seem to be joined. The bugs must go somewhere, and there are so many, they must have made their presence felt. Is there anything new on the landscape that could be associated with them?"

"I will find out. Your continued presence here may depend on the gatekeeper. If he will not allow you to stay, then there will be nothing you can do to help us here, nothing you can do for the land. I will then need to reconsider our existence here. A promise was made to us by the leader of The Green Valley, that were we ever in danger, you would assist us in every way possible. Would you agree to keep that promise and allow us to move to Athesha?"

27

Oak Speaks

Ubree returned soon after dawn. He, Vashetha, and Kirym spoke together until the sun was a hand-span above the horizon. We ate when they had finished. The trees provided us with a path to follow and sent us on our way.

The land changed quickly; thick forest gave way to open meadows with occasional groves of trees. Just before midday, we came to a sheer cliff. To our right, a path angled gently up and around a bluff.

Ubree shook his head. "Not that one. It's unstable and disappears halfway up the cliff." He turned left.

"How did you know about the path?" I asked.

"The sand-swimmers told me. They know a lot more about everything than anyone gives them credit for."

Ubree chose a wider path that rose gently up the cliff, and soon we had a good look over the land. We could see the extent of the fires in the distance to our left.

I could smell the smoke, and when the wind blew towards

us, I was sure I could hear the muted roar of the flames.

The path became more difficult. It steepened and became stony. Because the stones rolled as we stepped on them, we all spent some time on our hands and knees. Ubree went ahead to check the path.

The suns were bright and the air warm, but a thick mist descended, and the temperature plummeted. We rummaged through our packs to find our cloaks and robes.

By the time I pulled my robe from my pack I was chilled to the bone. Kirym was still fastening Trethia's robe and wrapping her shawl around her shoulders. I opened Kirym's pack and found her robe and cloak. She was shivering violently and smiled gratefully when I slipped her cloak around her shoulders. I knew better than to remonstrate with her; I also would have tended to Trethia first.

"Are you all right, Ubree?" Kirym asked, when he returned.

"Yes, extremes of weather don't affect me as it does you." He breathed over all of us, blissfully warm in the achingly cold mist.

The path, tenuous at best, got steeper. Ubree helped all of us, but he too climbed, retaining his balance with the occasional flap of his wings. His claws made easier work of it than our fingers and toes. Faltryn and Trethia, both being far too small, were carried. Faltryn was again stuffed into Sundas' tunic, while Trethia clung to Kirym, held safe with a shawl tied as a sling, for Kirym had no ability to hold her. While traversing a vertical face six times Sundas' height, I wondered if Ubree had perhaps chosen the wrong path.

The best path is not always the obvious nor the easiest route, Oak. Other paths are always there, this one moves, but although it is never in the same place twice, it does reach its destination, Ubree told me. *It was good to question, though.*

Once the path flattened, we rested briefly. Kirym didn't

allow too long, the suns would have been close to the horizon, and we needed shelter of some sort through the night.

I was pleased to set off again. As hard as climbing was on my legs, ankles and knees, sitting on the steep path drained my body heat. As the mist thickened and the light began to fade, we found a cave to shelter in. It was deeper than the hollow scrape we used in the middle of the desert and I felt more at ease, although that disappeared when Kirym placed her bow and bolts nearby.

Kirym sent us all off to sleep just before Ubree left to again battle the bugs. I woke when he swooped back into the cave. It was still dark outside. Kirym and Mekrar were both awake; guard duty, I assumed.

I slept again, lulled by the murmur of their voices, waking to the smells of a delicious breakfast.

Still wrapped in a blanket, I sat beside Kirym and draped my cloak over her shoulders; hers was wrapped around Trethia. Dawn was breaking, although it wasn't obvious in the dark of the cave and with the mist still thick. "Did you do guard duty all night?"

"No," she said, "but when I couldn't sleep, I saw little point in having everyone else awake."

"We should all share it, Kirym. Ubree was back early. Was everything all right?"

"Oh yes. He and I made the decision last night," Kirym said. "We had to ensure there was no chance of him being seen."

"But the mist is still thick."

"We didn't know what we faced this morning."

"Can we be seen from down in the land, do you think? As we climb, I mean," I asked.

"Ubree believes not. We are very high. The valley we aim for is separate it seems, part of the gate area, not the land.

Quite mysterious."

We ate while we talked. When the sky lightened, we again shouldered our packs and began to climb. The path widened marginally, and I chose to walk with Kirym who carried Trethia.

I offered to take over Trethia's care full time, but Kirym refused.

"I need to keep her close, Oak. If I want help, I'll ask."

"What did you and Ubree talk about last night and this morning?" I asked.

"The bugs, mostly."

"He must have made a big impact in their numbers by now."

"Well, that's the problem. After the first night, he seems to have made no difference. In fact, he thinks the numbers have increased."

I felt the colour drain from my face. "Do you think they're sort of gathering from all over the land? Sort of increasing this swarm by reducing others?"

"We don't know. Ubree thought this was the only cloud. He can't take the time to find out because once we enter this valley, he can't leave until we are through. If the bugs continue to increase as they are, it will be too late within a moon to do anything."

"There are no bugs on the path here. Do they not come up this high?"

"Ubree destroyed them as he returned. He wanted to be sure we would be safe even if we started before dawn, and we wanted to move quickly, which would be harder if Ubree had to search the path and cliff walls for bugs."

28

Kirym Speaks

The sun rose a hand-span as we climbed out of the mist, and another as the path wound around the cliff. The path was wide enough for us to walk comfortably in groups. Trethia walked between Kirym and me. We all walked close to the rock face, the sheer drop on our left was deceptively softened by the sea of mist that stretched to the horizon.

The path was narrowing when I rounded a corner to find a solid wall ahead. "A dead end," I said and turned around. "I'm sorry Ubree, we'll have to go back."

Before we could move, there was a sudden rumble and the path behind us fell away. We were enveloped by dust, and when it began to clear, I could see Ashistar teetering on the edge, held safe only because Sundas had grabbed his tunic. We bunched up near the wall. As I turned back to study the cliff around us to see if there was any way up or down, words slowly appeared on the rock in front of us.

DO YOU WISH TO FIGHT
OR WILL YOU RUN AWAY
DO YOU HAVE THE COURAGE
TO SEE YOUR FUTURE DAY
WILL YOU ENTER, WILL YOU RUN
DO YOU FEAR OR CRAVE THE FUN
DO YOU HAVE THE COURAGE STRANGER
WILL YOU FLEE OR FACE THE DANGER."

I read the words out loud, and as I did, a door appeared, getting more and more distinct with every word. By the time I had finished, it was fully formed.

"It's all very well to imply we have a choice here," Oak said, "but there's no path back so we either stay here or go ahead."

The edge of the path behind us began to crumble. Involuntarily, everyone shuffled towards the door.

"Huh! Not even a choice," Sundas said. "I don't like this, Kirym."

"Nor do I, so for safety sake, let's get through the door and see what happens." No one needed more encouragement.

Dashlan suddenly gasped. I turned to see the path stretched out behind us, as complete as it had been before the rock fall.

"It seems we do have a choice. Do we return or go ahead?

"What do you want to do, Kirym?" Sundas asked. "This danger. Well, what sort of danger?"

"Perhaps the biggest danger is fear," I said.

Oak smiled. "We'll face it together then, Kirym. I'll go with you wherever you go."

"No one has to come with me. You can all return to the portal and go home."

"You say it as if you have no choice," Arbreu said.

"Of course, I have. But I want answers and going through

the door seems to be the only way to find them."

"I'll come with you, Kirym," Oak said. "But perhaps you should send Trethia back with Mekrar and Arbreu."

Trethia glowered at Oak and clung tightly to my hand.

"We're all staying," Sundas said. "It's safer together. We all have strengths that may be needed."

"Anyway, this is the adventure we came for, isn't it?" I pushed the door which opened onto a flower-strewn meadow. It looked safe enough; iridescent yellow and blue butterflies swooped from bloom to bloom, and birds flitted through the trees. There was a path, merely a worn track in the grass that disappeared to our right. *This must be the Gatekeepers Valley—of this world, but not part of it.*

With our knives in hand, we stepped over the threshold into a park-like garden. When I looked back, the door had disappeared, and the scene behind us was the same as that ahead.

I slipped my knife back in its sheath. "The sooner we start; the sooner we reach the end."

The end came quickly. A large stone sat beside the path. Words were engraved on it.

PLACE OF FOOTPRINTS

BE YOUR PASSAGE SHORT OR WIDE
TRAVEL TO THE OTHER SIDE
CHOOSE A PRINT TO FIT YOUR FEET
JOURNEY THROUGH—YOUR FRIENDS TO MEET
PATHS WILL MINGLE PATHS WILL TOUCH
BUT YOU MUST UNDERSTAND THIS MUCH
THAT EVEN IF YOU'RE WITH A FRIEND
YOUR PATH IS YOURS ALONE TO WEND

I read out the words.

"What does it mean?" Oak asked.

"Just what it says," Ubree said. "Here, we find footprints to fit each of us. We follow them, meet up and go on. The only way through is to follow your own path."

"Seems simple and fun, but what's the point?"

"To learn, Dashlan," I said, "or perhaps just to realise that not all journeys are meant to be taken together, even when they begin and end in the same place."

"And this is the beginning?" Sundas asked.

Trethia shook her head. "No, this is the middle, and we meet further in the middle."

"What? How?" Sundas frowned.

"Journeys begin at birth and end at death," I said. "Trethia's right, this is just part of the adventure in between."

"Why does it say short or wide? Surely, it's the same for everyone, isn't it?" Dashlan asked.

"The paths are like life," Ubree said. "As in life, we all go in different directions, even if we live together. The journey for each person is as long as it needs to be."

"We could just ignore it and fly over," Ashistar suggested.

"As I said while we journeyed here," Ubree said. "This part of our journey must be walked. Those are the rules. We can turn back, but that path will always take us to the gate. If we choose that path, we have no chance of changing anything or help anyone."

"I must go on. It's the only way to find the dragons, and the sooner I do, the sooner I find out what's wrong with Iryndal, Othyn, and Arymda," I said.

"You think the answer to their sleeping is here?" Ashistar asked.

"It would be the obvious place to find out. This is where they came from."

The pebbles making the path joined together to become nine stones of various sizes stood in a row across the beginning of the path. More words were engraved across each one.

TO CONTINUE YOUR JOURNEY, TAKE A STEP.

"Why only nine stones?" Dashlan asked. "There are ten of us."

I studied them for a while before the answer came. "Because our wee white dragon is a baby and must be carried."

Once I'd spoken, one stone got a bit bigger.

"Humph, still being a burden," Ubree said."

"Wonderful company," I said. "I'll take her."

Ubree sighed. "No, the stone nearest me increased in size when you spoke."

"It may not mean anything. If we decide differently, then perhaps the stones will accept our decision."

Ubree shook his head. "She's my sister, Kirym. When we came through here as we left Halavash, Borasyn was the eldest. She carried Arymda. I need to do the same for Faltryn. Anyway, you have Trethia and the tokens, and the load should be shared." He picked Faltryn up by the scruff of the neck and placed her on his back.

"You've been here before?" Oak said.

Ubree nodded. "Yes, when it was decided we should find a new home, we came through this valley. The gatekeeper travelled with us."

"Why did he stay here if his footprints—,"

"He accompanies everyone when they leave," interrupted Ubree, "but his steps stop at the gate."

"But we're entering the land, not leaving it. Why the change?" I asked.

"It may not be a change, Kirym. I knew nothing of the gate until it was time to leave. Maybe visitors normally enter through here."

"All right," I said. "So, the sooner we begin, the sooner we'll be able to carry on."

When I stepped onto a stone, it immediately changed to the size and shape of my boots. The same happened as the others took their first steps.

All nine paths were made of two lines of what looked like ancient footprints, all made of rock. It was uncanny. The paths meandered through a wood, trees towered over us, the ground beneath them covered with flowers. There was a peaceful air about the place. I couldn't see the sky. The light was dappled, but no sun shone through the trees.

Dashlan was the first to wander away. His path took him off into a grove of trees.

Arbreu frowned as Dashlan disappeared. "He should stay with us. I promised Ma."

"He has his own path, Arbreu. You took yours at a far younger age."

"But what if—"

"He needs some time to think and dream." Mekrar took his hand. "He likes to be solitary on occasion. He'll sort out how he feels, and we'll help him return when he's ready."

Arbreu wasn't convinced, but Sundas patted his shoulder and walked beside him for some distance.

A while later Dashlan returned. He slapped Arbreu on the back and smiled contentedly.

We continued through the trees, and then Sundas and Ashistar's paths moved to the left.

"Don't get lost," Arbreu called.

Sundas waved; Ashistar was already too far away to hear him. Mekrar and Arbreu were the next to wander away, and soon after, Dashlan again disappeared followed almost immediately by Ubree and Faltryn.

Oak, Trethia and I walked on as the light above us darkened. The paths ahead changed. Oak's prints stopped. His path didn't move off but came to a spot where there were no more steps for him to take.

"He'll join us later," Trethia said. "Maybe something else needs to happen before he can move on. He must get to the other side, it's the rule of the gate."

"Who told you that?" Oak asked.

"The sand-swimmers."

Her argument makes sense, I thought.

Oak hunkered down, kissed her on the cheek, stood and kissed my forehead, and Trethia and I wandered on together. We had a lovely walk picking flowers and fragrant herbs. Then my prints also stopped.

I kept hold of Trethia's hand. This didn't feel right, or good.

"We've no choice, Kirym." Trethia pulled her hand from mine and walked on.

She took five steps before I was able to follow, but there was something between us. I would have called it a wall, but I could see into it and Trethia was in the middle.

I panicked and beat on it. "No! Trethia, come back!" She didn't move. She appeared to be part of the wall, fading into it. The wall had the appearance of a stream when it iced over, but it felt like stone as I tried to beat it down.

I stamped my foot. I was furious. "This stops now!" I yelled. "You force us into this, but it's too much. She's just a baby."

The shadow of a man appeared near Trethia. "You'll be able to continue your journey presently. We will keep the egg. Thank you—"

"What do you mean, the egg?"

"That," he said pointing to Trethia, "is part of an egg we gave to Athesha. We now claim it back."

"How dare you! Trethia is ours—she's mine! She grew with our care and nurturing."

He became more distinct, although still grey and misty. "You cannot argue with me."

"Oh, yes I can! I have no idea what this egg was, but I know what Trethia is."

"Perhaps if I explain." He became clearer. "A great black beast appeared at the gate. It came from Athesha. We told him to go away. He beat on the gate and demanded we listen. He was nothing to do with us, so we walked away. He became so angry, roaring with rage. He beat the gate to pieces. Then he left."

"So, the black beast from my homeland of Athesha wanted help, and you sent it away with nothing. Did you actually—"

"We did give some advice, which we had no obligation to give."

"And what was this advice?

He took a deep breath, as if trying to contain his temper. "It was, 'Let fallow lie the ground you ploughed and see what seeds will grow'."

"Which meant?"

He shrugged dismissively. "Whatever he wanted it to mean."

"And what was his response?"

"That was when the beast broke down the gate. We fled. He eventually left. When we returned, we found a gift, so we decided to send something in exchange. The egg. Now part of it has returned. We presume he sent it back, so we will keep it." He looked quite smug.

"You say *we* when you mean *you* because only you make those decisions. You didn't try to find out why this beast came to you, but you gave him a piece of trite nonsense, pretended it was advice and sent him on his way. Then *you* sent something to Athesha. Did you have any knowledge of the effect the egg would have?"

The gatekeeper looked angry, and that was good. I wanted him to begin feeling something.

"I don't have to protect any other world," he said.

"When you send the problem, you do. When, in the past, you approached Athesha for help, we helped, and that alone gives you an obligation."

He now looked far more substantial, almost real, and he was looking most uncomfortable.

"You didn't recognise Trethia, did you?" I said.

"It is different," he said.

"She! She, not it! Look at her. She's a little girl—my little girl. She is *not* what you sent. Even if you had a claim, which you don't, for you to take back what you gave, you must leave what we formed with us. However, something given cannot be taken back, it no longer belongs to you. She belongs to us. What did this egg look like anyway?"

He waved his hand and an image floated in front of me, spiralled slowly downwards on wings similar to those on a sycamore seed. The bulb was fat and oval. I could see why it was called an egg. When it neared the ground, it disappeared.

I remembered something Borasyn had said. *Two eggs emerged from that blighted nest. One went to light the morning sun, the other brought darkness to the western lands.* What the old man showed me here was both familiar and foreign, but it all became clear.

"The egg you sent had a double yolk. It split apart when it reached Athesha. What happened the other yolk?"

Now the wall was very thin and Trethia's hand stretched towards mine.

"I didn't follow the egg. I just sent it."

"Rather irresponsible of you. I shall tell you the result of your actions. You were asked for advice. Your trite saying meant nothing, and that's exactly what the beast did. Nothing! So, a problem that could have been easily sorted, got completely out of hand. The egg you later sent without informing anyone, separated. Each portion went to a different part of Athesha. Trethia came into my care. She's a treasure, and I thank you for her. You gave her away, she is now mine. The other yolk went west where it too developed, but outside its natural environment, it grew beyond what it was and killed everything it encountered, including thousands of people. Almost an entire tribe died because you sent that yolk. Can you bring them back to life?"

The wall disappeared and Trethia ran to me. I hugged her close, determined never to let her go again. She clung to me as I stood and faced the man. He was now solid. He appeared ancient, his face grey and lined with knowledge of the past. Right now, he looked shaken at all I had told him, and a little resentful.

"You're the gatekeeper."

He nodded. "I can see you're fond of her. I never imagined anything we sent would have an effect on the people of a land. Surely something that size can't be bad."

He still isn't taking full responsibility for his actions.

"Each yolk took its own form, perhaps because of where it went. The two were not related and different in appearance and nature." An image of the fyrsha came to mind, the giant I had killed just a few seasons ago.

The gatekeeper flinched as he saw it. "It changed, grew even more," he whispered. "Why?" He shook his head. "What made it so evil?" he asked, aloud.

"Not evil," I said. "Things can change in different environments. When we transferred plants from The Land Between the Gorges to The Green Valley, we checked first to see they couldn't affect the plants and animals already there. Many of the plants we took, changed. Some of them didn't survive, but fush grass became hardier. The leaves grew thicker and wider. The yolks you sent from here have each reacted in their own way, coping with the environment they went to."

"So, you think this evil came from us, and you send worse back," he said. "Many of our people have been destroyed. Why should I feel any regrets?"

"We've sent nothing to you. The gate is wide open, I'm sure it has been used by many. My friends and I came because we received a request for help. It said your people were being destroyed."

"I forbade any to leave the land, therefore, any request does not require an answer."

"But your land needs help." I stared at him. He averted his eyes. "The request was sent, and I am here. There are things I need to know. You say the beast left something."

"Well," he looked uncomfortable. "The gift was just beyond the gate."

"How far?"

He again averted his eyes. "Not far, but between here and Athesha."

"So not left for you at all, and yet you took it. Do you have a right to claim things from the portal?"

He didn't answer me.

"Is it your job to stop the people of Halavash from leaving?"

"I did not see anyone use the gate."

"It's your job to see. A message was left in the Burl, but someone then sealed its entrance. Who did that? Not the person who left the message, because they wanted our help. Whoever sealed it, stole our archives. So, who else entered Athesha?"

"No one living in the land used the gate." He glanced away, and I knew.

"You! You sealed the Burl. Why? Were you trying to insure we would be blamed for all that happened here?"

"How dare you!" He looked sourly down his nose at me. "Oh, all right. There was a whisper that a message had been placed in the Burl and I went to retrieve it. I thought..." he paused, "I couldn't find it but somehow you did and arrived with a bunch of—"

"Be careful of insults. Whatever you think of our appearance, we are all you have."

I knelt to see how Trethia was and a hump of grass, similar to those I had seen when we visited Vashetha, huffled over and nudged my leg. I took the hint, sat on it, put my arm around Trethia and drew her close to me.

"Things have changed here. Your land so unsettled. What are you doing to sort it out?"

He shrugged. "Change is inevitable. Left to itself, it'll balance out."

"It won't! The bugs are fast growing out of all control. Everything on Halavash is being attacked, and when they die, the land will too."

He shook his head. "Trivial problems. A few new bugs arrive. They'll settle."

"Have you been anywhere near the trees and animals down there?" I asked.

"My job is to care for the gate, not meddle in the affairs of the land."

"Oh, really? I might have accepted your argument had you had cared for the gate, but you didn't. All of this happened because of your negligence."

"There are stories about those who stood up to the things that entered Halavash. I'd have been destroyed, just like the rest of the fools who chose to stand. Anyway, the fire-starters will destroy the bugs. Then that problem will be gone."

"So, you're happy that one of the two things destroying

this land may possibly destroy the other. Unless they both survive. Of course, then they'll continue to destroy everything else. None of this would have happened had they been stopped at the gate, as they should have been. The black monster who didn't enter wasn't a monster, was he? Just a creature who needed help in the same way, that when Vashetha and the Gatekeeper of the time approached us for help, we didn't dismiss them as monsters. We helped!"

He waved his hand, a rock appeared beside him. He sat on it.

He certainly had a power I had never seen before. I wished he would use it as he was meant to. I almost felt sorry for him, he had been thwarted by his own lies.

"You brought other monsters from Athesha. Send them away, and I'll study what's happening in the land."

"No!"

He looked shocked. "But—but!"

"You've lost the right to make demands. We were asked for help and we answered. I suspect we will all be needed to sort these problems here now, and that's if it's not too late."

The old man was silent for a long time. I finally got tired of waiting.

"Where are our archives?"

"Athesha has no gatekeeper. People enter at will. It could have been anyone. I didn't enter the Burl, I only sealed it. Someone else must have gone in and taken them."

"Who?"

He shrugged, but I knew he was lying.

"Where are the dragons?"

"We don't have dragons. We've never had them."

I sighed loudly. "This is the dragon planet. Vashetha and Malsavash have already told me dragons lived here. It's possible the dragons are the link we need to destroy the bugs, and the bugs must be destroyed before we can address the problem of the fire-lighters."

He shrugged. "The dragons disappeared one night. Maybe they left. They weren't my responsibility."

I was getting exasperated. "Where did they live?"

He shrugged. "They don't welcome visitors."

"If they're not there, they'll neither know nor care."

He sighed. "There's a path; it might lead there. Then again, it might not."

"Show me. We can begin there."

He looked annoyed. "It's not my place to lead you around the land."

"Who cares for the land if you don't?"

He shrugged. "If anything, the dragons did, but everyone looked after themselves."

"Except they can't. You have an obligation to care."

"Gatekeepers cannot lawfully leave the gate area. The gate—"

"Has managed by itself for a long time and will cope for a while longer. What happens when you die?"

"Gatekeepers don't die. At some stage, a new gatekeeper will come along. They get trained and one day, they take over. Then, I join my ancestors."

"And, where are they?"

He pointed behind me.

I turned, amazed to see the arch just a few steps away. Carved into the wall were ancient figures. Their flowing robes appeared to have been frozen, mid-movement.

"If there is trouble, I can call them to come and help."

"And why haven't you called them?"

"Because the problems are minor."

Now I was angry. "When do you think things'll be serious enough for you to call on them?" I asked icily. "Would it be, oh let me think. Perhaps when all animals and trees are dead? Would it be when an army of fire-starters leave here and attacks Athesha or some other land? Your arrogant complacency appals me."

He went pale, but I had no regrets about being so sharp.

"How long does it take to waken them?"

He shrugged. "Don't know. Never had to. I don't think anyone ever has."

"Do it!"

"No. It's my choice, and I won't."

I stood and, taking Trethia with me, walked over to stand in front of the nearest figure. As much as I didn't think he moved, I was sure he had been looking elsewhere when I first saw him.

"Gatekeepers of old," I said. "The world of Halavash is approaching crisis. Without your help many more innocents will die needlessly. It may already too late to save the land, but we must try. Please help us."

There was a long moment when nothing happened, and then one figure became more dimensional, and moments later, it floated down from the wall. His robes were a bright and vibrant blue. His face was intelligent, not bored and disagreeable as the present keeper was.

By the time I had studied him, he had been joined by two others. The second wore rose-pink, the third, bright yellow. They made the present gatekeeper in his grey robes, look tired, old and drab.

I introduced myself and Trethia. "Do you have names?"

"We are known by the colours we wear," Rose said. Her voice was soft and husky.

Blue glanced at the present doorman who was slowly drifting away. "Stay!" He turned back to me. "You are right in wanting to look for the dragons. Within the limits of our power, we will help." While speaking to the gatekeeper, the voice was sharp and hard. To me, it had the same soft husky sound as Rose's.

"You will be guided to them. If you find a way to align yourself to the land, then your right to call on us will be easier and everyone else here will have to help you." The three ancients sounded very similar, but I was beginning to pick up minor differences.

I smiled. Hopefully, they would give more than just words. "What can be done about the gate? It needs to be repaired."

A fourth figure stepped out of the wall, this dressed in a soft orange. "With help, I can repair it."

"What sort of help do you need?" I asked.

"Someone who is willing to learn about the ways of the gate and the portal. Someone who will care for it, give it a life. No one has applied, but then again, no one knows we are looking. The position is open."

"You can't replace me," snapped the present gatekeeper.

"Replace? Oh no," Yellow said. "You have the chance to do more, and you must before you earn your place on the wall beside us. But unless you do your job, you will not be there. Ever! It doesn't mean you will stay on as the gatekeeper. You now make choices."

"What choices?" He sounded sulky.

Blue glanced at the sky, or rather, at the soft orange above us. "Those are up to you."

Rose waved her hand, and the remnants of the wall that had trapped Trethia, disappeared. The path we had been following stretched into the distance.

"Follow the path," Rose said. "We will send signs. Beware though, not all signs you see will come from us. Do not be led astray."

"How will I know the difference?" I asked, but there was only silence. They were gone. I took Trethia's hand, and we followed the path.

Oak was again walking beside us. "Well," he said. "That

was decidedly weird."

I nodded. "I hope we didn't hold you up for too long."

He shook his head. "You were gone, I took a deep breath to call you, but suddenly you were there." He frowned. "However, I did learn a lot in between those moments."

Mekrar and Arbreu sat together in a small clearing ahead. We joined them and walked on. Soon Ashistar arrived, followed soon after by Sundas. Dashlan approached from our right, and a short time later Ubree and Faltryn arrived.

"Last, of course. Faltryn takes forever to do anything," Ubree grumbled. "Even walking has been painfully slow." He paused and smiled. "But watch. She finally learned something."

Faltryn climbed from Ubree's tail to his head. Then the wee dragon spread her wings and launched herself off, to float down to the ground.

"Now do it again and this time, flap your wings as I taught you."

Ubree picked Faltryn up and sat her on his back. She climbed up his neck, the ascent was made harder when Ubree raised his head, making the climb steeper.

Faltryn paused at the top and then jumped. This time, she flapped her wings and her flight extended.

"Turn on one wing," Ubree called, "unless you want to walk all the way back."

Faltryn flew in a wide circle, flapped her wings again on the way back. She landed, flopped onto her tummy and closed her eyes.

Trethia picked her up and cradled the sleeping dragon on her shoulder.

Together we followed, the path took us through more trees

and to another arch, the twin of the one we'd walked through to find our footprints, and here, the footprints ended.

Ubree heaved a sigh of relief. "Well, we can follow this path, try to get back to see Vashetha or—"

"First I learned some things you need to hear." I described my meeting with the gatekeeper. "So, we need to find the dragons next. Can you lead us there, Ubree?"

"If it's where we are meant to go, we will get there. From the gate, we each had our own path. Now we're together, we can make our own decisions."

"You know, last night, I was thinking about the gate," Dashlan said. "While it's broken, anyone can come or go. It needs to be repaired sooner rather than later simply to ensure there are no further problems between home and Halavash. Whatever is creating the problem here will not have the option to return to Ashetha. What if I go and help the gatekeeper repair it?"

"Why didn't you talk to us about it this morning?" Arbreu asked.

Dashlan looked at him strangely. "I would've if you'd been there. This is the first chance I've had."

"How long were you away, Dash?" Sundas asked.

Dashlan frowned and shrugged. "I dunno. Overnight at least. I think it was one night, but it might have been two."

"So, you sat in a tree and daydreamed," laughed Arbreu.

"Everyone's time here is different," Ubree said. "However, we all start and end at the same time. What brought the gate to mind, Dashlan?"

"Well, because it's over there." He pointed to the right.

Arbreu frowned. "But, Dash, it—"

"It seems, Dash, you have a job," I interrupted, "if you'd like to do it. We'll come and find you later."

He hugged Arbreu and Mekrar, kissed Trethia on the nose,

and shook Oak, Ashistar, and Sundas by the hand. Then he put his arms around me and hugged me and kissed my cheek.

He pulled Arech out of his bag and handed it to Mekrar. "Would you look after this for me? He's too irresponsible." He punched Arbreu lightly on the arm. "Take care of him, too." He turned and walked through the trees, soon out of sight.

"The gate isn't there," Arbreu said quietly. "Why did you let him go, Kirym?"

"Because it is there for him, and he wants to help fix it. He has the talent and the desire. Maybe that's why he came with us."

"I'm certain I saw someone with him," Mekrar said."

"Wearing orange?" I asked.

"How did you know? More an orange haze, but I had the impression of robes floating around a figure."

29

Oak Speaks

Our time on the path was very dreamlike. I didn't miss
Dashlan which surprised me; I had spent more time with
him than anyone else except Kirym and Trethia. I felt drowsy
even after we all joined up and Dashlan left to rebuild
the gate. It was as if I saw everything from a distance and
through a haze. The orange sky and the purple trunks were
perfect, even with pink leaves and grass. I couldn't see the
sun, it never appeared to get dark and I didn't feel hungry,
thirsty, or tired, although I had the impression of stopping,
eating and sleeping. The meals were provided by the trees,
although when I tried to think about them and pinpoint
an exact meal or a time period between any two meals, I
couldn't.

Once while we were resting, I watched Sundas become an
old man with long wild white hair. When I looked again, he
looked even more youthful than when I first saw him at my
fortress home of Faltryn.

Ashistar appeared to be hewn from the very trees he spent time with. Occasionally I couldn't find him, but did I imagine the extra tree squeezed into the group always surrounding us?

I watched Mekrar and Arbreu grow old and contented, surrounded by children and grandchildren. Mekrar ruled over a vast happy community. And yet moments later, they looked as they always had.

Kirym and Trethia though, were always the same, serene and contented. Each day Kirym led us on, seeking something only she knew of.

I woke with a sudden jolt. I felt as if I had been asleep for many seasons. We were in a roofless tunnel, the walls tall above us. The sky glowed deep orange as if the sun was setting.

"Where are we, Ubree?" I asked.

He frowned. "I'm just following Kirym. She seems to know."

"How could she? Surely you would know the way, you've been here before," I said. "She hasn't."

"Perhaps she has. Each journey is different, Oak. We follow the one who is leading, and right now that seems to be Kirym."

The tunnel ended at a cave. To the left, the ground fell steeply away. Instinctively, I picked Trethia up and settled her on my hip, slipping my pack up to my shoulder.

Kirym led us towards another tunnel but stopped suddenly and stared at the wall. I walked up behind her. She was staring at a long line of engraved scenes.

"These are pictures of the dragons. It proves they live here," she said and went back to the beginning. The first was a massive engraving showing their life during a day. Dragons gathered around the entrance of a cave along with many other animals. Small groups of dragons were scattered around a large area, some sleeping together under trees, heads together in the same way Iryndal, Othyn and Arymda had lain, others playing. Then we saw dragons lifting full grown trees and resetting them down in a new barren area. Other dragons carried animals, insects and small birds to join the trees. It was a contented happy scene.

"Oh, my stars, look." Kirym pointed to the next picture. "This is Borasyn's story about their birth."

The picture she pointed to, showed the nursery full of eggs sitting under the trees, the dragon mamas standing proudly beside them. One egg, larger and brighter than the others, sat in a distant corner.

Baby dragons began to hatch, cared for by their proud mamas.

One dark night, the large egg was secretly taken into hiding deep in a gully by one dragon, while the other dragons were gathered together.

Winter arrived. Through storm after storm, the large egg was protected by the dragon. At midwinter, seven dragons were born.

Their introduction to the flight was greeted with celebration, the next picture showed the sky festooned with shapes, similar to those made by our dragons at the festivals. Ashistar chuckled. "So, they did it here too.

However, some of the other dragons were obviously unhappy.

"Look at their faces," I said, pointing to the pleased look on some faces when the youngest of the seven died, and then the horror when he was reborn.

The engravings showed the seasons passing until all seven had died and been reborn. And then what looked like a formal meeting of all the dragons, which led to the seven being expelled.

The next engraving illustrated the flight of the seven through the valley and to the still intact portal gate.

"That's interesting," Kirym said. "This is a new artist."

"This artist is not so talented," Ubree said. "But they knew what happened on Athesha."

"That's the pool by our end of the portal," Kirym said, pointing to a group of people standing beside the pool, "Those are probably our ancestors. You and your siblings were obviously expected on Athesha, Ubree, and if that is the arrival, then either you were all much smaller, or those who greeted them, our ancestors, were giants. But most relevant," she pointed to a person standing to one side wearing robes, rather different to the hunting clothes worn by the Atheshans, "that's the gatekeeper."

"Does that mean he drew these?" Sundas asked.

"The artist may not have included himself," I said. "Or perhaps the artist drew this from someone else's description? Other than the fountainhead and the portal pool, there's no background, just those scribbly vertical lines."

Kirym gasped. "That's Vashetha. I wonder if this is when the Burl was presented. I have so many questions. Grey told me he hadn't been in the dragon's cave. He was lying. Who organised and negotiated the terms for the dragons to be sent to Athesha? Vashetha or the gatekeeper? And, were the dragons were barred by that gatekeeper or the present one."

The next pictures showed more hatching eggs, but these were not laid in a nursery as we had seen earlier, but seemingly laid in secret. The new-borns bodies appeared longer and slimmer and were shown with no wings. Their fire was also drawn differently, jagged lines rather than rounded.

"I wonder, is it a different beast, or is the artist

inexperienced?" Kirym asked.

More pictures showed life with the dragons, but the different talent made it hard to decide what was being portrayed. The last picture was not fully finished. It showed a land with no dragons, but many short vertical lines, each ended with an oval.

Kirym studied the carving far longer than I thought necessary, given the lack of detail.

"Are these the bugs? Without the subtlety of Borasyn's detail, I can't tell. And why did they stop carving their history?" Finally, she shook her head. "I'll have to think about it. Let's get moving."

The path through the caves soon angled down. It got darker for a while, and just as I thought we could go no further without lighting a lamp, a gentle glow lit the whole area up. I looked around for the source and couldn't find it.

Ahead were two tunnels. Both were dark and foreboding.

"Which one do we use, Kirym?" Arbreu asked.

In the right tunnel, a small sunset like flash lit the far end. It then appeared to be taken over by storm clouds.

"We saw that colour when Dashlan walked away," Mekrar said.

Kirym didn't move. She stared from one to the other. Occasionally the orange light would flare, but still, she didn't move.

Then she hoisted her pack higher on her shoulder and stepped into the left tunnel.

I itched to know why she didn't follow the orange light, and I knew the others also wondered.

She has good instincts, Oak, Ubree told me.

Slowly the tunnel lit up, a soft yellow light and just in time to show us another choice.

Again, Kirym chose to go to the left, ignoring a harsh red

flash in the right tunnel. I followed her without question, and again when she chose to follow a blue glow in the next left fork. We followed a long wide tunnel until we reached a dead end. Kirym advanced to the face of the rock. We waited in silence.

"This is where we should be," Kirym said. "There must be a key."

Rolliz was again grumbling in Kirym's pocket. Instead of ignoring him, she pulled him out and showed him the rock wall.

His eyes raced around his cone like a demented bee in a goblet.

"Orange token on green token on blue and held really high." He looked at Kirym from her head to her feet. "You won't be able to do it alone. You hold me and let me hold them."

She pulled the tokens from her pocket, unwrapped them, sat them on top of Rolliz who sent out vine-like tendrils to hold them safe. Kirym then lifted him high above her head.

After a long search, Rolliz sent another tendril from his head up through the tokens. Once through them, it grew into a miniature tree lit up by the rays of all three tokens. A twisted ray of light shot from the tokens through three of the branches and following Rolliz eye movements, eventually each pointing to different darkened crevices up near the roof. Moments passed, and the lights intensified. The rays disappeared although the tokens still glowed. The branches reached into the crevices and I heard a distinct series of clicks and clunks, followed by an indistinct rasp of rock grinding across rock.

Ashistar beat me to stand by Kirym's right shoulder, Mekrar was at her left. I found myself behind her, Arbreu behind and to my left, Sundas at my right shoulder. Ubree blocked the tunnel behind us. The cave darkened, and my hand moved to my knife.

"We don't need weapons," Kirym said, and I wondered how she knew I was about to draw mine.

Kirym returned the tokens and Rolliz to her pocket. Before I was fully aware of her movement, she walked through what I was sure had been solid stone.

Sundas prodded me in the back. "Oak! The walls are moving."

I glanced to one side. He was right. Even as I paused, they widened further. I would have liked to check them, but Kirym didn't stop and I didn't want to hold things up. I glanced behind but couldn't see past Ubree.

Kirym stopped when the tokens began to hum, although this was different, deeper and richer than when I'd last heard them, and quite echoey.

We had reached a massive cave, and ahead, the floor was littered with hundreds of large misshapen rocks.

"Wait here, I'll be back in a moment," Kirym said as she went to explore.

Kirym led us down the wall on the right, past a large arch to a place to leave our packs. "I need you all to help me with the tokens," she said.

Further along the side wall was a flat rock. It was shaped like a half circle and sat at about waist height. The sides were rough, but the top was unnaturally smooth and shiny. In the middle, right against the wall was a great column of rock that reached up to the roof of the cave. It gave the impression of a thick beeswax candle, with solidified globules oozing down the sides. I was tempted to touch it, but I'd have had to lean over, and it didn't seem right.

Kirym opened her token pocket. "Choose a token and place them somewhere around this rock. Ubree, you and Faltryn as well."

With two packages left in the pocket, Mekrar paused.

"I hold Arech," she said. "You should place the two tokens, Kirym." Kirym nodded and picked them up.

Faltryn climbed laboriously up the wall beside the rock and, with Mekrar's help, placed the rainbow token on the left side of the half circle. Trethia sat the purple next to it. Then Sundas placed the yellow. Ashistar left a space in the middle at the front and put the green token down, Arbreu the red, and Ubree placed the orange token against the far-right hand wall.

Mekrar held Arech, Kirym held the blue token and Valycraag. I held the black.

There was no balance with the colours, and I waited for Kirym to move them, but she didn't. Instead, she placed Valycraag in the centre of the curved rock and asked me to place the black.

I hesitated. "It doesn't balance. Where will you put the blue?"

"Where it needs to be after you place the black. Where do you feel it should sit, Oak?" she asked.

"I'm not sure. You've always made those decisions."

She shook her head. "I've always let the tokens decide. What was your initial instinct about placing it?"

"On Valycraag, but you'll need to put the blue there first."

"Why?" She looked genuinely mystified.

"Well—it's what you did at the portal pool."

"Ahh!"

I was relieved, she understood.

"This isn't the portal pool, Oak. No two situations are the same. But I feel the blue should sit on Valycraag, but atop another stone. Your initial thought was right."

It didn't make sense to me, but I placed the black stone in Valycraags hole and Kirym sat the blue token on top of it. Then she stepped back and allowed Mekrar to sit Arech so the three prongs sat in the small indentations on the top of Valycraag.

As the tokens began to vibrate, Kirym called us over to an area to the left of the rock, where we could watch. I picked Trethia up to ensure she could see and checked that Sundas held Faltryn. The light faded and the sounds from the tokens were so low, I could scarcely hear them. As we waited, Ashistar began to sing. This was Churnyg's dragon song, the one that called Borasyn to Kirym, after she and Churnyg escaped from Gynbere's rock prison. As Ashistar paused to take a breath, Mekrar, Arbreu, and Sundas began a Green Valley song, one sung to welcome the family when it came together. I joined in with a song Wind Runner had taught me when I was young, a song our whole family sang when a child was born. Then Kirym and Trethia began to sing. Their song was unusual. It was in no language I had heard before. Their song made more sense when Ubree joined in. Dragonese, I presumed, although I wondered how they both knew it.

The singing could have been a cacophony, but the four songs wove together beautifully, often meeting on a note, separating again, one building as another paused, but always complimentary. When the tokens joined in, the whole cave vibrated with sound.

As we harmonised, the blue token lit up. Instead of connecting to the other tokens, it sent a beam of light out to each of us. It felt warm on my forehead. Trethia giggled, had I been younger, I would have done the same.

Those who wore tokens, returned the beam of light to Arech, although only one of Kirym's tokens—the white—

did. Her green token shot a light up to touch a spot high on the column, while her blue sent a beam to touch Faltryn, Ubree, and Trethia. Where they touched, I was surprised to see different blues.

Ubree's and Faltryn's token spots pulsed, and appeared bigger, although it may have been an illusion of the light.

Kirym's blue token then sent another ray to the black token, and the shaft of light at the top of the column did the same. A beam of light shot down through the black and then into each of the other tokens.

The lights went out as we finished our song, but after a few moments, the tokens lit up again, began to pulse, and with each beat, they grew. This was different to anything I had seen before, although I'd heard Teema describe something similar to Loul and Veld. While this was as amazing as his experience had sounded, I feared the tokens would explode. I wondered what would happen if they did.

They won't, came Ubree's comforting thought.

Just when I feared he must be wrong; they each sent a beam in towards the base of the column. The light licked the outer surface of it as flames do when meeting a large piece of wood.

A flicker of movement at the base of the column caught my eye. Faltryn struggled out of Sundas' arms and flew over to stand at the edge of the rock facing the column. For a moment, I thought she was coughing or choking. Then I realised she was trying to breathe fire.

Kirym grasped it faster than I did. "Ubree, breathe fire on the column," Kirym said. "Faltryn can't do it by herself, she's too little."

Ubree's flame made a huge difference. A flash of fire lit up the cave, there was a rumble and the flames began to roar.

It was a magnificent sight; the rock absorbed the flames. They were channelled up the inside of the column and then moved out across the roof of the cave, along thick grooves that fed into smaller ones. It reminded me of intertwined tree roots or the braiding of the river I had lived beside for most of my life. The noise of the fire intensified; the column was pulsing and appeared to bulge in the centre. Lines appeared in it—the fire glowed through them—and I wondered if it would fracture. If it did, we would be hit by the blazing fragments.

I glanced around for somewhere safe, I wanted to protect Trethia, but my attention was pulled back to the column when the noises changed. The column gave the impression it was taking a deep breath and holding it, forcing the flames back down towards the rock where the tokens sat, although they still crisscrossed the ceiling.

Kirym and Ubree both looked serene, I figured there were things they knew that I didn't. Ubree wouldn't allow us to be in danger.

As if a dam had broken, flames shot through small holes in the front of the stone the tokens sat on. I was surprised at how controlled the flames behaved. They didn't touch the ground but gently caressed the humps. Had we been standing amongst them, we would not have been touched. The moving flames made it look as if the humps were moving. I glanced around as the rock shapes cast shadows on the walls. A very clever effect.

The flames slowly died.

The tokens were intact, we were all unharmed, and for a short time, so amazed by the sights we had seen, we were silent.

"Is everyone all right?" Mekrar asked.

Before anyone could answer, the biggest rock in the middle of the floor shivered. I thought of Mekroe's description of an earthquake, but even as the notion came to mind, I knew it wasn't. Mekroe had described sounds and there were none here. Nor did I feel any movement in the ground. However, the hump expanded in all directions. It heaved upwards and suddenly I was staring up at a dragon.

Then the next largest hump moved, then another and another. Every one of the rocks was a dragon.

The first dragon stared at Ubree, glanced at the rest of us, and then back to Ubree.

"Who are you and why have you woken us?"

"I am Ubree of Athesha. We woke you because you were asleep.

I smiled quietly to myself, thinking it an answer I'd more expect from Borasyn.

"We have no reason to be awake."

"I call on your Grand Council to convene."

In the silence that followed, I tried to get a good look at the dragons, but in the dimness, all I could tell was they were uniform in colour, greyish, and almost identical in appearance, the only obvious difference being size. As far as I could tell, they came in four different sizes. The largest was about the size of Arymda, while the smallest, half the size of Borasyn.

"You have no right to call our Council. Go away."

"Anyone can call it and if called, it must convene."

The dragon shook his head, more in annoyance, I thought, than denial.

"Oh, very well then, let's get it over with. There's a place we do it." He turned and walked down the cave, followed by the others.

Ubree shook his head in disgust. "No manners at all." He motioned Kirym forward. She leaned over to pick Faltryn up off the ledge, Ubree walked beside her, and we followed.

"What happens to the tokens?" Sundas asked.

"They'll wait until we need them," Kirym said.

30

Kirym Speaks

We followed the dragons along a wide tunnel, and out into an open area, surrounded by cliffs. It reminded me of our canyon, although it was much smaller. There were three galleries on the walls, all were soon crowded with the smaller, or more probably younger dragons. The smallest had scrambled to the top.

Those who stayed on the ground opened a narrow aisle through to where the dragon who'd spoken to us stood with two others.

In daylight, the dragons were a uniform grey, although the smaller dragons had lighter grey splodges on their skin. They looked drab compared to Ubree and Faltryn.

There is no indication of bugs here, Ubree.

"Welcome, Ubree of Athesha. I am the Arqha, Dax. It's a long time since we had visitors, you must forgive us for not being prepared." He looked at Faltryn. "This would be your—grandchild? Great-grandchild?"

"Faltryn is my sister. And this is Kirym—"

"Oh, don't bother us with your attendants. Send them back to the cave or over by the wall while we speak."

Ubree drew himself up to full height and glared down at Dax. "Kirym of The Green Valley, daughter of Loul, Lady of Athesha and Monarch. Kirym is teller of the old stories, carrier of the ancient weapons, and Dragon. Leader." Without waiting for Dax to respond he continued, motioning to Mekrar. "Mekrar of Athesha, Lady of Athesha, eldest daughter of Loul of The Green Valley, and heir apparent."

He continued on through all of us, giving our names with a dazzling array of titles."

Dax looked shocked. He obviously didn't expect this. "Well," he blustered. "Well, what do you want?"

"Halavash is in danger. Its inhabitants are being killed. Why are you sleeping instead of helping?" Kirym asked.

"What we did, didn't work, so we..." he paused, "well, stopped!"

"If what you did didn't work, why did you not try something else or ask for help?"

"There was no one to ask. Our fire failed. The bugs kill us as readily as they killed the other creatures of the land. We were reluctant to put more of our children at risk. As it was, we lost too many. We couldn't ask for help. The gatekeeper said we couldn't use the gate."

"The gate was broken and unattended," I said, "so you could have used it as you liked. The bugs only flew in spring."

"I'm Zillib," a dragon who sat on the lowest gallery said. "All this was suggested. Dax did not call the gatekeeper to face us formally. He approached him alone. He did not allow us to question him, to demand he help us, although some of us tried. Dax then bound us here, so none could venture beyond the cave. We can't leave here until Dax is no longer leader or dies." He sounded exasperated.

"Why not allow others to find a solution, Dax?" Ubree asked. "It's my understanding they're entitled—"

"I had others approach the gatekeeper; they did not return. As the Arqha, I am obligated to protect the flight. My law ensured their safety."

"Under the old law, you are first obligated to help those of the land. We've seen the bugs. I suspect it will take a flight of dragons and a lot of coordination to destroy them. There may have been other ways even if you had no fire."

Dax eyed Ubree suspiciously.

Faltryn squirmed around in my arms until she could see everyone. Then she coughed. She did it again and again. Initially, a tiny wisp of smoke came from her mouth, and on the fifth cough, a tiny flame.

I glanced up at Ubree and saw his face change as he understood what she was trying to tell him.

"Perhaps you should try to reignite your fire. When we arrived, the column was cold. It happens when you don't follow the usual ceremonies."

"This disaster was foretold," Dax said. "We cannot alter nature's forces."

Ubree frowned. "Relate the prophecy that says you would cease to be dragons. As I understand it, on Halavash, the word dragon means protector."

Dax drew himself up to his full height. "Cursed reborns! They caused this. Dragons who refused to die. History said they'd be our demise. Although we sent them away, I knew we should have destroyed them when we first laid eyes on them. We didn't, and this is the price we pay."

"As I understood the prophecy," Ubree said, "the arrival of reborns heralded an era of great change. It said nothing of destruction, although if you can show me, I'd acknowledge my error. If I'm right though, then it may very well be that these are the changes the reborns were sent to assist with, to ensure you were able to continue to do the job you were born to. Can you send for them?"

Dax looked annoyed. "Even had the prophecy said that, the reborns were never of a nature to help. They were vicious and created their own mayhem. They were as happy to leave, as we were to see them go, and we had no idea what their plans were, they rejected every suggestion we made."

I glanced up at Ubree. He looked amused.

"How long between them leaving and the bugs arriving?" I asked.

"They left the bugs as a reminder of their power."

"The trees tell a different timeline."

Zillib flew across and landed beside Dax. "When Arqha the Ancient, breathed his last, he told us we would need to find help. That was after the reborns left, and before the bugs arrived."

Dax nudged him aside. "Return to your place Zillib. Leave this to your elders." He turned again to Ubree. "The ancient told me we would never be able to breathe fire again. I brought my people here and we slept."

Arqha is a title meaning head dragon, Ubree told me.

"Who is Arqha now?" I asked.

"I was asked to take the position," Dax said. "I am known as Arqha the Great."

"There was no vote?" Ubree asked.

"There were no worthwhile objections."

Zillib and some of the others looked annoyed.

"An Arqha must be voted in to enhance the power and wisdom that goes with the title. Then they can renew your fire," Ubree said to the gathered dragons.

Dax looked around. "Well, as all will vote for me—"

"No," Zillib said. "We do it properly. Votes are individual."

"It'll take too long," Dax said.

"Not necessarily." Zillib turned to the other dragons. "Who, among the eldest of their family, wishes to be considered?" He paused. "Come on, quickly. I'll place my wing on the rock. Anyone else?"

No one answered.

"You're too young," Dax said.

"As the oldest of my family, I have a right to stand. Would you like to recheck the law?"

"Just two of us then," Dax said. "We will vote in twenty days after—"

"We will vote now," interrupted Zillib. "Give two sentences to tell everyone what you hold dear. Same for me and then we vote. It is allowed in law."

Dax looked annoyed, but many of the other dragons nodded their agreement. He flew onto a low ledge on the cliff. It was the one place with no galleries above.

"I will make cautious consideration of all available avenues ahead, and check information from all possible sources to decide carefully what the best path for us all would be while noting our present abilities as the moons pass by. I will protect you, so you can bring your families safely into the flight to nurture and care for contentedly into your old age, ensuring you can die happily with the knowledge that your line will continue and so that those who follow us have the chance to—"

"That's fast becoming ten sentences," a large dragon who stood nearby said. "The same as we heard for the fifty moons after our fire died. There will be no new families unless there is agreement, and with the bugs out there, my family for one won't agree. Now leave the rock and let others use it. Zillib, what say you?"

Dax growled. "You have no right to order me about, Conysh," but the other dragons had all turned their attention to Zillib, who didn't fly to the rock, but stayed put and raised his voice.

"Our responsibility is to protect our neighbours and we've been sent help to learn the role anew. We will attempt to again breathe fire, and if unsuccessful, find a way to hold our heads high, and ensure everyone's safety."

Conysh stood. "Right! Now we each make a choice and make it fast."

She, Zillib, and a few others rose into the sky and circled the area between the cliffs. One dropped back to the ground, but about half of those on the ground joined Zillib.

They flew with their eyes shut. I watched, expecting any number of them to crash into each other or the wall. However, they slowly formed a wedge behind Zillib, and flying wing-tips touching, continued to circle.

More joined them; a few dropped back to the ground where they gathered around Dax. One by one the dragons on the ground rose to join the back of the wedge until there were only five left.

Dax finally flapped his wings, and followed by the other four, rose into the air, flying in the opposite direction.

It means they will never vote with the majority. Ubree told me. *However, it makes no difference. The vote for Zillib is overwhelming. Dax and his followers must agree to accept the majority decision or remove their wings and go into exile.*

"The decision is made," intoned the two dragons, flying just behind Zillib, and they all settled back to the ground, or their galleries.

"Ubree, what do we do now? Can we get the reborns to at least visit to help us?" Zillib asked.

Ubree inclined his head to Zillib. "You may not need them. You must each go through the fire-breathing exercises you used to teach your children."

"As simple as that?"

"It's a start. I'd like to watch how you do it. We can change the style if there is a problem."

Everyone trouped back to the cave.

Five dragons, with Zillib in the middle, stood in a half circle in front of the column. We gathered in the same place we had been while watching the dragons waken.

"Are we safe?" Sundas asked.

"If we weren't, Ubree wouldn't let us stand here," I said.

Each of the dragons took a deep breath and coughed.

Nothing happened.

"Stare at the column," Ubree said. "Draw your fire from your belly."

They tried again and a few produced wisps of smoke.

"As you breathe and cough, hum from your belly. Like this." Ubree demonstrated.

Zillib stood taller, started to hum as he took a deep breath and coughed. A small flame shot from his mouth. The column sparked.

He did it again and the others copied him, with similar results. Again, and this time, the fire was spectacular. Their flames tickled the base of the fire column, and again it roared.

They moved aside, and a larger group took their places in front of the column.

With Zillib also coaching and the fire now burning, they learned faster. Very soon, they were all breathing fire.

"What now?" Zillib asked.

The dragons all turned expectantly to Ubree who described the best way for the dragons to work together to attack the bugs.

"There is another problem here, though," I said. "Kultria flies in spring. That's when you can kill the bugs in the air. But they're multiplying elsewhere. To destroy them completely, we must to find those places. We've asked

Vashetha to search but if you see any unusual landmark as you fly the land, we will investigate."

"Would the bugs be causing the fires?" Zillib asked.

"Unlikely," Ubree said. "They wouldn't want fires to burn the plants and animals they eat."

The ground began to shake gently. The soil on the far side of the fire rock cracked as tree roots pushed their way up. Within moments a miniature and transparent version of Vashetha stood before us.

I stepped forward. "Thank you for coming, Vashetha."

"Just a small part of my root system," she said. "I appreciate the invitation from you. Zillib, it's good to see you awake again. I have spoken to every root in my family," she continued, "and there are things we have no real knowledge of. Nine areas talk of a growing death. A portion of the land already dead; devoid of plants, insects, and animals. Anything walking across this ground is pulled down into the soil, dead before they disappear. Something has drained the lives of our sisters who lived close by leaving nothing but dust. Those who had the chance, left the area. Having listened to your conversations, I now wonder if these places are where the bugs," she paused, "well not hibernate, because they are eating ravenously. Perhaps evolve would be a better description. The areas are expanding rapidly."

"Can you show us?" I asked.

"Of course. I just wonder how you will destroy them if these are indeed the places they live."

"Let's look first," Ubree said.

Vashetha reached out to Ubree with one of her more solid-looking branches. The branch twined around his neck and up to touch his token-spot. He concentrated for a short time and then nodded. "Yes, I can find that."

A picture of a wide barren area came from Vashetha. The surface moved slightly as if something underground was breathing. No insects moved across it, no blades of grass grew, and when a fallen leaf drifted across the surface, it turned black and became dust.

"Can you tell if it's the bugs under there?" Oak asked.

Ubree shook his head. "I need to go and look. What do you think, Kirym?"

"Until we have more knowledge, we can do nothing. What lives there?"

Ubree concentrated for a long time. Finally, he shook his head. "It's huge and nebulous, made up of many thousands of very small pieces swarming together. For ease, I would call it a nest. It goes very deep into the ground."

"How can we destroy whatever it is?" asked Zillib.

"I have an idea."

Everyone stared at me.

"Really? One that would work?" Zillib sounded hopeful.

"Well, no guarantees, but we need to do something, and I think my idea could work, and this is—well if someone else has a better idea..." Everyone simultaneously shook their head. "Well then, let's give it a try."

31

Arbreu

The expanse we looked over was big, bigger than Arbreu had thought it would be. He went over Kirym's plan in his head and wondered if it could possibly work.

Without knowing what they would deal with, it was all unknown.

Ubree had not been happy when Kirym suggested she stand and watch from a nearby hill. She had rejected his suggestion of a protective circle around her, pointing out that he had so many other things to do. She always has a solid point, Arbreu smiled to himself.

Ubree would be overseeing everything, shielding the view of the operation from everyone else in the land, backing up the other dragons as and where necessary, and doing whatever else needed to be done.

Kirym's plan was relatively simple. The dragons each had a specific job and she would be able to send Ubree a message if something changed. Her view may be important for destroying the next nest they attacked, if indeed the plan was successful.

It was agreed that in the event things went wrong, shielding the view would be secondary to protecting everyone there.

The flight hovered in a large circle just above the nest. Levels within the flight was decided on by age and ability, with the more mature at the lower levels, and the younger up high. A few of the dragons were given the job of watching from the side to ensure nothing escaped. The very youngest were further out and on the ground. Their job was to destroy anything escaping at ground level, although they all hoped that none would.

Arbreu didn't hear Ubree's signal, but the lowest ring of dragons breathed their fire onto the outside edge of the pit.

Moments later, the next ring did the same a little further in, and the next and the next until they were all projecting their flame down into the nest, and the whole nest was covered with fire. The heat billowed out, Arbreu could feel it even where he stood on the hill near Kirym.

Just as Arbreu registered the smell of burning sand, there was a curious hollow roar. A huge pillar of what looked like green leaves streamed up out of the ground trying to reach beyond the layers of flames. Because of the sheer number of leaf-like critters, their attempt was almost successful, but Ubree was waiting there, and with a single breath of blue flame, was able to topple the pillar of bugs back towards the burning ground. The dragon fire burned hot with no smoke.

There was so much to look at for the short time of the attack, Arbreu knew he would have trouble remembering many of the specifics, but Kirym's plan was working.

The dragons on the ground darted around spitting fire at the few bugs that managed to crawl out of the pit, some singed, but a few, intact.

One small creature dodged them all. Just when Arbreu thought it would disappear back into the soil, a nearby tree reached out and speared it onto the end of a sharp twig. The bug struggled briefly and then went limp. The tree then slowly climbed the hill towards Kirym.

The upper tiers of dragons now stopped breathing fire and were excitedly talking about the adventure. However, Arbreu noted, they stayed where they were, and kept an eye on the nest.

The lower tiers continued pouring flames into the ground, making sure everything deep down was destroyed. Eventually, the firestorm stopped. The dragons hovered above watching to see if there was any more movement. When all was still for quite a while, most of the dragons settled on the ground, waiting eagerly to see when they would get to repeat the action at the other eight nests.

The soil where the nest had been now formed a deep blackened bowl. Ubree hovered just above it, searching and listening for any signs of life. Eventually he accepted that all had been destroyed and joined those on the rise.

Now the trees moved in. They pushed their roots deep into the ground to see if there was anything left that shouldn't be. When they were sure the area was clean, ten trees brought in more soil and a variety of plants.

The tree who captured the escaping bug hadn't moved to set down its roots. It had been standing quietly beside Kirym for some time. She now held out the creature she had stabbed.

"Don't touch it," the tree said. "It's covered with fine hairs. They're quite irritating."

The bug was an iridescent green, with the appearance of a curled leaf. The tree used four twigs to carefully break it in half. Nestled in the centre was a small lump. We could see movement under the surface membrane.

"Whatever it is, it's about to reproduce, despite being stabbed," I said.

Ubree looked at it closely. "Put it down, it's best destroyed."

Even with those words, he waited as the membrane split, and the small creamy creature crawled out. It was covered with long silky hairs interspersed with thicker spikes.

"Why are the bugs born two different ways?" Mekrar asked.

"Perhaps," Kirym said, "one lot are female and the others male, or maybe it's just their life cycle."

"That would make sense," Ubree said, as he snorted a small ball of fire at it. "Now, can we attack more of the nests before dark?"

"We're ready for it," Zillib said. "Our fire is strong; we are all enthusiastic and ready to go."

32

Kirym Speaks

Three nests were destroyed before the second sun began to set. Zillib discussed continuing into the night, but Ubree explained he wouldn't be able to adequately shield the flames. The reflection of so much fire could invite investigation of the curious. Anyway, Kultria would be bringing more bugs, and their destruction was the priority.

Back in the cave, I collected the tokens and our packs, and we were given into the care of Sefan, an ancient dragon who had volunteered to care for us until Ubree returned in the morning. Ubree and the dragons left at full dark to attack the web.

Sefan, led us through a maze of tunnels to where we were to eat and sleep. In the dim light, it was difficult to see where we were going. Sefan chatted in a very sing-song voice which quickly became very annoying.

"Just along the tunnel," she warbled. "Around the corner, up the rise and down again, back this way, and here we are."

She stopped in the middle of a wide, windy tunnel. "Eat now, and then I'll show you a nice cosy place where you can sleep peacefully."

I glanced around. The wall we were opposite had several holes and burrows. Five of the larger holes were high in the tunnel wall; three more were at about shoulder height, and two at ground level. Sefan watched as a group of young dragons raced through the tunnel. While we were never stepped on, we were jostled as the young dragons raced past. Despite saying a lot, Sefan gave little information and avoided all questions, generally by starting a story about some irrelevant occasion from the past.

"Eat up and I'll show you your lovely cosy tunnel," she said. "There'll be plenty of room in there, you'll be very comfortable. You won't be bothered by the young ones playing through the tunnels. They are so energetic since they woke up."

It was cold, and we were eager to get to a warmer place. Realising we would go no further until we had eaten, we sat and shared some food. When we had finished eating, Sefan pointed us towards the smallest of the floor level tunnels. "Leave your packs out here, you won't need them until tomorrow." She pointed to a small inlet in the rock wall. Anything left there would be away from the path, no one could walk over them or crush them. I was reluctant to leave our packs, but it did seem a sensible suggestion.

We still wore our cloaks and carried a knife each. The ancient weapons were attached to the baldric and hidden under my cloak along with the tokens and my remedy pocket. Everything else was in the packs.

The tunnel was so small only Trethia didn't have to stoop to enter. The men did it on their knees; Sundas on his belly. I was the last to enter. I tried again to ask questions, however, Sefan ignored me and pushed me towards the tunnel. It was longer than I expected, but it opened out at the end. What to was unknown, it was too dark to see. Our lamps were in our packs. I began to crawl back, calling to Sefan as I did. Her voice warbled through somewhat indistinctly, "You'll be safe there," and the dim light at the end of the tunnel disappeared. I heard rock scraping on rock and scrambled backwards as a large rock was pushed towards me.

I crawled back to the others.

"She sealed the tunnel with a large rock."

"Oh," Sundas said. "I didn't expect that. Why? What danger is there? Not the bugs, and there isn't anything else."

"From what she said, I assumed there would be food, water and light in here," Mekrar said. "Without light, we're at a distinct disadvantage."

Sundas went to the tunnel and yelled to Sefan but received no reply. "This worries me, Kirym. She must o' heard us," he said, "unless she's deaf."

Mekrar laughed shortly. "Zelriff is deaf, and yet she can hear someone talking about pamchii nuts from the far side of the settlement."

"What can we do? Their place, their rules," Ashistar said.

"Oh no! I don't think so. Not after all we've done for them." I opened my pocket and picked up the first token I touched.

It glowed immediately—green—and I held it high. It shone enough for me to see our surrounds.

It was not a widened section of the tunnel, nor a cave, but a room. A niche in the wall beside the entrance caught my eye, although more accurately, what sat in the niche. A lamp! Sundas lifted it down. It was empty, but behind it sat a well-stoppered flask of oil and a small flint. With light, we began to explore.

The walls were straight and there were low platforms dotted about; useful for both sitting and sleeping.

"Wow, these walls and ledges are hewn from the rock," Ashistar said. "But there are no tool marks. Whoever made this room was an artist."

A narrow doorway in the right-hand corner of the back wall led into another room. It was long, narrow, and featureless, except for nine indented shelves spaced along the shared wall. Diagonally opposite the door was a set of large shelves holding various containers and packages.

Oak looked around. "Why didn't Sefan tell us about these rooms?"

"It might have suited her not to tell us, but more likely she didn't know," I said. "Only the smallest dragon would fit through the tunnel, and if they thought it was just a tunnel, why would they look. What strikes you as unusual about these rooms?"

"It's so different to any other place in Halavash," Oak said.

I nodded. "Yes, but more importantly, there's only one exit. Now, I can't believe anyone would create an area this well made with only one way in and out, especially as the entrance is so awkward. If that entrance been made specifically to keep the dragons out, there must be another entrance."

"Perhaps they thought there was no need. They could call on the dragons if there was a problem," Ashistar said.

"How could the dragons help? They couldn't enter, and it'd be hard to get out in an emergency. So, if it isn't a dragon area, what is it?"

"What'd ya mean, Kirym?" Arbreu looked bleary eyed in the gloom.

"This room belonged to someone else. But who, and where are they? Go and get some sleep, Arbreu. You look dead on your feet."

Everyone except Sundas and Ashistar settled down to sleep. I tried to send a message to Ubree. Either he didn't receive it or chose not to answer. I lay with my eyes closed, but my mind was too active for sleep.

The moon would have moved about one hand-span when I gave up all pretence of sleep. I tucked Faltryn in with Trethia, hoping to keep them both asleep, eased away, stood and stretched.

"I'm going to explore the other room. Can you two make sure everything we have is together in case we need to move in a hurry? I'd hate to lose anything. Ashistar, can you sit in the doorway and watch both rooms."

"Do you think Sefan will know what we are doing?" Sundas asked. "What if she's there to spy on us?"

"Then she's going about it the wrong way. She should have her ear against the tunnel, just as effective for keeping us in here, and she would hear everything."

The first container held knives, the second dyes; I recognised three of them, which were very scarce, and assumed they all were. Other containers held dried food, most of it I didn't recognise. Two packages held dried herbs, powdered bark and woods; many were remedies we used. There were also the usual items needed in a dwelling, platters and containers for water. Bigger packages held rugs, soft boots identical to those we wore inside, some simple robes similar to our night robes, short cloaks, and packs.

A small package had been pushed into the back corner on the lowest shelf. It was small enough to be easily overlooked but left in a spot easy to get to if one was in a hurry. Had I not been sitting to inspect the containers; I would have missed it. Intrigued, I unwrapped it, and found a small scroll in a cloth bag, which I slipped into my bodice planning to read it later. It was more important to figure out what the inset shelves were for.

I studied them for a long time. They were placed in three groups of three, obvious because the end two groups sat slightly higher than those in the middle. The centre space was taller than any of the others. Its top was level with the higher groups, the bottom with those on either side of it.

Trethia came and sat beside me. I was pleased to have her there, put my arm around her and kissed the top of her head. I tried to pull her closer to me, but the token pocket was in the way. I untied it to make Trethia more comfortable, and while I had it there, I pulled Rolliz out and sat him on the ground in front of me. He had been surprisingly quiet. I had expected him to complain about being kept in darkness for so long.

One of his eyes stared up at me. "Thank you for keeping me safe. Why didn't you tell them I was with you?"

"There was no need for anyone to know what I carried in my pocket."

"What if they had asked?"

"Then it would have depended on how they asked, and whether they had good intent. Mind you, had they asked, I suspect they would not have had good intent."

"Vashetha wouldn't have been happy to see me. She supported the decision to keep Malsavash and his brothers away from her and her daughters."

"When was that decision made, and why?"

"That was after the dragons had disappeared. The grey gatekeeper and his friend visited. Malsavash and his brothers were happy, the decision meant my brothers and I were no longer needed. Of course, we weren't asked." His eye swivelled around to the tokens as they began to vibrate.

The vibrations woke everyone, and they came to see what was happening.

Trethia helped me lay the wrapped tokens on the floor in front of us. "They sound different, as if they're happy, but they shouldn't be because we're prisoners."

Mekrar's eyes widened. She opened her mouth to say something but changed her mind, pulled Arech from the pocket in her cloak and sat it on the floor beside the tokens.

"Which shelf will we fill first, Trethia?" I asked as I picked up a wrapped token.

"In the middle on the left." We unwrapped the token, black, and when I placed it on the shelf, it glowed.

Trethia handed me another token and pointed to the shelf to the left of the black. The blue glowed before I had finished unwrapping it.

When I turned back, Trethia had handed a token to each of the others. Each person chose a spot niche and unwrapped their token. Sundas placed his orange in the niche on the far right. Ashistar chose a niche two places to the left of the orange and unwrapped the green.

Mekrar wanted her red on the far left, Oak placed his purple next to it. Arbreu chose to place the yellow in between the orange and green. A perfect rainbow of colours, with two spaces left.

Two spaces. One token, Valycraag, and Arech to place. I leaned over to pick up the token but Faltryn pushed Valycraag towards me instead.

"For the right-hand side?" I asked.

She shook her head.

"The centre?" She nodded. I unwrapped it, set it in place and reached for the rainbow token.

Faltryn placed her front paw on my hand as it closed over the token. She pushed the stone around me to my left.

I frowned, wondering what she meant.

"Put it on top of Valycraag," Trethia said.

Faltryn nodded.

"That leaves one place empty," I said.

Again, she nodded.

"The shelf is too small for them both. With Valycraag there, Arech won't fit."

She shrugged.

Trethia interrupted again as I was about to place the rainbow token. "Put it in Valycraag, as before. In it, not on it."

I turned the token over and sat it face down in the hole on the top of the desert stone.

The tokens were singing together before I had resumed my seat. This time their song was soft and more of a chant.

Mekrar sat beside me, unwrapped Arech, and sat it on the floor in front of the centre niche.

All but the rainbow token lit up. They each sent a sheet of colour rolling across the ceiling, down the far wall and then looping back to envelop us, before oozing into the rainbow token.

The lamp flickered out, and for a few moments, we sat with just the light from the tokens. It faded to nothing, and we sat in the dark with the tokens chanting softly.

A ball of blue light shot up from Arech. As the glow increased, each token shot coloured balls to sit above the rainbow token. The colour balls spun together until they merged—a big rainbow ball. They spun faster and faster until the colours disappeared, and a single white ball of light hovered above the rainbow token. It died, and we sat in the darkness again until Sundas relit the lamp.

A large white token sat on top of the rainbow token.

The other tokens chanted their welcome and their colours enveloped the new one and washed over us.

I picked the new token up; it linked, first to my white token, and for a moment, I heard Amethyst gurgling and chattering. Then it expanded to encompass my three small tokens. The glow faded until only the white remained.

I placed it in the empty niche in the wall and returned to sit between Trethia and Mekrar. The light from the tokens and the lamp faded with their song, and again we sat in darkness. I counted slowly to eighty, there was a low hollow thud, followed by a few quiet gasps from around the room.

When the lamp next glowed, Trethia and I were the only ones not holding a knife. As they all sheepishly re-sheathed their knives, I studied the wall. A niche, larger than those below it, had opened above the centre shelf where the rainbow token sat on Valycraag.

"Is that for the white token, Kirym?" Mekrar asked.

"I don't think so," I said. "It's big enough for Arech. What do you think?"

When Mekrar sat Arech in the niche, the token rays met on a spot on the ceiling just above me and a multicoloured ray jumped over to the wall behind us. We twisted around to watch as it appeared to bore a hole into the wall. It was a delightful illusion, the darkest colour, black in the centre, out to the white around the outside edge.

With a deep sigh, the tokens stopped glowing. We sat in darkness until the lamp glowed. I stood and turned around. In the wall where the tokens had shown their illusion, was a door, a straight-edged door big enough for even Sundas.

"How did that get there?" Oak asked. "More important, do we use it? What if we're wrong about Sefan, and she's just doing what she thinks is right?"

"I'd say this is the back door, the bolt-hole," I said, as I began to collect the tokens together and put them away.

"How long do we wait to see what the dragons plan for us? No matter how we look at it, Sefan acted strangely. I wonder where her loyalties lie. As the tokens showed us the door, I must assume it's the safest option and we should take the initiative and use it. We must be prepared, so gather what we need to from the shelves here. Bring the water containers and let's get going."

It was only a matter of moments before everyone was ready. I was still wrapping the tokens. I studied the white token. It was beautiful. Various shades of pearled white swirled through it.

I felt the black stone now made sense as a token. I had always thought of the tokens in terms of the rainbow colours, but I had nothing to base the assumption on. Both the black and the white belonged, and I realised there were probably others we had not yet found.

Trethia pushed a square of soft material into my hand. "Wrap it in this."

Mekrar had promised Trethia she'd teacher her how to piece together a blanket, and this was one of the special pieces Trethia had chosen for it. She'd been carrying it along with a few others in her pocket, but this was her favourite. It was a generous gift, and I thanked her profusely.

I picked Rolliz up. "I quite like those tokens. Uncomfortable, but entertaining." He closed his mouths and eyes and sighed contentedly.

I did a final check to see we had everything and led everyone through the door. Arbreu came through last and once he was in the tunnel, the door closed.

"There's no handle on this side, Kirym," he said. "That means we can't go back, so I hope we're doing the right thing."

33

Oak Speaks

The tunnel turned right almost immediately. One hundred and fifty steps later, it widened and turned left. Nearby I could hear the gurgle of running water.

Sundas held up the lamp; it reflected off a small cascade of water running down the wall and splashing onto the ground. We gathered around it and drank. While the water containers were being filled, I took the lamp and checked the passage ahead for a short distance. As I returned, Trethia came running to meet me. "I found something. Come and look." She grabbed my hand and urged me to hurry.

Kirym knelt in front of a small dark opening near the base of the wall just past the waterfall. I hadn't noticed it when I walked past. The blue token sat glowing beside her.

I lay on my belly and peered in. All I saw was a jumble of rocks, and then Kirym moved the blue token to light the space better, and I realised what else was there. Our packs.

"A way out," Arbreu said. "If we can get through—"

"That's not where we left them," Kirym said.

"They might've just been moved."

"But why would they, Arbreu? They weren't in the way."

Arbreu shrugged. "I suppose it doesn't matter. We can use the same way to get out. It'll be a squeeze for Sundas, but I'm sure he can do it."

"Let's check first and then discuss it."

Trethia crawled into the tunnel and pushed out the packs one by one so I could grab them. Then she carefully pushed the weapons and extra rugs to me.

"Kirym, you need to go in and look up," she said, as she crawled out. "Take one of the lamps, you may need it."

Amid questioning looks, Kirym did as she was instructed.

"You remember back along the tunnel where Sefan had us eat our last meal," she said when she returned. "Remember the holes high in the cliff? Well, this is the bottom of one of them."

"Can we climb up to get out?" I asked.

She shook her head. "The walls are too smooth. Anyway, it would put us back with the dragons, and their next solution to contain us might be more permanent, Oak. The packs being here tells us they didn't intend to let us out."

"How do you figure that?" Ashistar asked.

"Because they were irretrievable from the top. Sefan obviously didn't think we would find them and it's pure luck we did, but it means they don't expect Ubree to be back either."

"What!"

"Think about it, Oak. If he returned and couldn't find us, he'd tear this place apart to find us, and there'd be other repercussions. So, they must assume he's not coming back."

I knew Kirym was right.

"Could they kill him?" Mekrar asked.

"I suspect it would be difficult, but nothing is impossible. He isn't dead yet. I'm sure he knows we are now safe. We must get to where he can find us, and in here, well, it'd be difficult, although not impossible. However, that would take a lot of energy, so it'd be easier for us to get out."

"And you think there is a way," Mekrar said.

Kirym nodded. "No one builds a door to nowhere. These tunnels have been well used in the past. They must go somewhere. Let's see where."

Kirym decided we would continue to use one lamp only. I walked with one hand brushing the wall, knowing the path was safe, because Kirym, who led, would warn me if the path became uneven. It continued straight for quite a distance and then began to climb.

"We're going deeper into the hill," Ashistar said.

"Are you sure?" Arbreu asked. "The path is rising."

"Aye, that's as may be, but the rock above us rises more. We have a long way to go."

It was a long exhausting climb. Kirym eventually found a small cave to our right and suggested we stop and rest. "The moon must be past the meridian, and we need to be at our best when we get out of here."

Everyone looked tired, and we set out rugs and cloaks to lie on. Kirym took the first watch with Sundas. She woke me to take over from him and he lay his rug out and carefully placed his weapons beside it.

"I've been sitting there thinking about the things that have happened since we arrived," he said. "You know Vashetha said if we couldn't stop the bugs or the fire-starters, she would look at relocating to Athesha."

Kirym and I nodded.

"Will Loul allow that?"

"She'd probably insist on it," Kirym said, "but it would be

better if we could make Halavash safe for them."

He nodded. "I don't like Ubree and Dashlan being away. I wonder if our separating was a good idea."

"Why does that worry you?" Kirym asked.

"When Malsavash saw Kultria and took us to the cave, I was there first. I thought they'd separated us for good. Even when everyone turned up, they held you for much longer, Kirym. I was scared they had taken you away."

"Who arrived after you?"

"Dashlan first. Ashistar and then Ubree but almost together. A while later, Oak and Trethia together. More time passed and finally Mekrar and Arbreu. Eventually, they delivered you, but I think we give them too much power when we let them separate us."

"Oh my, I wish I'd known. Perhaps I've made a mistake."

"What sort of mistake?" I asked.

"I didn't ask any of you about that journey. Of course, lots of things happened in a short time. The trees had walked and talked, the bugs fell, and then we needed to cross the desert. So many other things became important. I thought we had all arrived at about the same time. It seems the trees distorted my view of the journey. I wonder why?"

"Do you want to ask Mekrar? She may know something," I said.

"No. She can't answer the question I should have asked, Oak."

"What question and who can answer it?"

She sighed. "Malsavash. I didn't ask him to describe the monster he spoke of."

"But he meant Ubree, didn't he?"

Kirym laughed dryly. "I assumed he did but I now wonder if my assumption was a mistake. On top of that, he mentioned monsters, not monster. I need to talk to Vashetha."

"I'm sorry, Kirym, I've worried you more. I should have

talked about it sooner." Sundas sounded upset.

"I hear you, Kirym." Vashetha was just a shadow against the cave entrance. "I will ask Malsavash, but it will take time. He never answers immediately." She faded away to nothing."

"Could she find Ubree?" Sundas asked.

"Possibly, but I don't feel he is in danger, and if he was, we could do nothing to help him. He will be in touch when he's ready.

"Why do you think this tunnel doesn't belong to the dragons?" I asked.

"I doubt the dragons even know about this particular area we're in. They couldn't have smoothed the stone and unless the dragons were a whole lot smaller once, I really don't think they could even enter the room. It points to someone else living here."

Sundas settled and Kirym and I chatted for a while about the new token. Sometime after that, she woke Ashistar. Then she too slept.

We decided to leave Kirym to sleep until she woke naturally. She had been awake for far longer than anyone else, and we felt the sleep was more important. She slept for a long time, and when she finally stirred, we had a meal ready.

"While it makes no difference in here," I said. "Ashistar thinks it's midmorning. We'll be ready to leave when you've eaten. Ubree should be looking for us by now. I wonder what the dragons will tell him when he finds we're gone."

"He knows we're safe, but he'll need to protect himself first. Before we left The Green Valley, he and I talked about situations we may encounter."

I shouldered my pack and Kirym led us along the passage.

Again, we travelled for a long time until Kirym found an almost white cave—uniquely different to the blue of all other rock we had seen before this—and suggested we stop for a meal. She lay three rugs on the cold rock; we set out the food and ate quickly. As we packed our platters away, a token began to sing. Its song sounded enticing, different to the songs we were used to. Kirym opened her pocket, unwrapped the stone that glowed—the white one—and sat it in the middle of the rug. I wondered if it sang differently because it came from here while the others came from The Green Valley. Arbreu turned off the lamp. Small lights shone from the walls around us.

As Kirym laid the other tokens in a circle with the white, they joined in the song. Although they all glowed, their light looked more like shadows of what they normally were. A single light, high in the ceiling, shot a beam down and touched everyone on the forehead. Four small white tokens dropped onto the rug in the centre of the token circle.

"Look!" Trethia pointed to the cave opening.

Dashlan stood there, but a very different Dashlan.

I could see the wall behind him through the flowing robe he wore. As we watched, a small white token appeared on his forehead.

I glanced down, only three remained in the circle.

Dashlan smiled, bowed, and slowly faded away.

"What—what was that about?" Arbreu asked.

"One of the tokens was for Dashlan," Kirym said.

"And the others? Who are they for?"

Kirym studied them. "This one is for Ashistar." She handed it over. "Oak, this is yours, and the third is for Trethia. Are there any spare token holders in the pack?"

"Always," Mekrar said. She delved into one of the packs and handed a holder each to Ashistar and me. Kirym helped Trethia adjust hers and placed the token into it.

I placed the holder on my forehead. It felt strange, but when I pushed the token into it, it felt as if I had worn it forever. The token was warm against my forehead although in my hand it had felt cold. I felt as if I had absorbed it, although possibly it absorbed me.

Trethia clicked Kirym's token first, then she came to click mine. Next, she touched hers to Faltryn's token mark, then she went to Mekrar, Sundas, Ashistar, and Arbreu. By then I was pressing mine to Kirym's and continued around the circle of my friends.

Ashistar followed me to Kirym, turned to Mekrar, Arbreu, Sundas, me and then Trethia.

I was intrigued that with each of the connections, my token changed just a little. I saw each person differently. But when I picked up the wee dragon and clicked my token to hers, my token changed a lot. I took a moment to analyse it. Some of the connections, Kirym, Trethia, Sundas, and Faltryn, had more impact than others. I wondered why. My token felt strange but familiar. I felt different, and I knew I never wanted to be without my token again.

As Kirym packed away the large tokens, I glanced at the small token Trethia wore. The white centre had a black band around the edge. It was quite different to all others I'd seen. Ashistar's had a green inclusion with a small dot of yellow in the centre, and although I had seen inclusions before, I had never seen them in quite the way I did now.

"When will we link to Dashlan's token?" Trethia asked.

"Think about connecting your token to his now. When we see him again, we will already have the connection, but it will then strengthen," Kirym said. She leaned over to me. "Yours is half green, half blue, with a white band across the centre, and a small black inclusion."

Arbreu looked unhappy. "Dashlan's become the gatekeeper. That means he'll stay here when we leave. How do I tell Ma and Pa? They left him in my care."

"They didn't, you know," Ashistar said. "You volunteered to care for him. Dash is old enough to make his own decisions—they know that. Anyway, clothes mean nothing. It comes down to what's in his heart."

Kirym nodded. "He's right. Jeresaya and Bryn will accept whatever decision Dashlan makes. Blue told the grey gatekeeper he could do more, but even if Dashlan does stay, there's no reason he couldn't visit us, and we him, I guess. If it's meant to happen, it will."

"The gatekeeper told you they couldn't leave here," Arbreu said.

"I'm not sure I'm ready to believe anything yet." Kirym paused, then picked up her pack. "Come on. Let's go."

We continued along the tunnel. After a while, the path began to slope downwards. There were more caves on each side of the tunnel and a lot more corners. It slowed us down and was a lot more tiring. We shared the lead. Whoever was in front checked each corner and cave we came to, knowing if there was someone there, they would have already seen the light we carried. However, we met no one.

We spent the night in another cave and continued through the next day.

It was late afternoon, by Ashistar's reckoning, when my token throbbed. Kirym was leading us—her tokens glowed red!

Around me, I heard the hiss of swords and knives as they were unsheathed. Sundas extinguished the lamp and Kirym's token faded. It took time to adjust our eyes to the darkness.

Far ahead a faint light reflected on the wall, allowing us to see each other indistinctly. Kirym grasped her knife, pointed to Ashistar and me and beckoned us to follow her.

I glanced behind. Mekrar stood at point watching us.

Arbreu was behind and to her left, against the wall and watching both directions. Sundas, with a small bulge in his tunic where Faltryn lay, was to Mekrar's right. He too stood against the wall, watching the way we had come. All had their weapons drawn.

Trethia, her bow and arrow in her hand, stood behind and slightly to Mekrar's left. She watched us as we walked away.

Kirym peered around the corner, nodded shortly and we followed her. Now the light was stronger, but there was another corner between us and it.

We spanned out across the tunnel, Kirym a step ahead of Ashistar and me.

Halfway down on the left was an opening, possibly a cave, but it could equally have been another tunnel or just a deep indent in the wall.

Kirym watched and listened carefully before moving forward. Just short of the opening, she paused, and after listening again, peered around the corner.

34

Kirym Speaks

The cave felt unused. I opened the lamp a little and played it around the open area. It was big and empty except for a large statue to my left. The implication of the statue was huge, but I had no time to think about it yet. I handed the shuttered lamp to Ashistar, walked quickly down to the next corner in the tunnel, and peered around.

Ashistar had been right, it was late afternoon, I could see the sky and a hill beyond the entrance. But this wasn't the time to go further because in the centre of the entrance lay a large dragon. It faced away from me and the cave entrance was so narrow, no one could get past without disturbing it, if it was alive.

I watched for a long time and eventually saw its tail twitch. *Why here of all places? And where do its loyalties lie?*

I returned to Oak and Ashistar who waited on the far side of the cave and asked Ashistar to get the others. "Warn them to be very quiet, we don't want to alert the dragon."

The packs were placed together opposite the entrance the statue's tunnel; weapons were checked and laid ready to grab if needed.

Sundas still held Trethia and Faltryn; he wouldn't put them down until he knew everything was safe. That decision was his alone, and I knew Trethia would be quietly discussing it with him, or perhaps arguing if she felt he was being too cautious.

I turned my attention to the statue. He stood much taller than me, was slender, handsome, and looked intelligent. Very life-like.

I was intrigued by his face; the lines were fine and chiselled. He wore a hood with a short cape; a thick plait dangled over his shoulder. His left arm hung at his side, his right held up near his face, palm out.

Parts of the statue were covered with a growth I had never seen before, a small dry-looking spiny plant. One sat in the centre of his palm; a couple on his shoulder, others dotted around. One protruded from his eye. I wanted to wipe it off. The face was so lifelike, the growth gave the impression of blinding the statue.

A tiny movement caught my peripheral vision. I snapped my hand up to sit in front of my eyes, just in time, as something touched my hand. I heard the hiss of a knife being pulled from its scabbard from behind me.

"No weapons!" I commanded, and at the same moment, something twined around my neck.

Whatever hit my palm moved up, and numerous tiny eyes peered over my hand.

"Are you sure, Kirym?" Oak asked.

"Yes." I moved my hand aside to get a good look at the creature.

It pulled back a bit and looked at me in the same way I studied it. They came from the growths I had been examining. The long spikes were made up of hundreds of smaller prongs, each ending in an eye. Each eye moved independently. Despite growing in length, it didn't get thinner.

They twined around my fingers, my neck, down my back and at the same time a few of them crawled up my left sleeve. Some were crawling through my hair, into my ears, and around my tokens.

The one up my sleeve slowly lengthened as I eased my arm downwards. They seemed to be harmless but were very inquisitive.

"What are you?" I asked.

"They are eyes." The voice was rusty from lack of use.

I was aware of the others staring around the cave. They had no idea where the voice came from, neither had I, for that matter. The statue was still a statue, and nothing else in the room moved except the plant-like eyes, which continued to study me from all angles.

"I asked what you were. I know they're eyes." The eye that had crawled up my sleeve reached my shoulder, and moments later peered from the neckline of my dress. It quickly withdrew and joined its friends staring at my face and head. The one that had crawled down my back, touched my waistband and was also returning, another three studied the baldric. Those around my neck were still holding me gently, but firmly. Some of those pulling back towards the statue, suddenly puffed up to the thickness of my wrist. It was the strangest creature I had ever seen.

They pulled back, thin again, still watching, but no longer quite as close to me.

"Why are you here?" the voice asked.

"Come and talk to us," I said. "We mean you no harm,

and it's nicer when we can see each other."

For a long moment, there was silence. I heard a soft noise behind me and looked around. There was nothing there, but when I turned back, a second statue stood alongside the first. It took a lot of willpower not to flinch.

He stood as still as the statue and looked almost identical, except his colouring was similar to ours while the statue was of the blue rock of this land.

He was as tall as Oak, and I had the distinct impression I knew him—his face looked familiar—I wondered if he was related to the gatekeepers, although his clothing was quite different. Then again, he could have come from any of the families in The Green Valley.

There were differences, his plait was longer, the hood was a slightly different cut, and he had none of the eyes growing on him.

He was dressed as the statue had been. His clothing, under the dark green hooded cloak, was simple. His brown trousers, side-laced to his knee with cord, were covered by a light-green knee-length tabard. A similar cord fastened his sleeves from elbow to wrist.

He put his hands together and bowed. The movement was remarkably similar to that made by Dashlan when he was given his token.

"The outside world always looks different in reality." He studied each of us; a thoughtful investigation that, I felt, told him an awful lot.

"I am Tilysh. Why are you here? What do you want?"

I explained who we were and where we came from. "I want to know why there is so much death in Halavash, and what can stop it."

He didn't answer, and the silence lengthened.

Trethia squirmed out of Sundas' arms and came to stand beside me. "Everything here is unhappy. We want to help.

Dashlan is repairing the gate, Kirym woke the dragons, and Ubree is leading them to destroy the firebugs. What was your place here? Why are you hiding?"

Tilysh glanced down at her but directed his response to me. "You woke the dragons?"

I nodded.

"We, my people, came here to facilitate peace," he said, "and hopefully be allowed to settle. But everything here was angry, and the dragons encouraged everyone to fight. We finally convinced the dragons to meet and talk, but the dominant group wanted war, and they wouldn't explain why they held that as a goal. When we refused to leave, they gave us a shallow scrape off a windy tunnel to stay in. It was most uncomfortable."

"How did you end up here?" Sundas asked.

"When we could, we spoke to the dragons of peace, and when we couldn't, we carefully extended and enlarged the scrape, and eventually broke through to a room. We used it and were grateful for the protection it gave us. One morning we found the entrance to the scrape had been blocked. We didn't know what to think and called for the dragons. When we were sure they did not intend to release us, we explored and eventually found a door with a tunnel beyond it. We followed it and when we finally found an exit," he shook his head sadly, "there was no war, and that was good, but there was also no heart. No—" he paused. "Well, no anything. We called for an accounting, but nobody came. We looked for the dragons, but they had disappeared. We explored the tunnels found this cave, set up a base and decided to send searchers out into the land. Initially, they returned to update us, but as time passed, they stopped returning. Now, they have disappeared. I suspect they are dying or dead. I cannot go to check on them, if I leave here and am killed, there is no way for anyone to return."

"Where do you come from?" Sundas asked.

"We were wanderers looking for a place to settle. We approached the Guardians, and they were the ones to suggest we broker peace here in return for a home."

I wondered if the Guardians he spoke if were the same Guardians who had guided The Green Valley in the past. If they were, I had a huge responsibility to this man, his family, and all those who lived in this land.

I thought over the implications of what I had heard. "It adds another level to the mystery of the issues on Halavash."

"But it doesn't really help us much, does it Kirym? What do we do now?" Sundas asked.

"Change guards. Ashistar can you watch the passage, check the dragon occasionally. The rest of you, relax. We can't stay here forever so I will soon need to decide on how to approach the dragon."

Trethia asked Tilysh many questions. He answered her readily, and we all watched and listened.

"What will you do now, Kirym?" Oak asked quietly.

"I need more information. I must read the scroll."

He frowned. "Scroll?"

"I found it with the supplies back in the room where we were given the white token."

"Oh, do you want another lamp?"

"Yes, please." I pulled my pack over, found the scroll, and made myself comfortable on a folded rug. I pulled the lamp close, trimmed the wick, and began to unroll the scroll cylinder.

"Oh, you've found the Halavash history. Where was it?"

I looked up.

Tilysh still stared at the scroll. "It disappeared long ago. I never knew where it went."

"I didn't realise it was yours. Please—" I handed it to him.

"No, no, no. The dragons held it, and although they read us parts, we were never permitted to view it. Later when I found it, I read it. By then, the dragons had gone. I placed it with some other scrolls. Later I searched for it but couldn't find it. Where was it?"

I explained our time with the dragons and where I found the scroll.

Tilysh nodded. "Their treatment of us was the same. Why did you bring the scroll with you?"

"Knowledge is power. We have less chance of successfully helping those on Halavash if we don't understand what happened here over time. This," I indicated the scroll, "may tell us something."

"You really want to help?"

"We wouldn't be here if we didn't. People generally ask for help as a last resort, and I think whoever asked was desperate."

"If it's really your desire, I would not approach the dragon out there. He received his instructions from Dax. You will be returned to a prison of some sort, and it will be more secure than the last."

"So how do we get out of here?" Sundas asked. "Do other tunnels lead…"

"There are five others, and all are guarded by those loyal to Dax. Dax was instrumental in our imprisonment. He was claiming leadership when we arrived."

"Why do you say claiming leadership?" I asked.

"Because he wasn't entitled to it. The Arqha family were the leaders. Soon after the birth of the reborns, those of the Arqha family began to disappear. The reborns were accused, but they were far too young to have been involved."

I nodded; a few things were beginning to make sense. "Who was entitled to lead, if the Arqha disappeared?"

"The family tree would have told them, but it too disappeared. That caused lots of arguments."

"We can consider that later," I said. "Now, how do we leave here?"

Tilysh was silent for a few long moments, then he nodded as if he had made a decision. "There is a way. I have a place where you can read your scroll in comfort and make a proper assessment. Then we can discuss what to do next."

"We?" Oak asked.

"Oh yes. If you can solve the problems, then I want to be part of it. I want to know what happened to the rest of my family. I want to gather together those who still live, perhaps find them a home if the Guardians will allow me to. They wished us to help here, and if we can sort out the problems, then maybe I can face them with my head held high. I will be interested in your assessment of the dragon history. So," he stood, "please follow me. It's not far and there's room there for all of you."

"That's a generous offer. Thank you, we'd be honoured." I glanced around.

Already, the rugs were being placed into the packs. As with any stop we made, we were always ready to leave in moments, in case danger threated.

Oak picked Trethia up, Sundas still held Faltryn.

"You feel no danger here?" Mekrar asked quietly.

"None at all," I said.

I followed Tilysh to the wall where I had first seen him and watched as he leaned forward, melted into the stones, and was gone.

"Kirym, this is creepy," Arbreu said. "We can't do that. It's solid stone."

"If we can't, we will know soon enough, and we'll call

Tilysh back. But let's try it." I copied Tilysh's stance and leaned forward. The wall melted away.

A tunnel stretched out ahead of me, different to the others we had walked down. This was hewn from rough stone, more like those in The Rock, where Churnyg and Ashistar came from, whereas the other tunnels had been much smoother.

I glanced back to where I had been. Behind me, the wall was rock, but I could see through it to where my friends stood.

Moments later, Oak and Trethia stepped through.

Oak's face glowing with awe. "Oh, my goodness, that was unbelievable. It's as if it wasn't there."

We all stepped away from the wall as Mekrar and Arbreu stepped through. They were followed by the others, Ashistar, coming last.

"Where's Tilysh?" Ashistar asked. "Why didn't he wait?"

"If I had visitors for the first time after hundreds of moons, I think I would want to look at my place with new eyes, and perhaps move a few things around or put them away," Mekrar said.

Sundas laughed. "It's not as if we can get lost, Arb. One path only, and it's lighted. We've spent a lot of time in the dark, so let's make the most of it.

35

Kirym Speaks

To begin with the tunnel was blue, much as I would expect the rock of Halavash to be, however, as we moved along, it changed. It wasn't just the colour; I felt the rock itself had changed.

Many colours washed over the rock, and soon they began to show us scenes. Trees, sand-swimmers, although they were not in the sand, aqua dragons of all different kinds, along with many other creatures.

Trethia pointed to one dragon. "Look, it's Ubree. He was here once before, just like he said."

She was right, and before long, we identified the other dragons. Iryndal was the hardest to find, she was sitting amongst a pile of rocks.

We continued down the tunnel, turned a corner and then we were there. Tilysh, who had been standing at a short bench with his back to us, turned, bowed and gestured us to enter.

The cave, dwelling, or room was a visual feast. There was so much to look at, so much to take in. It was a huge open area with smaller rooms leading off to the sides.

I stepped across the threshold and felt a wave of warmth wash over me. This was so different to the other caves we had been in.

I studied the room as I unpinned my cloak.

Within the large space, areas were set up for different activities, sitting, studying, reading—there were a lot of books and scrolls—and eating.

The end wall was different, straight, divided into similar size sections, and each with a different picture on it. I wanted a close look at them and hoped I would get the opportunity. Curtains appeared to grow out of the cave ceiling, falling partway down the walls.

Tilysh showed us where to leave our packs. Mekrar raised an eyebrow when I added the baldric to the pile. "Are you sure?"

I smiled. "He needn't have invited us here, but mainly, Faltryn likes him."

"Oh, you're right."

Faltryn who had climbed from Sundas' tunic and walked over to our host. She sat on the ground in front of him. Tilysh hunkered down and touched his hand to her forehead.

After a short time, he stood. "I've never seen such a small dragon. She makes your coming most special."

We settled in a comfortable area to the right of the entrance. The seats were the softest I had ever sat on. I opened the scroll and spread out the first section. Their writing was a little different to ours but similar enough for me to understand.

Trethia came and snuggled close to me. "Can you read it to me?"

"Perhaps Kirym wishes to read it privately, darling,"

Mekrar said.

Tilysh smiled. "I have many other things to do, so read your scroll to your friends." He turned to walk away.

I called him back. "You may be able to enlighten us further. This scroll belongs here, as do you. We have no secrets."

He smiled and turned back. "Allow me to offer a meal first. I usually eat at this time."

The meal he prepared was different to anything we had ever seen or tasted. Made up of small bite-sized parcels of various colours. The blue, green, and purple parcels, were savoury, while orange, red, and yellow, were sweet. It was one of the most exciting meals I had ever eaten. Each small mouthful was different, all were tasty.

The liquids were also diverse colours and Tilysh made a special drink for each of us. Mine was a sweet and sour fruit juice, well diluted with water, and perfectly suiting my taste.

Oak explained his, more savoury, and rather rich. From the comments, everyone had something that suited them.

Finally, I pulled the scroll to me and settled back. The light brightened, perfect for reading. It was almost as if the light, wherever it came from, knew what we needed and obliged.

The scroll was made of a beaten material. At a casual glance, I would have said it was dragon skin for the similar colours and appearance, but it was definitely a fibre. The words were uneven and gave me the impression of being written quickly and with little care. The surface felt rough and was deteriorating along the edges.

The scroll hadn't been made with the care I had seen in other histories. It was in the cloth bag, but the scroll was in such bad condition, I didn't think it had ever had the protection of a container. The same writing instrument had been used throughout, the same ink, and I felt it was written by one hand only.

"But could it be a copy of the original?" Mekrar asked, when I explained my thoughts.

"We were told it was the original and only copy of the Halavash history," Tilysh said. He busied himself collecting platters together and taking them to the bench where he had prepared the meal.

Trethia snuggled close to me as she did when I told her stories, and I began to read.

The rollers were wooden, the scroll rods were dry, one had split. The first words were;

The Official written History of Halavash

Our peaceful existence has been upset by the arrival of the Fhelian.

Although they looked unlike any creature we had ever sighted before and were ugly beyond belief, we welcomed them, made them part of us. we tried to teach them who and what we were.

Once they realised we wanted to be friends, they changed their form to mirror ours, although they had different colours. Their initial overtures of peace were quickly shown to be false when there were a number of attacks on the weakest of our kind. However, many of the dead were the hatchlings of the Argha family.

we mourned with the parents, and approached the Fhelian, to ensure it wouldn't happen again. when challenged, the Fhelian denied involvement, but when that was proven to be untrue, they claimed they had been attacked by those they killed.

Their scribbled plans for the future, which they carelessly dropped, showed their desire to kill us all, that whatever else they claimed to be, they were in fact, dragon eaters. when we showed them the document, they claimed that someone was trying to create problems between our families. we found them unwilling to agree on a behaviour plan and as the talks deteriorated they declared war.

still we tried but as easy as we made it for them they were either unable or incapable of agreeing to anything. Nor could they change although we worked hard to show them what a life of peace was like.

Eventually having been told it was our beautiful land they wanted we made preparations to leave. we were sure there must be a new place we could go to. Many of our adventurers had gone out from our land and returned talking of the welcome they had received from other lands. we planned to follow them.

somehow the Fhelian discovered our plans and raced to the portal-gate and broke it into pieces. some of them left to wreak havoc on those other lands determined to blame us for their actions.

But now we could not leave and we really feared them. The fighting started and we defended ourselves but they attacked our weakest point our hatchlings.

when an egg we thought to be infertile suddenly broke open and disgorged seven dragons we cheered. Our history spoke of how multiple births occurred to support us when times were hard.

The seven took time to grow so we protected them nurtured them as they matured. when they were of a size to join our fighting groups they led seven armies to challenge and destroy the Fhelian.

This time the Fhelian were reluctant to fight and we watched in horror as our seven approached the enemy and told them of our defensive plans.

we urged them to return to us but they laughed and jeered their colours changed and we realised we had nurtured and raised the first-born of the Fhelian.

understanding that they now knew our future actions we had no choice but to enter our secret places and hibernate until times were better.

Before we did that we searched the land and checked on our unhatched eggs. All were shattered and we had no way of knowing if the eggs had hatched or been destroyed. Our family heads worried that these young were somehow contaminated by the Fhelian.

Occasionally over time we would sneak out from our secret places to see if there was any change. The Fhelian were always there and over time we watched them get fat on the creatures of the land.

Then having overharvested the land they fought each other feasting on those they vanquished and they subsequently began to die out.

Eventually the land was free of them and we ventured out to live again in freedom. But the Fhelian had destroyed it. All they left was a flat barren waste baking in the heat of a massive red sun. We mourned the loss of the creatures we remembered.

Eons passed and we again built our homes but once we had we discovered the Fhelian had left their spawn deep in the dust.

These creatures grew as ugly as their ancestors. But without the previous influences we hoped they could become part of us. If we could teach them what we held dear they could become part of our families and we would all be at peace.

It was not to be. Even when small they showed carnivorous tendencies and one ghastly day we discovered many of the older Fhelian ingesting on the flesh of our hatchlings. Thankfully because they were still young they did not have the thinking capacity to yet attack and kill us.

Using all the strength we had we herded them into a prison and locked them in.

However in the last moments they signed our death warrant. Even as we sealed them in they somehow stole our fire. While they could never escape we were also locked into a prison that would eventually mean our death. Now with no way to protect ourselves we have agreed on returning to our hibernation possibly never to emerge. It matters not the land is dead it will never sustain life again and all we can hope for is that when the land dissolves into nothing it will be painless.

We will die but we know we have left the land safe for those coming after us.

"Wow, how tragic," Arbreu said, as I got to the end of the scroll. "What a history."

"What do you think, Kirym?" Mekrar asked.

"It was interesting," I said, as I rerolled the scroll, "but they didn't really put too much thought into their lies."

"Lies? What do you mean?" Tilysh sat forward, his face stony, but there was something in his eyes—an eager expectancy I hadn't seen in him before.

"It's not well put together. I wonder why they even bothered to write it."

"Explain!"

I watched Tilysh as I gave my reasons. "It's written as a story, a justification for their actions, I suspect. The Fhelian destroyed the gate, evidently making it unusable, but then they left to ravage other communities. There's no mention of the gatekeeper at all. It said the land was a barren waste with a massive red sun. But the suns are normal, and the land is full of ancient growth, trees, insects, animals, birds. Where did they come from?"

"Through the portal, just as we did?" Ashistar asked.

"Why would they come to a land as described in here?" I flicked the scroll. "The dragons wrote of their fire being stolen. How? And why didn't they just get it back? And that's just the tip of it."

Tilysh nodded. "I met one of the Fhelian. She told me a different story; I chronicled it at the time."

"Would you allow me to read it?"

He smiled. "I think it may tell you a lot."

Tilysh disappeared into one of the smaller cave areas behind us. A short time later, he appeared with a box, which he laid on the low table in front of me.

"I've not looked at it for a long time. It is, I think, a true rendition of the tale told me. Whether it is a true story, well perhaps you are wise enough to tell. As I said, I simply copied down what was said."

I opened the lid—it opened as the cover of a book would—but was in fact, a box. Ribbons secured the soft green material which wrapped the oblong content. Tilysh used them to lift it out and lay it beside the box. He slipped the ribbons away. A final flip of the wrappings released the material and placed a pile of coloured sheets in front of me.

I lifted the first and studied it. It was stiff, very thin, almost transparent, and yet not. The top sheet was cerise in colour, the second was dark blue, and each beyond was a different colour. The writing on the cerise was black, on the blue, it was white, and on each other sheet, the writing was a colour easily seen.

"This is different to anything I've seen before, Tilysh. What do you call it?"

"I have no name for it. There is a large store of the sheets here; I use it as needed. As I understand my history, when more is required, someone is born who knows how to make it. Sadly, this may be the last; my people are gone. There will be no more births." He stood and walked away, busying himself at a bench on the far side of the room. Trethia scrambled off the set and followed him.

She spoke quietly to him, and he lifted her onto the bench beside him.

I returned to studying the documents in front of me, knowing the others would watch her carefully and intervene if she appeared to need help.

The first sheet was simply titled;

The Fhelian

I placed it on the material and picked up the second sheet.

"What are you thinking, Kirym," Oak asked quietly.

"It's a copy, and this is not the language it was originally written in."

"Do you think Tilysh is lying?"

"No," I said. "But I'm wondering what made him copy it into a form we could understand."

"Do you trust him?" Sundas asked.

"Yes. Already he has given us a lot of help, and he's put himself at risk by inviting us here." I shrugged. "Anyway, let's see what it says."

When I found the Fhelian, she appeared to be almost at the end of her life. The majestic beast was old beyond belief, but extremely beautiful, despite her age.

No one had visited her for eons. I suspect she didn't realise I was not one of her own. I cooled her brow but could do naught else. To my knowledge, her kind must find their own food, and she had no desire to do so. She was trapped by a slide of rocks, and I wondered if she could break out, had she the desire. Her colours were strange, mottled green and yellow; unusual for this land. I remarked on it, and with a deep sigh, she began to speak.

She had much to say.

I noted what I could as she spoke and enlarged on my notes when she rested.

Her story did not agree with the official history I had previously read. When I questioned her about the history the dragons swore was a true reflection of all that happened, I realised they had lied to me.

"The changes came with the reborns," the Fhelian said, with an inward look of one who has watched the scene a thousand times. "The multiple birth, unknown to my flight, was the first issue. As siblings, they should have been identical to each other and the other members of their family. Indeed, that was the way of identifying families here. These though were coloured in the manner of the gatekeepers. We knew Farynth had laid the egg. Even though she took the seven be hatched in secret, that was the fault of the flight, who sort to destroy the egg because it was different."

"Farynth. It's a pretty name," interrupted Mekrar. "Do

you think the seven mentioned are your seven, Kirym?"

I laughed. "No more mine than ours, but yes, and now we know their mama's name. It has never been mentioned, but it may bring back more memories."

"They looked unlike any dragon in our flight, but initially, we saw enough family markings on them to know they belonged to Farynth and Bogryn.

Hatchlings markings always intensified after birth, whereas these seven lost theirs within days of our meeting the flight. And so, even as hatchlings, they were distrusted and avoided by many who should have cared for them.

I found them interesting. They had a knowledge unusual in their age-group. They were quick to pick up things spoken of. They thought ahead, anticipated actions, and could protect themselves.

Then, however, the youngest died, and sadly, many in the flight rejoiced. To their horror, when his sister and mama sang him their history—usual when a dragon here dies—he woke from death. A short time later he again died, and his sister with him. They too re-lived, and next, three died, then four, five, and six. Finally, the eldest died, and the flight leaders talked happily of this being the beginning of the end of them.

It was not, and when he awoke from his death, although somewhat different in appearance to the dragon he had died as.

The flight was in an uproar.

With much loose talk and stupid speculation, the fear increased exponentially. There was some talk of trying to kill them. A number cautioned against this, for they felt that could unleash forces we could not control. There was panic and much of it originated from a section of our flight leaders.

Meetings were called, and as the arguments raged, the cycle of death and rebirth continued. Finally, our leaders decreed there would be one final meeting where a decision must be made. The arguments continued through the day and into the night, from the long black night and on until the three moons appeared in spring.

At the instigation of a few, talk blossomed at the idea of banishing the seven.

Many opposed the idea. We had always been a family, we needed to stay as one, and together, face the unknown that lay ahead. Four family leaders supported Farynth and Bogryn when they argued that the reborns had done no harm and had been a boon to the flight. The argument was not accepted, and those leaders were ousted from their position, and soon after disappeared.

Stories abounded, each more preposterous than the last. We, who thought caution the best step, were ignored. The gatekeeper was called and the seven were banished. The gate was sealed by the Keeper to ensure they could never return.

Soon after, things again changed.

The dragon flight lost its colour and took on the colour of the dead stones of Karynsh. However, the markings of some from the newest hatching morphed into tones of greenish-yellow.

The flight leaders dubbed these the Fhelian and initially, they were shunned by many. For the hatchlings, it was hard; some were rejected by their parents. Others turned away, often driven by force and intimidation.

Farynth and Bogryn, still bereft at the loss of their own family, took the hatchlings under their wings. They thrived and proved as healthy as any in the flights. As they aged, the young yellow Fhelian took on tones of green. Whether it was the close association, or a quirk of nature, some who cared for the young Fhelian also began to change, taking on the mottled green of the new flight.

I was an anomaly within the anomaly; my mature green was interspersed with yellow. Despite the difference, I was still accepted by the Fhelian.

Instead of needing to learn to breathe fire as the dragon hatchlings did, the Fhelian had the art from birth, however, after exercising their wings on their first flight, their breath changed.

As news of these changes spread; more fear grew. The Fhelian and all who looked like them were forbidden to fly. We were sent to live in the lush flat grasslands of Morutha.

A number of young Fhelian died before we realised groups of dragons were attacking surreptitiously, aiming to kill us off one by one. Our colour was our downfall. In the pink flatlands, our green and yellow was easily spotted.

In the darkness before the spring moons rose, we fled to the sands of Abithka. There we were welcomed by the sand-swimmers. They taught us to float on the surface and to swim beneath the sandy waves. Because our colour was so different to those of the desert, we had to hide carefully, and even under the sands, it was difficult.

Before long, the dragons were actively searching for us and eventually, we were found. The wrath of the dragon flight descended.

I knew the ancient prophecies talked of the reborns being the sign of great change, and these changes were the biggest I had seen. I wanted the reborns called back, and so, when a renewed attack began on the Fhelian, I fled to speak to the gatekeeper.

Initially, he refused to speak to me, saying he only dealt with the dragon flight. However, he could not oust me from his porch. I sang mournfully, and tunelessly I must admit, *of the deaths, of old law, and I kept it up through the whole season.*

Eventually, sick of the noise, he came to see me. I asked him to call the reborns back. He refused, saying the gate was sealed and would never be unsealed.

I objected; he had sealed it, he could reverse it. It was his choice.

He then declared it was his choice—not to. He would never ever consider it because his life was easier with no one using it. No one could enter or exit without his authorisation, he intended to never give consent.

I was appalled, and I continued to sing my mournful history describing the persecution of the Fhelian, but there was no reasoning with him.

Two days later, the gatekeeper disappeared. I searched and sang until the three moons had merged twice. Eventually, he returned and said my request no longer mattered. The The dragons could no longer kill the Fhelian who were now imprisoned. Only the dragons could reverse their imprisonment.

'My problems are over,' he said. 'Now I will have no more issues with any of you. Nothing you do, neither your singing nor your calling will have any effect on me again.'

He turned himself into a rock, and slowly melted into the ground.

I raced back to Abithka to be told by the sand-swimmers that my Fhelian family had been rounded up by a shadow, who, with the help of the dragon flight, had taken them away. The birds took me to Empeat, the mountains to the west. I found the cave where my family were imprisoned and talked to them through the thick ice that sealed the door. They had tried to melt their way out, but their fire failed them. They intended to sleep until something could be done to liberate them, or until death took them.

With their warning that fire made their prison worse, I tried all else I could think of to open their prison from the outside, but as with their attempts, nothing worked.

As each called their goodbyes, I was overcome with grief and fear. My grief was the loss of my family, my fear was of being alone.

I crept back to the dragon's area, wondering how they were celebrating. I heard someone coming along the tunnel, and hid. It was the gatekeeper. He wasn't escorted, but then again, he had spent a lot of time with the dragons over the past moons. Once he had left, I continued my cautious journey.

To my surprise, there were no sentries. Perhaps they were all celebrating.

I reasoned that perhaps they felt the surveillance was no longer needed—although I knew it had never been needed. I crept closer, wondering what they would do if they found me, but decided that the worst would be death, but perhaps they would open the cave and allow me to join my family.

Closer and closer I edged to the area's they normally congregated in, but there was no joyful celebration, and eventually, when I reached the very heart of the fire cave, I discovered what the gatekeeper had done. He had taken the dragon's fire. With no fire, they had no protection. For some reason, rather than rekindle it, they chose to hibernate.

The Gatekeeper's revenge was complete, and now I knew my family was lost forever. The gatekeeper didn't even care that I was still free. I continued to occasionally search for an answer, but no one answered my plea.

I now lie here and wait for death to take me. Then perhaps I will be at peace."

I lay the last sheet on the others and added the back cover.

36

Kirym Speaks

"Interesting," Oak said. "Does it help us?"

I thought about what I had read. "I think it clarifies a few things, although there is so much not said, and those things are important. Without that knowledge..." I shrugged.

"Perhaps Tilysh will know," Oak said. "Maybe there were a few things he didn't note."

Tilysh and Trethia approached carrying a tray with small bites of food, and a jug of fluid.

"Thank you for reading loud enough so Trethia and I could hear. It was the first time I'd heard someone else read it, and it brought back many memories."

"Was there anything more; minor comments the Fhelian made that you didn't note, or perhaps something missed in the translation?"

He shook his head. "No. I was meticulous in my copying. While I visited her many times, she spoke only a few sentences each time. I wrote every word."

Oak shook his head. "It's the words she took with her that are the problem. Why didn't she tell you everything?"

"Perhaps because I didn't ask," Tilysh said. "But then I didn't know what to ask, nor what might be important in the future. I didn't see the point of asking her to be specific. She mentioned Empeat but was no more precise; the mountain range is massive. After my last visit, I knew there would be little point in my visiting her again."

"Why? Why did you stop visiting?" Mekrar asked.

"For a while, I thought she'd died. But eventually, she spoke again. I took her two final words to be a dismissal."

Oak leaned forward, his eyes shining with anticipation. "What were they?"

Tilysh glanced at him and shook his head. "She simply said, 'Goodbye,'."

"Oh, that's sooo sad," Mekrar said. "To not want someone who cares nearby; to die all alone."

"She isn't dead," Trethia said.

"Oh, she must be, by now, little one," Tilysh said gently. "It's been such a long time since I visited her."

"She's not dead," Trethia insisted.

I studied Trethia's face. She seemed to be very sure of it.

"Perhaps it's worth visiting her once again to see. Tilysh, can you take me to her, or perhaps tell me how to get there. Is there any exit not being guarded by a dragon?"

He shook his head. "Five tunnels leave this part of the maze system, and all are guarded, however, there is another way to the Fhelian." He beckoned me to follow him and went to the left edge of the strange wall at the back of the cave.

Once I was close, I realised it was made of the same material the Fhelian's story had been written on. The pictures on the panels were bright, the first I studied was of a misty landscape, with layers of hills drifting into the distance. The second showed a large pool, with water bubbling up in the centre. It looked remarkably like the fountainhead at the beginning of the river that ran along the top of the ridge and into our canyon. The third showed a wide clearing, surrounded by a wall of rock. A large number of dragons lay together near the rock face. I remembered seeing a similar picture in the tunnel leading to the dragon cave, and it gave me something to think about.

Tilysh touched the edge of the first panel; it moved away from the wall. He pushed it, and the line between the first two panels bent so the beginning of the first met the end of the second. One by one, each of the panels folded against its neighbour, until all sat together against the far wall.

As intriguing as this folding wall was, what the wall had hidden took my attention now. A long covered bench ran the length of the area, broken by a set of steps in the middle. Above the bench, the whole wall was covered with different sized circles within circles—web-like—in various shades of cream and green.

The outer area of the whole web structure was pale green, the centre area was almost black. It looked as if a mass of demented spiders had decided to spin their webs together, creating this amazing illusion. It was huge.

Tilysh went to the bench on the right of the steps and removed some of the covers. "This is my secret," he said. "When we found this area, we made a point of studying it. I had an instinctive aptitude for its working."

"What is it?" Sundas asked.

Tilysh shrugged. "I have no name for it, but watch."

Set into the bench in front of him was a large concave bowl. He moved his hands over it, and although he didn't touch it, small lines of flickering light jumped up to his fingers. As he tracked the lights into one small area of the bowl, the circles began to move. They moved around each other as well as around the wall. Some moved forward, some appeared to slip away.

Finally, Tilysh lifted his hands higher, and the light that had been flickering to and from his fingertips, became thicker, until it covered the entire bowl. Then it rushed up past his fingers to settle on the top of his hands. He turned his palms to face each other, and the light shimmered between his palms, still getting thicker until it was a dense cylinder of pulsing light. He clapped his hands, and the light cascaded down into the bowl.

The bowl was now convex.

Again, Tilysh collected the light from around the bowl area and concentrated it onto one sector. One set of circles in the webbed wall began to grow until it filled the whole wall. The dark centre created the illusion of distance.

I glanced back at Tilysh. He slowly lifted his hands and the lights thickened. When his hands were at about the level of his chin, he carefully brought his palms together, effectively trapping the light between his palms. I could see the bones of his hands through his skin. It was weird.

He pointed at the circles in the middle of the wall, opened his middle fingers, and the light streamed into the centre of a small circle. It darkened momentarily and seemed to jump forward—I might have imagined it, maybe I jumped—and then it settled, covering the whole wall.

A strange hum vibrated around the room; I was sure it came from the circles but couldn't see how. The circle in the centre lightened, and there was a flash of other colours.

I stepped closer and stared at the circles. "Oh, my stars, those are the eyes." I swung around to Tilysh. "They are, aren't they? Why are they so big here, and yet so small there?"

37

Arbreu

Tilysh stepped back from the bowl and rubbed his hands. "Yes. This is how I knew you were in the cave. I first saw you in the white cave. It was quite a show, although I didn't really know what to make of the stones dropping from the ceiling, or why you chose to use them as you did."

Kirym stared at him, not speaking. It was one of those silences we all knew not to break. It wasn't easy and would be even harder for Tilysh.

He broke. "I didn't know what to make of you. I wondered if you were looking for me?"

"Why would we look for you?"

Tilysh was still rubbing his hands, although Arbreu thought it was more to do with Kirym's intense scrutiny than the aftermath of working the lights.

"Very occasionally, a group of eyes would stop working. I've never known why. I always assumed we were the only people who knew about them and what they do. Over the last few days, several eyes have disappeared. If someone else who knew what they did, realised how they were being used, that could explain why they disappeared."

"Who would realise, and what would it have to do with us?" Kirym asked.

"The fire-starters and the gatekeeper were the first to come to mind, but I saw a strange green dragon and added it to my list. Then I saw you in the white cave and that had more implications."

"What sort of implications?"

"You could have been aligned to any of those who had done damage to the land. And you were following the tunnels quite accurately. You never veered into the labyrinth of minor tunnels that would take you away from me. You came straight to the statue cave."

"If you hadn't spoken, I would never have known about you. What made you decide to trust us?"

"Two things. I saw a new gatekeeper visit you in the white cave. I was still rather wary, it may have meant nothing, but then I saw him repairing the gate. He's brought colour back, flowers, butterflies, rainbows; even the birds and insects are streaming back there. So, things are changing for the better."

"The second thing?" Kirym asked.

"The eyes liked you. They made that decision. The only other time they did it was when they found the Fhelian."

Kirym nodded. "Was the old gatekeeper helping Dashlan?"

"No, he was in the desert with Dax."

"What was he doing there?" Kirym asked.

Tilysh shrugged. "Arguing."

"Could you hear the argument?" Sundas asked.

"Only bits in passing. Dax said the Fhelian were still trapped and couldn't escape without his help, and that no one else knew where they were. The other three who'd helped imprison the Fhelian had long since died. Later they talked about a new monster. Dax wanted Grey to find it and destroy it. The gatekeeper laughed at him; asked why he should soil his hands to again accommodate Dax. They also talked of trouble at the gate—a new apprentice. Grey demanded Dax help get rid of him. The rest was an argument about who owed who and should the dragons help get rid of the new apprentice if Dax wouldn't help with the monster."

Kirym was quiet for a long time. No one moved, no one spoke. She looked troubled.

"Tilysh, we need to return to the outer cave for a short time. I need to make sure Dashlan has protection."

"What will you do to protect this new gatekeeper?" Tilysh asked. "Are you aligned to them?"

"To Dashlan, but not the gatekeepers in general. Dashlan is just helping to fix the gate to ensure the land is protected. Grey is supposed to be there. Dashlan knows nothing of what's happening here, but I want to call one of the previous gatekeepers and explain."

"Why do you need to return to the cave?"

"To keep you and your home secret. You'll be able to watch. I will tell him nothing other than what is needed to keep Dashlan safe."

"All right, I'll accept that. Will all of you go?"

"Yes. The gatekeepers know who came through the gate with me. If we're not together, they may ask questions."

Tilysh nodded.

"What about Ubree?" Oak asked.

"He can look after himself," she said, with a laugh.

"But we've not heard from him for so long. What if they already—"

"Then they wouldn't still be looking for him, Oak."

"Look!" Trethia pointed to the wall of eyes.

One of the eyes had changed—it expanded until half the wall was one large opaque eye.

Tilysh looked shocked. "What? That's never happened before. What's going on?"

"I don't know," Kirym said, watching intently.

A blue mist appeared in the eye, it got bigger and soon spilled into the cave, swirled and slowly solidified into Blue.

Tilysh stepped between Blue and his guests. "Who are you, and why are you here?"

Blue bowed towards Tilysh and Kirym.

"Forgive my invasion," he said. "It was easier than having you all troupe out to the cave to call me. Tilysh, I have always been aware you were here, and I've always watched over you. I care for the land; you are part of this land." He turned again to Kirym. "Orange is helping Dashlan. She will protect him. The gate is becoming secure, Dashlan is doing well. He wishes to make it look attractive. If you desire him here, I will bring him, but he is as safe there as he would be with you."

"Leave him to finish the job he is doing," Kirym said. "He would worry if he hadn't attained the result he is aiming for."

"If you care for the land," interrupted Tilysh, "what happened to the eyes that have disappeared?"

"Not everything lives the life we desire for them, Tilysh. Your care has helped them, but some have been caught up in the fires in the south-east. Three groups of eyes are on rocks and were submerged when a river changed course. Eventually, they will return, but they wait for nature. Two groups simply gave in to age. Some do, some don't."

"How do you know about me?"

Blue smiled gently. "Initially the Observers, you call them eyes, told me. They liked you and showed me where you and your people were imprisoned by the dragons. They wanted you to escape. I guided you here and helped you to learn how to use the Observers. It was easier for me if you worked with them. Other things needed my assistance."

Tilysh nodded. "Why didn't you come to me sooner?"

"Because you were rightly suspicious of others. Lack of trust is not a good beginning to a friendship. Now you know of me, I will visit often, if I am allowed."

"It would be my pleasure."

"Blue, in caring for the land and the creatures, why do you allow the trees to stay apart?" Kirym asked.

"I assist and encourage. I cannot force. It was their decision, and although I advised against it, I was ignored."

"Who leads the dragons? Dax or Zillib?"

"Officially Zillib, but Dax is trying to eliminate him. A few dragons have defaulted on their vows and joined Dax in his plans. Zillib and his followers are in hiding. They're safe as long as they don't move for now. Ubree is caring for them."

Kirym nodded. "What overall influence does Grey have?"

"He no longer keeps the gate, but he is still resident in the land, and he still has the abilities he has always had."

"Is Dashlan now the gatekeeper?" Arbreu asked.

"Why do you fear that, Arbreu?" Blue paused and studied Arbreu closely. "Dashlan cannot take the place you left open when you left your family. Everyone has their own path to walk. However, no, Dashlan has not had enough training to become a gatekeeper, and he has not said he wants to. He may—or may not—take that position in the future, but right now, he is assisting other ancient carers of the land to ensure our gate area is all we wish it to be."

Blue switched his attention to everyone. "Now, I believe you are off to meet the Fhelian. What happens there will make a difference in the future of the planet. Kirym, go alone. Alone, she may respond to you. You must get her to return here with you."

"All is ready," Tilysh said.

"Go?" gasped Arbreu. "What do you mean, go?"

"The only way to find out if the Fhelian will help us is to go and convince her too," Kirym said.

"I don't like this, Kirym," Ashistar said. "We shouldn't split up."

"The journey is safe enough, Tilysh has done it before."

"But what if the Fhelian doesn't want you there?" Arbreu asked. "What if this is just a—?"

"I'll come straight back. I will be safe," Kirym said.

"Fhelian are peaceful creatures, Arbreu," Tilysh said.

"What will I need, Tilysh?"

"Take a cloak and rugs. The rock chills if sat on for extended periods. You won't need any weapons."

He handed Kirym a pack of food and a flask. "I have no advice to offer except to be patient. If you run out of food, you must return."

"Can I bring her back through the eye?" Kirym asked.

"Yes, although she has never accepted my invitation in the past."

"But then, she had no hope and wanted to die. I plan to change that."

"Where's Blue?" Arbreu asked.

Kirym glanced around. "He has returned to watching the land."

38

Arbreu

Arbreu wished he was going with Kirym, but he knew he would also want to take a knife.

Kirym stood in front of the eye and studied it carefully. She wore the crown she had been given when she found the ancient weapons.

Arbreu knew she valued it more than the great sword and shield. He wondered what knowledge she had about it. It seemed a frivolous thing to wear, and yet, she wore it frequently.

"What now?" Kirym asked.

Tilysh moved up to the bowl again. "Stand on the top step." Kirym did so. He placed his finger in the middle of the bowl and stroked it towards the outside edge. "Concentrate on the Fhelian and merge with the web."

Kirym took a step and the web seemed to swallow her. She glided away from them, paused for a moment, turned back and waved. She was smiling.

Arbreu felt empty. He remembered Teemas comment about her, that she so often trusted people she didn't know, and one day, one would turn on her. *Will the Fhelian be the one to hurt her? I wish Teema was here. I'd have someone to talk to.*

He reddened slightly when he realised he could equally speak to Mekrar, Sundas, or Ashistar. Any of them would give him a far more balanced view of the burdens he felt.

Kirym looked very small now, but she was moving off to the right.

"Tilysh, she's going off the path. Can you warn her?"

"She follows the path truly, Arbreu. The path we see is an illusion. All paths curve to a greater or lesser degree. They need to, they curve with the land and lead to different places. Some turn quite sharply as soon as you enter."

"That makes sense," Sundas said.

Kirym stopped moving.

"What's wrong?" Arbreu asked.

"She has reached a junction web," Tilysh said. "She must work out how to pass it, or she must return."

"What sort of junction? Could it hurt her?" Ashistar asked.

Tilysh shook his head. "It's just part of the web. I'll show you." He moved his hands over the bowl, and the entrance into the tunnel shimmered.

It looked like the surface of a bubble caught in the sunlight. Fine lines appeared, initially net-like, but they pulsed and thickened.

Everyone crowded around to study it. The main strands were thick. They glistened as if covered by morning dew. Between them were smaller strands, and Arbreu had the impression of webs within webs; of hundreds of spiders of all sizes, busily weaving strand after strand until it was almost a solid wall.

"A spider's web. Could one that big hurt Kirym?" he asked. "Some eat—"

"It's not made by a spider," Trethia said. "It's just a web."

Arbreu carefully touched it, almost expecting it to be sticky, but the strand flexed slightly and held, first a small push, and then his entire weight, as he leaned against it with both hands.

"She'll never get through it," he said, relieved. "I doubt even Sundas could." He looked up and gasped. Kirym had disappeared. "What—where is she?"

Trethia touched his hand. "She discovered how to pass it. Everyone can." Suddenly, Trethia was on the far side of the web.

Arbreu tried to grab her, but the web was solid, more like a wall than a web.

He gasped. "Blue said only Kirym could approach the Fhelian."

"The eye isn't open to us. This single web is here so we can understand what Kirym faces," Trethia said, patiently.

Again, Arbreu put his weight on the web, but it held firm. Then Mekrar was beside Trethia, and moments later they were at his side again.

Trethia slipped through to the other side again.

"Close your eyes," Mekrar said, "and imagine the opening is clear."

"Like this," Trethia said. She leaned her forehead against the web and was standing beside him as if the web wasn't even there.

Arbreu took a deep breath and copied her.

"Just lean forward," Mekrar said.

Arbreu did as ordered.

Trethia laughed. "Open your eyes."

Arbreu was shocked. He stood on the tunnel side of the web. He pushed back against the web but was held fast.

"You have to forget it's there," Sundas said, as he stepped through to stand by him. "That's why it can work when your eyes are closed. It's simple when you know. Once you accept it, it's easy even when you can see the web."

39

Kirym Speaks

I thought about how I walked through the wall of the statue cave when we followed Tilysh. I leaned into the web and took a step. It felt as if I was being catapulted forwards. Another web and another pause. It was a strange feeling. I needed to take a step to pass through each web, but between them, my movement just happened. Before I could think about where I was going, I came to an abrupt halt at the edge of a brilliant green and yellow cave.

The walls were reflective; I could see hundreds of me looking back from various angles. It appeared to be otherwise, empty. I glanced around, distracted by my movements. I had the impression of something else there, but it was elusive. Finally, I stopped trying to see it, concentrated on the centre of the cave and thought about what I knew of the Fhelian. Green and yellow.

A shape came into focus, disappeared, reappeared, and this time it stayed put.

I took a few moments to bring it into some sort of perspective. The reflective nature of the cave made it hard to see her properly. Her tail was wrapped around her body, her head on the far side of the cave. Her colours reflected in the walls and she was so bright, I understood why they were hunted down so easily.

I walked around the edge of the cave, until I reached her head, chose a spot, and spread the rugs. I sat and studied the massive face. She was beautiful. She lay very still and could have been dead, although I felt there was an energy in her body that wouldn't be there if she was.

It was hard to know where to begin. I had to get her to speak to me, and I wanted it to happen quickly.

I took a deep breath and began.

"My name is Kirym. I need your help to save the creatures of this land."

There was no response, no movement at all. I supposed it was too much to expect one sentence to rouse her into action, or even give me a response. The drawn-out silence became overwhelming. It was not going to encourage her to speak. I needed to offer her more.

"More importantly, I want to free the other Fhelian."

She moved. It was slow and subtle, but her body became more alive. Eventually, she lifted her head and turned to look at me.

"What could an insect like you do to overcome our enemies and free my family?"

"Nothing, without your help."

She looked almost amused. "What is the point? The dragons will just round us up again, and they'll make sure I'm with them. Unless they decide to kill me first."

"Dax is too busy trying to regain his position. Even if he does manage to, he doesn't know you still live."

"If the Fhelian are released, what's to stop Dax from re-imprisoning us?" I was pleased she was at least talking to me.

"He won't have the help he had then. He lied to his flight and they now know that. They feel he overstepped his position. They now understand that he could easily treat them the same way he treated you and the other Fhelian."

"But would they support us against him, even if we did again approach them?"

"I can't make that promise, but if there is even a hint of antagonism towards you, the people from the land of Athesha would welcome you there." I paused. "Bogryn and Farynth have the right to see their children who live there, but it can't happen unless they are released."

The Fhelian stared at me. "The seven are dead. Dax said the people in the world they went to, hated any connection to us, and killed them on sight."

I laughed. "So how would Dax know what happened on Athesha?"

"The gatekeeper told him."

"And yet Grey told me he wasn't allowed to leave this land, so we can agree he lies. Anyway, Grey is no longer the gatekeeper. The seven reborns live happily on Athesha, although two are here with me."

"So, you think you can quell the anger of hundreds of dragons and all of the other things out there that would kill us?"

"I haven't come alone, and there are others who will help," I said.

"The reborns live on Athesha?"

"Yes."

"They're slaves?" she asked.

"No. They are part of our family."

"I see no reason yet, to do as you bid. I've heard too many lies over the eons."

"Tilysh told me how to find you, and I came through the Observers, the eyes, with Blue's blessing."

"They both knew I wanted to be left alone. I intend to stay here until I die. Leave me be."

She sank down again, into the position she had been in when I arrived.

"So, your family will die because you want to be left alone. You're as bad as Dax and his cronies. Perhaps I am wasting my time here. I'll find your family without you. The eyes can guide me as far as they're able; then I'll ask the birds and keep searching." I stood, picked up the rug and started to fold it.

"You'll never find them, and you'll die while looking."

"At least I'd have tried," I said. "There are threats to everyone on Halavash. Vashetha has requested refuge on Athesha for those who wish to leave. If everyone dies or leaves, no one will be able to help your family. They would be welcome on Athesha."

"With everyone gone my family will be in peace where they are."

"Really? Dax will stay. Owning Fhelian slaves would be the incentive for his followers to remain with him. The gate would be locked, the ancient gatekeepers will come with us to Athesha."

She growled deep in the back of her throat. "Your arguments are compelling, but do you actually have a plan?"

"First, we return to Tilysh. We need your knowledge before we can finalise our plans." I pushed the rug into my pack. "You weren't always known as The Fhelian, and to me, it doesn't seem right to dismiss you in that way. What is your name?"

She was quiet for a few moments. "It's a long time since I was asked. I'd almost forgotten. I'm Shalinba."

"That's beautiful. Why did you stop using it?"

"We were collectively called Fhelian. I imagine they insisted on it to remove our personal identity. It made it easier for them to destroy us. I accepted their maxim when I realised they had won."

The journey back to Tilysh's quarters took longer. I was tired, I was sure I had now missed another night of sleep. We were taken on a different route with even more webs to go through.

Shalinba followed me. She didn't seem to notice the webs at all, although I had to consciously step through each one.

I paused before stepping through the last membrane. My companions rose from their sleep—something must have alerted them to our arrival. I took this time to study Shalinba because now I was finally able to see her in detail. She was big, not as big as Ubree, but bigger than Arymda. She looked noble. Her body was more worm than dragon, although her legs were like Ubree's. Rather than the disc-shaped scales I was used to, she had fine lines running the length of her body, interspersed with vertical ridges. Her head was different, finer, a more pointed muzzle, delicate eye ridges, and fanned webbing from her jaw and up around the crown of her head.

We stepped through the last web. Shalinba bowed her head to Tilysh when I introduced her by name, but her attention went straight to Faltryn. The two approached each other, touched noses, and stared at each other for a time.

"You said you had reborns back here, but there is a strange difference about this one. I don't see how such an immature creature can help in any plan you might have."

"You will be surprised at what reborns can do. Faltryn may be small, but her oldest brother Ubree, is very capable."

"And a lot bigger," Oak said.

"I've said I will get your family from their prison and I will. However, to do so, we must first go to where they are. How do we do that?"

"I could carry you, but Dax's dragons will see me as soon as I leave the caves. They'll capture me long before we get to our destination."

"Yes, all the tunnel entrances are guarded," Tilysh said. "The eyes will take you, but it rather depends on where you wish to go. Some areas have few eyes."

"Could you get us to Vashmilla?"

Tilysh shook his head. "She lives in her daughters, but as she was, she is no more. She stood fast in defiance of the fires, while her daughters escaped. The eyes she protected went far to the south and are only now beginning to rebuild their antennae back to me."

Shalinba looked bereft. "She was a noble tree; I would have expected little else from her. How close to her memory can we safely go?"

"To the river by Magdesh bend."

"Too far to the west. I need to be on the southern face of the Empeat mountains."

"There is a shallow cave opposite Chagolt," Tilysh said. "It's disguised but Dax doesn't know about the tunnel behind it. Between it and Chagolt is a barren wasteland. It's a little boggy in places, but it should be easy to cross. Exposed though."

"It matters not. We'd cross it as evening approaches and be on the mountain before full dark. But what can you do, Kirym, that I couldn't?"

"You'll see when we get there. How many of us can go through the eye, Tilysh?"

"The filament is fairly new, so resilient. You and Shalinba. Are there any others who must be with you?"

I glanced at the group around me. "I need Trethia. How many more can I take?"

"Two."

"I'll go." Oak spoke first, but only moments before the others.

I thought about who would be most useful in the circumstances. "I'll take Oak, and Mekrar. I know the rest of you would love to be with me, but Oak is familiar with ice and snow, and his knowledge could be vital."

There was argument, but it was half-hearted. They knew I would not change my mind, and Sundas at least saw the sense of my reasoning.

"What should we do if we're attacked, Tilysh?" Oak asked.

"Fight!"

"How, if we have no weapons?"

Tilysh stared at him. "Why wouldn't you carry weapons?"

"Because you said," he paused. "You wouldn't let Kirym take even a knife—"

His comment was drowned by Tilysh's laughter; the first time he had really relaxed with us.

"I was thinking of Shalinba. A weapon may have made her feel uncomfortable."

"If you thought one little knife would make me feel threatened, then you truly underestimated me," Shalinba said.

"Truthfully," Tilysh said, his face red, "I thought if you detected a weapon, you may be desperate enough to attack Kirym, and force her to take your life."

Mekrar and Sundas helped me gather together the things we needed, Oak sorted them into packs for each of us. I decided to sacrifice a rug to make warm clothes for Trethia, but Tilysh stopped me as I contemplated the most economical way to cut it.

"It would be more useful intact," he said. "I have garments she can use."

He had warmer clothes for all of us. They were perfect for the trip, and I wondered where they came from. Once I had put them on, I realised just how much colder it would be on the mountain.

The material was different to anything I had seen before. The boots were lined with it, but the outsides of the boots, including the soles, were almost fur-like. It reminded me of the coarse coat Iryndal had stripped off the giant fyrsha I had killed in the desert sands of Valythia.

"It comes from another land," Tilysh said. "Made from a plant found high in a mountain range. Snow and ice won't cling to it, but they grip it and walking is easier."

I tied the baldric to my hip and hooked the token pocket and my healing pouch into place. Tilysh had prepared food and flasks for each of us. Oak added them to the packs he had put together and handed one to me.

Shalinba carried two packs, Oak and Mekrar, one each. Sundas double checked Trethia's clothes, made sure all the ties were correctly linked. She touched her token to his and hugged him tightly.

"Are you sure Oak and Mekrar are all you need, Kirym?" Arbreu asked. "I could try to convince Tilysh to let me come too."

I shook my head. "I need you here. If we're not back in three days, call Blue and have him lead you all back to the gate. Talk to Mama about allowing those who are in danger to move to Athesha. With Mama's approval, Borasyn and Egrym will help it happen. Between them, Blue and Tilysh, you will manage everyone. Don't let anyone leave the gate area once they are there. Invite Blue and the other ancients to move also."

"And leave you here?"

"I will do all I can to get back in time, but nothing is guaranteed. We have connections, Arbreu. Mek and I will let you know what is happening if we can, but don't expect much. This journey is very secret. If you need to, you and Sundas can contact Findlow and possibly Mama before you leave here." I raised my voice, although I knew everyone had heard what I had been saying. "Ashistar's sword is a mighty protection. Allow him to organise your defence."

"And Ubree?" Sundas asked.

"He will know what's happening," I said.

Ashistar nodded and clicked my token. Arbreu was less happy, but Mekrar spoke softly to him as she hugged him goodbye and he relaxed.

"Tilysh, what has happened with the Kultria bugs? Do they still fly at night?" Kirym asked.

"Fewer bugs fall every time Kultria crosses the night sky. Two large nests remain, but a new nest has started. With Dax again plotting, Ubree and Zillib no longer have the numbers to continue destroying them. The trees warned Dax, but none were destroyed these last three nights." He paused. "Kirym, when you leave the cave at Chagolt, take care to mark the entrance in your mind. You may need to return there. It is well hidden."

40

Oak Speaks

The journey through the fibre was surreal. The path was crisscrossed with webs, and once through a web, we were flung forward until stopped by the next.

"Why are the webs here, Kirym?" I asked.

"I suspect they're junctions where we change from one eye filament to another."

Eventually, we slowed and stopped. The wall in front of us was hazy, a substantial shadow of a real wall. I knew it would look solid from the cave beyond, as had the wall Tilysh first took us through.

The view into and beyond this cave was different though. It reminded me of Wind Runner's wedding dress. Each of the many sheer layers had a scene woven into it. Together, they gave the impression of a landscape; a river, trees, and hills receding into the distance. When she hung the dress up for me to study, I had the impression of looking through an oddly shaped window. I'd never seen the likes of it since, but here was the nearest thing. The cave looked out to a wide plain. In the distance was a line of mountains with higher peaks behind them.

I was so lost in the scene, I didn't realise Kirym was speaking.

"...and because the cave is empty. Waiting in it would be less strenuous for the eye fibre. We'll keep guard at all times, but if there is any movement out there, we can come back through the wall."

"Anyone passing could see us. Is it worth the possible exposure?" Mekrar asked.

"Tilysh says the outer opening is also camouflaged, as the entrance to his cave is," Kirym said. "Unless someone knows of the cave, they couldn't gain entrance. I do intend to post a guard."

Kirym went first, her knife held loosely beside her leg. From the entrance, she studied the land outside. Moments passed, and she beckoned us to join her.

The cave was small but big enough for us to be comfortable. Mekrar joined Kirym at the cave entrance.

I helped Trethia from Shalinba's back.

"I can do guard duty," Trethia said.

I was surprised when Kirym said yes, but, I reasoned, we would all be watching with her.

Kirym lay her rug on the floor, her knife beside it. "The rest of us should sleep until we leave. We'll be awake all night."

I was surprised—doubly so when Mekrar joined her. Shalinba had already closed her eyes and gave every impression of already being asleep.

Trethia sat in the middle of the cave facing the entrance,

her knife, bow and arrows set out in front of her.

"She's quite capable of doing it, Oak," Kirym said, softly. "She's not the age she looks and was guarding herself when she lived in The Rock. Had she failed then, she would have died. She knows what she's doing, now let her do it."

I woke when Mekrar touched my shoulder. I was on my feet, my knife in my hand before I had time to draw a breath. I was astonished I slept at all, although I had spent much less time with my eyes shut since we came to Halavash. Perhaps Kirym's relaxed attitude and her trust in Trethia was all I really needed.

The cave was huge, empty. "Where's Shalinba?"

"She's checking to see what's out there," Kirym said.

"How long has she been gone?"

"Not long," Trethia said. "She'll be back before dark."

A single sun sat low in the sky, although I couldn't figure which sun it was. The air was cooler than I expected.

Kirym set platters of food out for us. "Let's eat while we have the chance. Trethia has done us proud."

"She prepared this while guarding us?"

"It's what the guard usually does," Trethia said, "unless of course there is danger nearby, in which case, I would have woken you all long ago."

I felt conflicted. She was so tiny, I wanted her to be playing safely back in Tilysh's cave.

I suddenly understood Teema's feelings toward Kirym. I knew I was as wrong as he was, and I knew I had to change my view. Trethia was older than I was and had a wealth of experience. However, it didn't stop me feeling protective of her. But she was here because Kirym felt she was needed, probably more than I was.

"It's hard to believe this was once a vibrant forest," Mekrar said. "All life now dead or in hiding. So tragic."

I looked out at the wide plain. It was a dark blue barren area with an occasional burned stump and a few dying clumps of scorched grass.

"It'll be a hard journey, Kirym," I said. "We'll be easily seen crossing that. It'll take a long time. The mountain—it's massive. The Fhelian could be anywhere up there."

"We cross at night, less chance of being seen, and Shalinba knows exactly where her family were imprisoned."

"It'll take more than one night. What if Shalinba doesn't come back?" I said.

Kirym looked at me, frowning. "Of course, she will. Otherwise, she wouldn't have brought us here."

The temperature dropped, and I was pleased with the trousers and hooded tunic Tilysh had given us. My tunic, belted at the waist, also had ties in the front, with an extra panel to cover them and fastened nearer my right side. The tunic ended at my thighs. The large collar turned up to cover my mouth and nose.

Mekrar's tunic reached her knees; was more fitted to the waist before flaring out. It had no belt. Trethia's was almost identical.

We also had hand covers. Although I thought they would be too thin to be of any use, I found them to be as warm as the rest of the outfit and they enabled me to easily use my weapons. Everything we wore was white.

Kirym's tunic resembled Mekrar's but reached her ankles. The stand-up cowl covered her lower face when she attached the accompanying heel length cloak and hood. With the baldric at her hip, she had ready access to her weapons should she need them, although the cloak hid them if she so wished. Her tunic and cloak were decorated with what looked like plants, made of the same white material. I knew she would be hard to see in the snow.

Shalinba returned as the moon peeped over the horizon, and I was astonished by how the area around her body rippled and sparkled. She had looked beautiful before, but this was stunning.

She turned to face us. The shimmering effect stretched out on either side of her.

"Wings," Trethia whispered. "She has wings."

They were quite unlike anything I'd seen before, and very different to our dragons. The membrane was mostly transparent and shimmered even in the ghostly light of the moon. I suspected it would sparkle even if there was no light. However, the effect wasn't just her wings.

"If you're ready, it's time to leave," Kirym said quietly.

"Wear everything Tilysh gave you," I said, "and make sure all the ties are tight. Attach the face coverings but we won't need them until we begin to climb the mountain."

Kirym nodded. "Secure your weapons; if you drop anything, we won't have time to stop and look for it. We probably wouldn't find it anyway. When we leave here, Shalinba will manoeuvre as she sees fit. She will keep us safe. When we stop, stay on her back unless she tells you otherwise."

The shimmering effect around Shalinba became larger. I stepped closer and realised the membrane covering her body was layered. Each layer lifted in sections, almost like frills.

"We sit between the raised membranes," Kirym said.

I had intended to carry Trethia with me, but Kirym placed her between two membranes in front of me. The membranes were initially quite narrow, but they stretched up around us, and soon I was enclosed in a breathable cocoon. It was weird. Fully supported, I could lean back or forward, see and hear what was happening around us. The only thing I couldn't do was leave the cocoon.

Before Kirym entered her own cocoon, she pressed her

tokens to Shalinba's forehead. Although there was no corresponding token lump, as our dragons had, I was aware of a change in them both. It was as if Shalinba became part of Kirym's family. It impacted on my connection to Kirym as well.

I had expected Shalinba to fly but, with her wings streaming behind her, she ran. We covered the ground at such speed, the landscape was just a blur. Despite our destination being far to the right, she aimed for a point straight across from the cave.

The first moon of the three had travelled less than a quarter of its journey across the sky when we arrived at the base of the mountain.

The top third of the mountain glowed. It would rarely become dark enough for the stark whiteness of the mountain-face to not be visible. The reflected light created a false twilight, which I was used to. I knew it would produce strange shadows and distort our view.

We were in a small sheltered recess surrounded by almost vertical walls. I could feel the cold radiating out even through Shalinba's membrane.

"Shalinba is allowing us to feel a little of the cold, so we are aware of one of the dangers we face on the mountain," Kirym said.

We tightened the coverings over our faces, checked our weapons, and then Shalinba extended her wings and began to climb. She appeared to be running fast although her wings added to her speed. When she was well above the plain, she turned and aimed for a bluff. We were in the shadow of the mountain and I could no longer gauge her speed.

Distances here are distorted. Because of the massive height of the mountain the bluff looks closer than it is.

I was startled to hear Kirym's thought. Before this, I heard her only because of Ubree's presence. I wondered if it was because I now had a token. I glanced behind me. Mekrar's eyes crinkled as she smiled. Beyond her, Shalinba's tail was almost invisible. Her mottled colouring looked like snow and shadows; hard to see, and the glimmer effect just looked like moonlight flickering on ice-crystals.

The journey became monotonous. It was too dark on the plain below us, to pick out details, and snow is snow. Visibility had decreased as a thick layer of cloud covered us. I hated not knowing what was happening but realised no one else could see us this way—if they were indeed looking for us.

I dozed.

I woke when Shalinba slowed, and moments later, stopped.

We were still in dark shadow on the mountain, but the cloud had thinned a little. Windblown snow had built up into a massive ridge above us, extending as far into the distance as I could see.

Shalinba settled in a cleft between the mountain and what I took to be a large ice-covered rock which extended down to a large ledge below us. I wondered why Shalinba hadn't stopped on the ledge. If the overhang above us fell, we would be entombed, and although it would hit the ledge as well, there was a chance there that we would escape.

Kirym quietly explained why we were where we were. "Three dragons are approaching. I don't want them knowing about Shalinba, so this is the safest place for her now."

"Is Ubree one of the dragons? I asked.

"No. He would have let me know if he was here."

"So, what should we do?" Mekrar asked.

"Stay put, do nothing. The ledge below fronts the cave where the Fhelian are trapped. The approaching dragons are probably aiming for there. I'm going closer."

"Why? If they don't see us, they'll go away," I said.

Kirym shook her head. "Those coming here will have a plan, and I doubt it's to save the Fhelian."

"I'll come with you," I said.

"No. They may accept me being here alone, but not if you're with me. We're not ready to take them on just yet; not without Ubree. So, just wait and watch. If there's danger, Shalinba will take you to the safety of the gate."

Kirym slid off Shalinba's back and melted into the shadows. Her tunic was excellent camouflage, as it was meant to be, but that had a serious downside—I couldn't see her. I was left wondering where Ubree could possibly be.

Mountains are noisy places at best. The ice and snow whispers, grunts, and groans as it settles. It slithers from one place to another. The wind roars and dustings of snow shower onto whatever is below it. The ridge above us creaked and groaned as the wind gusted against it. I knew from experience, there would be a myriad of cracks and flaws under the smooth surface.

The wind strengthened, and amid the other sounds, I heard what may have been the murmur of voices. However, I knew snow is devious to the mind and ear, giving us what we want or fear most.

A strange whistle coalesced into a bolt of fire. It streaked towards the ridge where I knew Kirym stood. My heart was in my mouth, but before it hit, it reversed.

Shalinba eased forwards, and although she kept in deep shadow, this allowed us to have a better view of what was happening below.

41

Kirym Speaks

From behind a mound of snow, I watched the three dragons hover near the edge of the flat area. Dax, who had the assurance of someone who knew what to expect, led them, but the other two were hesitant.

When the second fireball deflected from the ridge, the younger two looked around fearfully.

"It's just the wind," snarled Dax. "Put more force into it."

"Then why didn't you tell us first?" the larger of the two asked. "Anyway, why not leave well enough alone. They've been hidden all these ages. The outworlders are locked in the cave, and you said no one knows what's here. So why bother?"

"Because the outworlders may at some stage, manage to escape."

"Even so, you said no one knew about this secret."

"Grey does, and he's stupid. He talks to himself, and if

one of the old gatekeepers hears him, they might tell the outlanders or come looking. If the ledge isn't here, they'll never find it. So, we weaken the overhang, and the snow will fall down to cover the ledge."

"But it's just a ledge. There must be hundreds o' them."

Dax slapped his tail across the small dragon's nose. "You were told to keep quiet, Kwarfo. Would you prefer to…" His anger was obvious, and he struggled to contain it. The younger dragons were visibly shaken, and Dax made a huge effort to control himself. "I'll explain later. We need to get closer and try this together. Teonarl, you wait here, and you Kwarfo, over here." He pushed the smaller dragon closer to the ledge.

"I'll show you what to do and then we'll do it together." Dax breathed a shot of fire towards the middle of the overhang.

For the third time, I flicked the shield up to intercept it. The ball hit the curved surface and deflected back towards Dax.

He darted away, more shaken than he let on. However, this time, he didn't fly back to his position between the other two. He began to peer into nearby cracks and crevices. Sooner or later, he would find me, or worse, Shalinba and the others.

I stepped out of the shadows.

"You!" Dax was shocked. "How did you get out of the tunnel?"

"You thought paltry stone would hold me? You know nothing!"

"But Grey said…"

"Oh, he has no idea who he's dealing with. You and Grey between you could destroy everyone on Halavash. Your names will be forever aligned with death and destruction. For the short time your children live, they will curse you, unless we can undo the damage you've done."

"I didn't destroy the gate."

"You could have insisted Grey fix it. You could have helped protect the gate area, but instead, you tried to destroy those who could save the land."

"You've no proof o' that, and soon you won't be here to accuse me. Your silly games with my fire-bolt won't stop you from being buried with the Fhelian. Then I'll hunt down your friends. No one will know what happened in the past, so no one will blame me."

"Your two friends here know. But of course, you plan to kill them, don't you?"

"They support me. Why would I hurt them?"

"So, why did you place Kwarfo where he would be buried when the overhang came down?"

"I didn't…"

His protests were drowned by gasps of outrage from Kwarfo and Teonarl.

"She's lying," Dax said quickly "The snow would be deflected towards me."

"It wouldn't," I said. "Kwarfo, the snow would hit you directly. At best it'd bury you, but it could knock you down the mountain and crush you or break your bones and rip your wing membranes. You'd never fly again, and you wouldn't be able to leave the mountain. You'd freeze to death if you weren't killed outright."

"Why would I kill my friends?"

"Why would you turn against Zillib, your rightful leader?" I challenged.

"Sefan is the oldest and she wanted me to rule"

"Only one of the oldest, and the choice wasn't hers alone. The whole flight voted. When given the chance, Sefan didn't speak up. But it explains why she tried to imprison me."

Kwarfo edged away from the cliff. Dax flicked his tail in the small dragon's face and he scuttled back into place.

"Don't believe her." Dax snarled. "If she releases the Fhelian, we'll all be destroyed. Other things might live, but not us. You were told what they did to us in the past. Your loyalty belongs to me, Teonarl. You heard the history."

"An invented story. A lie. Not history. Dax, why use inexperienced young dragons to help you? Because the more experienced would know your lies for what they are. Why not use those who helped you bury the Fhelian originally? Of course, you ensured none of them lived beyond the imprisonment, didn't you?"

"The reborns killed them. Fortunately, I managed to ensure those aberrations could not return. The Fhelian are dead, and you're about to join them!"

Kwarfo and Teonarl looked at each other uncertainly. "But historians said the reborns had long gone from the land when the Fhelian were born," Teonarl said.

Dax's face hardened. "The historians didn't go out to discover what really happened. The reborns came and went as they wished, despite the agreements. We knew they would continue returning until they had killed us all. They came at the behest of the Fhelian. When the Fhelian were imprisoned, the reborns had no reason to return. If we don't do this now, it'll be too late. You two, bring down the overhang!"

The single ball of fire that hit the snow above me didn't penetrate the ridge as I thought it would. Instead of boring in and destabilising the ridge, the fire simply slithered across the snow, as if it had hit thick ice. Dax's next fireball came straight at me. With no time to react, I steeled myself for the inevitable impact and wondered how the material of my coat would react to the flames, but the ball stopped in front of me and dropped to the ground, spitting and spluttering in the snow.

Dax sent a second and a third fireball; they too slid to the ground. He stared in disbelief but pressed forward and fired a stream of fire towards me. It paused mid-blast, hit the fireballs—they erupted into life and sped back towards him. He raced towards the thick cloud, but the fireballs caught up with him despite his twists and turns and stayed with him.

"Stop," I called. I was surprised when he obeyed. The fireballs hovered just above his neck and shoulders.

"Stop trying to hurt others and you'll be safe," I said.

He snarled and spat out another fireball. It flicked around and tapped him on the shoulder. He squealed with anger, sending another ribbon of fire out. Again, it turned on him.

Suddenly the air around him was full of dragons, with Ubree and Zillib in the centre.

Dax backed away but came to a sudden halt when he banged into a snow-covered rock that jutted out from the mountain. Lumps of snow peppered down on him. He dodged them and snarling, darted towards Kwarfo. The young dragon cowered away, his eyes shut.

Before Dax reached him, he came to an abrupt stop. Realising the smaller dragon was beyond his reach, he turned in the opposite direction, but his frantic wing-flapping made no difference. He was slowly moved backward until he was tucked in against an ice wall.

"You will remain there," Zillib said, "until I'm ready to deal with you."

Teonarl and Kwarfo cowered together when Zillib approached them.

"Why are you helping Dax?"

"He holds our families," Teonarl said. "He said he'll have them killed if we object."

Ubree glanced at Dax, who stared back defiantly. "Where are they?"

He shrugged. "Free me and I'll look for them."

Ubree looked amused. "Your help isn't needed. As of now, they are free and returning to the dragon caves."

Teonol and Kwarfo looked relieved and edged themselves into the dragon pack.

Ubree settled on the ice beside me; I climbed onto his back.

We hovered to the right of the dragons as they set up to attack the snow and ice that blocked the cave entrance. Zillib took the position in the centre, just above and out from the ledge. The others gathered around him. I didn't hear a starting signal, but they all blew their fire into the entrance at the same moment. Suddenly, a great wave of melt exploded from the wall of snow and ice, hit the ledge and cascaded over the edge.

With so much melt in the cold mountain air, we were quickly surrounded by thick fog which Ubree blew away. I had the perfect position to view the work on Ubree's back. The icy conditions refroze the water as it cascaded over the ledge. A frozen waterfall formed at the lip of the shelf to fall majestically out of sight.

Can Trethia, Mekrar, and Oak see this, Ubree?

Yes, Shalinba has moved to allow them a better view.

The deeper the dragons bored into the snow, the more pronounced the overhang became, and eventually, it fell, doing exactly what Dax had envisioned, although no one was caught in the fall. The flat area in front of the cave was piled high with snow and huge chunks of ice.

The dragons began again, and eventually, the ledge was

cleared of the fallen debris. Then they continued lengthening and widening the tunnel through the ancient ice.

As the tunnel in the ice became deeper, the dragon's fire became less effective, even when they moved closer and concentrated the fire in a small area. Zillib called a halt, and the settled on the ledge to take a much-needed breather.

Dax sniggered. "Even with your pathetic attempts, nothing will change. My plan will stay in place."

"Ubree, is there anything you can do?" Zillib asked. "It seems our fire is not enough."

Ubree glanced at Dax and shot his fire deep into the hole. Again, water gushed out, some refreezing on the way; the rest disappearing over the cliff. Ubree showed me what he could see in the cave. A thin wall of ice sat between us and the Fhelian, but he was unable to melt it.

"There's something more to this than I can understand, Kirym. Perhaps you can find a way through." He hunkered down, and I climbed onto the ice.

The surface of the ledge was slick with newly frozen water, but the fibre on the soles of my boots clung to the surface. With no fire, the tunnel was dark.

"Could you invite Shalinba to join us, Ubree? I need my pack." Above all, I wanted to see the reaction of the other dragons to Shalinba. It would dictate where the Fhelian eventually lived.

Shalinba's entrance was grand. She came from high above us, keeping her hiding place hidden. She still didn't trust them, and I didn't blame her. Even though clouds covered the moons, she sparkled as she descended. Hers was a spectacular entrance.

Most of the dragons backed away, but Zillib and five others came to meet her. Slowly, the other dragons came closer and although the greetings were restrained; I felt it heralded a good beginning.

As the dragons spoke, Mekrar, Trethia, Oak, and Faltryn joined me at the mouth of the ice tunnel.

Lamps in hand, we walked into the tunnel. It was huge, but it had to be to accommodate dragons and Fhelian created to accommodate Fhelian and dragons the size of Ubree.

The ice-wall holding the Fhelian in was opaque. It seemed flimsy. I wondered why it hadn't melted.

Oak pressed his weight against it, but the fragility was in look only. It didn't even flex. He removed his glove to feel the wall and quickly returned his hand to his glove. "How can we get through this? It's definitely ice so why couldn't Ubree melt it?"

42

Oak Speaks

We could see shadowy shapes massed together behind the thin sheet of ice.

"We can't be this close to them and fail," Kirym murmured, frowning. "We've come so far."

"Perhaps the solutions we need are back on Athesha," Mekrar said.

Kirym smiled. "And maybe the solutions came with us. Come on, I need a bit of distance."

We returned to the ledge and stood beside Shalinba, Zillib, and Ubree. The other dragons formed a large circle around us, an air of nervous expectation about them.

Kirym flicked her cloak back and pulled three bolts from her quiver. She had found them in the great rock where Churnyg and his people had been imprisoned for many hundreds of season-cycles. She last used the bolts as the keys to open the burl where, once inside, we found the request to come to Halavash. She now unhooked her small bow from the baldric.

The bolts sparkled as she nocked the first to her bow and fired. The bolt hit the ice wall, a clear crisp note that hung in the air. With nothing to indicate if the ice had even cracked, I waited to hear a clatter of the bolt hitting the ground, but the note continued uninterrupted.

Kirym already had a second bolt nocked. She fired, and another musical note joined the first. The sound of the third bolt hitting the ice was more bird-like. As the notes continued my token vibrated with the sound, but still I hadn't heard the ice break.

Kirym didn't seem at all worried, and we again followed her in to inspect the ice-wall. The three bolts sat, embedded in the ice, in a wide triangle, two above the third. No cracks radiated out from the impact, but the three notes continued to resonate around the tunnel.

"Any other ideas?" I asked, as I grabbed the nearest bolt and gave it a sharp tug. It didn't move, and nor could I spin it in the ice. I had the same results with the other two bolts when I tried to move them.

"They worked together at the tor, perhaps they need to do the same here," Kirym said.

"What do you mean?" Mekrar leaned forward and studied the arrows. "Oh, that's right, nothing happened until the third bolt slotted into place. Then the Burl opened. But here, they are all embedded. So, what now?"

"We do the next step together," Trethia said. She gripped the shaft of the lowest bolt.

Mekrar and I waited for Kirym to choose one of us, but she shook her head. "One for each of you. Just pull steadily."

I was prepared to put all my energy into pulling the bolt, but before I could do more than grab the shaft, Kirym touched a point in the centre of the triangle with the white token. The ice cracked and collapsed inwards.

We stared into the cave. The walls and ceiling sparkled in the light of the lamps, giving the impression of more light than there really was. The floor was littered with mottled, dark grey rock-like shapes. They reminded me of when we first entered the dragon's fire-cave, although each of these were covered with a slick film of ice.

"Are they dead?" Mekrar asked the question I dreaded hearing the answer to.

"I suspect they sleep deeply. I hope so anyway," Kirym said.

There were narrow spaces between some of them, and we made our way towards the back of the cave. It wasn't an easy path, they were squashed together tightly, more so the further back we went. We made sure we avoided the many stalactites that hung from the roof. Some of them looked fragile, and had they fallen, would have hit the grey shapes. I wondered if a direct hit from one would pierce and kill a Fhelian lying below it, or whether the ice would be a protection.

"How did three dragons overpower so many?" Mekrar asked.

"Grey helped them. He and Dax took their youngest first, but the Fhelian would not have fought. They're peaceful creatures." Ubree's voice sounded so close, I looked around to see where he was, but neither he nor Shalinba were behind us. It was for us, or rather Kirym, to waken them if she could.

At the back of the cave, we found a smaller cave, ice fragments littered the floor at its entrance. About sixty smaller shapes were huddled beyond.

"This wall held the young ones in," Kirym said. "With them imprisoned, the mature Fhelian were beaten."

The small shapes were huddled closely together, some were piled on top of others. I suspected they had tried to protect the very youngest. We could go no further; we turned back towards the cave entrance.

Mekrar slowed so she was walking beside her sister. "How will you waken them, Kirym?"

"We use what brought us here, and what we were given when we came to Halavash."

So many of Kirym's answers seemed to be riddles, although the meanings became obvious in retrospect.

"What were we given?" I asked. "Well, other than the white token."

Kirym stopped beside a large stalactite. Most of the stalactites were smooth, tapering to a point, although a few had met the ground and thickened to become columns, this one though was full of fissures and holes; quite misshapen.

"The air up here is so dry, the condensation from the Fhelian's breath must have created the stalactites but why is this is this one different?" Kirym asked. "Ah well, let's start here."

One by one she unwrapped the tokens, and together we helped her place them in the crevices in the stalactite.

Trethia sat the white token at the bottom. "It comes from here and needs to be closest to them."

Kirym asked me to place the rainbow token at the top with the black just under it. By the time I had secure niches for them both, she, Trethia, and Mekrar had placed all but the orange token in various crannies curving around and down the ice spike leaving one large hole left in the middle.

"Will you use the orange in the centre with Arech and Valycraag?"

"If that is your instinct, Mekrar, then yes, put them there."

"It needs something else," Trethia said when everything was settled. The tokens weren't singing, and we knew they would if everything was whole.

"Is there a token we haven't found yet?" I asked.

I was sure Kirym was smiling, although I couldn't see her mouth behind the cowl, but her eyes had a way of crinkling at the corners when she laughed at me. She rummaged again in the pocket and brought out one more wrapped bundle. "It's not always tokens, Oak. We need everything Halavash has given us, and we were given Rolliz."

Rolliz was complaining even before Kirym had taken his wrappings away.

"Ya leave us stuck in there without seeing anything for days on end when things are going well. No one talks to us, no one cares, ya don' even ask if we're comfortable. Then when it's so cold, I'll freeze an' fall ta bits, ya decide to bring us out. What's ya plan? You gonna leave us on the ice to freeze to death?"

Followed by; "Well she's not going to leave me to freeze. She likes me, and she promised."

"Idiot. She doesn't like me, so you'll freeze along with me."

"I like all of you. No one's going to freeze. If you're not happy here, I'll ask Ubree to take you back to Sundas," Kirym said.

"Humph! We may as well sort out all ya problems while we're here," he grumbled. "Ya won't solve anything unless we do it." He paused and looked around. "So whaddya expect me to do?"

"Don't you know?" I asked.

Kirym elbowed me in the ribs. "Do what you do best, Rolliz."

"How will moaning and grumbling help the Fhelian?" I muttered.

"Sing," Kirym said.

Mekrar and I stared at her. Only Trethia was unfazed by her suggestion.

"Sing?" Rolliz gasped. "In this cold? It'll ruin my throats."

"All right. I'll ask Ubree to take you back to Malsavash. He can send a seed-cone who has a stronger throat."

"Ya won't find one. Malsavash used us all for target practice. Not to be outdone, the other trees stupidly copied him."

"What do you mean?" I asked.

"He threw us! If he didn't like something, he threw one of us at it, and there were a lot of things he didn't like."

"Why?"

"He had no other use for us. Not after he took us away from Vashetha's influence."

"Oh dear. Well in that case, the Fhelian will have to remain here. We'll seal the cave up. Malsavash will value you as his remaining seeds."

"Value us? Not likely! We were an irritation. The only reason we weren't thrown away, was because 'e didn't know we was there. We, sensibly, didn't move. He can't throw what he don't know."

"And yet he found you easily enough when he needed to," I said.

Rolliz sneered. "We wanted to be found. We moved and annoyed him. We saw it as our first chance to get away from him without being crushed against a rock."

I was intrigued. "How did you manage to not move for all those eons?"

"Sing? You really want me to sing? To these lumps? What song?" Rolliz asked, ignoring my question.

"Any song you wish. When the Fhelian waken, they'll hail you a hero."

Rolliz brightened considerably. "Not doing it for that," he grumped. "Doing it because we wants to."

I was a little surprised at the look of adoration he gave Kirym. Perhaps I shouldn't have been; everyone loved Kirym. Well, almost everyone.

43

Kirym Speaks

Rolliz's first note was more a vibration, but it quickly expanded. The picture it painted for me was of trees talking and laughing together, flowing water, birds chirping, the whir of butterfly and dragon wings.

The tokens joined in and colour flowed from the rainbow token, down through the black and emerged, still a rainbow—but much darker. The colours coursed further down the column, mingling and changing to gather in the white token. There they swirled and roiled, moving faster and faster until all I could see was white. Slowly, a black nodule formed in the centre of the stone, exploded and we were enveloped in a dark mist, through which the tokens still glowed brightly. The white token was intact, the colours still swirling in its centre

Through the mist, a dark shadow to my right, enlarged. The first Fhelian had woken.

He loomed out of the mist. His grey head was shaped

like Shalinba's, but they couldn't have been less alike. This Fhelian was gaunt to the point of emaciation. As large raw wound down his neck and right shoulder. He moved defensively between us and the rest of the sleeping beasts.

I stepped forward. "We're here to free you and your family."

"Really? Death is the only real freedom for us in this land."

"My name is Kirym. I come from Athesha. If there is no peace for the Fhelian here, you can leave Halavash and live with us. What is your name, and how can we waken the rest of your family?"

He, still unsure of us, edged back until he was tight against the nearest sleeping bodies. "I'm Thenne. They'll awaken if I deem it safe. What of the dragons and their cohorts?"

"Dax no longer leads the dragons, Zillib does. He supports you and is outside with others who agree with him. Grey is no longer the gatekeeper."

"I have very little trust in words, Kirym of Athesha. The dragons lied many times, and even bringing us here was wrapped in promises they didn't intend to keep."

"Who would you trust? Shalinba? One of the reborns?"

"Shalinba was killed, Grey delighted in telling me the gruesome details, and reborns? Well, it's hard to trust a fable."

"Would ya trust me?" Rolliz asked. "I woke you. I wouldn't have done it if there'd been any chance you'd be hurt. I'm the easiest to destroy here. Trust Kirym. She keeps her word. She kept me with her when she could easily have dumped me when I was no longer needed." He paused. "Anyway, why would you believe those who lied to you, against Kirym, who is offering you a real life? She has a reborn here to answer your questions."

Thenne frowned. "A real reborn?"

"Yes," Rolliz said. "Two of them, although you only need one."

"What can a reborn do?"

"Ubree can heal your wound, if you'll let him," I said. "Once you're healed, we can waken your family and discuss your future."

Thenne frowned, obviously still unsure.

"Ubree arranged for the snow plug to be removed from the cave entrance. We needed the dragon's help for that. Had we not wished to help you, Thenne, we would not have unsealed the door to your prison nor broken the ice-walls that separated you from your hatchlings and from freedom."

Thenne whipped around, and disappeared towards the back of the cave, reappearing after a few moments.

"The wall is shattered. You did it?"

"Kirym did," Mekrar said.

Thenne looked around at the sleeping Fhelian, then back at Kirym. "All right. Bring your reborn, let's see what it can do. However, even then, there are many who'd kill us."

"The land needs you," I said. "Without you, everything will need to leave or die. While that may still happen, you will at least have the choice of a new home."

Ubree approached, explained what he wished to do, and touched Thenne's shoulder with his nose. The wound slowly faded, to reappear on Ubree's shoulder, looking even nastier on his dark skin. He sank to his belly, his eyes closed, panting with pain. Slowly, his breathing deepened, and eventually, the wound began to lessen. It took a long time.

Are you all right, Ubree? I asked.

Yes, he replied. *After so many seasons, the poisons from the wound had built up in his body, and they needed to be removed before the burn would heal.*

Finally, with a deep breath, he opened his eyes and stood.

The wound had healed, but a scar remained, similar to that on his left shoulder, although not as long nor as deep.

Thenne carefully reached out and touched the scar. "You took my wound? I thought you would give me a salve or use healing leaves. But," he paused, "you took the wound and the pain."

"It was little compared to the time you've suffered with it. Do others have similar wounds? It would be best I heal them before they waken."

"Can we really be free?" Thenne now sounded hopeful.

"Everything Kirym promised will happen. First, let's awaken your family. I'd like to be finished by dawn," Ubree said.

Healing the rest of the Fhelian before they woke ensured the healing went faster. None had been as damaged as Thenne. The oldest were woken first and by the time the babies stirred, the mist had cleared, and we could see them properly. They were snakelike and except for their grey skin, it was obvious they were related to Shalinba.

Ubree, where are their wings? Could the cold have damaged them?

I don't know, but best we get them away from this icy tomb. If need be, I can carry them all to safety.

We led everyone out to the ledge, arriving as the sun rose. The dragons had disappeared, *so,* Ubree told me, *the Fhelian could heal in peace and not feel threatened.*

Before we could do or say anything, the Fhelian turned, as one, towards the morning sun.

I watched in wonder as they all seemed to breathe in the light and warmth. Their colour changed, the adults green, the babies yellow.

"Shalinba is a mixture of both," Oak said. "Why?"

"Perhaps she was keeping the memory of the whole family alive," I murmured.

Once the Fhelian had acquired their colour, their bodies began to fill out. They all looked much healthier.

Shalinba tells me they thrive on light and warmth, Ubree said. *The incarceration in the icy darkness was the worst sort of torture anyone could inflict on them.*

Shalinba climbed down the mountain as she had before. She cautiously approached her family. There was a long moment before there was any reaction, but then Thenne's entire body shook as he recognised her, and he stretched forward. As their noses touched Thenne wrapped himself around Shalinba. With a mighty thrust of her wings, she propelled them both into the air, twisting around each other until both were far above us. My fears that Thenne would at some point fall were proven wrong when, as he pulled away from Shalinba, his wings and frills sprouted. They gracefully swooped back down to land on the ledge beside us.

I had looked for Farynth or Bogryn as Ubree healed the Fhelian, not finding them and nothing was mentioned. No dragons were entombed with the Fhelian, and Ubree also made no mention of them. I wondered if they had been killed during those last fraught days before the remnants of the family were imprisoned.

The Fhelian sorted themselves into family groups. Reunited after so many eons was an emotional process, those with babies, had them nestled close, between their legs, or on their backs. When everyone had settled, Shalinba explained what she had planned for them—to go somewhere safe and warm so they could rest and hear what options were available to them.

"I'm, Jomm. Who is the gatekeeper, if not Grey?" Jomm was a little smaller than Thenne.

Before I could speak, a blue haze engulfed the ledge and moments later, Blue appeared in front of us.

"The previous gatekeepers have returned until the land

and gate is settled."

"What has happened to Grey?" Thenne asked.

"We don't know. Once he ceased to be a gatekeeper, we have no specific way of observing him. However, we are watching to ensure he cannot hurt you again."

"What holds us in Halavash?" Jomm asked. "Can we leave right now?"

"Yes," Blue said. "The decision is yours."

"What's the haze over there?" asked a juvenile, her skin touched with tinges of adult green.

"Smoke, and the fires causing them are one of the things you need to consider before you can make a decision," I said. "Many of those living here are in danger from the fires, many have been killed already."

"Why don't they move elsewhere until the flames have died?" Thenne asked.

"You're not the only captives Grey took," Blue said.

Jomm rounded on Kirym. "So, we're expected to rescue them. None came to our help when we needed it. Why should we even consider it."

"Many tried to help you, and some gave their lives in the process," Blue said. "Others were lied to and many were ignorant of what was done to you."

"There is no obligation for you to help anyone, Jomm," I said. "What you do beyond here is up to you, but I would ask that you understand what is happening here on Halavash before you make a decision. It may be that you can't help anyone, even if you want to. We would not put you in any more danger."

Thenne was quiet, listening to the many comments made around him, some wanting action, others wanting to flee. Finally, he raised his voice and hushed them.

"The dragons have the same gifts we have. Why have they not handled this?"

I suddenly had doubts. Had my assumptions based on a picture and a myth, been wrong?

You can but ask, Kirym, but later, please. "We need to get away from the cold here to a safe place where we can discuss your future. Shalinba feels the meadow outside Tilysh's tunnel will be the best place for you. It's set to catch the warmth of the suns," Ubree said. "You can finish healing there while you make your decisions."

Dax has a guard there, Ubree.

I can handle him, Ubree told me, *if he needs handling.*

The Fhelian launched themselves off the ledge. As they did so, their wings appeared. The older Fhelian floated gently down, their heads together. I was sure they were discussing what they would do next. I was pleased Thenne included Blue in the conversation. Most of the younger ones soared exuberantly around the group. They were a joy to watch.

As they approached the ground, they saw the dragons and stopped in mid-air.

"They won't hurt you," Ubree said. He showed the dragons the condition of the Fhelian when they emerged from the cave.

The dragons looked genuinely shocked when they saw what had been done to them. "They have also been imprisoned by Grey and Dax, although their conditions were not as bad as yours. You're all free, but from now on, you need to work together."

Zillib flew up to meet them and added his reassurances to Ubree's, Blue's, and mine. While Shalinba, Thenne, and Jomm accepted the rest of the dragons, they eyed Dax with suspicion.

"While his prison is not as onerous as yours was, it is

every bit as confining. He will remain constrained until you consent to his release, and until we can ensure he will no longer hurt anyone." Ubree blew a stream of smoke over the invisible circle binding Dax, showing its tight size and shape.

44

Kirym Speaks

The Fhelian, with their snake-like bodies, swam through the air. Shalinba's movement mirrored theirs, quite different to her run across the plains and up into the mountains. Like them, she used her wings to stabilise her body and change direction. I could tell that flying for the first time in eons was a joy for them all. It looked leisurely and even the youngest kept up without complaint.

Tilysh, Sundas, Arbreu, and Faltryn stood at the entrance of the tunnel. The dragon who had been guarding the entrance for Dax was trying, without success, to usher them away from the tunnel opening.

He thrust out his chest and snarled aggressively when he saw the flight of dragons but backed away when Zillib and Ubree landed beside him.

Oak handed Trethia to Sundas, and we slid off Ubree's back.

"Why are you out here?" I asked, "and where's Ashistar?"

"We saw your approach through the eyes," Sundas said. "We though it sensible to come out and watch the Fhelian land. Ling here captured us, but he's ineffectual—" Ling looked embarrassed, "—and Ashistar went off to fill his water flask. He'll be back soon."

Ling sidled away from Dax.

"Dax no longer holds your family, Ling," Ubree explained. "They will be here soon." He raised his voice. "Dax controlled many of his followers by imprisoning their families. With all now released, the vows the dragons took mean you will all now follow Zillib. Those who choose not to will face the consequences stated in old law."

While the Fhelian and dragons intermingled, I approached Thenne. "Can you tell me what happened to Faranth and Bogryn?"

He smiled. "Parents to all of us. Without them, we would've been killed or captured long before we did. Their advice ensured we survived to be rescued. Faranth distracted Dax when he was checking we were all captured. Without her interruptions, they would have realised Shalinba was missing."

"Farynth was in the cave with you?"

He nodded. "

"And is still alive?"

"Yes."

"It's time they met their dragon children."

Thenne disappeared into the crowd while I collected Faltryn and took her to Ubree.

"It's time you both talked to Farynth and Bogryn."

The flight parted leaving two larger Fhelian alone. The smaller, Farynth I assumed, stared intently at Faltryn for a few brief moments, then ran to her. She placed her face alongside her daughters and closed her eyes. Moments later, her eyes and mouth flew open, and she stared up at Ubree.

"You are also my son?"

He inclined his head. "Somewhat overgrown, but yes, your third child. The other five are on Athesha."

Bogryn joined her, greeted Ubree, and turned to the rest of the Fhelian. "We always said they'd return if they could. My sons Ubree and Faltryn." Farynth nudged him and whispered in his ear. He looked a bit sheepish and cleared his throat. "Um, no, it seems Faltryn is my daughter."

Ubree's head whipped around as another Fhelian pushed through the crowd. They spent some time together as Tilysh prepared another meal for us. Eventually, Ubree introduced us to his parents and his sister, Ilarth.

They remember and recognise Faltryn, although to get used to the reality that the full-size child they bade farewell, has returned to less than his, he paused, well her birth-size, will take some time. I gather they didn't anticipate any of us to grow bigger than Arymda, so they find my size a little intimidating.

Ashistar hauled a filled water-trolley to the grassy meadow in front of the cave. Tilysh brought a large basket of food from his cave. While we ate, the Fhelian discussed whether they should help quell the fires or leave for Athesha immediately.

Meanwhile, Trethia and Faltryn had befriended Sarheet, the youngest Fhelian, who was slightly bigger than Faltryn. Trethia had gathered a large pile of twigs together. She placed a twig on a flat rock in front of Faltryn.

"You need to practice your breathing," she commanded.

Faltryn coughed at the twig and spat a small flame out. The end of the twig sparked.

"Do it again," Trethia said.

Faltryn did and on the third cough, the end of the twig caught alight and burned for a few moments. As it fizzled out, she placed a twig in front of Sarheet, who coughed, as Faltryn had.

I leaned forward in anticipation. This would tell me if my hunch about the Fhelian was right, which could dramatically alter what may happen in the future.

Despair washed over me when the twig caught alight. My assumption, that although they came from the same eggs, they had grown differently, was wrong. My plan wouldn't work, and now, I would need to begin arranging the mass exodus from Halavash.

Trethia encouraged both little ones to light twig after twig. Then as they rested, she built up a small mound of twigs. Faltryn blew on them, and as they smouldered, blew again. The flames roared and the Fhelian took a breath and copied her.

The flames died instantly.

My heart leaped. I leaned forward. "Do it again, little ones."

This time, Sarheet went first; starting a fire, and Faltryn's added breath made the flames roar. When the little Fhelian copied her, they died.

"Again!"

They did; Faltryn created a fire, and Sarheet quenched it.

Thenne leaned forward, staring in shock. "How does she do that?"

Now, everyone was watching.

"I think it's something you can all do, Thenne," I said. "If so, you could possibly extinguish the fires, and release those still imprisoned. Will you try?"

Thenne stared at Faltryn and Sarheet. "Yes, I will try, but it might just be a gift for the young ones, or possibly only Sarheet."

A large pile of thick branches appeared in front of us, the shadow of Vashetha hovering behind them. "With my compliments. If this works, many of my daughters may be returned to me."

Ubree breathed on the brushwood to ignite it.

Thenne took a deep breath, held it momentarily, and breathed on the fire.

It died instantly.

Excited, he breathed again. And the branches flamed up. He reared back in shock, realised what had happened and doused the flames.

"Why? How? Why did we not know this before?"

"Oh, I knew," Farynth said, "but I never realised it was important, and we were imprisoned soon after."

"The birth of reborn dragons heralded a time of great change, although the change may not have arrived at the time of their birth. I think they were needed to lead the destruction of the firebugs. Now a different sort of firebug is here. You encompassed some of what the dragons could do, but the needs ahead had changed. So, you did also."

"How did you know, Kirym?"

"There is always a little truth in the myths, Mekrar. Starshine's myth spoke of a dragon whose fire turned to ice. I thought the pictures we saw at the entrance of the dragon caves were the work of an inexperienced artist. But what if I was wrong? When I saw Shalinba, I started to rethink my ideas."

"What if it only works with dragon fire, Kirym?" Ashistar asked.

"We'll find out, but if we encounter any problems, we'll begin the evacuation immediately."

"And then," Blue said, "we gatekeepers will seal the gate, ensuring those who have ruined the land, cannot leave."

"You'll take everyone else?"

"All who wish to come, Thenne, provided they intend no harm to those already living in Athesha's Green Valley," I said.

"If you are willing to do this for so many, Kirym," Shalinba said, "we must at least try to help here first."

45

Kirym Speaks

The decision was made to attack the fires and whoever was behind them. The dragons opted to come along and while many of them just wanted to watch, Zillib and several others wanted to ensure there was no outside interference from any of Dax's uncaptured followers. Dax and two of his supporters were in the custody of a number of Vashetha's trees. Ubree had sealed their fire within them.

Faltryn, Sarheet and other babies stayed with Tilysh. He could guide his people back to the cave if we managed to free them. It also meant he could direct us to one of the eyes, should the need arise. Oak suggested Trethia remain with Tilysh and Faltryn but she refused.

We left late in the day and hoped to approach the fires unseen, although if our plans worked, the fire-starter would soon be aware of our presence. We rode on Ubree as was usual.

The flight covered the land quickly. The fires glowed

against the darkening sky, and smoke hung over the land. The smell of burning wood and flesh increased as we neared them.

Vashetha had ensured there was a wide sandy area between her trees and the fires, to stop the fires from gaining more fuel, however, we saw small groups struggling over the sand towards the fires.

"Why would anyone go towards the fires?" Oak asked. "Should we go down and check?"

"Fire, by its nature, needs new victims," Ubree said. "Vashetha told me that the fire-starter has supporters and they provide victims as they can. Some are taken by force, others tricked into going. We will help them better by doing what we are here for. Those who have sworn allegiance to the fire-starter will be handled better once they have no support."

The view in the distance was strange. Although the trees behind us proudly waved their pink leaves and purple branches, those ahead were grey. The whole area was covered by a black centred grey mist. The fireballs continually erupted from the black centre. We lost the general greyness when the sun dipped below the horizon. With darkness, the flashes from the centre became brighter and more frequent.

Blue had advised us to begin our attack on the fires to the right of the dark area where the fireballs came from, and work in a circle. We would attack the fire maker last. This would allow the Fhelian a chance to practice and work out the best way to use their talent.

The Fhelian approached the flames in a wide arc. The oldest of them flew in front, the younger followed a few dragon-lengths behind them. Ubree, carrying us, flew above them, ready to assist in any way, although the other dragons stayed behind on the outlook for any unexpected danger.

The first small swoop across the flaming area had surprising results. The flames died instantly, and the younger Fhelian swarmed down to take care of the few remaining pockets of glowing embers.

Buoyed by the initial success, the Fhelian moved on, pivoting their arc successively from each end. As we moved forwards, I realised it was mainly trees burning, and in the eerie light of distant flames, I noticed movement behind us. Already, some of the blackened stumps had begun a race across the sand to safety.

Thank goodness there are no sand-swimmers there.

But there are, Kirym, and strange things are happening down there, Ubree replied.

He told me no more, and I thought nothing more of it, but concentrated on the work at hand.

The night was long, but the Fhelian appeared to have unlimited energy. I watched them carefully to see if they were affected by the colder air they were creating with their breath, knowing how hard it had been for them in the mountain cave.

They seem immune when it comes from them, Kirym, came Ubree's thought. *They appear to absorb the heat below them, and that helps cool the fire as much as their icy breath.*

The Fhelian's attempts were better than I had hoped. Behind us, a huge area was empty of trees.

At my request, Ubree swooped across the area. I was surprised to see that even those with massive burns had decamped and were fleeing, and they were moving surprisingly fast across the sand. *They have no wish to be recaptured, Ubree told me. Their sister trees are waiting to care for them.*

Closer to the core, the flames burned with more intensity. Extinguishing them took longer, and the line of Fhelian closed ranks, to ensure nothing reignited after they had passed. Now the younger Fhelian had more to do, but as they practiced, their icy breath became stronger and more consistent. Whirlwinds of fire formed, and these targeted the Fhelian, although we all had to dodge occasional fireballs. Every breath was now a massive struggle for the Fhelian, but despite all these problems, they struggled on.

Ahead, a massive wall of fire suddenly appeared. Its brightness almost blinded us to everything else. Even from a distance, I could see it pulsing, intensifying, the centre slowly changing from red to white, and condensing into a flaming blue ball. It moved towards us at incredible speed, so big and so fast, there was no escaping.

And then it was gone!

Ubree had disappeared from under us. Oak, Mekrar, Arbreu, Sundas, Trethia, and I suddenly found ourselves astride Zillib. The other dragons and the Fhelian had scattered.

The fireball shot straight up, the intense heat slowly dissipated. We waited and watched.

Cover your eyes!

Although I obeyed Ubree's order, I still saw an intense white flash. I could see the bones of my fingers, through my closed eyes.

I waited, my hands over my eyes until I stopped seeing lights, then gingerly parted my fingers and peered upwards. The sky was dark; the area around us seemed darker also, and while I initially thought that was because of the intense flash, I quickly realised the flames on the ground were weaker than they had been.

I called the Fhelian and dragons together.

"What was that? How did it not affect us?" Shalinba asked.

"I'd say the fireball exploded," Oak said. "Why it went up instead of through us, well it seems that was down to Ubree."

"Where is he?" Zillib asked.

"Ubree took the fireball a long way above the land. He'll be back as soon as he can. Now, let's carry on extinguishing the smaller fires and releasing more captives."

"The fire under us is easy, but we need to concentrate to douse the flames," Shalinba said. "We don't see the new fireballs until they are on top of us. Coping with both together is tiring. And then there are the fire whirls. They come out of nowhere. It's unsettling."

"Could we dragons can help there?" Zillib asked tentatively. "We can warn you when the fireballs are coming. Their paths are quite obvious. There are few areas where a fire revives, so if the younger Fhelian concentrate on the fire whirls and occasionally, you all pause to check for glowing spots and deal with them together."

Moments later, the Fhelian were again quenching fires and freeing the trees. Now there were other fire victims as well. Animals and birds had been captured and tethered close to the burning trees. As the fire was doused, Zillib swooped down to see what we could do.

I analysed what I held in my remedy kit. *Oh Ubree, I could really use you now,* I thought, and then he was beside me. Before he could begin healing anything, healthy twigs grew up around us. A forest of healthy tree roots arrived.

"Vashetha bids you continue with the Fhelian. We will care for the children of the forest."

As Ubree rose into the air, I glanced down to see the roots roll each creature into a cocoon of fine roots and new leaves, and slowly sink into the ground with them.

"Oh no! They're burying them all." Ashistar said. "Did we come too late?"

"Many are still alive," Ubree said. "Vashetha will do what is best for them. They can begin the process of healing them as they take them to safety. That keeps the rest of her trees safe too."

What happened with the fireball? I asked Ubree.

I needed to ensure the explosion didn't affect other worlds up there and that no debris from it fell onto other parts of the land here. But as a flame, it shouldn't have exploded like that. There is something evil here and we need to destroy it.

Again, quenching the fires became harder as the Fhelian neared the black, cloud-covered centre. It was a massive effort to free each burning tree. To do what each previous breath did, took twice the energy, but although the progress was slow, it was continuous. As we advanced, it got darker, until even the flames became difficult to see. There were fewer fireballs now, a relief, as all the Fhelian were needed to push against the grey cloud.

From Ubree's back, even I could feel something pushing against us. Suddenly, with a loud bang, the grey cloud disappeared. Only Ubree's quick action in placing his own wall in front of the Fhelian and dragons, stopped them being catapulted forward into a wall of fire, hidden by the smoke and cloud. Then it vanished and some of the darkness went with it.

The flames were now sharp against the night sky. After a long moment of shock, the Fhelian gathered themselves together and attacked the wall of fire. Thankfully, this fire was normal and only needed to be quenched.

As the flames diminished, I glanced to my right. In the greying light of dawn, I could see a huge dark cloud drift across the desert. I was amazed at how heavy it appeared.

The cloud and the core are two different things. The core is no longer here, Ubree told me.

The remaining fires burned even more intensely now, but the Fhelian attacked with renewed vigour and their advance, for a short time, was spectacular, until a barrage of fireballs began to rain down on them.

Thenne pulled everyone back to rest while he and Ubree

decided how to proceed. "We're now losing ground. Every fire we quench is replaced by two more."

"We need to concentrate on destroying whatever is generating the fireballs," Ubree said. "A concerted effort to close down whatever is in the centre could help if only to allow the burning trees to escape."

"Escape while still burning?" Oak asked. "Won't that spread the fires across the land?"

Thenne nodded. "Ubree is right. If we don't attack what creates the fires, we'll forever be putting out small fires. Once that's sorted, we can easily mop up the rest."

"What if your younger ones took responsibility for quenching the fires in the escaping trees, Thenne," I said.

Thenne looked troubled. "They're terribly young."

"Overnight, they've gained a lot of experience," I said, "Allow Shalinba to watch over them, and if they need help, she can call Ubree and one or two of the others."

Thenne was silent for a short time as he thought over the plan. Then he nodded and the young Fhelian peeled away from the group, while the rest swooped over the outer rings of trees and continued their attack on the centre.

A large part of the outer ring of burning trees immediately began their trek across the desert, and as soon as they were clear of the fireballs, the young Fhelian began to quench their burning branches.

The nearer we came to the core of the fires, the more trees and animals remained, they made no move even when urged to.

Why don't they go?

Something holds them. Concentrate on the fireballs, we'll work on the other problems later, Ubree told me.

The fireballs continued coming, and although there were fewer, the heat was as intense as ever. The Fhelian concentrated their icy breath on each fireball as it powered towards us, and we slowly moved closer to whatever was creating them.

As the sun rose, I finally saw the creature. It was massive and had the look of a tree. It lacked the elegance of a tree, was stiff and ungainly. All its branches pointed towards us, the fireballs and flames erupted from these branches.

The Fhelian's icy breath changed again. Ice-balls flew straight to the ends of the branches, attacking the fire as it left them. The Fhelian were so fast in their attack, they managed to block the firing tubes.

A group of Fhelian raced off to help the youngsters, while others put out the fires around us. However, even with the fires quenched, the trees nearest the fire-starter, didn't move away, and the healthy trees who had been so active in caring for those hurt did not appear.

The creature shook its trunk and rid itself of the icy snow. It straightened its trunk, become taller and straighter. And now, it had a face.

"Danth!"

"Oh, my stars! It is, isn't it?" Mekrar said. "What have you done?"

46

Arbreu

"Created immortality!" Danth screamed. "And I've ruled a world for eons! I'm the supreme leader here! You may have stopped my fire, but you will never stop me. My influence is massive, and I will continue to rule, long after you're dead. All that has happened here, did so because I decided it would. The few who are not my followers are prisoners. They will remain prisoners forever unless they join me."

"What utter rubbish," Kirym said. "Forcing someone or something to join you or be burned to death, is not ruling them. Nothing is imprisoned any longer."

"But do they leave? They don't! They never will, and more will join them because they want me as their ruler."

The Danth tree was huge but had none of the elegance of any other tree Arbreu had seen. With ugly grey and black streaks, it couldn't be more different from the gorgeous rich purple of Vashetha and her daughters. Danth's face, taking up the middle of the trunk, was massive, many times bigger than it had been, flattened grotesquely, its movements were wooden. The deep gouges of an aged tree scared his face, and branches grew from the outer points of his eyebrows—now made of spiky moss—eyes, ears, and mouth. His branches, which fired the fireballs, had very limited movement. His other appendages, hundreds of them, were more fluid in their movement. They reminded Arbreu of tentacles he had seen on an octopus. These didn't have suckers on them, but they did have groups of small holes scattered down each limb.

There was something more about this mixture of man and tree. It took Arbreu a while before he realised there was a rock-like aspect to the figure. Arbreu wondered how Danth had achieved it but wasn't going to give him any satisfaction by asking.

Danth was still boasting.

"The male trees refuse contact with the female because I decreed it. The separation gave me power over them all. Those I don't want will die out as will all the things dependant on them. The fyrsha, mighty warriors of Athesha's Valythian desert and created by me, now stalk the sands here. They'll destroy all those there who won't swear allegiance to me. My firebugs' control everything else."

"If all happens as you decree it, you'll eventually rule a dead land," Kirym said.

"Then I'll take my followers, enter another land, and rule there. Because of your interference, Kirym, daughter of Loul, Athesha will be next. Prepare for the destruction of those who have denied my dominance."

"Locked up here in your own tiny part of this world, you have no idea what's happening out there, Danth. The firebugs no longer fly, their nests have been destroyed. There are no fyrsha in the deserts of Halavash and most of your prisoners have now escaped. Those who stand beside you do nothing to assist you."

"I need no help," Danth sneered.

Perhaps now you should all see why he is so sure those around him will stay. He swooped down to the ground and allowed us to dismount.

Among the trees were men, women, children, and animals. Arbreu had seen some horrible things in his life: men killed in battle and anger, men hunted and killed like animals for sport, families burned to death in their homes, but this was different. Arbreu felt sick at the sight of hundreds of people, probably Tilysh's family. The ragged clothing hanging off their emaciated bodies couldn't hide the large burns and sores on their bodies. Many looked ancient, and he wondered why they still lived.

Danth has reduced them to this condition, but he also sustains them. Just. Ubree told us.

Each person was tethered by a tentacle, Danth's tentacles, encircling their neck, arm, or leg.

The trees with them aren't tethered, but they remain to support and shelter the prisoners. Ubree continued. *Without them, the people wouldn't have the energy to stand, and would burn under the suns.*

Why don't they just rip the tentacles off and leave? Arbreu asked.

Intentional damage is punished, and damaged limbs are evidently replaced.

In one quick movement, Danth grabbed Kirym and Trethia with his long grey tentacles and lifted them off the ground.

"All lives in this land are mine. You're worth nothing here, although perhaps I'll keep you all for a few eons, just to prove I can."

Tentacles swarmed around Kirym. One plucked her cloak and flung it into the trees, another her shawl. One grabbed her stone knife from its sheath and whipped it away, but almost immediately, the tentacle wilted, and the knife fell to the ground. Oak quietly picked it up and slipped it into his belt.

Another tentacle attempted to take Kirym's knife from her baldric, but when it touched the handle, that also shrivelled away.

Danth cursed, and one of the tentacles punched an imprisoned man in the shoulder. Blood spouted from the wound and he slumped towards the ground. The nearest tree whipped a branch out to catch him, but missed, as the ground shifted them apart. Another tentacle punched at a tree. It shuddered, folded in half, and would also have collapsed, had other trees not reached out and given it support. Two other trees moved to the fallen man and lifted him to his feet.

Arbreu tasted vomit in the back of his throat. *Why is Danth doing this to them? Ubree, can you help them?*

"Kirym!" Ashistar whipped out his sword and threw it. It somersaulted towards her, and although Danth's tentacles reached for it, the sword evaded them, and slipped easily into Kirym's outstretched hand.

Danth snarled and the tentacle holding Trethia began to squeeze the wee girl. She made no sound, but moments later, Danth screamed and dropped her, the tentacle writhing in agony. Other tentacles moved to help it, but the contagion passed to them, and they too began to waste away. One of them, attempting to save itself, grasped a branch just above Danth's eyes and hauled itself erect. It continued to shrivel, and the strain ripped the branch from the trunk.

Whatever affected the tentacles was also impacting Danth. His whole trunk was writhing, he twisted and turned, moaning and groaning.

Using tentacles from the other side of the tree, he forcibly ripped the section of trunk with the affected tentacles off

and hurled it over the trees and into the desert beyond.
He again stood straight.

47

Kirym Speaks

I stared down into the dust and debris, trying in vain to catch a glimpse of Trethia. *Oak, find Trethia!*

He has her. She's safe. They're both protected, Kirym. Ubree told me.

Danth growled and twisted the tentacle holding me until I was in front of his face.

"I am invincible! You cannot prevail." His face contorted, pain and anger, I thought. "You're beginning to bore me already. Your friends, I will keep to amuse me, but you— well you are untrustworthy. So, breathe your last, daughter of Loul."

"You're not as invincible as you claim," I said.

"My appendages are replaceable. I could rip them all off and new ones will grow, stronger and even more venomous than those they replace. He plucked one and flung it over the trees. Almost instantly, a new tentacle began to grow. "Are you willing to watch more people die? Perhaps one or

342

two of your friends?"

"What would ensure their safety?"

"You have more tokens than I remember," he said, "and they're different. Perhaps I'll take those, along with the sword you hold. Your family couldn't face me if I wore those tokens and carried that sword against them."

"If you free these people, you can have it." I held out the sword.

A tentacle reached for it but pulled back. "Oh, you're too eager to hand it over. What do you hide, spawn of Athesha?"

One of the tentacles dived down, and before I could speak, punched Ashistar between his eyes. He stood still for a moment, blood trickled down his nose. His eyes clouded over, and he slowly crumpled. A long needle had pierced his forehead and exited through the back of his head.

The tentacle tightened its hold on me and began to speed towards the massive face. I wondered if it was attempting to crush me against the trunk. I instinctively swung the sword forward to give me whatever protection it could.

The sword slammed into Danth's eye. Black slime oozed out, he groaned as the gelatinous liquid ate into his face. His nose and cheek began to dissolve, his trunk writhed in agony, and the groaning got louder, rising to a screaming crescendo. He dug at his eye, pulling half of it away from his face and dropping it to the ground where it scrabbled through the dust towards his roots. A streak of yellow mould grew from wherever the eye touched.

Just as I thought Danth might be destroyed, more tentacles began to grow. But all the while, the scream continued.

A patch of white flashed past me; Faltryn, half flying, half climbing, zigzagged her way up the trunk, deftly avoiding the few tentacles trying to brush her off. When she reached the gash where a branch had earlier been torn away, she coughed a small spurt of fire into it. A few sparks spilled from the hole, Faltryn took another breath, but before she could try again, a tentacle brushed her off the trunk.

She fell.

Branches and tentacles whipped around trying to grab her, but all missed. One branch was more accurate, but as it was about to hit her, she extended her wings, swooped around it, over one tentacle, under another, and disappeared into the dust rising from the ground.

More sparks shot from the hole Faltryn had breathed in and smoke began to billow out. The fire caught and roared towards the sky.

Danth's screech was inhuman. Tentacles whipped around in a frenzy, and although none touched me, they tried to rip the tentacle holding me away. I suspected Ubree was protecting it and me, it was the only logical reason why I wasn't lying broken in the desert.

Slowly, Danth began to crumble from around the sword wound, his face, what was left of it, contorted with pain and rage. Branches thrashed around in the same agony Danth felt, but they dissolved as the scream faded.

I waited for the tentacle holding me to tighten, pierce me with its needles or drop me, but I was gently deposited on the ground before it disintegrated. Soon, all that remained was dust, a pile of rocks, and the sour smell of burnt mouldy wood. The ground where the ooze had spilled, smoked, and the soil under it heaved and roiled.

The massive mutant tree slowly turned to dust.

As soon as my feet touched the ground, the tentacle released me and dissolved away. I stabbed the dusty, slime-covered sword into the ground, raced over to Ashistar, and dropped to my knees beside him. Tree roots had wrapped around his body. These were being covered in a cocoon of moss and leaves, all that was left uncovered was his face.

"I am so sorry, Ashistar. What do I say to Churnyg? I should never have…" I sobbed.

Oak hunkered down, put his arms around me and hugged me.

"Tell Churnyg the truth. That he died protecting you and Trethia. His actions allowed me to get to Trethia."

Recriminations I could have coped with. I knew no one would blame me for this, but I was at fault. I was responsible for everyone here.

Trethia put her arms around my neck; I hugged her close, my tears smeared her dust covered face.

I looked up at Ubree.

"Some things happen so fast, even I can't help. His death was instant."

Moss crept over Ashistar's face and the roots sank into the ground taking Ashistar with them. All around me, hundreds of trees had arrived; Vashetha's daughters and granddaughters were caring for those who had been tortured by Danth, in the same way as they had for the fire victims. Ashistar was the first they had taken, and although I appreciated that, I hoped the time spent on a dead body didn't mean someone else died.

"Where's Faltryn?"

"She's here, Kirym," Sundas said.

The wee dragon looked exhausted. She was streaked with dust.

"Well, she's finally justified being a burden for the entire journey so far." Ubree said. "Mind you, despite showing she can be useful, I'm sure she'll still expect me to carry her everywhere for the next hundred season-cycles or so."

He looked genuinely proud of his small sister, blew gently on her to get rid of the dust, and placed her on his back.

A sharp bang reverberated across the land.

"Look!" One of Vashetha's daughters pointed back across

the open area towards the hills in the distance. The trees standing in that direction parted to allow us to see a cloud of smoke rising in the distance. It grew bigger and bigger as we watched.

"That comes from the gate," Vashetha's daughter said. "You will be needed there. We will care for everyone here."

I raced to where I had left the sword but stopped short. I had stabbed the tip of it into the ground, as I had done many times in the past, but here, it had sunk to its hilt, and was now rising to meet my hand. The slime and dust had gone, now it was bright and clean. My shawl and cloak were folded beside it.

I grabbed them and sheathed the sword as I raced towards Ubree to take my place in front of the others on his back. I didn't bother tying the harness, just clung to Ubree's neck as he took off.

Getting to the gate took longer than I thought it would; the distance was as deceptive as time was in the portal. Ahead of us, the cloud grew. It was immense. What caused it?

We all felt the same concern for Dashlan.

The gate area was vastly different to when I last walked through it. It was much bigger than I remembered, lighter, and was a mass of vibrant colour. However, the colour made no sense, although the order of what some of it had become, was still obvious. There were deep gouges in the pink grass, and the vibrant blue soil glowed in the strange light. Flowers and bushes had been ripped from the ground and littered the area, but the ground appeared to be covered with coloured shadows, and I was unsure what had caused them.

The ornate double-wing gate had again been ripped off its hinges. One side of it was lying half out of the gateway, dented and broken as if stomped on by a great force. The other half was deeply embedded in a large tree on the far side of the gate area. It had hit the tree with such force, part of it had punched right through the trunk.

Two bodies lay on the ground, one dressed in white, the other in a motley assortment of dirty grey rags.

I hit the ground moments after Ubree landed, and raced to the white-clad body, having assumed, rightly, that it was Dashlan. He was almost as pale as his robes, but the token still held colour, and the pulse in his neck was beating.

I left him to Ubree and Arbreu's care and went to see if Mekrar and Sundas needed help with the other man. From his clothes, I took him to be one of Tilysh's men, although as he was here in the gate area, I was unsure where his loyalties lay. He was unconscious, thick blood on his clothes indicated wounds, and Mekrar and Sundas were attempting to stem the blood until Ubree could deal with him. I regretted asking him to heal Dashlan first, this man could die waiting. I wondered how long Ubree would be.

Soon, Kirym, soon. Dashlan couldn't have waited, his damage was internal and life-threatening.

I looked carefully at Ubree. His eyes were unfocused, but I could see little else to tell me what Dashlan's problem had been. There was nothing I could do until he was healed.

"I need something to plug a wound, Kirym," Sundas gasped.

Near the gate was a large patch of the same moss that had covered Ashistar. I raced over and grabbed a large handful. "Sorry," I whispered, hoping I wasn't destroying a life form here on Halavash.

Back with Sundas, I thrust the moss into his hands, watched as he expertly pressed it to one of the wounds, and put pressure on it to help stem the blood.

I sat back and wondered why the grass was such an odd

assortment of colours.

"Can you bring them back?" Trethia asked as she slipped her hand into mine. "The land desperately needs them."

"Them? Oh, my stars! These are the gatekeepers? What happened here?"

Trethia touched the nearest stain, stroking her hand through it. The colour roiled, moved faster and faster, and slowly, the form of a person emerged.

I was awed by her ability but wondered if she alone could bring them back; she had, after all, originated in Halavash.

As if she could read my mind, she looked up. "Anyone who wants them here can call them back."

I kissed the top of her head. "Thank you, darling."

Mekrar was not needed with the stranger, Sundas would manage by himself, so I explained what was needed to recover the gatekeepers.

As she watched Trethia, I moved to a peach stain, the nearest colour. When I first touched the shadow, it felt as if nothing was there, but my fingers left silky trails as they moved over the surface. The trails slowly thickened and soon, it felt as if I was stirring honey. It changed again, became silky, it was as if a soft wind caressed my hands. The colour then solidified under my hands and a figure began to grow. Little time passed once before it was fully formed and moving.

"Thank you," Peach said. "I'm fine now. Please help me find the others."

I turned to a brown shadow and began again, although I kept my eye on Peach, until he sat up and began to help a light blue stain.

Time appeared to stand still. The sun didn't shine here. I

didn't feel the lack of it, it was warm and bright, different from the cold grey we had been greeted with when we first stepped across the threshold such a short time earlier. The gate area had grown with the care and attention given it by Dashlan.

I glanced around to check our progress. Gatekeepers of all colours were in partial stages of regeneration. Ubree moved from Dashlan to the stranger, leaving Arbreu to continue fussing over his still pale brother. Sundas and Faltryn moved on to help with the gatekeepers.

Some of them were very hard to find. Dark Blue was almost invisible against the damp soil, Pink went missing in a patch of grass, and one of the Greens was almost indistinguishable amongst a pile of uprooted flowers.

Dashlan's face had some colour in it when I finally approached him and asked what happened.

"There's a place here where we can see over the land. Sometime before dawn, a shadow covered the moons. As dawn approached, it settled on the ground. It looked like a dark mist, although Orange said it wasn't normal. There was lightning in the middle of it, but the lightning bolts were strange colours. Then the whole system raced towards us.

It felt as if I was hit by a wall. Whatever the shadow was, it just ran over me. When Orange began to process them in the usual way before entering the portal, they became violent.

I went to help him but we were both attacked. I felt I was being battered from all sides and nothing I did, made any difference at all. The other gatekeepers arrived to help us, and that's all I can remember."

"What was trying to leave?" I asked.

"Mainly residents of the land, but they seemed to be part of the shadow. They were led by the one named Rabbit," Orange said.

"That makes sense," I said. "Was there a reason she couldn't leave?"

"No. We rarely stop anyone leaving. Our job is to ensure no one is forced to leave. One person in the group didn't know there was a choice. Dashlan and I fought to give him the right to choose."

"There were other things in there though," Purple said. "Things I've never come across before."

"What sort of things?" Oak asked.

"I don't know. Initially, they were in cages, but they broke out and disappeared through the gate. They were strong creatures and vicious beyond belief. I initially thought they were dragons, but there were differences. The violence was uncalled for. Everything that wanted to leave, could, but the gatekeeper's job is to know who was leaving."

"You haven't mentioned Grey." I said.

Orange frowned. "I would swear he didn't go through the gate as I knew him."

"Equally so, he is no longer in the land," Blue said. "So, we must assume he left with Rabbit," Blue said. "Now, we need to ensure they can never return."

"Does the gate need to be stronger?" I asked.

Orange shrugged noncommittedly. "Not stronger, just different."

We anticipated someone wanting to enter unwanted," Rose said. "Leaving has never been a problem in the past, but now, we must look at the situation anew. It won't take very long, but it will keep us and others safe."

"But, it's over," Arbreu said, "They're gone, so now we can take Dashlan home."

"It's not over, Arb. The gate isn't secure and Halavash isn't safe. I need to make sure that whatever went through the gate, can't return," Dashlan said.

"Can't the gatekeepers do that? I promised Ma and Pa I'd get you back safely. They'll be worried."

"You could always go and reassure them, if you think they're so worried."

"Dash is right, Arbeu, and I have also more to do," I said gently.

"Danth is dead, Rabbit and Grey have left. What more do they want of you?"

"They want nothing, which is why you can return to Athesha, but the problems Danth caused still remain. I have to make it right."

I turned away, picked up a platter of food from among those Mekrar and Sundas were preparing.

The man who had been freed by the gatekeepers was emaciated beyond belief, his skin the pallid white of someone who had not seen the sun in many seasons.

I hunkered down in front of him and handed him the platter of food. "My name is Kirym. Is there anything I can do for you?"

"I'm Lartherin. Thank you, the food is much appreciated. It's a long time since I ate. I require
nothing more."

"We'll then get you back to your family, although if you wish, I can have them brought here for you."

He shook his head. "They won't want me. Against advice, I approached Danth and Rabbit. The family members who came to rescue me, all died."

"As much as that isn't true, it would be a shame if the sacrifice of those who did die in their attempt to save you was not rewarded with your return. Had they been captured, would you not have tried to save them? Anyway, you weren't the only person they attempted to rescue."

He gave no response, but closed his eyes and leaned forward, his elbows on his knees.

Sundas brought over flasks for us to share; I was pleased when Lartherin took one and drank.

"What made you decide to stay on Halavash?" I asked.

"I didn't know we were leaving until I was asked if I wanted to stay. I knew I'd rather die than go anywhere with Rabbit."

"How did you come to be with her?" I asked.

"She lured me into the heart of a hollow tree thousands of moons past. Once there, I realised it was a prison. She said I was to guard her treasures, but in reality, she found it amusing to keep me there. When the tree disintegrated. I hoped I'd be freed, but I was made to carry some large containers. I put them down when I was told I didn't have to leave. They were snatched away, and I felt pain and knew nothing more, until now."

"Do you know what Rabbit took with her?"

"Scrolls and papers, mainly."

"Where did she get them?"

"Most belonged to Danth and Grey. They asked her to keep them safe, from each other, I think, but then she refused to return them. Rabbit had powerful knowledge of her own and experimented on trees and animals. After she read the scrolls, her results improved, well she was happier with them anyway. Danth and Grey initially disregarded her knowledge. When they realised she had outgrown them, it was too late. She refused to share her knowledge. Danth had fused a fish to his body, but the connection was very unstable. Rabbit had been experimenting with trees and suggested he allow her to put him into one. He felt vulnerable and demanded something that couldn't be easily destroyed. She chose a rock that was part of the land. It worked but took his mobility. That pleased her, she was tired of him."

"What happened to her other experiments?" I asked.

He nodded. "Her first experiment was the tree she imprisoned me in. There was only so much she could do to trees, so, she worked on two sand-swimmers. Those experiments were unsuccessful, but she made huge strides forward when she used birds. Then she began to try things on people...some of my brothers. She was delighted with the advances she made, but she still killed them. To my knowledge, she eventually killed all her experiments except Danth."

"So, why are you still alive?" Arbreu asked.

"I was never an experiment. She just kept me to guard her scrolls and the containers."

"Why was Danth fused with so many things?"

"He asked for them. He thought they would make him invincible. When Rabbit heard the dragons had woken and saw the fires being extinguished, she decided to leave him to his fate."

"Why did she wait out in the desert?" Oak asked.

"Grey went to collect other containers. He wanted to leave with Rabbit, they thought they would be able to destroy the gate, allowing them free access out and in. Everything became chaotic, and when I woke up, he," he pointed to Ubree, "told me I was safe, and that you'd help me."

"What did Grey hold that he valued so much, Blue?" I asked.

"We're not sure," Blue said. "Grey was secretive about his possessions, and we didn't pry. However, we know he took items he didn't own, among them, the history of the gate. That would be one box, Kirym, but what about the others? Does anyone know?"

"When Trethia and I met Grey initially, he admitted taking something belonging to Faltryn. Our family history was stolen. As Grey locked the Burl where our history was stored, and he has stolen from others, the theft points to him. We need to find everything and return it."

"Why didn't you tell me all of this before? Mekrar asked.

"I wasn't totally sure, but now," I shrugged. "He admitted

to sealing the Burl, and although he denied taking the histories, no one else had the opportunity."

"So, who did ask for help?"

"I did, Mekrar," Blue said. "Grey had forbidden any of us to leave Halavash, but my main concern was for the land, and anyway, the gate was open."

"When you were in the Burl, were the shelves full of books?" I asked.

"Oh yes. I was very tempted to stay and read them, but I had no right to be there. I had hoped to find your people but leaving a note was the best I could come up with. I placed the request in what I took to be the book most likely to be used next."

Lartherin gingerly stood, stretched and looked around.

"Would you like to return to your people now?" I asked. "I'll go with you if you would like, to ensure there are no problems."

He shook his head. "If there are no objections, I'd like to stay here for a while. Help for a bit. I've been watching the man in white, he is doing a great job, but the work would go faster if he had help."

"Dashlan will appreciate that, Lartherin."

48

Kirym Speaks

Ubree swooped out of the dawn mist to land in front of
Vashetha. When I had last seen her, her daughters had been
gathered around her, and I'd not been totally aware of her
great height and girth. Now, alone at the edge of the desert,
I realised I had never seen a bigger tree, she must have seen
thousands of season cycles. She looked short, but that was
simply because of her immense width. As we landed, even
Ubree looked small compared to the majestic tree that
towered over us.

I was surprised she had personally attended my invitation,
although I had rather demanded she attend. She was alone.
I was aware she was ancient and thought at best, I'd see
her shadow, a figure of her from her root system as we had
seen before. She could even have sent one of her daughters,
and I would have accepted that. I was grateful she had
acknowledged the request. Without her, any plans for
Halavash would not work.

No one else had yet arrived; my request for their presence was still recent. Vashetha had travelled extremely fast.

We greeted the great tree, who was gracious in her acknowledgements.

"Who else are you hoping will attend?" she asked.

"Malsavash, Blue, Shalinba, Zillib, and Tilysh. They may bring others, but they at least are needed."

She nodded. "Malsavash may not attend. He rarely gets to this side of the desert. He has refused to appear over the seasons because the journey around is so arduous. In the past, when I have insisted he attend me, he took more than sixty days to arrive."

"Vashetha, why do the male and female trees live so far apart?" I asked. I'd wondered how to ask this question. I didn't want to accuse anyone of anything, but I needed answers.

Vashetha frowned. "It wasn't always so, you know. We lived happily together until Grey introduced the creature called Danth.

Danth despised females and refused to meet with us, although there was a delightful camaraderie between him, Grey, and the male trees. I was pleased to see Grey take an interest in the land and I personally thought he might settle into his job as gatekeeper properly. Eventually, we were invited to one meeting, but we were ignored by everyone. On the second day of the meeting, the trees accused us of trying to kill them. The charge was laughable until twenty-three trees we had most contact with, became very sick. Nine of them died. That was when they decided to put a desert between us and them."

"Why would the death of a few trees cause such a massive decision?" Oak asked.

"The leading Malsavash was the second to die, and soon after, his successor joined him. They had been the more rational voices. Without them, the arguments were one-sided."

"How did they all get to the far side of the desert?"

"They gathered at the edge of the Vumborta cliffs and released a family of Yiffions. Yiffions produce sand and reproduce until they've made a desert of the required size. We females were pushed back towards where the black sun rises. We thought the males would soon sort themselves out, that wisdom would prevail, so we allowed them time. Instead, they enlarged the desert, finally settling it at the size it is. Now, it's too big to cross."

"The sand-swimmers may know his plans," Ubree said. He slipped into the sand. After the initial ripple, we saw nothing more.

Blue arrived as the second sun tipped the horizon, although it was hardly visible through the mist. Ubree returned moments later. He rose out from the sand in front of us and stepped onto the grass.

"Malsavash is on his way, according to the sand-swimmers."

"What did you say to get Malsavash to agree to meet you here, Kirym?" Blue asked.

"I said firm decisions for the future of everyone on Halavash would be made, and if he wasn't here, would be made without him."

"Did you tell him who else would be here, Kirym?" Vashetha asked.

"I didn't want to give him any excuses to stay away. The Kultria bugs have all been destroyed, and you've confirmed that he can get here, Vashetha. It's just a matter of time." I wondered how long I should wait for him.

As we talked, Shalinba, Thenne, Zillib, Conysh, and Tilysh arrived, with another of Tilysh's family. He was introduced as Dorchym.

"What do yiffions look like?" Oak asked. "I mean, I've been trying to figure out how a creature does that, creates desert from normal land, that is."

"You've never seen them? I'll try to find one." Vashetha shook one of her branches out as one would shake water off a hand. The leaves scuttled up the twigs and joined those on the branch in a general migration towards her trunk, leaving the end leafless. She began to sift through the sand with the twigs at the end of the branch. Malsavash had done something similar when looking for a sand-swimmer.

When Vashetha eventually lifted her branch from the sand, she held two small cream creatures.

"It's a fyrsha!" Trethia said

These though, were half the size of my fist and without the massive horns.

"Are they vicious?" I asked.

"On the contrary, they're very gentle," Vashetha said.

"So, Danth lied?" Mekrar asked.

I nodded. "On just about everything, Mek."

"How did you know?"

"Fysha on Athesha are so vicious, there is no way he could have brought one with him. More probably, he heard a vague description and made assumptions. What do they eat, Vashetha?"

"They draw the moisture out of the ground, and they'll eat green vegetation if it's there. When the desert is barren, they eat wind-blown debris, seeds, and bits of dead matter."

"Why is the whole of Halavash not a desert, then?" Oak asked.

"I've been told they're kept in check by rock and the sand-swimmers. This desert has remained static for thousands of moons. You called them fyrsha, Trethia. What are your fyrsha like?"

"They're opposite in nature," I said. "Those on Ashetha

are huge, almost as big as Ubree. They're ferocious. They eat every breathing thing they find, including people. However, they're relatively new to the land, although possibly still hundreds or thousands of season-cycles."

"As hard as it is to admit," Blue said, "I think they might have been part of something Grey and Rabbit created."

I shook my head. "They can't have been. The fyrsha were in Athesha long before Rabbit and Danth met."

There was a long silence.

"I fear Blue is right, Kirym," Tilysh said. "The portal does strange things with time. You can enter the portal after someone, and arrive eons before them, at the same time, or eons after. The portal can take you forward or back in time, as well as staying true. Tell me about Danth's use of the portal."

"He discovered the entrance to the portal about eight seasons ago. He was hauled out within moments of falling in."

"And yet he was here for hundreds of moons. Then he disappeared, and hundreds of seasons passed before he returned with Rabbit. His arrival the second time was thousands of seasons ago."

I nodded. "There's so much we don't understand. How could Grey create the fyrsha, Blue?"

"Long ago a traveller visited. He was a storyteller," Blue said. "He told amazing tales, many are still told on dark nights. Some were tales of joining two or three creatures together. Occasionally, some have tried to copy his tales, although generally they just repeated those he told, with minor variations. When Grey quit being gatekeeper, he left behind a few items. One was a scroll. I thought it was ideas for stories. Some were very original. Now, well in view of what Danth became, I think it was a list of their experiments, although possibly not a complete list, and maybe Grey included some of what Rabbit had done. He wrote of what he called mixes, taking parts of two or three creatures or things, and fusing them together. If his notes are to be believed, he succeeded many times. His early creations lived for only a short time. When they began living longer, he chose to kill them. Most, it seems, were quite vicious. He had the idea of keeping some of them in the portal, so he could watch their progress. This was why I thought these were stories, because he must have known that couldn't work. Nothing stays stationary in the portal. Portals take things from one place to another. Grey did write of visiting the creatures. Most had disappeared, he assumed they had died. One he found, had prospered, and he was shocked at its size and viciousness. It scared him. He never went back. That creature could very well be the fyrsha, alive on Athesha."

"Hold on," I said, "Faltryn put something into the portal; Grey said he found it between Halavash and Athesha. It must have stayed stationary."

"It couldn't have," Vashetha said. "More likely, Faltryn left it beside the portal and Grey took it. Kirym, could other things have arrived in your land?"

I thought about the journal I had recently retrieved from Gynbere, who had stolen it from my ancestors. I nodded slowly, as one entry in it came to mind; an outlying community was attacked by a huge creature. Even the dragons had problems destroying it. The size and viciousness made the creature stand out, but there had only ever been one, which was noted in the journal as unusual. I described what was written and drew an image of it in the sand.

Vashetha stared at the picture. "Blue, does that remind you a little of a zillast? They're very small of course, but my, they are vicious. Being small, they're reasonably harmless, the worst you could expect would be a nasty nip."

"So, if Grey mixed the zillast with something else, he could have created that monster?" I asked.

"It would make sense with the information we have," Blue said. "I suspect he made the firebug, too."

"Danth said he made it," I said, "but he hadn't the knowledge. More likely Rabbit and Grey were its creators."

Blue nodded. "Grey wrote that he was uncomfortable with the unsurpassed viciousness of putting two creatures together, so he wondered about adding a third, one having a sweet nature. I'm not sure whether he ever tried though."

"Oh!" I said. "He did. He recognized Trethia and tried to claim her back. He implied she came from an egg he sent to Athesha. A gift, he called it. Borasyn said it had two yolks, but the yokes split. But what if it was made of three parts, two stayed merged and the third broke away. That would explain some of it. Except for Trethia, none of their natures could stay true because they were so mixed up."

"It seems to me, they made mistakes with every foul experiment. Why did it work with Danth?" Oak asked.

"Did it?" I asked. "The other parts of the experiment were so different and may have made it stable, but it was still a foul mistake. Tree, rock, fire, and whatever the tentacles came from. There was little of Danth left, just his face and desire for power. The other difference was Rabbit. She had knowledge of her own, perhaps saw something Grey and Danth missed."

"There's one thing we haven't thought about yet," I said. "We know some of their experiments went to Athesha, but what if others went elsewhere? To lands further down the portal."

"Grey did note they shouldn't be released into Halavash. Perhaps that was experience speaking," Blue said.

"Meaning?" Sundas asked.

"Something was released here and went wrong. Any ideas?"

"Kultria bugs," Oak said. "They've been destroyed now, haven't they?"

"Yes. We destroyed the final nest on the day the three suns merged on the horizon," Zillib said.

"Could there be anything else unexplainable here?" Oak asked.

"Only male trees," Vashetha said, "but I suspect we're stuck with them."

"Wait-wait-wait," Oak said. "One thing we didn't talk about. If all this has been assisted by Danth and Rabbit, they've been here for many thousands of moons. So, our families will be long dead when we return home."

Mekrar gasped. "Oh! We'll never see them again."

"Not necessarily," Blue said. "The portal has its own intelligence. It can make decisions depending on what is needed or what the traveller wants. For example, had you arrived here much later than you did, the bugs would have already decimated our land. They were intelligent and learning to thwart our defences. Had you arrived soon after Danth, few would have been aware of the bugs. You may not have even seen them. Even if you had, you wouldn't have taken the actions you did, thinking them part of our ecology. You came at precisely the right moment to do the best thing for Halavash. So, wherever you go when you leave, the portal will do the right thing for you. No history is truly written until *you* have lived it."

I laughed. Maletta said something similar when I saw her last.

"What will you do about Dax, Zillib?" I asked

Conysh laughed. "He didn't need to do anything. Dax formally challenged his leadership, claiming Zillib's refusal to stand on the leader's rock to give his speech negated the vote. He demanded a new election. The results were as before, but this time, our three eldest dragons suggested everyone swear loyalty to Zillib in front of the rock. Dax refused. He was asked three times and was warned there would be repercussions. He ignored all advice, and on his third denial, his wings shrivelled, and his fire died. His attempts to rekindle his fire at the fire column, failed. After that, everyone realised the seriousness of his stance, and his followers deserted him."

"What will happen to Dax now?" Oak asked.

"Oh, he will be cared for," Zillib said, "for he is one of us. His lack of wings has taken away his position in the family. He is pitied, and he hates that. With no wings and no fire, there is much he can't do. If he wishes to join us on journeys, he needs to accept help. He refuses all offers so, he misses out on a lot. Of course, no other dragon will mate with him, so his line will die out unless he can change his behaviour. Then his wings will regrow. I believe it is possible, but he is stubborn. It may be a long time before he sees sense."

Discussions continued until, as the third sun passed the meridian, Malsavash staggered along the edge of the grass towards us. He had numerous gashes on his trunk, a section of bark had been torn off, his leaves were ripped or gone, and three of his branches were broken—one at the trunk. He gasped as he sank to the ground in front of us.

"Oh, I never expected to make it here alive," he gasped. "Greetings, Vashetha, I didn't realise you would be here. I need not have come."

"Hmmm, I am surprised to see you. I was only informed of the meeting yesterday. When were you notified?"

Malsavash ignored the question; he was bent double still gasping for breath. Eventually, he straightened and pointed to Tilysh and Dorchym. "Who are they?"

As everyone was introduced, a mass of sand-swimmers

gathered on the edge of the sand. Malsavash glowered and moved away from them.

"Kirym, you have concerns about Halavash," Vashetha said.

"Yes. First, a general note for everyone. The fire-starter and the Kultria bugs have been destroyed. The bug nests have gone, so they will no longer decimate those who live on Halavash."

"You had me risk my life to tell me there is no longer a danger here and all is back to normal?" Malsavash was outraged.

"Oh no, that's minor news. Halavash is in as much danger as it has ever been. And that's what we need to discuss," I said.

"What danger is there?"

"Vashetha, you introduced us to your daughters and granddaughters, but I suspect they are great granddaughters and their daughters and granddaughters. Am I right?"

She nodded. "Numerous generations of my family fought the fires and were killed outright. Many of those who escaped, along with some of those you so bravely rescued, were damaged to the extend they died soon after they returned to us. As much as I didn't want any of them to go into battle, we had no other choice. The decision was initially made by Vashmitta, who led the family then. She was a great strategist and I supported her completely. Those who died are remembered in the following generations."

"Have the male trees ever lived as long as the female trees?" I asked.

"They used to," Vashetha said, "but their age is reducing drastically for some reason."

I nodded.

"Why did you call us here, Kirym? Surely, it wasn't to talk about the relative ages of our trees," Tilysh said.

"Halavash is dying and although it may still last for many season-cycles, it will die sooner rather than later."

"But you've rid us of the fires and the bugs. Everything is back to normal," Malsavash said.

"Am I right in assuming that Halavash means The Land of Vash, or Land of the Trees of Vash?"

"Yes," Blue said. "Occasionally, lands die. The survivors of those lands looked for new homes. The trees of Vash were sent here, to a land that needed them to keep its inhabitants alive. Why?"

"The trees have a limited lifespan, and even the youngest are now ancient. With no new trees growing, there'll be nothing to keep the land alive when the last tree dies."

Vashetha frowned. "I hadn't foreseen that from the present situation, but yes, I feel you are right."

"What can we do to change it?" Blue asked.

"The trees must reproduce! It'll never happen if the male and female trees remain apart. The male trees must now return to the forests of Vashetha."

"And we would welcome you," Vashetha said.

"It won't work," Malsavash said. "You need seeds, and we've none left."

"None!" Vashetha sounded outraged. "They don't dissolve with age. They remain stored in you."

He shook his head. "With no chance of being used they became an irritant. It became fashionable to destroy them. I would guarantee there are none left at all."

"And whose *stupid* idea was that?" Vashetha asked.

"Can we bring a male tree from another land?" Oak asked."

"No," Vashetha said. "We are a special species. There's a basic difference between us and other trees. Kirym is right, we will die out and the land will follow. We must find a new home for those who rely on us."

"How many seeds could one cone produce? Oak asked.

"Hundreds," Vashetha said.

"Thousands," Malsavash boasted. "Hundreds of thousands."

"Numbers matter little if there are none left," Vashetha said. "We need a plan to leave Halavash."

"There is one other option," I said.

I opened my token pocket, hauled Rolliz out, and introduced him.

For all that he had been snorting with amusement while in my pocket, now he was straight-faced and formal. He respectfully acknowledged Vashetha, Blue, and Tilysh, and stuck three tongues out at Malsavash.

"Fool. You held the last seed cone on Halavash, and you told Kirym to destroy me. Fortunately, she wasn't as stupid as you are."

"That's enough, Rolliz," I said. "Now, Rolliz has agreed to help here, but he needs someone to take care of him."

Malsavash lurched forward. "He's mine, I'll take him."

"No, no, no, no, no! You gave me away and I have no desire to be cared for by the thing that assassinated my siblings," Rolliz said.

"Would you be happy staying with Vashetha?" I asked.

"She might be encouraged to milk me dry and then dispose of me."

"I'm dedicated to caring for the land," Tilysh said. "Would you like to live with me. When you choose to meet the trees, I will take you to them and ensure your safety. I will care for you as my own, and I'll enjoy conversing with you in between our journeys into the land."

"The birth of one male tree will make you redundant, Mouth! Then they'll be happy to destroy you," Malsavash said

Vashetha snorted. "Male trees need time to mature. Many,

many seasons, by my memory. Even when they reach their maturity, Rolliz, you will be held in the highest esteem for your whole existence, which I'm sure will be lengthy."

"I'll accept your offer, Tilysh, but if I want to return to Kirym, I want assurance someone will take me to her."

"I will guarantee your freedom and take you to Kirym whenever you wish," Blue said.

"Fine," Malsavash said. "I'll return to my brothers now and let them know we can stay where we are, and not bother with any of this nonsense."

"No! You must return to the place of your heritage," I said. "The male trees are living shorter and shorter lives, and your absence may affect the lifespan of the new trees as well."

"Why should we?"

"Tell me about the monster you sent into the land," I asked.

Malsavash was surprised by my change in subject.

"Why? What do you want to know?"

"What did it look like?"

He shrugged. "Like the two you brought with you."

"Two?" Mekrar murmured in my ear. "So, he did know Faltryn was—" stopping when I grasped her hand.

"Like that one," he pointed to Oak. "Taller though."

"How is Oak a monster? What are you talking about, you idiot?" Rolliz asked.

"Like him, the Danth monster had two heads."

Then I understood. Oak was carrying Trethia.

Oak also realised, lifted Trethia off his back, and stood her beside him. "You thought we were one?"

"Well, umm, how would we know? Danth was my friend when he first visited. The monster, when it arrived, had two heads, one of them looked like my friend Danth."

I tried to keep a straight face. "It's an understandable mistake when you have nothing to gauge it by."

Malsavash shrugged. "I saw what I saw. When my friend Danth returned, he had a second head. Later I was told that he had become a monster."

"Was Grey always with Danth?" I asked.

"Yes."

"Did they bring containers with them?"

"The monster carried two chests, a big one and a small one. Grey wanted them to be left in the gate area with his boxes."

"Important, Kirym?" Blue asked.

I nodded. "Maletta, one of our ancients, told me our history had been stolen. I suspect Rabbit and Grey took your history too, and whatever Faltryn left by the pool."

"So, we have to follow them?" Mekrar asked.

"Eventually. First, I'd like to go home. I want to tell Mama about Ashistar. She should know what happened here and why. Her input will be important. But before we leave, the male trees must return to their traditional place."

"No! The routes are too dangerous. I will not chance the death of even one of my brothers in the mountains or the desert."

Vashetha, I want you to trust me. Walk out onto the sand? I promise you'll be safe.

I glanced around and realised that everyone except Malsavash received Ubree's message.

Vashetha slid forward and tentatively moved onto the sand.

"No!" Malsavash lurched forward and tried to grab her. "They'll kill you!"

Vashetha evaded him, took one step and another. The sand, initially solid, began to swirl beneath her roots. As when we crossed the sand, she began to sink before rising to the surface of the sand. She moved away from us, gathering speed as she went.

Ubree passed his vision to us. Vashetha was gliding on the surface of the sand, her extensive root system was visible although she wasn't using them at all. Rather, she occasionally leaned her body to one side or the other to change direction. Her enjoyment was obvious as she swooped in circles and zigzagging across the sand.

"How does she do that?" Tilysh asked the question we were all thinking.

"Wow, I would love to do it," Oak said, mirroring my thought.

"You'll all get the opportunity to ride the sand," Ubree said.

Watching Vashetha from behind, I realised the massive gift she had given us. She had a huge scar on the base of her trunk where a massive section had been cut off.

Oak glanced at me. "What's wrong?"

"I've just realised. Vashetha gave us the Burl. It's part of her."

"That was generous," Mekrar said. "It's so beautiful."

"No, no, it was part of her! She gave us a section of her trunk."

The sand-swimmers pushed up onto the grass in their eagerness to carry us. Sundas put his foot on the sand but quickly pulled back.

"Are you sure this is safe, Ubree?"

"Believe me, Sundas. The swimmers are pleased to have the chance to carry you. They were quite frustrated when we crossed their domain."

I rounded on Malsavash. "You lied to us. Why?"

"I didn't. It only works for the female trees," he said.

"The sand-swimmers tell me you've used them many

times," Ubree said. "It's how you crossed to meet us here today. They also told me how fast they can do the journey, should speed be required, although you spent most of yesterday and all of last night riding the sands." He turned to me. "The sand-swimmers carry everyone who wish it. They would have carried us but were specifically ordered not to. In fact, the instability they created was also done at Malsavash's order."

Malsavash took a deep breath, shook his branches and the damage he displayed, disappeared.

I was furious, but Vashetha returned before I could say more.

"All males will return to this side of the desert within two moons. Ralimvash, you are no longer Malsavash and will not be until you have again earned the position. The position as the first contact to those who enter the land is one of hospitality. To specifically scare our guests, to lie to them, and put their lives in danger is almost unforgivable. I've asked the sand-swimmers to bring Uguvash over. He will take your place and organise the trees back to where they belong." She turned to me. "The sand-swimmers are upset they could not help you cross their domain. They invite you to travel with them for a time now; they will return you when you wish. You are welcome to ride the sands at any time."

"Thank you, Vashetha. We'd be happy to accept their invitation. We will leave you to care for the trees and land." I stepped closer to her. "I have only just realised the source of the great gift we received so long ago. I wish I had known sooner. Please visit us soon. I know Mama would love to meet the giver of our burl."

She smiled down at me. "It was just a token, my dear. Your people saved us from war, and again, you have returned to ensure the continuation of our life here. We will be forever grateful to you for your gift."

"For our family also, Kirym," Shalinba said. "Without your insistence, we would have died out. You are always welcome, and if you ever need our help, you have only to ask."

49

Arbreu

Vashetha, Tilysh, Dorshym, Shalinba, Thenne, Zillib, and
Conysh returned to the gate with us, eager to see what had
been done. Lartherin and Dashlan were seeing to the final
touches. Everyone volunteered to help but were neither
wanted nor needed.

The change in Lartherin since they had first seen
him was stunning. He had filled out and lost the pallid
colouring caused by many seasons of imprisonment and ill-
treatment.

Finally, the work was finished, and everyone gathered
together near the gate.

"It looks wonderful, Dashlan," Blue said. "You've given
Halavash a great gift, a welcoming and secure gate. Will you
stay on as gatekeeper?"

Arbreu glanced across at Kirym. He knew he couldn't try
to influence Dashlan's response, as much as he wanted to.

Dashlan looked around the gate area. "You know, it's been

a grand adventure being here. I feel I've done something worthwhile. I've had great help, Orange, Lartherin, and others who have passed by. I'm delighted the gate is now secure, no one can arrive without approval, and the gatekeeper now has the power to remove any visitor who doesn't have the best interest of the land in their heart. However, my path leads away from Halavash, although I'm sure I'll return. As much as I wouldn't leave the gate unmanned, there is someone who would be a better gatekeeper, one who wants and needs the land. I think you should ask Lartherin to be gatekeeper."

Blue nodded and turned to Lartherin. "If you have the desire to become a gatekeeper, we would welcome you. You would be taking on an important job. Will you do it?"

Lartherin finally managed to close his mouth. "I would be honoured to accept, but I must talk to my family first. I've not even spoken to them yet." He eyed Tilysh sheepishly.

"I've watched you since I arrived and think you're well suited to this place," Tilysh said, after hugging him warmly. "I remember you when you were young. You always had the desire to make tiny changes that, while seeming to be insignificant, made a huge difference, not in the usual way of our people. Perhaps this is the perfect place for you. You won't be alone though. We, your family, will visit you often."

"Then I'd like to do it," Lartherin said. Immediately, his clothing changed. Now he wore a flowing robe, the colour of the sea on a summer's day.

At the same time, Dashlan's robe faded, and he was again dressed in the clothing he had arrived in.

"It's decided, then," Blue said. "Welcome, Summer Blue."

"Before I forget, Kirym," Vashetha said, "I have something for you." She reached into a hole in her trunk and brought out a large package wrapped in a pliant dark pink material.

Many of the lines on it were leaf-shaped, made of what Arbreu suspected were her leaves.

"Ashistar wished you to have these. You'll know what to do with them."

Kirym carefully unwrapped the package. Ashistar's cloak was wrapped around his hood, dagger, the scabbard he had held the sword in, a scroll, a small pocket carrying ten silver buttons and a chain holding a heavy acorn.

"The scroll is for you, Kirym."

"He was still alive?" Sundas asked.

"No. His desire for you to have these things remained with him."

As Kirym sat to read the scroll aloud, Vashetha began to sing. Her song, deep and earthy, reminded Arbreu of something he had heard before.

"If you are reading this, Kirym," she read, *"I am dead. I am not surprised, I have always known I would not live to be old.*

However, I am amazed at what I have accomplished, and I hope my Sire is proud of me. Please ask Rosisha not to give our child my name, nor allow Churnyg to name him, but choose one to suit herself.

My cloak, hood, and dagger should be passed to Churnyg to give to whomever he feels needs it. My acorn should go to Varitza with my love, for the loyalty and care she showed me. Ask Churnyg to teach her how to use it correctly. Rosisha has instructions for the other items I left behind. Particularly she has a gift from me for our child.

Kirym, I am sorry I could not serve you longer and better, but I held the weapons with pride.

I urge you to choose someone new to help you carry them NOW· Having more weapons than you can use and not having a person to hold a weapon at your side is not sensible· You have the right people with you· The weight needs to be shared·

You have always had my respect· Now, surprisingly, I also pass on my love·

Qwerben Ashistar, Weapon holder, Follower of Kirym, and proudly, son of Churnyg Oak"

"His name was Qwerben?"

"Yes, Arbreu. It means Son of The Great Oak."

"Wow! It's impressive," Mekrar said. "Why didn't he use it once he left The Rock?"

"He felt it would make the other dwarves wary of him. Although they now know him as Churnyg's son, he didn't want to create any antagonism."

Vashetha's song ended when Kirym stopped speaking. Kirym looked up. "Thank you, my friend. It was a wonderful tribute to Ashistar. He would have felt honoured, as we all were when we first heard it at the portal before we came here. It was slightly different this time, wasn't it?"

Her leaves rustled as she bowed an acknowledgement. "I wondered if you heard it originally. Yes. I heard your request to come to Halavash, and I sent the invitation to ensure you would get here. I have another gift, a special thank you for your help, Kirym."

She handed Kirym another package. Kirym opened it and displayed a length of material. It was deep purple, soft, pliant and marked in the same way as the Burl.

She brushed aside Kirym's refusal. "Without your help, our home would be dead. My children, who helped me make this for you, are aware that nothing would truly pay the debt we owe you. My daughters collected my sap, made it into thread and wove it. You will find it has some interesting properties, but it's something you can discover when you need to use it."

Kirym graciously accepted the gift.

"Who will you choose to help you with the weapons, Kirym?" Vashetha asked. "As I understand it, it is both a privilege and an honour to assist you."

"Before you begin to reflect, Kirym," Mekrar said, "and as sad as I am to say it, I couldn't consider the honour. I will have more than enough responsibility facing me when we get home."

"The same goes for me, I suppose" Arbreu added.

"I too have many responsibilities, although I am pledged to serve you always," Ubree said. "I do not need a weapon to tie me to you, and I suspect I would find it awkward to use."

"The same can be said for all of us, Kirym," Sundas said.

Kirym looked around the group, her gaze pausing on each of them. Arbreu could see her considering their values, the strengths, the weaknesses. He was surprised she included Mekrar and himself in her assessment and wondered what they would say if Kirym chose either of them. He knew that if chosen, he would be unable to say, no.

50

Kirym Speaks

I hated choosing. It put so much responsibility on one person. Ashistar would still be alive had I not chosen him all those seasons back. I remembered our discussion in the dark, dusty tunnels of The Rock, while Churnyg was helping us escape. Churnyg had called him a traitor to his face and I saw the hurt it caused. And yet his loyalty to everyone would become renown in ballads in the future.

Ashistar had argued when I asked him to carry the weapons but accepted my reasoning when I gave it. He had not surrendered us to Gynbere, even though it could have cost him his life had his duplicity been discovered. He had already helped ensure the tunnels were clear to secure our escape. But more than that, he had tried to assist his people in The Rock, feeding the hungry when he could, and stopping any brutality he saw. For that, he had given up the life he was born to and deserved. He was lonely and shunned by many who should have supported him. Even those he helped seemed to have little love for him. He had lived in constant fear, knowing both sides of the families he lived with would kill him, given half a chance.

Now, having had only a few seasons of happy family life, he had been killed. Had I not chosen him to help me with the weapons, he could have stayed with his family and lived to be ancient, his children and grandchildren around him.

He wouldn't have, Kirym. Ubree's thought interrupted my inner turmoil. *Ashistar would have joined you because always, he saw the need to care for those in trouble. All else would have happened in the same way. He would have thrown whatever sword he held, and Danth would have killed him for it. The fortune possibly lay in his sword being the sword it was and thank goodness it destroyed Danth. Ashistar helped to ensure no one else would die at Danth's hand.*

I glanced up at Ubree, quietly thanking him for his care and common sense, but knowing I would always grieve for the man who had given his life to save mine.

You have three people to consider. Oak, Dashlan, and Sundas.

Ubree was right. I studied each of them and I instantly knew. I stabbed the sword into the ground and took a step back.

"Understanding that you can say no, would you help me carry the weapons," I paused, "Dashlan."

In the moments before he spoke, I glanced at Sundas and Oak. Sundas looked relieved.

He didn't want it. He would have refused, had I asked him.

Oak's expression hadn't changed. *Oak would have accepted, but it would have been a waste. He would always be there for me.*

Dashlan stared at the sword, the silence lengthened. "Kirym, I've had many dreams over the seasons. None of them ever included a sword." He glanced at his brother. "Arbreu, you would keep me safe, wrapped up and close to our parents. However, that's a place you'll have to fill, because..." He stepped forward and grasped the handle of the sword, pulled it from the earth, and wielded it, getting an idea of its balance. "I'll happily support you, Kirym, and hold the weapons as you desire."

I clicked his token. At once, it settled onto his forehead, looking far more part of him than it had before. This was what had been missing. I regretted I had not connected to his token sooner. However, there was no more than that between us, and although I wondered why, I knew I had made the right choice. The place beside me was his, simply because he held the sword and lived.

Trethia skipped up to him. He stabbed the sword into the ground, picked her up and hugged her. She clicked his token. There was a flash of light, and a tiny black inclusion appeared in the centre of Dashlan's token.

He leaned over to me and again touched his token to mine. Six tiny points of colour appeared around the black inclusion—one for each of the large tokens, and now, I felt the connection.

I hugged him and handed him the scabbard. He sheathed the sword, added the shield, and slipped the belt over his head to sit against his shoulder. He sheathed and unsheathed the sword a few times to get used to it, then picked up his pack and hooked it to his belt. Smiling, he again drew the sword and studied it, first the handle, then the blade, before again replacing it.

Arbreu grabbed his shoulder. "Do the job properly, don't mess up, and don't get killed! That's all I ask." They hugged and clicked tokens.

Arbreu was followed by Mekrar, Oak, Sundas, and Ubree. I was intrigued to note that other than settling, connection with the other tokens didn't change Dashlan's token in any way.

Faltryn was last in the line. Dashlan picked the little dragon up, hugged him and clicked his token mark.

Suddenly, the two of them were sucked into the portal.

The End

If you have enjoyed The Portal to Halavash, please leave a review on the website of the seller you purchased it from. Good reviews are the life blood of independently-published authors, so please take a few moments to let others know what you thought of the book.

Thank you for reading.

Do look for further adventures as
The Token Bearer series continues.

www.wordlypress.com

Made in the USA
San Bernardino, CA
19 February 2020